Henry Nixon

THE JEW FROM
Berlin

This edition first published in paperback by
Michael Terence Publishing in 2025
www.mtp.agency

Copyright © 2025 Henry Nixon

Henry Nixon has asserted the right to be identified as
the author of this work in accordance with the
Copyright, Designs and Patents Act 1988

ISBN 9781800949645

No part of this publication may be reproduced, stored
in a retrieval system, or transmitted, in any form or
by any means, electronic, mechanical, photocopying,
recording or otherwise, without the prior
permission of the publisher

Cover design (AI)
Michael Terence Publishing

1

1925–Lyon France

For several years Andre Dupont's small production unit had turned in a healthy profit; but when receiving recent bad news was devastated. The ailing German motor company Daimler Puchs, was to locate both Germany and France production units in Austria. The Frenchman shifted uncomfortably in his chair, nursing nervously a tepid cup of tea as he awaited the year-end report. Black rain clouds chased by a North Easterly wind, hovered like a bad omen over the production unit of the pensive Frenchman. Nervous anticipation ran rampant through Andres slender frame as shaking hands raised a lukewarm cup of tea to his trembling lips. Sleep filled eyes flashed door-ward as squeaking hinges announced the entry of his Accountants with the eagerly awaited report.

Trembling hands flicked cautiously the first page as overhead black clouds clashed. Beads of worried sweat trickled liberally down the forehead of Andre, claps of thunder resounded *angrily* from the threatening clouds sweeping their slow progression over darkened heavens. Forked lightning strobed the ageing slatted blinds addressing the factories office windows as Andre turned to the second page of the report. Gale force winds whistled through the warped blinds of the office window onto a worried filled Andre Dupont. Flesh quivered in the corner of worried eyes almost as a pre-cursor to ripples of apprehension gripping his spine. With the eagerness of a body whose life depended on it, he scanned the report. A mood of negativity floated ominously the cool air: a bubble of corrosive nervous apprehension consumed him.

The ageing grandfather clock standing partially hidden in the shadows of the office chimed with monotonous regularity the time of the hour. A large space of time elapsed very, very slowly, worried sweats ran down Andre's spine. The steely fingers of doubt grabbing his gut unwound as weary eyes landed on the final sheet. Euphoria swept over him replacing soul sapping negative vibes. His skinny torso shook with excitement; the doom-laden situation that had lingered for so long dissipated, an electric positivity now clung to the cool air. Euphoria enveloped the twenty-one-year-old Andre Dupont. Youthful exuberance welled up inside his trembling body when re-scanning the welcoming financial figures. His small production unit hugging the outer extremities of Lyon, for the second consecutive year, showed profits had increased. Draining his cup of now cold tea, the young Frenchman embraced optimism; with a spring in his step, he skipped joyously into the chilled evening air.

Young legs propelled him forth in excited strides to his business meeting with the area manager of the German Motor Company. Armed with his uplifting data revealing the health of his company, he hoped to sway Daimlers mind; and move total production to France instead of Austria. The business meeting overran, the young Frenchman stared in dismay at his watch. He was late for a hospital appointment with his wife Ann Marie, and birth of their baby.

The dark of evening rushed in cooling the warm air, earlier threatening rain clouds had disappeared. Weak rays from a full moon fell upon a swirling north easterly wind chasing dry leaves down that dusty lifeless road. Along which the Frenchman progressed hurriedly towards the hospital, pausing only at the florist to buy a bunch of red roses. On arrival at the hospital, the flustered Frenchman rushed into the ward. "Anne Marie, Anne Marie; please accept my deepest apologies." The Frenchman blurted meekly, before in a subservient, apologetic gesture handed his wife a bunch of broken-headed flowers. The sleek figure of Ann Marie, glistening black hair flowing down her back, smiled weakly whilst gazing at the freshly cut headless blooms.

The troublesome birth had sapped her energy, left her weak, too tired to chastise her husband. In an upbeat voice she whispered softly. "You're here Andre that's all that matters." Ann Marie reached for his hand almost as a sign of forgiveness. "You were alright with the birth and everything? Andre blurted in youthful exuberance. "The midwife was very helpful during the birth so yes; all went smoothly a baby boy awaits you. I trawled through many names for a son; to no avail." She murmured frustration lacing her sad tone. A flustered Andre gushed excitedly. "My engineer and I agonised for hours over a name, if a boy we arrived at Jean Pierre. What do you think, do you agree?"

Squeaking hinges announced the entrance of a buxom nurse, who in low authoritative tones, advised visiting time was over. "See you tomorrow; promise I'll be early, Bye." Andre spluttered walking in a backward motion, his retreat from the ward. Outside the hospital an elated Andre screamed with joy. "I'm a father." He shouted in a euphoric cry to everyone passing by. His arms shot upward to the darkened sky gesticulating his joy.

Hitler signed the Concordat, a document negotiated between the Vatican, and German Army. This document allowed Catholics free movement in Germany. Hitler reneged on this treaty two years later by launching an attack on Catholicism. Catholic priests disagreeing with Hitler's policies, and daring to voice their concerns; were immediately shot. The Vatican aware of these atrocities chose not to complain, but overlook the tragic incidents. The German army advanced upon the Vatican to kidnap, imprison, Pope Pacelli. General Karl Wolff, leading the army, dissuaded Hitler from this plan. Urging Hitler to concentrate their evil assaults on persecuting the Jews.

2

1935

Berlin–Aaron's interview

Fluffy white clouds drifted aimlessly across the sun blessed sky of Berlin. The hot midday sun cast its rays upon the broad shoulders of twenty-six-year-old Jew, Aaron Yitzchak, as he progressed his lean muscular body through the oncoming throng of students. Cocooned within thoughts of his future The Jew remained blissfully ignorant of Hitler's threatening warmongering. Or of his ideological army of blood-thirsty brownshirts engineering antisemitism within the disillusioned German masses. That this bloodthirsty maniacal crowd would be instrumental in destroying his ambitions, by engineering anarchy, insanity, leading to devastating destruction and bringing total ruin upon his family and his blossoming career.

From his ageing valise Aaron selected the vital criteria that would help him on that exciting, slippery path of ambition. With hope dressing his eyes, he stared with hopeful conviction for a large space of time at his certificate before placing the treasured economics degree back into his valise. Excitement flowed through his veins when tackling the worn stone steps trodden by Erwin Stronger, the renowned Austrian Scientist that had graced the same walkway many decades earlier.

A sour taste exploded in his throat; this was not nervousness, but fear. His father had invested his total savings into his son's university education, failure, therefore, was not an option. Aaron's impending interview introduced a cocktail of stress and havoc into his overactive mind. The young Jew skirted the rhododendron bushes lining the ageing walls of the A.E.G. High Tension factory. A company that would later provide electrical products to what would prove to be; a notorious, infamous death camp; AUSCHWITZ.

Aaron had been summoned to the hallowed halls of the Bundesbank, and interview with Herr Schmidt the ageing Vice President of the Bundesbank (Germany's Federal bank). The Vice President and president basked in the twilight of their career; both entered the final phase of their working lives. Consequently, the bank urgently sought highly qualified students as replacements. Men with ideological financial nous enhanced with the ability to solve complex economic problems. Deal with highly intricately financially woven dilemma's the successful candidate would encounter

3

The Vice President

Bright rays of sunshine streamed through vents of the pristine venetian blinds gracing the bowed windows of that spacious room of the vice president. A solemn, funereal silence blanketed the office, a mischievous glint sprang to the blue eyes of Herr Schmidt. The ageing gentleman swivelled in his large black leather chair; blue eyes dancing with pleasure when thoughts of retirement sprang into his mind. The solid oak panelled door glided silently open to the secretary, ushering in the interviewee. An overawed Aaron swept his deferential gaze of admiration over the red rose cornices peppering symmetrically, a magnificent white ornate ceiling. His overwhelmed gaze of bewilderment; transferred seamlessly to respectful awe. From under his winged eyebrows, Aaron's warm brown eyes fell upon the respected economist, and interviewer. The vice president, with Pince-nez perched precariously on the end of his bulbous nostrils, he began in calibrated tones, the interview. "Good morning! Herr Yitzchak; please sit." Resounded the authoritative amiable tones of welcome. The vice presidents' hand like a sword cut authoritatively through the air, before pointing to a vacant chair. His balding head dropped to the highly polished mahogany top of his well-organised; paper-laden desk and Aaron's job application.

Black shiny shoes squeaked the progression of Aaron sheepishly forward to the chair. Aaron sank like a rag doll onto the chair as Schmidt's balding head rose slowly. He held his interviewee in an interrogative stare; before launching into an intensive interrogation. "I've been researching your expansive dissertation,"

Schmidt remarked appreciatively. Waving sheets of paper through the air like a sword before replacing them on the desk. "I found your auspicious, enlightening interpretation of lending, extremely interesting; vibrant and refreshing whilst seamlessly integrating with our policies." A benign smile of approval bent his lips; his podgy forefinger poked the precariously balanced pince-nez to a safer resting-place; on his oversize nose.

The muscles of Aaron's arms twitched. The Jew engaged nervous apprehension; in tones marinated with shy confidence he replied with respectful diffidence. "And good morning to you sir! Expansive you say?" The Jew queried foggily, his brown eyes dilating, eyebrows winging in surprise. "That is correct... but, of course, you will elaborate?" The ageing Schmidt countered in the form of a question as he strummed podgy fingers upon Aaron's application forms.

Aaron's face clouded apprehensively; a strange challenging excitement gripped his stomach; the concerned Jew replied calmly. "By expansive I take it you refer to the inclusion of the crucial relevant peripheral issues; issues we refer to as the small print." Light perspiration danced freely upon his forehead. The vice president coughed, swallowed water; replied. "Yes, that is so." Schmidt stuttered in a voice low... driven. His clear blue eyes penetrated the young Jew with an intimidating stare. Aaron uncrossed his legs, leaned forward almost provocatively; the corners of his brown eyes twinkled almost as a challenge. Something the size of a small boulder slipped down his throat, probably a gulp, he launched into his reply. "Sir the length of my dissertation, was not my intention to introduce duplicity or ambiguity. The inclusion of peripherals were primarily there to stress the importance within the detail. I sir hold dearly the belief, that by analysing peripheral information. Such information releases one's analytical nous; provides one with the necessary freedom to be critically subjective. This surely would bolster the recipient's confidence... convictions. His economic prowess would no doubt instruct him of the corrective action. By allying this progression to diligent research, it would reveal the bigger picture."

A pregnant pause filled the air, the Jew took a deep welcome breath; sipped water then continued, "I hope sir, at the risk of sounding facetious, you appreciate these peripherals, do not trivialise or misconstrue the cohesion of my complex financial considerations. That the embodiment of small print; can assist greatly in one's summation of his final prognosis." The Jews throat tightened with nerves; another drink of water cleared his throat. "Finally, you will sir accept that the small print, would release your highly tuned business acumen to access the finer points of the core issue, profit. May I, at the risk of upsetting my illustrious mentor, be allowed to quote an overworked cliché. That the devil is in the detail." Aaron sank gratefully back in his chair, visual relief swept over him, a feeling of accomplishment warmed his gut.

4

1918

Germany–Post World War One

A decimated Germany lay entrenched in negativity; the devastated Teutonic nation plumbed the soul-destroying air of poverty, disbelief. This once proud Germanic working-class nation wallowed in self-pity. The disgruntled populace pleaded the government for support; heartrending noises that fell on deaf ears. The indifferent support from the governing hierarchy manifested unrest. The suffering populous made a herculean effort to restore a modicum of normality to their miserable life of austerity. The comedic irony of the prevailing situation, being solely attributed to the mindless exploits of the middle and upper class. Germany was officially bankrupt. But the ruling hierarchy chose to dwell in a bubble of blissful ignorance. Their perilous financial dichotomy ignored by those in power, who continued their financial recklessness, ignoring the dire warnings of worldly financial indicators.

Shares bottomed out; the economy weakened; investment became non-existent. The governments misunderstanding of the dire situation being evident by their continuance of borrowing abroad to sustain a ridiculously opulent lifestyle. This unnecessary extravagance festered retribution amongst the downtrodden working class; those despairing people struggling to exist. Several demeaning years elapsed; Germany never having embraced the ignominy of poverty found difficulty in accepting their impoverished situation. Feverishly they sought to pigeonhole blame, these negative vibes plagued the troubled minds of the downbeat populace. Without wanting to blame the government for their intolerable position? They pointed their finger of retribution on religion; the ruling body of Catholicism.

Unsightly bombed buildings proliferated Germany's landscape, the once great country lay in ruins, barring one exception. Amidst rampant depravity, prospered the Jewish enclave an area that remained untouched by austerity. Were Jews profiteering whilst we the general populous fought the uphill battle to control poverty? This unanswered question provoked yet more anger.

The affluent Jewish quarter of Berlin continued to flourish; wealthy Jews grew stronger. The imbalance of lifestyles produced an untenable situation for the struggling masses, invoking dissatisfaction amongst the restless public. Igniting lurking retributive juices engendering instant action. Their dilemma raised provocative, condemning questions. Fermented vengeful feelings within the anguished, suspicious minds of the starving Germans. Fresh doubts invaded beleaguered minds attempting to digest that highly divisive information. The troubled, revenge-seeking masses, exonerated Catholicism, swiftly shifting their condemning indictment. That hostile finger of blame, with the rapidity of a striking snake; was pointed squarely at the wealthy Jews. Hostilities towards the race intensified, escalated vengeful retributive emotions into hysteria. Anti-Semitism reared its ugly head, manifesting revenge within the sorely troubled minds of the starving, Germanic race.

More problematical years drifted passed, their insufferable position remained unchanged, until an accusative voice laced with hostility rang out. "Those bloody Jews. Why aren't they suffering?" The angry voice questioned in wild accusatory recrimination.

Volatile, vengeful emotions ran amok, festered further acts of hostile confrontations. That restless unruly crowd began chanting for an equitable response. "Why don't we rectify the position? They should be made to pay, bloody foreigners in our country." The leader goaded in high pitched tones of rebellion. These acrimonious accusations instigated a revolutionary incitement, created a wave of hostility, vengeance; of unruly dissatisfaction. The disturbing murmurings gathered pace within that restless crowd. If only that provocative, unsettled crowd of warmongers knew. Within twelve years they were to be dealt a far worse blow.

5

Aaron's Delight

Cocooned within the stringent constraints of Germanic intransigence the vice president allowed briefly the Jews challenging criteria to sway him. Before the vice president replied abrasively, in a tone of hostility he grunted. "Yes." Herr Schmidt issued in a cold hard monosyllable before continuing, "regarding your implied toxicity; marginalisation." Schmidt questioned in rather hurriedly quizzical mechanical tones. Then in a disconcerting swift movement the vice president swivelled his chair forty-five degrees to face the slatted window. A movement injecting fleeting disengagement within Aaron from his comfort zone of positive thought. A stony silence of reflection ensued pushing the Jew into the unwelcome position of uncertainty. An air of frustration swept over the jew; he shook his head foggily before re-engaging the vice president's hostile attack. His fertile imagination sent thought processes searching frantically for relevant criteria. Pertinent criteria that would allow him to bring dominance to the discussion, counterbalance the uninvited hostility injected by Herr Schmidt. The Jew re-installed his earlier confidence; with an authoritative voice of assertion he introduced challenging abrasiveness. "The passage you quote sir is based on short term issues; not ones of greater longevity," Aaron responded in a voice quivering with protest; his shaking hands grabbed a glass of water.

The Jew injected toughness into a voice that had accessed mediocrity and lacked conviction. "To introduce my hypothetical dilemma, I quote a poverty-stricken family. This family are dependent upon handouts, benefits, for their very existence. These unfortunates wish to improve their house. To accomplish this expensive project, they would require a large injection of capital. This sir is where your toxicity raises its ugly head. That substantial amount of money raises tenuous, provocative questions. Would you, hypothetically of course, loan them money?"

The Jews throat tightened cutting off his breath, leading to a poignant hesitancy. The pause injected gravity to his challenging proposition; positive nuances engaged a voice resonating belief. "No, of course, you wouldn't. They have, unfortunately, because of their situation; have been ostracised;

marginalised by society." Aaron paused to drink water, continued his deliberation. "By marginalisation, my inference is that sadly, their situation advertises a brutal but obvious fact. That because these needy people do not have the necessary finance, there is no chance of them repaying your loan why? Because of their financial situation, they have been made outcasts, pariahs by our society; there lies your toxicity... their obvious inability to repay your loan." Sweats of worried anticipation wetted Aaron's brow, cocooned in uncertainty he hung anxiously between indignation, jubilation, and anger.

Herr Schmidt stroked his chin studiously; his clear blue eyes entrenched in indecision. He launched into a challenging subjective reply. "So, you take the cowards way out, seek higher safer ground; insist banks should not assist these unfortunate individuals?" Schmidt's scathing tones challenged. His vitriolic riposte clung icily to the already cool air. Instantly, the Jews earlier excitement vanished, a frown of worry knitted Aaron's brow. Exasperation clouded his eyes glaring vacantly the desktop; the fear of failure and his father's life savings festered hotly his gut. The Jew swept an agitated gaze at the interviewer, suddenly emboldened eyes housed emotional conviction. Frustration vanished, replaced by an attacking decisiveness, this injected into his voice, an arrogant confidence. "No sir, indeed, you are missing the point, if you considered reflecting upon the current way of expediting money you may agree with my financial hypothesis. I am merely stating the creation of wealth and poverty are generated from diametrically opposite extremities. Surely you would agree that we economists must promote a degree of greed. Furthermore, we accomplish this feat by engineering demand... promotion of profit. However, sir to deviate from your current policies requires backbone and foresight allied with the ability of foresight." Aaron's throat dried, he sipped water before continuing, "To be more direct, if we are considering lending to these poverty-stricken people; the following steps must be strictly adhered to. Step one, prepare a balance sheet followed with profit and loss account from whence you will introduce your apparently toxic loan. From the relevant accounts, select taxable gross figures. Using these figures, trawl company tax laws; lastly, ascertain the amount of tax disappearing from your profit. Then select the amount of investment offsetting your higher rate of tax arising within your trial balance. That sir will probably equate to the amount your generosity will provide to your preferred charity; your toxic loan." Emotional excitement closed his throat, he paused coughed gently; continued, "then prepare a second Balance sheet, the figure selected for investment should almost fully manifest, from tax saved onto the balance sheet. So, as you see sir, investing in the worse off can pay... enhance the bank's reputation. In conclusion of this lengthy process, you will find, due to your extensive research into the tax laws. You will emerge the victor; a knight in shining armour... everyone is a winner." Aaron stated with disingenuous disarming simplicity. The Jew indulged himself by engaging a renewed bolstered confidence. Then in thankful relief, his euphoria dissipated. Once again, he allowed his body to crumple like a rag doll back in his chair; the air sizzled with positivity

6

Germany's 1930 Inflation

1930. Hyperinflation inflicted a tragedy of cataclysmic proportions upon the deflated German populous. Economic ruin decimated what little the downbeat... struggling working class still clung to. Jobless figures escalated exponentially. Out of work pitiful souls unable to meet mortgage repayments lost their only treasured possession, their homes. The prospering Jewish bank owners repossessed them. That once proud nation sank ignominiously to its knees, plumbed the depths of devastation. Inevitably these downtrodden souls were sucked mercilessly into a downward spiralling vortex, of soul-destroying austerity.

German banks, run by affluent Jews, refused to extend credit to increasing ailing German businesses; this was a pivotal death blow leading an en-masse- closure. Meanwhile the overspending bourgeois; frustrated in their inability to extract more loans from abroad languished apathetically in total devastation. Their inexcusable inaction manifested, once more, amongst the German populous, a fearsome anger. This raging dissatisfaction festered retribution among the lawless restless hordes. Slowly awareness accessed the proletariat who sought change. The bourgeois fearing the retributive mood of the unsettled masses, changed course. Ironically, the redirection of their apathetic energies was to throw their support behind a young rebellious upstart, Adolph Hitler.

The Jewish quarter, naively relaxed in their comfort zone, enjoyed total domination over all Germanies financial outgoings. The bourgeois poured money into building brand new houses for the masses; money borrowed from the Jews. The Jews used their newfound prosperity to build grand new houses for themselves within their already upmarket complex. Meanwhile, the starving masses scratched out a miserable existence, within their run down impoverished, overcrowded ghettos. Anti-Semitic slogans proliferated; the cost of food soared; that once-mighty people were reduced to social handouts. The all-powerful Mark plummeted yet further; oblivion beckoned; bankruptcies accelerated. Even the mundane task of providing food for the table was proving to be a Herculean task. Soup kitchens populated the main thoroughfares, this demeaning hand out became the norm for the destitute starving Germans. Rampant poverty prevailed, spreading yet more disillusionment. Ambivalence created still more anguish within the already tortured minds of those downtrodden, despairing souls. The starving populous strove fruitlessly to cope with their demeaning oppression. During this period of humiliation, fingers of retribution spread like wildfire. Dissatisfaction vaulted itself into the ascendancy, revenge became paramount. Nationalistic fervour fed by starvation fuelled reprisals; huge unruly mobs urged action.

Conflicting emotions heightened Anti-Semitism, the proletariats proclivity for vengeance gathered momentum. Like an invisible contagious disease, revenge became paramount within the agitated warlike crowds. Inflammatory accusations pinpointed the Jews as being the antagonists for their present demise. This anger further incensed the hostile air sizzling with rebellious indignation. Disgruntled ex-soldiers having lost their livelihood, were the most vociferous in their desire for rebellion, they joined the brownshirts. Vengeful hate instigated reactive action within the ever-growing hostile crowds; ignited further their insurgency. Intense dislike fanned the flames of hate, encouraged their yearning... hunger for justice; inflamed emotions further engendered their desire for action. This inflammatory negativity tortured every occupant of those war-torn, ravaged streets. The saber-rattling emanating from the reactionary crowds reached the ears of the prospering Jewish communities. These warlike evocative outpourings, permeated uncertainty within the elite. This devastating, unseen enemy, spread unnervingly through the troubled wealthy, Jewish community.

7

1936 – The Bundesbank Job

The querulous face of the vice president held the Jew in an interrogative stare. Which softened with a gratifying smile of recognition dressing his thin lips. Reclining in a black leather swivel chair; he boomed in a positive calibrated tone of assurance. "Your process was highly commendable, your financial pragmatism impeccable. Your pursuance of selecting the pertinent criteria, accessing the correct channels, almost left me breathless; we return to your paper. We have at length scrutinised your extensive or should I say comprehensive financial projections. By we, I mean the president and myself; we both find them faultless." Platitudes dropped with ease from the tight lips of the overweight German, his lined face beaming with a wry smile of admiration.

An overjoyed Aaron accessed a triumphant blanket of euphoria that banished his lingering negativity. A gamut of emotions ran rampant through his mind cocooned in joyous celebrations; but his churning stomach was beset with nerves. The young Jews dissertation having surpassed expectations, allowed celebrations to embrace him. Aaron wallowed in the Germans complimentary platitudes, propelling his renewed confidence to a new high.

After a quick inhalation of much-needed breath, Aaron accessed seamlessly top gear; words flowed like a fast-moving stream. "Humboldt University lecturers repeatedly stressed, that wise investors, will always bend their ears when solid financial information begins to flow. Would you not agree?" Aaron questioned; an electric apprehensive quality embraced his question.

Herr Schmidt responded nodding positively, lined ruddy face gleamed with admiration. "But of course, I do, allow me to state that I'm heartily glad that we both sing from the same hymn sheet." The Vice President gushed with pleasurable ease. Schmidt's bony hand stroked his thinning grey hair, he coughed to clear the throat.

Alert blue calculating eyes held Aaron in a prolonged stare of inquisition. "This morning the president and I, held an in-depth conversation with your tutor at Humboldt University. He informs us you were, without doubt, his best pupil, showered you with glittering recommendations. Indeed, he sang the highest praise for your obvious abilities. As a result, the President and I were in full accord, that on your interview proving successful. By that we mean, you pursue the same financial beliefs that we practise. Well, you do. We would like to offer you a junior post starting seven-o-clock Monday morning." Aaron's muscles tensed; his skinny hand nervously gripped the chair. Anxious eyes twitched with disbelief, nervous trepidation. Nervous disbelieving eyes swept searchingly the ceiling; searching for confirmation from a greater source; he longed to shout for relief.

The Jew relaxed, allowing the Vice Presidents glowing statement to warm his gut. The air sizzled with positivity, expectation; exciting vivid pictures of his new job swam into an overactive mind. Negativity was banished replaced by a satisfying sense of gratification, fulfilment. "Thank you." Aaron's grateful response shot forth in a nervous stutter of jubilant gratitude. The Jews eyes once again shot heavenward with thoughts of thankfulness for his parents backing. "Father, we did it." He whispered as tears of relief streamed his ruddy cheeks, the vice president tactfully pushed forward a box of tissues, Aaron nodded tacit gratitude. The vice president leaned forward, thrusting forward a welcoming hand before employing a more sombre tone grunted. "Until seven-o-clock Monday." Herr Schmidt issued quietly whilst pressing a button. Coincidentally the central heating clattered into action. Gurgling... hissing the progression of hot water surging through the ageing system. Once again, the Oak door swept silently, effortlessly open to a staid secretary sporting grey flecked hair; attired in a brown tweed suit. She took Aaron gently, but firmly, by the arm, leading him from the palatial room.

Surprise shock and horror sprang to secretary's numbed eyes staring at the water streaming from the radiator. "Herr Schmidt; the water." She gasped in horror. Schmidt's gaze followed hers to a pool of water. The ageing Vice President engaged a jocular disposition. His Blue eyes twinkled mischievously replied humorously. "Ah! The aggravating; irritating hostilities of inanimate objects." Herr Schmidt chortled mirthfully; through a snigger he added, "call the plumber." But Schmidt's attempt at joviality met with scarce appreciation from the strait-laced secretary, forcibly ushering Aaron from the room. The Jew, face aglow, paused hesitantly at the door; turned abruptly as though to speak. But the brevity of meeting followed by his swift engagement; swept him into a reverie of pleasurable silence. His brain engaged perplexity struggled for the right words; the exuberant open-mouthed Jew remained speechless.

# 8

The Office

A typical working day at the Bundesbank starts at seven a.m. finishing at eight p.m. with a handsome forty-minute dinner break. It was Aaron's third day and to his utter amazement, a lucrative account serving one of their biggest customers landed on his desk. This highly prized account, historically, was dealt exclusively by Herr Schmidt, a group of inquisitive workmates gathered closely around Aaron's desk. "You are indeed honoured." Echoed an admiring bystander mingling with curious office work-colleagues encircling Aaron. Sheer incredulity sprang to their faces as the young Jew transposed figures. Aaron's dexterity in juggling, manipulation of complex, financial figures from the balance sheet, held the attendant group in awe.

The midday sun shone brightly through the office windows as Aaron, after a short spurt of frenetic activity sat upright; face beaming with delight. Closer scrutiny of the document revealed significant savings on the account; awestruck colleagues stepped back in stunned amazement. Management appreciation filtered in double quick time from the elite of the board room to the office. An appreciative Vice President ensured Aaron received further lucrative accounts. Yet again the Jew impressed his fellow colleagues with his analytical dexterity bringing the account to a satisfactory conclusion. Through this entangled mass, of complex financial configurations, his magical touch had provided yet another impressive profitable result.

Unsurprisingly, this bright young Jew was held in the highest esteem by workmates. The young man's financial nous without exception; surpassed all work colleagues. After a mere six months? The young Jew was plucked from obscurity, jettisoned to the penultimate seat of power; the chair of Vice President.

The young Jew found sleep to be at a premium that Sunday night. The following morning it was an excited, tired and overwhelmed Aaron, that reported for his new position. The young Jew opened the impressive wooden doors to the bank at exactly six fifty-five that first scary morning.

Apprehension aligned itself to uncertainty... excitement; injected a cocktail of emotions to course his shaking body, introducing lingering fingers of doubts to surge his skinny torso as Aaron climbed cautiously the stairs leading to his office. Where he found the nameplate on the door of Herr Schmidt, he knocked; entered under a cloud of nervous apprehension. "Good morning, Vice President Aaron Yitshack." Herr Schmidt boomed. Aaron's well-shaped hairy eyebrows winged with embarrassment. A wave of achievement swept over him; adrenalin coursed his body; confidence surged to the fore. "Yes! and good morning to you Herr Schmidt." Resounded his perplexed stuttering's in confused consternation. Schmidt's finely tuned mind honed in on the worrying concerns littering Aaron's voice; he replied softly. "I'm here for but a few days, primarily to accustom you to your hectic schedule: familiarise you with your new surroundings." The Vice President muttered as he playfully twisted the sign, "this will be put on the door later today." Early morning rain rattled the windows of the office as the retiring vice president swivelled about, smiling. Aaron's cheeks reddened at sight of his name aligned to the sign of Vice President, "I will be out of your hair by Thursday; I then officially retire to the peace, quiet of my bungalow in the Bavarian mountains." The corner of his mouth lifted wryly as a staidly dressed secretary entered; laid refreshments on the table to a funereal silence, "meet your new secretary." The vice president voiced somewhat lazily, waving a bony hand at lady exiting subserviently. The present and retiring Vice Presidents lapsed into a conspiratorial conversation. But even this remarkable achievement of the young Jew; was to be eclipsed.

9

1932–Winston Churchill

A post-war demoralised Germany fought poverty valiantly for its very survival. Over Germany dark clouds amassed over the hordes of starving Germans making a herculean effort to escape the unforgiving, cast-iron grip of poverty. Their dire situation perpetuated by WW1. was now being made even worse by the Great Depression; unemployment escalated to an unprecedented four million. September 1932, an insignificant British visitor embraced the German culture on a research visit to Munich. A back bench conservative minister, Winston Churchill, researched a biography, this being the very reason for his visit to Germany. He attempted to script the life of his famous ancestor, John Churchill Duke of Marlborough. John Churchill's famous victory over the French in the battle of Blenheim, is still being celebrated by historians. The backbencher, Winston Churchill, would write three volumes. Consisting of over one million words recording the outstanding feats; of the greatest general Britain ever produced.

Adolf Hitler's entry into the political arena gained the ascendancy; indeed, he became the most talked-about political figure. Coinciding with Churchill arranging to meet Putzi Hansfstaengl German economist, also amateur history buff. Putzi worked for Lutz von Krosig Hitlers Financial minister. Putzi advised Churchill that Hitler frequented his hotel daily and would gladly arrange a meet.

A buoyant Churchill cocooned in boyish enthusiasm readily agreed. The following day, during a financial meeting with Hitler;

Putzi muttered hopefully. "Heir Hitler, I have a friend who would like to meet you," Putzi suggested. "And who might this friend be? Hitler replied airily. Hope built within Putzi. "Winston Churchill." The amateur historian mouthed enthusiastically. "And what would be the benefit to me if I were to meet this, Winston Churchill; is he not a mere backbencher in English politics," Hitler replied derisively. "Yes," Putzi replied in muted tones of disquiet; knowing his request had slipped into the dark recesses of the Fuehrer's mind. A grimace of dissatisfaction lined Hitler's brow, who replied with obvious irritation. "This Winston Churchill is a nobody; I have not got time." The German leader grated impatiently whilst stroking his ridiculous moustache; Hitler flashed the Nazi salute and marched from the room.

The French General and leader Louis X1V, whom John Churchill defeated at the battle of Blenheim, bore striking similarities to Hitler. The General too tried to expand his countries boundaries; exactly what Hitler would eventually aspire to. This meeting with Churchill would have been ideal preparation for determining world events when they were to meet in a decisive confrontation twelve years later. If only the German leader knew, he'd just refused to meet the man about to play a pivotal role in his eventual downfall; his nemesis.

10

1935 – The Bundesbank Hitler and his Brownshirts

1935. Aaron attended a meeting presided over by the seventy-five-year-old president. The Jew had been informed that he was to replace the president on his retirement; in six months hence. It was the day Aaron the president interview him for that treasured position, within the young Jew built up an unnerving dilemma. Running the bank had been his boyhood dream. But warring mobs, and the anti-Semitism slogans running amok within the city created niggling, disturbing doubts within an already worried clouded mind. Glumly he shot an agonising stare at foreboding black clouds negotiating sluggishly their progress across Berlin's angry skies. The moment he had been planning for had arrived. His boyhood dream was about to become a reality. Tragically this burning issue between him and his precious dream, stood the German populaces increasing hostility towards the Jewish race. Auschwitz and Birkenau death camps had been established with millions of Jews being dispatched there. The situation further destabilized judgement on his dilemma, on top of those worries was his father's ill health.

The President was only too aware of his successor troubled disposition, so offered the Jew a lift home. "You think about our proposition overnight, leave your car at the bank. I'll take you home, pick you up in the morning; in what is to be your new car." The president proposed somewhat seriously, in his eyes... concern:

they approached what was to be his new automobile. "Many thanks." A troubled Aaron replied, positioning his skinny bottom onto the white leathered upholstery of the passenger seat; of the new luxurious three-litre-Volkswagen. Later that evening at home a sullen Aaron glared again at the same type of black clouds he had witnessed earlier.

The menacing clouds unleashed torrential rain upon the luxurious detached houses in the Jewish enclave; Aaron returned inside the house to protest with his parents who wanted him to leave Germany. "But Mama, Papa I cannot; I have given your proposal a great deal of thought but the answer remains the same; I cannot leave without you both." The Jew spluttered; to further dampen his mood torrential rain pounded heavily their Georgian style windows. In a stiff jerky movement, the ageing Aaron's proud father rose unsteadily to his feet in protestation of his son's stubbornness. "Son your mother and I, have spent eighty joyful years; on God's earth." He paused... took a much-needed inhalation of breath; tired bloodshot eyes held his wife with a loving conviction. Aaron's elderly mother with grey hair flopping over her creased brow was already mouthing her brave intransigent response, "We are ready to face those damn warring brown shirts." She croaked her supportive reply. "You must go, Aaron, you can travel much faster without us." Pleaded his fragile Silver-haired mother, "you, your wife must leave Germany, Austria will be much safer. Go now before the murdering militia arrives." She urged urgency littering her failing croaking voice.

Aaron's father gripped his troubled chest; violent coughing robbed him of much-needed air. His eyes dilated, head shot ceiling-ward, before drifting into a fugue state and collapsing to the fetal position on the floor. Fear cloaked the disbelieving eyes of the worried frustrated Aaron. Dropping to his knees beside his father, he gentled the ageing greying head into the crook of his arm.

"Mama, fathers' car is outside, get into the back seat I'll bring father," Aaron yelled. "But what about our clothes... belongings." The ageing voice stuttered.

"Don't worry I'll buy what you need in Austria, now hurry." Replied Aaron impatiently. The ever-present rain-bearing clouds gathered ominously over the dark angry heavens. Forks of lightning shot across an angry sky illuminating torrential rain slicking the dirty grey pavements. Aaron with father in arms, negotiated passage to the ageing vehicle on that traumatic rain sodden evening. Unmitigated dread filled the family as loud staccato gunfire echoed its deathly rattle through the rain-filled cold night air. The gravity of their situation grabbed them... held the frightened Jews in a spine-chilling dilemma. A frightening gripping fear chilled Aaron's spine. The young Jew stood as though in suspended animation.

He stood for what seemed an eternity in soaked clothing, holding his unconscious ailing father in his arms. Aaron leant his father on the back seat of the car beside his wife. The fear-stricken family remained motionless in their bubble of uncertainty. There had been expectancy of a bloodthirsty backlash from German brownshirts, but these atrocities the brown shirts were executing were barbaric, inhumane, instilled a terrible fear within their frightened minds. The gunshots injected a fearsome terror into their fragile bodies. A dense black smoke spiralled heavenwards as the group sat staring from the rain-soaked windows into the blackened heavens.

The terrified Jews stared open-mouthed from their stationary vehicle at the raging inferno. As two hundred yards further down the avenue a newly built detached house of a senior bank clerk lay engulfed in flames surrounded by looting, bloodthirsty brown shirts. The foul stench of death; lingered threateningly in the air. Tortured, blood-curdling screams from Jews trapped in the house only grew louder as the hot flames licked ever closer to their bodies; their cries for help fell upon deaf ears that dark horrific night. That sorrowful wail of death pangs chilled the bones of Aaron and family safely ensconced in their ageing Volkswagen beetle.

Eyes of fear stared into the rear-view mirror at the rapidly approaching brownshirts progressing menacingly towards their car. Shooting pains of urgency gripped the gut of Aaron as the advancing bloodthirsty brown-shirts neared. They charged, waving their weapons towards the stationary, ageing car. The Jew, with fingers trembling turned the key feverishly several times, before getting spark plugs to splutter with uncertainty. The rusting car struggled to gain momentum before exploding into life, then almost immediately collapsed back to the silence of inactivity. The occupant's heartbeats rose rapidly to unhealthy levels.

Aaron felt the cold clammy fingers of sweat chase his spine; the fearsome brown-shirts charged ever closer to their stationary vehicle. Would the ageing Volkswagen's engine fail? Would the terrorising brown-shirts ensnare them? Just a few of the torturous provocative questions troubling the frightened occupants sitting defenceless, unarmed in that ageing vehicle. The torrential driving rain pounding mercilessly their rusting vehicle only increasing their stress levels. Ever increasing forks of lightning crashed earthward. Into Aarons worried face crept a determination. His head shot heavenward as though he sought divine inspiration. As gently he coaxed the accelerator pedal up and down; the blood- spattered brown-shirts reached the car. They surrounded the motionless vehicle, rifle butts banged threateningly against the roof of the car; bloodied hands tried to force open the fly window. The Jews sat cocooned in terror as Aaron attempted many times to start the engine; Aaron's shaking body froze in a bubble of petrification. The frightened occupants trembled as brown-shirts levered rifle butts between the seals of the door to force it open. The vehicle chose that terrifying moment to engage, jerkily exploding into life with a forward movement. The bloodthirsty group of brown-shirts standing arrogantly in front of the car were mowed down to the ground.

Aaron momentarily reflected dismally on the tragic irony of the situation. His brand new three-litre company Volkswagen car; remained motionless in the Bundesbank car park. Thoughts of the glittering career, he was leaving behind haunted him as he negotiated the ancient machine over bomb craters littering the road. Aaron's knuckles whitened as his vice-like grip held tightly the steering wheel of his ageing machine, maneuvering with uncertainty over rubble-strewn roads leading to Austria.

From the back of the car cries of anguish were released by his father, the ageing Jew fought for breath. With his health rapidly deteriorating Aaron's father was scared of sleep, he forced heavy eyelids open in an effort to stay awake. Weakness invaded his skinny torso, he fainted; collapsing limply upon the skinny bony knees of his wife. With silver hair flopping upon her brow, she with loving affection nursed her husband with the caring only a wife could provide, stroking the sweating forehead of her husband's balding head.

Aaron attempted to inject a modicum of hope into the maudlin air of despair, defeatism. The vehicle shuddered, bumped ungainly its progression over the potholed dusty road to safety. "We've escaped the animalistic rage of the militia." He chirped, as the ageing Volkswagen beetle progressed safely, its perilous advancement. The car rattled across the German border into

Poland, through the unsettled Czech Republic into Linz, Austria, before arriving at their destination; Steyr. A tired, exhausted Aaron endured many hours of stress-filled driving, before killing the ignition, in joyous euphoric claims, he mouthed. "Mama, Papa, we made it." But these excited victorious acclamations were to fall unheard upon deaf ears. His travel-weary passengers were cocooned within the safety afforded by the oblivion of peaceful sleep.

11

1938–Kristall Nicht

It was the 9th and 10th of November, a carefully orchestrated violence erupted; the night of broken glass exploded. German brownshirts attacked Jews homes and properties. Daubing what few shop windows remained with large letters of JUDE. Thousands of Jews properties were broken into, ransacked, 35000 Jews were arrested and ushered forcefully into filthy-run down ghettos, swelling the ever increasing numbers of death bound Jews. The German hierarchy (backed by Hitler) had placed Germanys defeat in World War one squarely upon the shoulders of the Jews.

12

1929–Lyon

A euphoric Andre was positive he had clinched the production contract. He stood proudly with his son beside their new factory. Five-year-old Jean Pierre clutched excitedly his father's hand. The couple entered the factories frenetic atmosphere; generated by the toiling workforce at their machines. The youngster gazed in awe, at the dexterity of workers operating machines. "Papa, what are they doing?" Young Jean Pierre questioned, bewilderment lacing his young voice. "The men operating the machines, are semi-skilled; they are producing parts for motor cars. Whilst the men wearing white coats and supervising operations are engineers. The engineers, using a micrometer, ensure the measurement of parts produced is within required tolerances." Andre's chest swelled with pride in his technical expertise. "Can I operate a machine?" Jean Pierre questioned in boyish enthusiasm. "Maybe, when you're older, finished school." Andre laughed grabbing his sons' hand, "come, Jean Pierre, it's getting late we must go now. We told mama we'd be home in time for dinner; and I have an important meeting to attend."

1939 Germany invaded Poland killing six million Poles, half were Jews. Rape and pillaging of expensive artefacts proliferated the Jewish quarter. On completion of their robbery, the Nazis set light to the buildings. The devastated Jews were forcibly rounded up into dirty ghettos before being sent to a death camp and gassed.

13

Austria

An exhausted Aaron and family on completion of their fraught journey from Germany booked into a cheap hotel bordering the outskirts of the third largest town in upper Austria; Steyr. The towns two rivers, Enns and Steyr, flowed into one at Babenberg castle. It was within this imposing building, lunchtime the following day. Threatening wintry rain clouds lumbered their cumbersome progress against dark angry skies. Thick cold grey damp mist blanketed the picturesque town bristling with midday shoppers. It was in the Castles coffee shop, Aaron literally bumped into his first bit of luck. Whilst returning from the counter, coffee in hand, he collided with a young Austrian.

"My apologies!" Aaron spluttered, his cheeks flushing a deep red. Hans smiled benignly, replied courteously. "No please I was not looking where..." Silence blanketed the air before the shy Austrian cut into Aaron's apology as in a restrained, polite voice said, "reckon we could call a truce; my name is Hans." The young Austrian intervened in gushing tones of enthusiasm, his outstretched hand shooting forward. "Pleased to meet you, my name is Aaron." The Jew replied grasping the hand of friendship.

Entrepreneur Hans longed to run his own company; he had heard that a large Automotive Company wanted to outsource part of its production. This German car company presently sourced fifty per cent of its production in France.

Due to Germany's financial problems, the manager wanted to outsource the remaining 50% outside of Germany. Schmidt had already researched the possibility of sourcing cheaper suppliers in France/Austria. Hans was graced with generous amounts of capital but lacked business nous. The financial expertise needed to launch such a venture. Heavy droplets of rain pounded the walls of the castle, bouncing onto the proud Oak's hovering perilously at the side of the moat surrounding the castle. The once green leaves of the trees, now a fading crisp brown, were displaced by rain forcing them to flutter in a spiral motion; earthwards.

Meanwhile back in the cafeteria, the seated Aaron and Hans gravitated apprehensively into small talk. Hans rose from the table to collect their second coffee, the young Austrian returned to the Jew coffees in hand, but Aaron's face was masked in a query. "You got a problem?" Hans queried the glum face of Aaron. "I arrived with my family from Germany two days ago and need a job. I was wondering, do you know of any banks currently employing?" Aaron blurted. Hans eyes widened in expectation and blurted. "If you want a job at a bank, I take it you have knowledge on the complexities of finance. You do know about finance?" The unbelieving Hans gasped. "Well, yes... I have a degree in economics, but I'm Jewish." Aaron's head dropped to his chest in dismay.

His questioning eyes levelled challengingly at Hans in an interrogative glare, "does that present a problem?" Aaron snarled angrily. A lump the size of small boulder slipped down his throat, probably a gulp of expectant dismay. "No, not in the least." The Austrian paused whilst seeking a tactful reply, "Hey I'm an entrepreneur in need of an economist, not a bloody racist. I may have this once in a lifetime opportunity to start a factory with a ready-made outlet for its products. But I need, seeking; someone to guide me through financial complexities surrounding the deal. Sorry I was being over presumptuous. Don't suppose you could?" Hans added dolefully, raising the cup to lips; his faltering voice reflected sad resignation. A warm smile graced Aaron's lips, the frowns of concern creasing his forehead vanished. "Well now I know I'm talking to a friend. You, sir, are talking to the man who advised Germany's biggest bank, on their financial policies; of course, I can." Aaron blurted to the stunned Austrian. A disbelieving Hans again threw forth his hand, excitement warmed his stomach, with eyes dilating in happiness he gushed enthusiastically. "You could be my silent partner, my financial Guru. I'll provide the cash, you your expertise." Hans gurgled in boyish enthusiasm. Aaron grabbed the Austrians hand optimism awash in his eyes; he whispered. "Well, I'm not completely broke, I have shares tied up in the Bundesbank. If push came to shove; I may be able to provide a little capital." Euphoria embraced the air, with a caffeine injection the duo slurped celebratory the beginning of what would prove to be a fruitful, profitable relationship.

"We'll set up a production company here; in Steyr. I have spotted the perfect place, an empty warehouse hugging the banks of the river Enns. In Steyr there's an excess of skilled labour, employing personnel will be no problem. But all this is dependent we get the contract, that of course, you will arbiter. We could be supplying the new automotive company "The Steyr branch of Daimler Puch" before the end of the year." Hans blurted excitedly before disappearing from the cafe returning minutes later. "I've contacted the motor company, set up a meeting with the director Meindl tomorrow." Hans blurted excitedly. "Why the urgency?" Aaron queried cautiously. "We need to get in quick before the opportunity is lost, there are other prospective bidders. I heard on the grapevine, Frenchman Andre Dupont, owner of several production units in Lyon. He has already made an approach to Meindl; proposing his unit taking on extra work." Hans's chest swelled with deep inhalation of worried breath; apprehension beset the Austrians shaking hand. Han's bid won the contract.

The first five years trading of the Auto company was hectic, problematical, but profitable beyond their wildest dreams. Aaron however, being the cautionary pragmatist, released only 70% of net profits to shareholders; 30% going to a separate account. The Jew harboured grave suspicions, regarding the credibility of their largest shareholder the Bundesbank. Germany's biggest bank had problems with its cash flow; it being immersed within financial frailties of its own. Another several fruitful years passed for Hans and Aaron.

Halfway through what proved to be a troubled year Aaron summoned Hans for a meet. "We've arrived at decision time," Aaron grunted to his partner as he strode into the boardroom. Hans produced an audible gasp of surprise. "Sorry! I thought the firm was doing well." The Austrian blurted reaching for his coffee. Aaron's head dropped; his mind raced to find the right criteria; his head jerked upward before levelling numbed eyes at Hans. "Yes, you're right, Schmidt of the Bundesbank phoned me, regarding contractual obligations, they are about to change dramatically," Aaron replied, warm brown eyes studying with rapt concentration, the latest production report of Daimler Puch Automotive Company. "So why the meeting, you deal with financial peculiarities, terms conditions?" Hans questioned. "To sustain growth next year; we need to invest heavily in machinery. Secondly, the Bundesbank, from whom we borrow money is in financial trouble. They state that to secure the contract; we've to buy the machinery with our own money. Daimler issued a statement quoting, by the end of the year we need to fulfil our contractual obligations. Their intention is to shift production from France to us; then close the Lyon branch. During the renegotiation of contracts, our quotations were cheaper than Dupont's; we won a new contract. However, this contract is on the proviso we supply one hundred per cent of parts by the end of next year; instead of present fifty per cent. If we cannot meet their requirements, the entire business will default to the Dupont's; meaning they will close us down. I have it on good authority, last week Meindl visited Lyon automotive manufacturer Dupont. No longer can we languish in our comfort zone; our choice is binary; invest in expansion... or lose the business." Aaron stared almost accusingly, handing the document to Hans who ignored the outstretched hands, waving away the papers. "Yeah, alright you're the financial expert; sort it." Hans snarled then stood and paused before turning to leave. Turning forty five degrees to his partner he introduced a warmer more cordial level into the conversation, "I'm buying a villa in Vienna, hope to move there soon you should too before it's too late." The disturbed Hans left.

14

Andre Dupont

A flustered Andre yet again was late for dinner, but the good-natured mild-mannered, slightly heavier wife; awaited at the door to welcome him. Ann Marie, with grey flecking the black locks sliding over her forehead; stared at Andre with a forgiving look. Andre nodded his apology before sliding into a vacant chair opposite his son. "Did your meeting with Herr Meindl go well, Papa?" The ten-year-old Jean Pierre enthused. "It could not have gone better son; Daimler outsources 50% of parts to the factory in Steyr of Austria; the factory is owned by a Jew and Austrian. We produce the other fifty per cent. Herr Meindll harbours an intense dislike of Jews and is looking to cut costs. This means sourcing one 100% of parts to the cheapest bidder; Meindll wants to concentrate total production in one unit. But even although the Jew is cheaper; I think we will still get the new contract." Andre gushed.

"That would be fantastic." Gushed Jean Pierre in youthful congratulatory tones. "Well even then; there is a catch." Andre paused for thought then continued, "it is common knowledge of the Germans hatred of Jews; that snippet of information could sway it in our favour. But winning the contract means doubling production; we would be sole producers for Meindll. The trouble with acceptance of the new contract; lies the snag." Andre's voice quieted.

Jean Pierre's eyes flashed in querulous anger towards his father. "What is that?" The teenager snapped with youthful impatience. "Herr Meindl agreed with the Commandant of the German concentration camp to use their prisoners as cheap labour. We would have to use these prisoners, provided by the camp. So being awarded the contract brings distasteful ethical problems; we must agree to use forced labour... Jews and Russians." "But surely Papa, if it means you make more money... principles, well they take a back seat, even if it means using Jewish or Russian prisoners." Young Jean proposed glibly, whilst in a seamless motion his spoon moved in robotic harmony; soup to mouth. Andre's eyes glinted with ironical cynicism at the cold calculating mean streak shown by his son. Even at the tender age of ten, the callous young Jean embraced a healthy disregard for human life; harboured a cruel nasty side. "Well, son instead of arguing the finer points, let us await the final result of the outcome." Ann Marie's emerged from kitchen toting dishes.

15

Hitler's Rise

Lurking in the middle echelons of Germany's unstable government, lay an increasing black hole. Apathetic policies sanctioned by the government; were summarily rejected by the disconsolate populous. A power vacuum was emerging. Charging into the challenging arena of discontent swept a little Austrian brimming with enthusiasm. This rebel Austrian was bolstered by his outrageous audacity, gritty ruthless tenacity. Qualities of primary importance for a contender to succeed filling the void; this poison chalice. This unknown Austrian with a ridiculous moustache, brownshirts leader was Adolf Hitler. A name to become synonymous with inhumane evil; this megalomaniac grabbed the mantle of power. Hitler's unshakeable faith feasted upon total ignorance within the half-starved audience. His warlike rhetoric gorged greedily on Teutonic fanaticism, dogma. This ridiculous self-confident little man placed himself in front of a rebellious, motley crowd pleading for change; gathered in front of the town hall to hear him speak.

In charged high vociferous squeaky overtones he deliberated caustically. "You empowered this government to serve the people." He challenged. The Austrians announcement was interrupted by a churlish voice of disagreement. "Yeah, our leaders are famed for their meaningless, ineffective rhetoric." The sarcastic, resigned tones replied disdainfully. Hitler stared contemptuously, before launching vociferously into his maniacal onslaught. "I would change these policies... shift power from the bourgeois to the working people." The irritated Austrian replied in a voice of indignation. "Yeah, where others have failed, how would you accomplish this?" Disbelieving tones questioned provocatively. "This government promotes ineffective policies riddled with ambiguity," Hitler yelled. "If you were in power, what would you change?" The voice challenged in derisory tones. "Our currency is worthless, regeneration is necessary." The perturbed Hitler screamed. "I ask again. In what way would your policies enact such promises." Iterated the goading, agitated words of dissatisfaction.

Hitler sought placatory words of pacification to satisfy... calm the antagonists. With an upward surge of confidence, his challenging eyes confronted his adversaries. The flesh quivered at the corner of those cold eyes staring accusingly, long, and hard at his inquisitors; he launched into an attacking fanatical tirade of condemnation. "This government's fatalistic lethargy exercised policies of predisposed negative action. That comrade is where your problem lies, I would counter their policies; take positive steps like the regeneration of our economy. I would ensure the common masses have work and revitalize our armies." Hitler paused to drink; arms gesticulated in wildly measured exaggeration. He promised not seismic, but apocalyptic changes, his promises were backed by over emphasised nuances. Coupled with inflections of speech and demonstrative body language which proved effective in winning over his warlike audience. His pre plotted moves proved a masterstroke; his convincing displays provided assurance. This pint-sized revolutionary promised to release a geopolitical bomb of such magnitude, it would propel Germany to its rightful place, amongst world leaders. "I repeat, I will rid the country of the ruling bourgeois, replacing them with the proletariat. This will lead to a true democracy; organised by the working class. We, without a doubt in our lifetime, will experience a renaissance, the re-birth of this great country. Together we will re-establish Germany as a world leader."

Hitler paused for a drink of water. "You promise to get Germany back to full time working. How would you achieve this?" The doubter questioned caustically. "I would get our comrades working building cars, not for the luxury market, but reliable vehicles the working class could afford. We must return Germany to full employment, rebuild its armies; its industries." Hitler ceased his confrontational deliberations when police in threatening moves surrounded his brown shirts. The Austrian cast a disgusted stare at the advancing black leather coated men. In a raised, antagonistic voice, the tiny Austrian launched into belligerent, provocative tones of defiance. "So, the government will not allow peaceful demonstrations. Could it be because these demonstrations are in direct conflict with their useless; ineffective policies." The Austrians belligerent outcry of confrontational challenges incensed the police, left them with no choice. Hitler was imprisoned for public disorder. On his release, Hitler once again resumed direct provocation, with outpourings of anti-government propaganda. He promoted further emphasis on the workers party's achievable goals. With the spellbound crowd totally under his control, he reiterated demands for Anti-Semitism policies. The downtrodden mass accessed euphoria, these desperate souls were ushered into a new belief, new hope. Hitler quieted after he'd provided exactly what the awestruck proletariat yearned for. His retributive rhetoric stirred ideological fervour; the adoring crowd voiced unanimously, their approval. The vociferous clamour for more from their leader accessed deafening proportions; ecstatically they launched into frenetic shouts of adoration. "Heil Hitler! Heil Hitler!" The crowd chanted with a tribal enthusiasm.

By 1933 Hitler's phenomenal popularity eclipsed the ruling bourgeois; soaring exponentially; such was the attraction of this little man... it unnerved the government. To counterbalance the Austrian's power the bourgeois government, installed Hitler into the chambers of power... made him Chancellor. The governing hierarchy although initially objecting to the Austrians entry. After subdued quiet reflection, concluded, if he entered the field; they could keep watchful eye on him. The government placed the poison chalice of the defeated German forces under his control, a blatant attempt to fragment Hitler's growing popularity.

16

Disaster

The catastrophic fall of the Mark exacerbated the financial problems facing the struggling Germany economy. Luckily for Hans and Aaron, this financial dichotomy took several years to affect them. Austria was heavily reliant upon the Bundesbank for financial input especially their Auto industry, to carry on backing Hans and Aarons company was proving problematical. The floundering Mark fragmented German businesses, trade with Austria stuttered to a dramatic halt. The Austrian Schilling plummeted into the vortex of free-fall. Hitler, unfazed by Germanys currencies volatility, accessed his precarious path with the skill of a mountain goat. He goaded the populous by inciting preaching, provocative racist policies. Tempting these disturbed hordes to the extreme, citing total extinction of the Jews being the answer to their darkest fears.

His inflammatory racist outpourings elevated antisemitism into the ascendancy. Within Austria, the resident Germans hatred of Jews escalated to new scary heights. Membership of the Nazi party rose exponentially; Austrians rushed to join Hitlers party in their thousands. Adding to Aaron's misery. Joseph Schiecher (an Austrian catholic priest) launched a tirade of Anti-Semitic slogans from his pulpit. Embracing the same sadistic, vitriolic virtues; promoted by Hitler's policies. Schiecher vociferated outright condemnation of Jews habituating the cities of Austria. "Why should these people who forced Pontius Pilate to free a robber, a murderous killer. Then hand Jesus to the masses for crucifixion. These religiously derelict people had a golden opportunity to change history; they ignored it. Well need I say more, why should these mindless, religiously devoid animals; be allowed to impregnate our children's minds with their lies; their foul untruths."

Aaron's tenuous situation had just worsened, uncertainty grabbed his gut. His troubled mind swam unnervingly into a sea of doubt. Had his family's crucial decision to leave Berlin been the correct roll of the dice. From above dark clouds rain sleeted down onto the dirty Grey pavements as stalwart partner Hans rose above the damning negativity, ignored the Nazi parties cry clamouring for Jewish blood. Hans stood behind his convictions, backed his friend and reliable Jewish partner Aaron, with unwavering resolution. The disconsolate pair shrouded in negativity; nursed their pent-up emotions in the board room, tired eyes glancing despondently over the financial column of the local rag.

They scanned their company shares; they'd plummeted even further. Wrapped within a blanket of despair the Austrian uttered in hope. "There's bound to be an update on television." Aaron choked as he flicked the switch to the television which exploded with sound; pictures sprang to life. With bated breath, the couple clung to their pathetic strand of hope. A desperate hope that the orator would reveal an upturn, improvement in their disappearing fortunes. "You're the boffin... financial genius; explain the dynamics of our dire situation." Hans groaned hands soared ceiling ward in frustration. Aaron spluttered with apathetic frustration. "Nothing could please me more than to paint a rosier picture.

Unfortunately, financial indicators predict yet further gloom and doom. Our dichotomy is, owning a thriving business; supported by a worthless economy meaning our loan repayments will increase dramatically. What with sales falling, debt repayments increasing as our company spirals into 'negative equity.' Putting it bluntly; we cannot afford to repay our creditors." Misery allied itself to the growing despondency blanketing the couple. Aaron rose, his ageing... arthritic bones progressed him in a series of lurches to the window. He swivelled his grimacing face, head nodding a tacit confirmation of their fears. An indication to his Austrian partner that there was no escaping their tangled web of poverty, "put simplistically, what we own is of less value than what we owe. When outgoings exceed income; you're heading for insolvency. The frustrating irony of our situation is that the new machinery lying in the factory. Machines that should have saved us drained our contingency fund; they bankrupted us. Short of a miracle our situation will worsen." Aaron stuttered in slow calibrated tones of resignation, his eyes dilated in despair, exasperation dressed his face. The Jews quivering fingers addressed the television screen spewing out endless streams of dismal figures. Han's eyes flared with hope. "What about the contingency fund." He gasped questioningly. "Were you not listening to a bloody word I've said," Aaron shouted. "The contingency fund, as I explained. Last year the Austrian government promised if machinery were bought locally; a tax break could be claimed. I withdrew that money to buy machinery for our expansion. Sorry, my friend that account is no more." An ironic smile soured the Jews lips. "And those are the brand-new machines lying idle in the factory." Hans wailed. "Yes... afraid so." Replied the downbeat Aaron

Although advertising their intention, large black clouds collided as they sent out there warning, they advanced sluggishly across the dark threatening sky. Aaron turned to Han's head falling forward to his chest in resignation. Vibes of defeatism consumed him; he blurted dolefully. "Who could have predicted Germany's financial collapse, that the failing Mark would have devastated our currency so rapidly. That we'd be sucked into the black orifices of oblivion." Then in more upbeat tones, the Jew blurted, "but we must hold on!" Hans, with bloodshot eyes dilating; groaned in disbelief. "I'm still digesting your impending gloomy scenario of our Armageddon. What the bloody hell do you mean, hold on: To what!" He paused then in more conciliatory tones. "But you anticipate the worst Aaron. We still have your money; albeit tied up in shares in Germany?" Hans's queried in hope. "My optimistic friend my shares in the Bundesbank are worthless. The Austrian economy is in the doldrums. Our company shares are heading towards the precipitous slope of oblivion; bankruptcy. Lastly our golden goose, the automotive company we supply, it is moving back to Stuttgart. I am not altogether sorry; I strongly oppose the use of slave labour; especially when that labour is to be supplied by Mauthaussen Gusen prison camp. That swine director Meindll, instructed Ernst Laltbrunner that a prison camp be built adjacent to the proposed new factory site. We are reliant on your input; let's be realistic." The Jew paused for a sip of brandy before recommencing, "I've seen your bank balance, it is struggling to stay in the black; how long could we last?"

Exhausted the Jew sank into the nearest seat. "We have enough money for another month's wages, we'll manage somehow." Hans paused for a moments solace, nervously he twiddled his thumbs, choked back moments of panic; continued, "sorry emotions got the better of me, it's this bedeviling insecurity; not knowing which way to turn." The air that once sizzled with condemning accusation; settled into the amicable warmth of conciliatory entreaty.

17

The Jews' Final Journey

Black rain clouds threatened the darkened angry skies; rusty hinges squeaked open the bedroom door of the ailing wife of Hans. Her ageing face etched with pain as with lurching movements, she negotiated progress to her husband. In that dramatic instant, her eyes glazed over; arms waved frantically in movements of hysteria; her limp body collapsed like a rag doll to the floor. Hans dropped to his knees, scooped his motionless wife lifeless torso into his arms; carried her to bed. The Austrians troubles had just escalated. With assets worthless, wages and debtors still to be paid... now his poorly wife. Hot tears of worry pricked the back of his eyes, his throat went dry. He drifted seamlessly into agonizing negativity, into a bubble of self-pity. Tears flooded his ashen cheeks when staring glumly at his pitiful bank balance; the situation was dire. His meagre funds would stretch no more than a week; he too now was penniless.

Aaron escorted Hans on that final journey, we plodded, cocooned within miserable nostalgia, the dusty road leading to our lifeless factory, took one last sorrowful look at the empty building. A poignant irony grabbed us as we stared glumly at our once thriving, now derelict, empty, workplace. Hans turned to Aaron. "Well old friend it is finally over, the good times have deserted us." The Austrian muttered in doleful acceptance of their dilemma. "Steady you're treading the boards of realism, beginning to sound like me. Of course, you're right we've to adjust." The pragmatic Aaron replied, he proffered outstretched hand towards Hans, "well old friend you will have already considered, that with our houses being mortgaged to the hilt; we'll have to move." Aaron blurted; a lonely tear ran down his bristled cheeks.

Hans allowed a half-smile to dress his lips; Hans withdrew a letter to brandish it like a sword in the air. I forgot to tell you I received this letter in the morning post from my brother. He's a director in the diamond mines of South Africa. He returned to Austria this morning and is willing to invest in another business; with us at the helm. He's in the country to meet Austria's Foreign Minister. On hearing our plight, he volunteered his support for any new business venture. So, I'll be giving you a call sooner rather than later." Hans blurted enthusiastically returning the missive to his pocket.

Aaron's face grimaced, he yelled in agony, collapsed limply to the ground; whilst bony fingers clutch his chest. Panic flickered in Hans eyes; hands kneaded together in worried absorption.

A cold chill encompassed Hans as he climbed, with the unconscious Aaron, into the ambulance for their journey to the hospital; Hans in despondent isolation sat in the waiting room. A diminutive, follically challenged doctor, face decorated in apology; burst into the room. The Austrian leaped from his seat worried anticipation covering his face. "How is he Doctor?" His enquiries floated in waves of uncertainty from the quivering lips of Hans. The doctor held me with a disappointing... knowing look. "You did know both his parents died in this hospital yesterday?" "No, he never said a word." Hans murmured. The bloodshot eyes of the balding doctor bubbled over his clipboard, whilst issuing in apologetic tones. "I'm sorry he was dead on arrival, we attempted resuscitation; but his weak heart couldn't cope." My head sank to the comfort of my chest, maybe to hide tears, but most likely with acceptance; I'd lost a very dear friend. My financial guru Aaron Horowitz, Jew, and trusted partner; was no more. Cocooned in self-pity, and through misted vision; I stumbled from the hospital to the taxi rank. Back in Vienna, and comfort of his front lounge, the six-o-clock chimes exploded loudly from the television.

The cool dark of evening rushed in; Hans pulled closed the curtains. Blasting from television, was more depressing financial news, cameras panned the outer government offices. Pessimism etched the grim faces of gathered businessmen, concerned eyes focussed upon government ministers attending the economic summit. The ministers entered in an organised shuffle, the conference hall. Outside, panning television cameras captured the turmoil. The confusion of an assembled, agitated crowd, surrounded the conference hall. In threatening movements of frustration, they waved frantically their placards. Condemning in protestation; the governments mismanagement of the economy.

Reclining uneasily, I raised whisky glass to mouth; eased my aching body onto cushions hugging the settee. Excitement surged my limp skinny frame, I jerked forward. Growing apprehension spawned beads of sweat to dampen my forehead when spotting my brother. His tall well-built torso progressed forcefully through the antagonistic crowd of dissenters to meet the awaiting foreign minister. The minister reciprocated when spotting my brother, he shouldered enthusiastically his way through the hostile crowd towards my brother. The Austrian government were optimistic, that a large financial investment was forthcoming from my brother. They met in congratulatory appeasement; shook vigorously the outstretched hands. He ushered his prospective benefactor through the crowd to the entrance and hall. A sharp crack whistled through the air; my brother collapsed to the ground. A bullet meant for the minister; hit and killed my brother.

I rose to my feet aghast, stood transfixed in utter disbelief, trembling hands dropping my whisky filled glass to the floor; tears ran amok down bristled cheeks. My throbbing disbelieving head, inadvertently shot ceiling-ward; in a voice of frustration, I wailed. "My brother, my only hope... my would-be Saviour." I choked in self-pitying tones of recrimination. Entering the bedroom, bloodshot eyes were veiled in sorrow. I beheld my bedridden wife's futile attempts at a smile. The ashen-faced grey-haired Esther; allowed cracked thin dry lips to part in a glimmer of a smile. "I heard you shout; your brothers been shot!" The weak tones issued sorrowfully "Yes, unfortunately confirming we'll have to move; the bank will probably send the bailiffs round next week."

It was within their "new" dwellings, situated in the squalor of less desirable residences of Vienna. Where Hans questioned his religion of Catholicism; contemplated a change. Whilst researching possible sects, religions. His roving attention was caught by local rag promoting an atheist sect, the Illuminati. His rapt attentive eyes lit up when dropping to the name of Baal. This sect could provide me with a different passage, new channels of hope, belief; Louis entered the room. "We should check out the Illuminati they worship Baal, seems a promising alternative." Hans urged handing findings to him. "Baalism. What the hell is Baalism?" Louis queried pessimistically. "The Illuminati is an atheist sect, they worship the God Baal, hence Baalism." A shriek cut me short.

We dashed into the bedroom, my wife's condition had rapidly deteriorated. The next several worrying hours my wife drifted in and out of consciousness. I was staring at damp running down the walls when my wife opened her eyes. "What happened?" She croaked weakly. "You fainted, suffered an epileptic seizure but you are alright now. I've good tidings, Louis is to have a new school." Hans blurted in subdued enthusiastic tones; he reached for her hand. "That is good news, but more to the point, how is the search progressing on the financial front?" Her brow furrowed; voice accessed an upbeat tone as she continued. "When I recover, I can work," Esther whispered, before engaging a heavy bout of coughing; her body fell limp; went cold. Her illness drained her of the vibrancy of life... sucked her into its black evil tentacles; peaceful abyss of finality.

Again, I was sucked into a vortex of instability, my world collapsed around me. Firstly, my friend and partner Aaron, my brother, now my loving wife. Could these deaths be signs; confirmation we really should start anew. I pondered our dire situation, turning to my red-eyed son Louis we hugged, shared our irreplaceable, immeasurable loss. Louis stared helplessly at his mother now released from the pressures of life; uttered in a shaky voice just above a whisper he said in words soaked in sorrow. "I'm sorry papa." Unashamedly Louis's head dropped crying to the chest. I stiffened with resolve. "We've to start anew son," I replied in a lame voice of desolation. That traumatic day, the delicately woven tapestry of life had become even more threadbare. Wrapped within an isolating bubble of cold loneliness Louis and I embraced.

We entered the third year of World War two, Jews were now disappearing in their thousands. Rumours abounded that Jews were being herded into trucks bound for the death camps, to be burned or gassed. In comparison our fate our painful existence paled into insignificance. Even so the immediate future for me and my son looked decidedly bleak. Louis and I joined the Illuminati; we embraced their beliefs; began our search for a new future. My beliefs in Catholicism deserted me; having been abruptly diverted from God. Our focus now was placed fully upon the Antichrist. Children of priests were given private tutoring, provided by ex-teacher now a pagan priest.

18

The Antichrist

Employing a genteel swagger, the teacher sauntered under a halo of confidence into the room blanketed with respectful funereal silence. "Good morning scholars, today we stretch our minds with the provocative subjects of, Evolution or Creation. To engage these challenging theories, comparisons need establishing. Today for confirmation of that controversial criteria we turn to the bible. The bible states God created all humans; starting with Adam followed by Eve. Once again, I iterate, good morning scholars, today we digress, no boring Math's or English. Instead, I invite your minds on a journey to the garden of Eden. A place that is synonymous not only with Jesus but also the traitor disciple, Judas. Christians cite God as the designer of everything surrounding us. Christians are intransigent in this belief, and outrightly refuse to accept the Darwinian theory. A bold theory claiming that life evolved from the single-celled invertebrate. That scenario however seems highly improbable, at the least highly dubious. Our body with such a vast complex interaction of interlinked parts would indeed necessitate the involvement of incredulously intricate detail. For a single cell to organise, deal with such complex innumerable interactions is beyond belief. This perfectly functioning structure would need to have been designed. The atheist's response was sheer outright indignation when considering this scenario. Their viewpoint or argument, was that if God is the designer; who designed God? The very definition designer is a contradiction in terms. As a design for the human race would have meant the participation of humans to accept the outcome; we atheists state emphatically that there is no god."

A bored Louis interrupted the speaker's oration. "But sir why are we even contemplating the study of the bible. Aren't we the very people whose motives you are now throwing into doubt?" The question slipped glibly from his tight lips. "Well perceived young man, a pertinent question relevant to its justification, however, the answer lies within the detail. Let us engage our discussion from a different perspective. For two and a half thousand years Christians have juggled with the conundrum... possibility. That the devil, after successfully tempting Eve to eat from the forbidden tree of knowledge in the Garden of Eden. Proceeded to have sex with her. That Cain, who killed his brother Abel, was the seed of the serpent, not of Adam. To further exacerbate their dilemma, Christians believe Jesus is their Saviour. Jews however believe Jesus, was not the promised one, but a misleading preacher; under the pretence of being gods son. Consequently, they put Jesus to death; yes, he was put to death on a stake... not a cross as many pictures portray. The Jews allowed their beliefs to fade; they became disillusioned; eventually this conundrum turned them against their Jewish faith.

Another interesting question is the exodus of Jews to Hitlers death camps. Catholicism turned a blind eye, a possible sign of tacit coercion to that earth-shattering momentous event. Could that have been because of the Jews misplaced beliefs? Ask yourself this very relevant question. Who in their right mind would give a concession to Hitler for the total extermination of the Jews? Whatever your answer, the resulting consequence was. Nazi concentration camps, in contravention of common human decency. Within these abominations Nazis gassed thousands upon thousands of helpless Jews. Could these inhumane actions have been avoided? Were the actions of the Nazi party purely a result of Jewish entrenchment in their dogmatic belief.

The belief that Jesus Christ was not the son of God? Now Louis after digesting these imponderable questions. We at this juncture, draw another presumptive parallel. Could it be possible that Hitler was, in fact, the seed of the devil?

Hitler tried to exterminate Gods chosen people the Jews, most of whom still await their Saviour to appear. You might conclude the only difference between the Illuminati and Christians; is that we seek a god called Satan not Jesus. From our lesson, you can draw yet another tenuous parallel. This Satan, that God and his cohorts threw down from the heavens in approximately 1914. Satan we strongly believe to be the Antichrist. So, although it may seem strange, by employing a stretch of the imagination. We are tenuously linked to the Jewish strands of belief. We both believe our Saviour has still to arrive. But that is enough learning for today, we shall resume tomorrow. Once more we shall return to more mundane lessons, Math's, and English. Good day." The priest slipped from the room as quietly as he'd arrived.

For ten fruitless years, Hans and Louis searched in vain for their savior the antichrist, before succumbing to ill health. It was from his death bed; Hans extracted a solemn promise from son Louis to continue his quest.

19

1938–Berchtesgaden

Insane flurries of swirling snowflakes swept earthward from angry heavens; a Christmas card white covering nestled upon the picturesque village of Berchtesgaden. This remote village nestled in the snow-covered Bavarian mountains of Germany. The village, an idyllic, quiet picture-postcard village, had being chosen by Hitler as his recluse. On that storm ridden black Monday morning of September 1938; the village bristled with Black Citroens sporting the feared swastika.

Silvery bone slants of moonlight flickered upon the village and snow-laden chalets. Through the half-light of evening, faint fingers of light pulsed the ageing windowpanes of that; "special" chalet. This snowbound village hosted vital talks. Two world leaders locked their horns in hostile... stale-mate negotiations. Should these critical talks fail, the outcome would ensure apocalyptic waves of unrest. Uncertainty would ignite disastrous repercussions rippling threateningly throughout the entire world. From the outset, their diametrically opposed views were to stutter to an inevitable impasse; were doomed to cataclysmic failure. Outside, the onslaught of a storm-driven snowfall, ensured the already freezing temperatures dropped even lower.

Within the snow laden wooden hut, a stress driven Hitler struggled to convince the English Prime Minister, that the incursion into Czechoslovakia; was merely reclaiming the lost land; Sudetenland. This stoic Englishman's eyes were blurred, confused; his frayed nerves created an icy knot in his stomach when questioning the validity of the German leader's statement. Claiming his intervention was at the least; blatantly controversial. That the despot's invasion, on the defenceless eastern Bloc of Poland's borders; was outrageous and bordering on the insane.

A north-easterly wind hastened heavy snow laden clouds on their threatening progression over angry heavens. Swathes of heavy Black clouds blanked out momentarily, weak silvery moons rays from reaching the village. That special village slipped dramatically into complete darkness. The extreme temperature sunk to minus ten degrees due to the disappearance of the moon; temperatures plummeted even further. Herr Flicks shivering finger, cleared ice lying in asymmetrical patterns on the weather barometer. Unrelenting howling arctic winds swept ice-covered street. Even the thick regulation Army overcoats proved insufficient to prevent Arctic wind penetrating, their thick grey fibres. The muscle-bound guards, Herr Flick and Schmidt; stamped feet to generate a modicum of heat into their frozen bodies. The unrelenting cold blasts of wind attacked the guards' bodies into a submissive cringe. Finger ends tingled before losing feeling; numbness invaded them. The frozen guards made a herculean attempt to control their mindset; remain positive.

Angry clouds parted allowing silver slants of light flicker on the building housing the leaders. Ice shards glistened upon the numb lips of Herr's Schmidt and Flick. The guards conjured pictures of themselves basking within warmer climes; to help combat their arctic conditions. Unfortunately, recollections of sun-blessed lands merely introduced deeper discontent. The unrelenting, penetrating cold, injected instability into their fragile minds; festered ambivalence. They shivered uncontrollably, concentrated thoughts on generating heat in the hope it may bring brief relief to their freezing pain-racked bodies.

Welcome early morning light crept over the Bavarian mountains, easing the freezing temperatures embracing the village. Droplets of ice formed on the eyebrows of the guard's nearing completion of their nightly vigil. That of guarding Herr Hitler's chalet, failure in guarding the hut correctly meant they could be transferred to the front lines. Herr's Schmidt and Flick struggled to keep tired eyelids open, tiredness corrupted their thoughts. The SS officers fought against sleep, snuggling for warmth deep into their snow-covered army issue trench coats. Freezing extremities borne on arctic gales ensured the guards did not escape that harsh blizzard sweeping in on that unforgiving cold Arctic wind; their bodies continued to shiver. Herr Flick threw a questioning glance to his comrade. "Herr Schmidt; we'd be much warmer sheltering under the eaves of the chalet. "Jawohl" Herr Flick grunted in agreement. Schmidt's tired eyes threw searching glances the length and breadth of the snowbound deserted street. "It's all clear," The trembling guard announced. The tired, discontented soldiers deserted their positions, sheltered under the wooden eaves of the porch. Pressing their bodies against the wood of the chalet afforded them a modicum of warmth; their newly found warmth however was heavily tainted with shame.

Within the "special chalet," Hitler and Chamberlain had spent the entire night in fruitless negotiation, their polarised thoughts split into selective intransigent positions. The leaders were tired, frustrated... exhausted; Hitler rang for refreshments. Within the fireplace of that sparsely furnished room, lay a lifeless smouldering log. The world leaders stubbornly languished within their opposed viewpoints. Both immersed within the heat of their vociferous disagreement remained oblivious of the chill blanketing the room. Hours of ill-tempered futile deliberations had proved disappointedly inconclusive; their disagreement being the only link to common ground between Chamberlain and Hitler. "For the third time in twenty years, Germany's people have been brought to their knees; this invasion will knit the working class together." The German leader hesitated in exasperation. "This incursion will create a camaraderie amongst the proletariat; banish negativity from their pitiful minds. Retrieval of our stolen land will help the German populous to rise; feel alive." Hitler screeched animatedly. "No Herr Hitler, what you're in fact suggesting, is England legitimise your unwarranted, unprovoked invasion; upon a defenceless regime. A contradiction in terms of your proposals." The stinging accusations of the bespectacled Prime Minister clung like a challenge, to that cold morning air. The veins in Chamberlains neck bulged, his lined face dressed in condemnation; flushed with conviction.

Chamberlain was acutely aware of what devastating consequences would follow; should he mishandle this finely balanced, precarious situation. Hitler cherished the thought of Germany and England striking an alliance, that with both countries uniting they could become a world power. To the utter disgust of the Fuhrer, talks floundered in the bowels of disagreement. The German leader stroked his ridiculous moustache whilst reflecting upon earlier considerations. Chamberlain entered a reverie of unease, accessing stubborn single-mindedness. That room that for so long had sizzled with angry charges of incrimination drifted into an eerie silence. The air that had spiked with animated frustration; now cocooned itself into a dismal finality. Rejection resounded loudly in the ears of the leaders. In unison, their heads dropped to their chests in sorrowful resignation. Tired minds struggled to accept failure; a funereal silence hung heavily in the air; the German leader sat despondently.

Chamberlain felt the tinge of an empiric victory; Hitler had failed to reply.

Rusty hinges squeaked the door open, enter a terrified ageing maid back bent, her lined face advertised her advancing years. She approached the table in tentative jerky movements of subservience. Within her eye's lay submission, her eyes projecting waves of uncertainty. Skirting the fireplace and excuse of a fire; she approached the two leaders. Her slight frame wilted under the weight of her tray laden with refreshments. Cowering nervously, she placed the tray on the table, anger welled within the German leader. "Mien Got." The pint-sized despot snarled; his body shook with agitation. Distress surged the terrified torso of the maid. Hitler growled gruffly, "danker." The frightened maid poured coffee, maintaining respectfully her stoop of humility withdrew, rusting hinges squeaked her exit.

An air of resignation sat uncomfortably on Hitler's face as he paced, like a caged tiger, the worn carpet. Fingers of frustration chased the spine of his numbed body; he wanted to scream, release his pent-up emotions. His mind trawled frantically for the relevant criteria that would make a convincing argument. "Mien Got," Hitler repeated in a snarl of frustration, pausing to attack the flameless log; kick it back to life. His tired eyes were re-energised by an explosion of hungry flames snaking the blackened chimney. Chamberlain maintained the renowned stiff upper lip of English impassivity. Sustaining the typical English aloofness; he calmly sipped warm strong coffee.

20
Hitler's Acceptance of Defeat

A fury filled Hitler gazed vacantly through the snow laden window; acceptance of defeat deflated his previously buoyant ego. Eyes shot skyward, to the throaty deafening growl of a swooping Messerschmitt. Vibrations from the plane shook the very foundations of the wooden building. Herr's Flick and Schmidt shifted hurriedly their frozen bodies in fright from their warm shelter to the safety of the snowbound street. The fighter plane injected new hope into Hitler. His pulse quickened; he spun to face Chamberlain... to launch one final conciliatory entreaty.

The leader allowed uncharacteristic warmth to embrace his voice as he addressed Chamberlain. "I ask you for the last time, Herr Chamberlain. When Germany invades Czechoslovakia, will England support the Fatherland in the recapture of Sudetenland?" This explosive challenge injected a deafening silence into the chilled air. Introducing an unambiguous negative response, the Prime Ministers nodded his tacit refusal. The flushed face of the distressed Fuhrer courted the negativities of desperation. With mind embroiled in rejection, he hung precariously between despair and dejection. Blood vessels on his neck stood proud as his volatile temper ran wild. His blood pressure escalated with alarming rapidity, into orbit. With a sour bitter taste lodged at the back of his throat and temples pounding, angry legs stormed him over the worn carpet to confront the Prime Minister. "Sir, you do realise how many Czech lives could depend on your answer." Hitler paused before continuing, "consider carefully your position, the importance of your reply and impact on England." Hitler snarled ungraciously.

Chamberlain replaced his coffee cup to the table, in a movement of negativity his head dropped to his bony chest, accumulative disapproval clouded his tired bloodshot eyes. His head swung slowly side to side in rejection of Hitler's ultimatum. Before launching into a stinging reply heavily veiled with an uncompromising threat. "Herr Fuhrer, I cannot over-stress, that if you insist on this invasion of Czechoslovakia. The fragile, fractious relations existing between our two countries; will become untenable." Chamberlain's chest swelled when snatching a precious lungful of air, "we are sir, because of our polarised views, astutely aware what catastrophic consequences would ensue. Should you choose to continue your present foolhardy course of action." The Prime ministers head dropped in the certain knowledge; his answer had inflamed an already delicate situation. Hot blood coursed Hitler's bulging veins. "So be it." Hitler snarled in cold menacing monosyllables of finality, "Herr Chamberlain I shall have your car brought to the front." Hitler screamed cold sweats of dissatisfaction chilled the spine of the disillusioned, dejected German leader.

This sabre-rattling Austrian upstart, still reeling in disbelief of the English Prime Ministers intransigence, clicked his heels, levelled the Nazi salute; then screeched animatedly. "Heil Hitler!" The ill-tempered despot barked, the leader cocooned within dejection, stormed from the room. Hitler begrudgingly accepted his wildest fears; open confrontation with the country he'd so much wanted to befriend. My conundrum to you the reader. I wonder at this point if Herr Hitler reflected with unease back to 1932, and his refusal to meet Churchill. Then a mere backbencher, now a warmongering... threatening minister hugging the front bench of government. Would his meeting with Prime Minister Chamberlain have ended differently?

Hitler's troops marched through Poland, reclaiming Sudetenland for the Greater Germany.

1938, the world encompassed a disheartening cocktail of dismay. Disbelief stirred with a healthy mixture of astonishment beset leaders looking on with bated breath. Bewildered countries withdrew quietly within their borders, shamed into their apathetic comfort zone. As though they awaited an instructive policy of justice, or was it that they awaited confirmation to enter the fray. Vociferous mutterings of discord rang loudly their discontent around the houses of Parliament. A tired, weary Chamberlain rose slowly to his feet to address the antagonists. The opposition launched vociferously their heated objections of Germany's unforgivable invasion, their provocative actions. So ferocious was the oppositions attack, the beleaguered Prime Minister conceded defeat; allowed his rear end to warm his seat. Winston Churchill, the then Foreign Secretary, sprang to his feet in defence of the Prime Minister. "My respected colleagues let us not shower blame on our Prime minister for this outrageous, despicable outcome. Instead let us in unison; praise his tireless energies. In his tireless intervention, in his very trying negotiations with this warmonger in his attempt to bring Germany's compliance, with the basic rules of humanity. Indeed, his strenuous efforts to stem the Nazi invasion extended beyond his call of duty. So please let the whole house unite as one in our platitudes of gratitude. Unified let us commend the Prime Ministers actions, his robust response. To Germany's unprovoked invasion of Poland; and their outright rejection of peace." Churchill issued gravely; loud applause echoed in total agreement in recognition of Foreign Ministers timely intervention. "May I take this opportunity to inform the house, this action is purely a safeguard and will start tomorrow morning. One million children, in nine hundred schools, will practise evacuation. I condemn out of hand these inhumane events of hostility; stand firmly with my colleagues; the opposition. But gentlemen, may I put your minds at rest. Should war result from the prime ministers meeting; by God, we'll be ready." Churchill guided his well-rounded rear end to his seat. Collective parties rose to their feet; the house erupted with solicitous applause. In overwhelming unison, the entire house shouted their appreciation for the foreign minister. For his creditable management of that explosive, volatile situation.

Then that dramatically stirring announcement; on the morning of the 3rd of September 1939. Sir Neville Henderson stated gravely. If hostilities engaged in by Germany, does not cease by 11.a.m; a state of war would exist between Great Britain and Germany, Germany failed to respond; England accepted the warlike confrontation with youthful; arrogant confidence. Hundreds of thousands eager young men; rushed to be first to sign on the dotted line in an overwhelming response to Hendersons chilling radio announcement. The official declaration of war between England and Germany. It was late 1939 and the onset of WW2. A weary Chamberlain resigned the seat to Churchill. Early 1940, the man who would prove to be Hitler's nemesis replaced Chamberlain as prime minister, Winston Churchill.

21

1940–Doctor Eugene Fischer

Hitler dispatched Eugene Fischer, a doctor of heredity and highly respected man famous for his documented work on the 'Basters of Namibia'. The doctor arrived in Gur's village jail in South-Western France. This notorious prison housed refugees of the Spanish war, gipsies, Basques, Cagots; and Jews. Eugene was to test, what Hitler referred to as the lower forms of human life. Prisoners of all nationalities were to be tested. Hitler wanted to confirm that Germans were irrefutably, the superior race. 1942, incontrovertible results arrived confirming that the Jews, being allowed to carry on. Would inevitably become the superior race. This devastating news enraged the leader, inflamed him as would a red rag to a bull. This unexpected revelation aggravated the burning need in Hitler to accelerate total extermination of this race. The German leader filed findings of Eugene Fischer to the bin; proceeded to spread his lies to the Germans that they were undisputedly; the superior race.

1941 war prepared the German army to march under the misgivings that the incursion onto Russia would be short. Due to Germany's inefficient planning for this invasion; which began during the fierce extremes of the Russian winter. This allied to the intransigence provided by the defending Russian troops led to an unexpected initial setback. But the beginning of 1942 heralded the return of clement weather. This assisted the German advance, propelling the German army five hundred miles forward; in two months. They reached river Volga and Stalingrad. Hitler ordered, that at any cost; Stalingrad must be taken. But due to the resilience of the Russians meant Stalingrad resulted in a humiliating defeat.

Hitler learned his mighty army had capitulated, in his despondency Hitler wrongly bemoaned soldiers for surrendering, for their total capitulation.

22

1945 – The Duponts

Forked lightning illuminated torrential rain pouring earthward upon Lyon and the Duponts' run-down chalet. Jean Pierre as though in suspended animation stood rooted to the spot. He stared in rapt concentration from the broken window at skeletal buildings opposite. Within the Dupont's ramshackle building, lived the once rich but now poverty-stricken Dupont family. The family consisted of seventeen-year-old Jean Pierre, mother Ann Marie, and his father Andre. This derelict desolate area of Lyon was a veritable haven for the underworld. Pre-second world war this bombsite was occupied by a thriving community, in what was now an impoverished slum. The Dupont's then were part of the rich elite, moved within a different circle of friends; lived an opulent lifestyle. Frequented with ease the lavish haunts of the financially independent class; enjoyed excesses only wealth could provide. The family of Dupont relaxed in their affluent surroundings... entered a bubble of security, accepted the belief that financially; the family was secure for life.

This bubble of their treasured security was before Hitler decided to unleash his bombers to flatten the area into submission. Dupont's dream was shattered, thrown into utter disarray. Andre remortgaged his house to raise sufficient funds to re-start his business. That too was bombed into oblivion as Hitler's bombers ensured he lost everything. In utter helplessness, Anne Marie with husband Andre and young son Jean stood apathetically by; watched the Germans planes bomb their production units into pulp. These precious units that had provided their wealth; all vanished when Nazi bombs flattened everything.

Their once ornate house brimming with opulence was now a bombed shell. They entered the despairing depths of poverty; were now paupers. Hitler's invasion had been the catalyst for Andre joining the French underground. These heroic men issued but a token resistance. But their insistence in disrupting troop movements proved but a thorn in the side of invaders, the unscrupulous Nazis. 1945, France welcomed its liberators, showered them their undying gratitude for their participation in securing their freedom. France now walked the path of a free country. With the resistance disbanding, Andre returned to family and chalet. That once-thriving community had been vacated by the rich friends; was deserted... empty. The chalet Andre returned to was a ramshackle shell of a building; situated on an abandoned squalid rat-infested bombsite.

Amongst the buildings surrounding Dupont's house, stood a skeletal building opposite occupied by the Mafia; this was their drug outlet. Within this building, dysfunctional thugs working for the Mafia organised and supplied the lucrative drug chains. Their primary functions were the distribution of drugs to immigrants, encouragement of aspiring drug runners, expansion of existing operations. It was to these clandestine meetings seventeen-year-old Jean Pierre would religiously attend. The disturbed teenager viewed the underworld of the Mafia, an escape route from his prison. That dirty ramshackle, run-down chalet his father seemed to so love; with the same passion he hated.

The door creaked open; the tired, forlorn figure of Andre entered the sparsely decorated room adorning peeling paintwork. A shade-less 40watt bulb swung randomly its shadows over three wooden chairs nestling against a welcoming spluttering fire: the squeaking hinges had prodded Ann Marie into action. "Dinners ready." Ann Marie's sombre tones boomed. Andre grunted acknowledgement of his wife's announcement; he removed his black beret from a balding head. Relentlessly, storm-driven rain pulsed their cracked windowpanes. "Winters come early." He complained, squinting over his rimless glasses at Ann Marie's rounded figure struggling with a pan of soup; she approached somewhat ungainly the table. Her black headscarf flattening her thick wavy grey hair. "Oui." She replied voice laced with boredom. "oui." She repeated ladling soup into a bowl.

A deafening crack of thunder preceded lightning blazing a jagged trail across darkened heavens. Dripping water formed a pool on the floor. Ann Marie's stared in disbelief at the dark patch on the ceiling, from which water navigated freely its path onto the ancient, threadbare carpet. With the agility of a woman half her age she placed a bucket beneath the falling water, before scolding her unruly teenage son. "Jean Pierre, stop daydreaming, come from the window, remember your manners; join papa at the table." "Oui mama, oui." The teenager replied in a voice of boredom, hands firmly planted in the pockets of his fading blue jeans. He resumed his arrogant posture, staring with envy from the window at two figures emerging from the ruins opposite. The taller, uglier thug wore an angled worn trilby over his forehead protecting his pot-marked face from the driving rain. His colleague struggled to control a salivating German shepherd dog. The muscle-bound dog strained at its leash, attempted to attack a passing black Citroen; that vanished without incident into the dark arms of night.

The young Frenchman stood engrossed... motionless. Rapt concentration engraved his brow. He gazed in awe as the thug struggled to control his overweight German Shepherd dog. The teenager gasped in disbelief, when a second thug approached from behind. Adjusted his wet trilby, before in one seamless movement; left hand slipped inside his jacket pocket. Withdrew a gun; fired several bullets into his colleague's forehead. The dead thug dropped to the ground into a dirty pool of water. That dirty water coloured a deep red as blood escaping from motionless corpse seeped liberally into the pool.

A third squat figure, waddled from the bombed building skirting the dead man, addressed the thug holding a smoking gun; in a piercing American drawl he ordered. "Here's your money now blow; don't forget to report to Scar." The fat American growled before disappearing into the dark shadows of night. In misplaced admiration, Jean Pierre muttered coldly. "What a way to live, make your own rules, when they're disobeyed shoot them; that's the third death this week." The bloodthirsty Frenchman cackled cynically. Jean Pierre stared at condensation forming pools at the base of the ageing window frame; before re-focussing on the action opposite, "one day, yes one day." Jean Pierre vowed through gritted teeth; eyes widening with envy, when spotting the thug struggling to control the victim's dog. The thug placed several thick wads of money into his inside pocket. Wheeled about into the driving rain, guiding the dog into the shadows of darkness.

"Jean Pierre! The table now!" Ann Marie screamed; her patience finally exhausted. Jean Pierre lingered, envious eyes staring into the empty darkness of space at the bombed building opposite supplying the nefarious life he yearned for. He turned slowly, deliberately, in his glacial world of quiet; approached his father and table.

23

Pearl Harbour

Japan allied itself to England in the first world war against Germany. But December 1941, Japanese bombed Pearl Harbour an unannounced, unprovoked attack. A direct sign Japan allegiance lay with Germany in World War two. On completion of their successful bombing raid, euphoric Japanese pilots returned to the deck of the aircraft carrier in a jubilant mood. Excited young pilots consumed within self-congratulatory acclamations; rejoiced triumphantly. Bringing the ecstatic celebrations to a subdued funereal silence was the commanders stern warning in unambiguous gravelly tones. From the loudspeaker, the commander advised his youthful triumphant troops their celebrations; were but fleeting. "Today actions will no doubt... have dramatic consequences, winning the battle today against an unprepared enemy was inevitable. But all our achievements have accomplished, is to awaken a reticent... sleeping giant from its comfort zone; America will now undoubtedly declare their entry into the war." Hitler when informed of Japanese incursions remained impassive, unmoved, re-focussed his energies on the invasion of Russia.

Problems escalated amongst German Generals; impassivity conveying tacitly thier dissatisfaction when strategically ill-contrived instructions given by a hysterical Hitler reached their ears. That their battle-weary soldiers were now to fight on two fronts. Within high-ranking officer's dissension festered; insurrection spread like wildfire through the ranks. Dissatisfied Generals openly expressed anger in mutinous narratives. Disruptive news reaching the ears of the dreaded SS and Hitler. To prevent a fractious insurrection, dispel the Generals fears, the Fuehrer delivered a stirring speech. "The Third Reich will last for a thousand years." Hitler screeched in maniacal warmongering incitement. 1934, Hitler promised to rid Germany of Jehovah's Witnesses. By1939 Jehovah'sWitnesses numbers had vastly increased. Accepting the abysmal failure, of his religious rout; he redirected energies on ridding Germany of Jews.

24

Disillusioned Hans

Gnostic priest Hans wearisome search for the Antichrist was proving fruitless; despair accessed frustration. Negative vibes drove the disappointed priest into uncertainty: Hans bent his ear to the radio. Screeching maniacal tones energized him; Hitler's powerful speech of the thousand-year reign exploded into the air. Hans enthusiastically recollected bible readings, books of Peter... Revelations; quoting Jesus would reign for a thousand years. "Could this be the parallel I've been searching for." Swinging excitedly to a seated son, "tonight, Louis, you and I will celebrate with a bottle or two of red wine; our quest has ended."

The priest bid a hurried goodbye, scurried off to a pre-arranged meeting. Returning two hours later he; shouldered open the door. "Louis, Louis." Hans called to no response, the grandfather clock chimes ricocheting eerily the bare stone walls of the house. Hans stared incredulously at the dial reading nine-o-clock, "strange... Louis is always home by this time." His twisted face screwing in bewilderment, the priest progressed room to room. He entered his son's bedroom and switched on the light.

Louis with Annette entwined in a passionate embrace; Hans stared in utter disbelief. The squeaking of rusty door hinges announced his father's entrance, the noise caught Louis's attention. In one seamless movement, Louis jerked his naked body from the compromising position; confronted the intruder. "Father." In confused embarrassment, Louis agitated apologetically. "I'm sorry to disturb you," Hans mumbled pulling the door closed, shoulders drooping the Gnostic priest shuffled his lonely path to the bedroom. Co-incidentally whilst opening a bottle of wine a searing pain grabbed the priest's chest. "Help!" Resounded his agonised cry as he slumped like a rag doll on the carpet; hands clutching his bony chest. These shouts were summarily dismissed as the embarrassed flustered Louis hurriedly dressed, escorted Annette from the house. Oblivious of his father's situation Louis returned to discover his father lying prone on the wine-stained carpet; the priest had experienced his first heart attack.

Annette's father, a devout Catholic priest; nursed a deflated ego. Despair mingled with fear, exacerbated his troubling worries of what the villager's reaction would be when they learnt of his daughter's romantic liaisons. "My daughter; bedded by an agnostic." He whined, "what effect will it have on my standing as village elder; I'm finished when these rumours circulate the village." He whimpered pathetically. He was not re-elected, the humiliated Annette's father decided to leave the village with family; they moved to Italy.

Hans, absorbed within the strict constraints of his faith; compared Louis's predicament against the Illuminati's stringent rules. He could not bring himself to condone the teenager's act of indecency. Seeking a solution to his dilemma dropped to his knees, prayed to Baal for direction. Whilst on his knees Hans experienced a more exacting second heart attack; struggled with his breathing. This worrying time injected urgency into to the fractious mind of Hans, time arrived for a meeting of minds, he needed his son to read from the same sheet as himself; Louis who entered the room. "Father, you sent for me." He whispered when seeing Hans lying prone on the floor. "Son, I beseech you." His throat closed with emotion. "Please continue our search for the antichrist." A reluctant Louis nodded. "Okay father, okay." He muttered in tones of resignation as rage, humiliation swept through him tightening his stomach. A tear of shame slid down the bristly cheeks of Hans, the priest was fully aware, his son and himself trod totally different paths. "I linked Hitler with being the Antichrist; I was wrong. What I search for has not yet arrived, once again I beseech you; ensure my search for the Antichrist has not been in vain." Hans gasped, clutched his chest; squirmed with pain.

After the recovery of his father Louis married Hannah, spent a two-week honeymoon abroad, his father's health deteriorated rapidly, the newly married returned to his dying father. 1945, after the death of his father, the Illuminati installed Louis as the Grand Master. The same year Hannah bore a son, bright red circles on his neck. The young Austrian misinterpreted circles to read 666 the sign of the devil. Could this be a sign, his son may be the Antichrist; this uplifting thought injected burning optimism. An emotion moving him to check birthmark once again; his body throbbed with nervous anticipation.

25

Nicky, Sunderland and The Pits

The rampant poverty of Sunderland's east end held Nicky and family in its vice-like grip; sucked them mercilessly into the vortex of the poverty spiral. This rundown dockland area of Hendon housed several shipyards producing ships for the war. These productive shipyards were proving a vital lifeline for the British navy; consequently, these yards became a prime target for Hitler's bombing raid. Bombed houses littered the landscape, these shell ravaged buildings were populated by skinny, poverty-stricken streetwise urchins. Their troubled existence within these downtrodden streets littered with bomb craters, instilled within youngsters... vital survival skills. These half-starved youngsters lived a daily challenged life for their very survival in that perilous area.

My parents raised me within this unforgiving regime, alongside street wise unruly kids. The camaraderie spawned by necessity, flourished in those bombs cratered streets. A strong bond of protectionism developed amongst these unfortunates; of which I was part. These scruffy streetwise urchins became my staunch friends; molded me into a fighting machine. Father had earlier informed me, that miner's sons were lucky as they were allowed to follow their fathers into the dark confines of the coal mine.

My father Ernie had received his call up papers. He had already arranged my entry to the pits, with the blessing of the pit overseer in Wearmouth colliery. At the age of fifteen school leavers attended an 'after school' meeting, where teachers directed pupils which career path to follow; I trudged awkwardly into the room. "And you boy." The teacher questioned in bored tones. I stood head drooping; replied glumly. "I'm to follow my dad into Wearmouth colliery," I answered sadly. The teacher shrugged shoulders, released a sardonic half-smile; shouted. "Next pupil." I'd accepted that one day I would die in that black miserable hole they called the pit; that dreadful day arrived; destiny beckoned.

Thunder clouds hugged angry heavens that morning, Ernie marching proudly in his khaki uniform led me up Bramwell Street to the mines. Being my first morning, Dad was allowed to accompany me into the dark dust filled tunnels of the pit. Those soulless, bleak, coal dust-filled bowels of Wearmouth Colliery; was where my proud father introduced me to my prospective ageing workmates. They reciprocated to my father wishing him well; hoped he would return safely. Dad threw a smile of farewell towards me; that welcoming smile lingered until he slipped into shadows. That critical moment my face dropped; cold reality introduced a dramatic trauma with the stark; mind-blowing fact. I would, for the rest of my life; ply trade as a miner in these dark unforgiving tunnels.

Four dreary, torturous uneventful years dragged by before that tragic day. It was a cold picturesque November morning, crisp white snow crunched under black leathered safety boots of miners approaching the cage. I squeezed my muscular torso to the rear of the lift, an eight-foot square space that filled instantly with hardened, grim-faced men, jostling for position. These hard-grim-faced miners shared a common bond, abject poverty. In eerie silence, the lift plummeted with frightening speed, the black hole before shuddering to a stop. Miners streamed from the lift, entered the dimly lit dust-filled tunnels... dropped to their knees after shuffling into a vacant position. I followed; dissatisfaction dressed my bored young face. Kneeling on the puddle ridden floor besides the iron track. I began wielding my pick at the veins of black gold forming a wall. Sweat streamed over the contours of my dust-laden torso, the high-pitched screeching of iron wheels attracted my attention. As it neared the volume intensified. I stared in disbelief as an out of control, over-laden coal trolley; hurtled towards us over the ageing track.

Dick, an ageing colleague knelt beside me, having just returned to work after hospitalisation. The frail ageing man was still weak from his operation, and lacked the strength to constantly wield his pick for eight hours. His operation had left him partially deaf, with the hearing aid batteries fading, the ageing miner slipped the hearing aid into his pocket; grabbed his pick and resumed work. Dick had informed me earlier how much he looked forward to enjoying his retirement with his wife. Within minute's exhaustion attacked his frail body; fatigue sapped what little energy he possessed. For support, he placed a hand on the steel track; oblivious of the two-ton trolley approaching them. A blood-curdling scream pierced that dust filled air; the trolley ran over the miner's hand. The following bloody mutilation caused several digits to fly from Dick's hand towards overhead beams. Blood spurted freely from the decimated hand; help progressed slowly along the darkened tunnel; towards the unconscious miner.

That evening Dicks loving wife had prepared a celebratory meal for her husband and patiently waited his return, unaware she'd just been widowed. That she would never again enjoy the love and company of her husband. That ageing shadow of a man died from shock, in those dirty dank tunnels. Tunnels he'd spent his total, young working life. This unfortunate event made me physically sick; I tendered my notice.

The welcoming sounds of the siren signalled the end of my final shift, I entered the shower room and the welcome relief brought by jets of hot water soothing my aching muscles. Sweat stenched miners jostled for position beneath the spray of the hot shower. "Coming to the pub, it is your final shift?" the gruff voice of Tommy Smith invited through the steam-filled room. "Naaah. I'm taking Nancy, my mother for a drink, I'm expected home early."

"Mammie's boy." The miner taunted.

With towels draping the broad muscle-bound shoulders of miner's, they emerged from the steamy shower room. Their sodden bare feet left a series of footprints marking their progress. I battled through the oncoming milling bodies to the pit doors. A biting cold North wind chilled my bones, that fateful Thursday night. My threadbare overcoat afforded little protection from the harsh extremities of the northeastern weather, I struggled to the terminus; 10.30 bus and the night I would never forget.

26

Louis meets the love of his life, Annette

Hysterical gratitude pulsed Louis's trembling body, an outpouring of thankful subservience followed; the exuberant pagan dropped meekly to his knees. He flashed glazed wild eyes of appreciation skyward, to Beelzebub.

"Thank you, master, for the treasured gift of your son; my Scar... my hope." Grovelling platitudes spilt with ease, from Louis's thin lips. Following the ecstatic outburst of hero-worship, a catastrophic... frustrating mood drop ensued. Frustrating uneventful months; followed uneventful months. During this period of funereal morbidity, his wife Hannah gave birth to a second child, a daughter. Frustrated Louis paid scarce attention to his beautiful baby daughter; his attention focussed solely on scarching daily the sky for confirmation. He needed a sign son Scar was the Antichrist; skies of the sun-blessed heaven remained empty.

The agnostic plumbed the depths of disillusionment, accessed the slippery slope of drink. During a drunken stupor, Louis stumbled into an old flame Annette. "We have a son," Annette screamed in excited tones. "What!" Why didn't you tell me?" His exasperated face lit up. "Well, you were happily married to Hannah; I knew my father longed for a son. It seemed right our son Paul should live with us; a consolation prize for my father." "But, but." He stammered. "Stop worrying, when I informed Paul, his father was an Illuminati high priest; he found it hard to contain his excitement; the boy can't wait to meet you." Annette squeezed Louis's hand, hormones raged, the couple entered her humble cottage; Louis paused at the bedroom door. "What about your father?" He blurted. "Father's attending a parish council meeting, will not be home for hours." The couple hastened inside the bedroom; Louis killed the lights to resounding slapping of bare flesh, against bare flesh. Annette's father once more was beset with indecision, when news of his wayward daughters renewed relationship with pagan Louis; reached him. Infuriated, her father decided to move once more, to Lyon France.

Annette's departure infuriated the frustrated Louis, who directed all this misguided wrath upon the unfortunate Scar; savage beatings were meted out daily. Scar's miserable life was bereft of comforts, being raised within the Illuminati's strict disciplinary code of conduct. This disillusioned teenager agonised within the bubble of fraught indecision. Louis, embroiled within the loss of female companionship endured a daily mental life of tortured anguish.

As he removed his thick black leather belt, flesh quivered with satanic glee the blood red corners of his fatigue ridden eyes. Louis struck the belt on Scar's back with such force, it lterally removed the boy's flesh. Scar fainted, his limp torso fell to the ground, head colliding with stone steps. Blood poured from the open wound on Scar's head, Louis stared impassively at the bleeding head of his son before calmly walking away. This 'incident' harmed Scar's ability to reason logically; shooting head pains became the norm or the teenager.

27

Jean Pierre Joins Mafia

Andre swallowed in grateful anticipation, a large gulp of cheap red wine, irritated glances from tired eyes slid over the top of his spectacles to his son.

"Come Jean Pierre; sit." He ordered whilst lightning forked ominously the angry heavens, a bright flash of lightning filled the room momentarily illuminating the ageing furniture cluttering the room of Jean Pierre's prison of austerity. "Oui father! Echoed a disgruntled response. "Oui." Jean Pierre repeated mechanically. The agitated... troubled teenager shuffled ungainly towards the table; slipped into a vacant chair. They bowed heads in silence, hands clasped; Andre began grace. "Father, we thank thee for the food you gave..." Andre's voice faded, paled further and further into the background as Jean Pierre's concentration wandered back to what he had seen through the window. His mind engaged conjuring scenarios of escape from that dreaded wooden chalet, his prison. The distant voice ceased; Jean Pierre was instantly jolted back to reality. Ann Marie and son held Andre with a questioning stare; looking for his approval to begin their meagre evening meal. His father took a spoon to his watery soup; the family followed. Jean Pierre attacked his crusty roll with animal gusto, spooning in robotic motions, soup from bowl to mouth.

"Slower Jean Pierre, eat slower." The silver speckled haired Anne Marie scolded, as in dignified movements she guided her spoon mouth-ward.

Only the pouring of cheap wine and clinking of glasses, interrupted that morbid funereal silence blanketing the Dupont family eagerly devouring their evening meal. Andre finished eating, produced a healthy appreciative, burp. His thin bony hand snaked table for the wine to refill empty glasses then turning to his wife. "Thank you." Andre commented gratefully in a voice just above a whisper, raising a filled glass in an appreciative salutation of wife's culinary efforts. In a jerky movement Jean Pierre jack-knifed himself from the chair. "Mama-Papa, I shall retire to my bedroom now." The teenager announced with controlled enthusiasm, kissing the greying locks falling upon his mother's forehead. "Thank you, Mama." Jean Pierre whispered, clicked his heels, launched his young head forward in a respectful gesture to his father. "Goodnight papa." He issued in a voice of solemnity, to the clip-clop of Jean Pierre's clogs rattling against bare boards. Andre nodded a tacit thank you to his son before opening another bottle of cheap red wine.

Jean Pierre lit the half-spent candle gracing the worn chipped veneer of his bedside cabinet, closed the door of his bedroom. He stripped; launched his naked lean muscular body beneath the sheets. Grabbing the tattered book, he guided it towards the flickering candle. Instantly his vivid imagination clicked into action, igniting a burning desire for excitement; a journey he longed for with every beat of his heart. He wanted dearly to experience the dangers his imaginary heroes tackled daily. With a boyish enthusiasm he entered eagerly his imaginary zone of danger. Sweat dripped liberally from his brow as he became engrossed when flicking enthusiastically the books well-worn pages.

The teenager absorbed the sordid bloody detail, wetting his lips with expectant-anticipation of the thugs next action. Seamlessly he entered the lawlesss dark underworld world of fiction. Imagining himself as a thug re-living the vicious actions of his bloodthirsty characters. With growing impatience, he flicked the well-worn pages of the gripping Mafia story. 'The Valentine Day Massacre'. "Line up against the wall, Mr. Capone rules this town; only our wagons deliver booze in this territory." The overweight thug ordered, priming his gun, releasing the safety catch; then a bawdy laugh before squeezing the trigger. Bullets spewed in quick succession from the automatic weapon. The thug emptied contents of the carbine, into the trembling bodies of his helpless victims; blood flowing liberally from dead bodies colouring the dirty... oil-smeared floor.

Perspiration stood proud on Jean Pierre's brow, the gangster's crude; inhumane action illuminated his overactive fertile imagination. Beads of sweat wound their way between the muscular contours of his body; the young Frenchman cocooned within a bubble of envy lay enthralled in the exciting grip of the story. Eagerly he flicked over the pages with an impatience, what further inhumane actions would his heroes inflict on their victims. The hours slipped past like minutes; tiredness invaded his mind slowed his reading capabilities. His vivid imagination fragmented; heavy eyelids shepherded the young Frenchman into the peaceful black oblivion of sleep.

Anne Marie staggered to the bedroom, a half-empty bottle of wine dangling precariously between her fingers. Meanwhile in unsteady erratic movements Andre rose clumsily from the table, stumbling in an alcoholic haze he made erratic progress bolting the doors of the wooden chalet. When convinced all was secure, he entered his son's bedroom; doused the flickering candle. Removing the book from sleeping son's clutches, he stared in loving admiration at the sleeping teenager; in a drunken slur, he mumbled. "Sleep well, Jean Pierre." Andre whispered through broken discoloured teeth, "sleep well, my son." A proud smile hugged his thin lips.

28

Pagan Sect Acknowledge High Priest's Achievements

1960, the Illuminati acknowledged the outstanding achievements of their high priest, Louis. Under him membership had doubled, Louis was promoted to be an elder. "Italy is experiencing a period of unrest." Resounded the head priest to the meeting. "It looks a ripe place for a conversion would you agree? It came as no surprise when this country was chosen for Louis and son to exert their influence. The Illuminati lived with the hope their new elder might replicate his earlier performance." The Pagans identified an Italian commercial outlet with offices nestling beside orange groves in the middle of the picturesque village; Diana Marina. It was within this business they set up twenty-year-old mentally impaired Scar, with his father Louis.

This idyllic village was marred by the strict control of the Church and Mafia. The Illuminati attempted to ease the path for Louis and phoned Mafia headquarters in Sicily; issued a friendly warning. "We have an elder, named Louis, about to become active in your area. He comes merely to expand our interests. I would like you to accommodate him the co-operation of our existing tri-partite agreement with yourselves and the church. If co-operation is forthcoming, I thank you; choose not to accept this hand of friendship; beware." Resounded threateningly the strong worded challenge.

Minor panic seized the imperturbable, Sicilian family. The head godfather unceremoniously grabbed the phone to warn the Diana Marina godfather. "Had a call from the Illuminati." The Sicilians headquarters issued. "Who the hell is the Illuminati?" Griped Diana Marinas godfather. "A powerful pagan sect; not to be messed with. One of their priests will be arriving in Diana Marina. There is to not be any strong-arm stuff with this guy; alright." Hairs bristled with indignation as the Diana Marina godfather entrenched within the old ways ignored Sicily's instructions. Took the decision to control the situation himself; he summoned his number one assassin. "Luigi, a pagan priest is arriving tomorrow. I want this guy checked out." The irritated Italian screamed.

The overweight Luigi was stunned into surprise by the ferocity of his boss tones, responded with a subservient cool. "Right boss." The thug replied trudging from the room, head drooping in resentful obeisance.

Louis with son embarked enthusiastically upon operations in the small,

beautiful village of Diana Marina with its lush orange groves. The newcomers tempted villagers, that by investing with them they could double their money; the response was encouraging. The atheists were rewarded with a modicum of success. The Illuminati had gained a foothold in the Catholic/Mafia stronghold. Catholics swopped allegiance in their hundreds from mafia investment companies to the atheist's company. Business expanded exponentially. News of the pagan's business meteoric explosion spread through the village like wildfire. The trilateral agreement between Catholics, Mafia and Illuminati had been restarted. But the serious inroads made by the Illuminati devastated the Mafias income. Louis and son Scar entered the tenuous, fractured co-existence with trepidation. Louis expanded operations. Lira poured into the Pagans coffers, leading to yet more heavy losses on the Mafia, customers left in their droves the Mafia controlled businesses to join the Pagans.

Mafia anger reverberated the small village. Villagers cowered in expectancy of a violent reaction from the Mafia. Uncharacteristically the shrewd Mafia Godfather opted for the pen not the sword. Threatening messages slipped through the letterboxes of villagers trading with the Illuminati. Coincidentally Louis released financial documents reflecting healthy returns. The village church bell pealed stridently announcing their monthly meeting was to begin.

The overweight godfather of Diana Marina lit his cigar, coerced his fat bottom onto the plumped-up cushions of his seat. A gratifying smile danced upon his lips, basking in self-confidence he sipped whisky in the assurance his threatening letters would provide the correct outcome. Cocooned within a sphere of bloated positivity he assumed his actions would result with villagers returning to mafia fold.

Within the villager's church meeting an unexpected turn of the event unfolded. The villagers decided unanimously to continue investing with the Pagans regardless of the Mafias threatening letters. They believed the Illuminati's power was equal to the might wielded by the Mafia. This disastrous news inflamed an already outraged Diana Marina's godfather. The godfather entrenched within the old ways needed to counterbalance these unexpected events. "The damn Austrian chose this confrontation." The godfather spat out angrily to Luigi. "Pay this pagan a visit tomorrow; inform him he contributes for our protection. Remind him refusing to do so, would be tantamount to challenging the Mafia. Nobody challenges the Mafia." Snarled the enraged Godfather grabbing the phone. Louis edged his way into the front room and grabbed the telephone. An aggravated voice chilled the line. "Pagan; a friendly warning, my boys will call on you tomorrow; pay." The Godfather threatened; the line clicked into silence. The heckles stood proud on the neck of Louis, a reaction to anger; not fear, he replaced the phone to its cradle. "This cheap Mafia hood dares challenge a servant of the all-powerful Illuminati." Snatching the phone, in a thin brittle voice he informed the Illuminati head priest of the Mafia's actions; the head priest immediately contacted Sicilian headquarters.

"My priest has been threatened by your godfather in Diana Marina; I expect an adequate response." The Illuminati threatened. With laboured delicacy Sicily replied with a touch of wistful desolation in his voice. "I'll settle the issue." The head Godfather spluttered. A meeting of the Mafia family was urgently convened. "That bloody damn fool in Diana Marina, he's ignored instructions. He has acted against our advice, threatened the Pagan priest. The Illuminati will not let this fool off lightly. We must act." The Sicilian head screamed. A note from the Illuminati arrived informing them of the dire consequences if the situation was not resolved to their satisfaction.

29

Consolidation/Confrontation; Church Dithers

News of the chaotic disorder existing between Mafia and the Illuminati filtered through to the Catholic Church. Would this dramatic shift of pagan power adversely affect the now fractious tripartite agreement. Mafia and Illuminati flexed their muscles in a display of superiority, the fracas unsettled the church hierarchy. An enraged Sicily phoned Diana Marina to serve the godfather an unambiguous ultimatum. Ordering the Godfather of Diana Marina to reach out to the Illuminati with an olive branch of peace; or else. The godfather shook his head in disbelief, irritation gathered within him. This threatening message undermined his authority, beliefs, challenged his fraying nerves. The devastating phone call left him hanging between disbelief and anger; his overweight torso quivered with rage. The contrary godfather slipped into quiet reflection. A tightening in his stomach ensued; he proffered his hand of friendship to Louis. This blatant pretence of friendliness by the godfather threw the Austrians contradictory situation into mistrust. Louis swam against the tide within this quagmire of misinformation. The quandary drove him to distraction, with a beating pulse he grabbed the phone. "I need advice, the Mafia propose a truce." His plea floated down the line in a voice of bewilderment and anger. "Louis, accept this situation for what it is; the godfather is acting under orders. Time for reciprocity; extend the hand of friendship." Advised Illuminati head priest. Louis replaced the receiver, begrudgingly wrote invitations to the godfather; Scar delivered. The distrusting Godfather, accompanied by Catholic priests, trickled single file into the room. Exasperation drained slowly from Louis, he relaxed; settled guests with friendly preliminaries, small talk. The door swung open; Scar staggered into the room carrying a tray laden with wine. Louis rose; called their meeting to order. "Gentlemen let us drink to our co-operation. I ask you, to please raise your glasses." Guests slipped into reluctant obeisance... raised and drained glasses, Scar swiftly replenished empty glasses. Guests shuffled with reticent unease, before obediently slipping into lame acceptance of the contrary situation. Free-flowing alcohol loosened tongues, washed away prevaricating small talk, enabling progress tackling the torturous journey of cooperation. Alcohol had seamlessly relieved inhibitions, differences melted into oblivion; with one exception.

The drunken Godfather allowed festering rage to incur aggravation to activate his irrational thought processes. A blanket of dissatisfaction nestled uncomfortably on his shoulders. He'd sat uneasily nursing displeasure throughout the unsavoury proceedings. The pressure of expectancy lay heavily with him; his temper jack-knifed out of control. "Louis, what the hell are we doing here?" Challenged the godfather in an confrontational, slurred voice; attritional distrust permeated the troubled air. Louis in slow deliberation drained his glass, stared back impassively at the angry Godfather, replied in icy tones of provocative facetiousness. "Why is that not obvious, was that not our objective... peace?" His lip curling in a snarl. Fury festered within the Italians stomach, leaning back in frustration the godfather brooded; through fiery eyes his temper escalated. "No Austrian bum tells me what to do; we're out of here." The godfather roared; his voice of anger rising high with protest. He withdrew his handkerchief, mopped his brow. Then in an air of intransigence stormed angrily from the room. His thugs and priests followed in meek subservience.

The Catholics priest's meek acquiescence to Mafia orders reached the ears of the villagers; irritation gathered within them; manifesting disgust. Church attendances dropped dramatically; villagers questioned their religion.

Catholic priests cowered in fear of a backlash from Rome. A conspiratorial conversation ensued as priests decided collaboration with the Italian gang to unseat their enemy... that damned Austrian. News of the unholy alliance between the church and Mafia reached Rome. The cosy tripartite that had ensured peaceful cohesion for many years between Mafia, church and Illuminati fell into chaotic disarray, was fractured with distrust. Meanwhile, in Rome the Pope, when informed of the massive upturn of Mafia personnel attending their churches; visually squirmed.

30

The Death of Luigi

The unnatural collaboration between the Catholic church and Mafia, held villagers in unease... silent; the coalition set a frightening precedence. This merger manifested confidence within the Godfather. To reinforce his earlier threats, the Italian stationed thugs on street corners to advertise his intent. Whilst Catholic priests made a futile attempt to counter their church's falling attendances.

Behind closed curtains Louis watched the unprecedented action unfold before informing the Illuminati. Several disturbing days slipped by, the Diana Marina Godfather whilst eating breakfast, signalled for a coffee refill, shouted for Luigi. An overweight thug barged unceremoniously through the open door, presenting the godfather a bloodstained parcel. "What the hell is this, where the hell is Luigi?" The Italian godfather shuffled uneasily in his seat, portrayed a picture of frustration. His shaking hands hovered over the blood-stained parcel, he moistened his pursed lips, in frantic movements he ripped the brown paper, revealing the head of his assassin. Pinned to the forehead of Luigi, was a bloodstained note with a single word written in blood, ILLUMINATI. The incensed Godfather snarled. "What happened?" The question chilled the air, his lips curled in frustration. "We found him lying on the main street, weapon still holstered; his gun had not been fired. This note was pinned to Luigi." The overweight thug grunted. The godfather's head dropped to his chest, with eyes dilating with anger he screamed at the gathered thugs. "Get out." Raged the godfather; the Italians eyes dropped to a second note in capital letters it challenged.

YOU WANT A WAR! YOU GOT IT. Louis.

There was a sour bitter taste festering in the Godfather throat when he phoned Sicily. But the powerful Illuminati had beaten him to it, they had already claimed responsibility for the decapitation of Luigi. More meetings with Sicilian family heads were arranged. With face three shades whiter, lips curled in bitter disappointment, the head of the family proposed icily. "The Diana Marina situation has spiralled out of control; I recommend the godfather be replaced." Heads nodded in tacit unison their confirmation; the outcome of the meeting was consensual.

Early morning sun's rays broke through fluffy white clouds to fall upon the picturesque Italian village. A cacophony of discord resounded the perfect sound of disharmony from birds chirping their morning chorus. The morning's rendition was rudely interrupted by a sharp knock on the door, an overweight thug answered. "Yeah." The thug grunted in an air of boredom. "I'm Louie from Sicily. Tell the godfather I want to see him." Snapped the visitor brushing specks of dust from his pristine well-pressed black suit. "The godfather knows you're coming?" The thug grated harshly. Louie drew his gun; pressed the weapon against the brow of the thug. "Now." The Sicilian grunted in stilted menacing tones. Stunned surprise leapt to the face of the thug, who scurried off; re-appearing minutes later. "Come with me." The thug issued tersely.

The godfather draped in a smoking jacket, relaxed in an air of cool, lit a cigar; as Louie entered the room. The Godfather produces a nervous... benign smile before in a quivering voice, asked just above a whisper. "Louie my friend, how is your wife and family? Word on the grapevine is you're in line for a promotion."

The words sprang unbidden to the godfather lips like an afterthought, unease crept into his voice. Louie dropped his head to his chest, swinging it with sadness side to side. His icy blue eyes flashed a quick appraisal of interrogation over the godfather. In a dramatic, though pleasant admission, Louie issued amiably. "I come bearing news; good and bad. The good news is yes, you're correct; I'm in line for a promotion." Louie paused; his throat tightened with emotion. Himself and the Godfather had been friends for many years. Louie coughed to clear his throat; continued. "The bad news is the job I am being lined up for... is yours." Louie paused again; his hand moved slowly to the bulge under his jacket. "This is unpleasant for me; we go back a long way; please believe me I take no pleasure and is with great regret." With pulse beating, Louie withdrew his pistol, muscles twitched like snakes in his arm.

The godfather gritted his teeth, drew in a deep breath of protest, light perspiration broke out on his top lip. Fear held him motionless; a strange foreboding chill fell upon him. "You're a good boy Louie; do what you have to." A sibilance of breath escaped him; a deep inhalation of smoke from his cigar ensued. Tears spiked the back of his eyes before bursting forth onto his ashen cheeks. He raised the decanter of Brandy to his trembling lips, warm yellow alcohol tripped over his tonsils. "I expected a reaction from Sicily, ever since that damn pagan arrived; but I never expected anything as dramatic as this." The Godfather issued; bitterness lacing his voice. Louie placed the gun against Godfathers head, an uncharacteristic emotion filled him, a lonely tear slid down his tanned cheek; he released the safety catch. "I hope I do a better job than you, cause if I fail someone similar to myself will be gunning for me," Louie grunted prophetically, his voice thin brittle, a lump slid down his throat when easing the hair-trigger backwards.

Doubting villagers entered a bubble of uncertainty; they courted somewhat warily, acceptance of Louis's claim. The outrageous claim he had fathered the antichrist; the air sizzled with acrimony. Once again church bells pealed stridently, heralding the beginning of their monthly community meetings. Within the semi crowded communal hall echoed murmurings of acrimonious disagreement, discontentment filled the air with protest. An elderly; grey-headed gentleman rose in jerky movements to speak; in a voice of incrimination issuing the following damning statements. "We are aware of our religious laxity, our inexcusable drift to paganism. Our dereliction of duty must greatly offend the Almighty. His wisdom could have been instrumental in bringing this ungodly person into our midst; this apparent antichrist Scar. This stranger may have been sent as a warning; we must repent... regain our religious obeisance, return to the focal point of our faith: the church." He returned his bony bottom to the seat. A frail old lady inhaled a deep troubled breath, stood shakily to her feet; delivered her damning indictment. "We cannot vindicate our unforgivable irreligious activities upon scapegoats; there aren't any as united, we stood together; all of us are committed investors with the pagans." She croaked accusingly her caustic vindictive accusations; her skinny backside returned shakily to the wooden seat. Excited babblings of discontent echoed vociferously their poignant differences, differences ringing out a warning into the still night air.

The villagers meeting escalated Scar's perilous situation to a higher plane, through the signals of their distrust. What little confidence the Austrian clung to; plummeted. Confusion wove threads of fear, festered a burning anger into his tormented mind.

These aggravating emotions triggered retributive hate into the unnerved teenager. To vent this explosive emotional turbulence, he directed his burning vengeance and total blame upon his father. His head dropped with a hurtful resignation into his hands, a strange chill fell over him as his troubled mind accessed the slippery path of fractious uncertainty; he juggled conflicting scenarios. His sorrowful huddled form lapsed into delirium; panic flickered in his eyes like ripples of water, a precarious predicament introduced into him perplexity. His head was ravaged with indecision, with his unbalanced mind in turmoil the tormented youngster stormed from the house. His emotionally disturbed state injected within him the corrosives vibes of hate towards his father. He drifted aimlessly in a bubble of frustration the orange groves of Diana Marina. His dire situation dictated action; actions that were to incur dangerous ramifications.

Black clouds rumbled angry skies; claps of thunder resounded; shafts of lightning forked menacingly their zig-zag path earthward, illuminating the interminable torrential rain. The incessant downpour soaking the frightened youngster stumbling blindly in his pursuit of safe refuge; friendship. Within this reverie of despair Scar staggered towards the large steel gates of Mafia H.Q. The gates squeaked open to a pock faced thug wielding an umbrella, who in surprised tones grunted. "You're the Pagans son." The overweight thug pulled the youngster under the protection of his brolly. "I'd like to see the Godfather." The frightened tones of Scar echoed in a whimper. The thug dragged Scar into the building, depositing the soaking torso in a darkened room. "You wait there." The thug grimaced through a half-smile; then disappeared. The despondent frame of Scar sat, shivering in utter disbelief of his situation, he entered a state of petrification.

An unnerving silence enveloped the room; punctuated only by the regular ticking of the grandfather clock. Ironically the constant tick injected calmness into the teenager. The ricochet of footsteps from Leather shoes clattering against wood; caught Scar's attention. The door flew open to the Silver-haired Godfather Louie. The Italian's jaw dropped in amazement. "Well, well, Louis's son." The Italian grated, his voice dropping to a low growl. "And bright enough to know you're not welcome. What the hell are you doing here?" His gravel voice spat out sarcastically. Scar shivered in his cold-soaked clothing that had long since banished any remaining body heat. The youngster sat emotionally disturbed ... angry.

A cloud of ambivalence shrouded Scar; allowing a tired mind to enter a vortex of confusion. "I don't know, I don't know how I ended up here. But who the hell are you? I need to see the godfather." Scar replied in exasperation. "I'm Louie, the new godfather. But more to the point what the hell are you doing here?" The Italian snarled impatiently. Scar's face filled with disbelief, he was talking to the Mafia, the bloody Godfather. "I've run away from home; from my life." Scar mumbled in confusion, "I've been drifting for hours; and here I am. Where is the old godfather, I want to join the Mafia?" Scar queried in bewilderment. Tears of frustration spilled onto his ashen cheeks. A pause of indecision hung in the stale air of cigar smoke. The Godfather mumbled unintelligible grunts to the attendant thug; before inhaling more smoke. Smoke that was to journey its destructive path through miles of his narrowing arteries. The Italian exhaled, sending wispy smoke snaking ceiling-ward; a scheming smile parted thin lips. His face beamed when realising the vast potential sitting in his front room; and all there for the taking.

This situation could be explosive; he must handle it with extreme care; his nerves twitched excitedly.

His podgy hand shot ceiling ward, signalling enthusiastically, the thug. "The godfather well he's taken a long vacation, I'm Louie, I will be replacing him for the time being." Focus turned to the thug, "where are your manners, fetch the boy hot coffee, a change of clothing; bed him down in the games room. I take it we have a change of clothing for him?" The Godfather remarked expectantly. His pock faced henchman, through a greasy grin of satisfaction; replied. "Sure boss." Sicily will be pleased thought the new Godfather, only one week in the job, already I may have the solution to the pagan crisis; the overweight thug ushered Scar from the room. The following morning Scar entered, bloodshot eyes fell upon Louie ravaging breakfast; apprehensively Scar approached, stood by the table; stiffened. "Sit boy, sit and eat." Louie's eyes narrowed with crafty speculation, floated ceiling-ward before returning to Scar, "the problem is young lad you are an unproven entity. The Mafia's run-on mutual trust: the question springing to my mind is; are you reliable?" Louie's uncompromising, questioning eyes flashed scowling; to a bewildered Scar, "well, are you?" Louie iterated, spitting toast from his Cholesterol lips. Scar stared in disbelief, slowly collecting his fractured senses, this was his chance, golden opportunity to join the Mafia.

The youngster's eyes sparkling with confidence; widened in confirmation. "Test me, test me… I'll do anything," Scar Begged in a tiny beseeching voice. Louie's cold blue eyes flashed to the whimpering youngster. "Prove to me you are trustworthy." Louie's questioning eyes planted firmly on Scar, "we do have a minor problem, it's your father." Louie signalled to the thug to replenish his cup. Scar's eyes void of emotion stared in disbelief at the Italian. "My father." The teenager replied nonplussed, "who in his right mind would dare challenge my father. The man basks within an impregnable blanket of protection. If I did rise to the challenge, how would I accomplish such a mission." Scar muttered silently to himself. "What was that? Do we have dissension in the ranks?" Louie rasped facetiously. "Nothing, it was nothing... I was thinking aloud." Replied Scar pensively.

Thoughts of confrontation with his father unnerved him, tested his resolve to distraction. The young Austrian shuffled uncomfortably in his seat. His mind wrestled with the dangerous, nigh on impossible scenario. The Godfather presented to him an impossible situation; metaphorically he'd placed Scar between a rock and a hard place. The question of joining the Mafia was a no brainer as the boy had no choice; but to solve this incredibly dangerous situation. "I realise this is a big ask, that you've problems of your own, but sort this problem; you're in." The Italians words hung in the air like an irresistible challenge. "You're asking me to kill the most powerful man in Diana Marina." Scar gulped. "I realise you're young and inexperienced, maybe even afraid. I killed my first when I was fifteen; if this task is beyond you, speak up now," Louie taunted; derision marinated his voice. Anger leapt into Scar's eyes, he jumped to his feet, eyes glistening with hostility. "I'll accept your assignment; complete it successfully or die in the attempt." The youngster committed rashly; his voice laden with conviction; but with hot juices of uncertainty burning his throat. "That's what I like to hear. Have you anywhere to sleep tonight?" "No! I just told you I've run away from home." Scar replied scathingly. "No problem, you can stay in the games room." Later that evening the couple entered the room, the thug pointed to a makeshift bed, The snooker table. "Boy, I know what you're going through. You feel unwelcome and friendless, nausea unsettles you... grips your stomach and saps your confidence. But come the time to kill, adrenalin takes over; you'll do good. I welcome you to our little group." The thug delivered a half-smile to Scar before leaving the room.

It was early evening, the dark Autumnal air leaden with rain stank with death. That smell cloaked Scar's shoulders like a wet blanket; the youngster trembled... was terrified. He snatched a worried breath when the petrifying thought he was about to kill his father; flashed intimidatingly before him injecting fear into his fragile, fraught mind. Shaking hands noiselessly turned the key. Opening the front door, he tiptoed into the half-lit lounge with the stealth of a preying tiger. Adeptly he slipped his trembling skinny torso into the protection of shadows. At the table in the sumptuous lounge his father Louis poured wine. Hannah entered the room silver salver in hand. Louis levelled cold questioning eyes at her. "Scar late for dinner again?" Louis blurted. "I've not seen the boy for two nights; his bed's not been slept in." She retorted. "The ungrateful wretch, one day he'll expect to replace me as the high Priest; the boy must learn to obey rules." Louis snarled throwing wine over his tonsils.

Cold sweat trickled Scar's spine, nervous apprehension gripped his gut, body trembled with excitement; or was it fear. Hannah poured soup into the bowls on the table; returned her overweight torso to the kitchen. Scar eased himself from the safety of the shadows. Crept silently to the unprotected back of his father; Louis busied himself replenishing his empty wine glass. Globules of perspiration gathered on the teenager's brow. His hands began to shake violently. His wiry torso trembled as he unsheathed his razor-sharp knife. Mouthing silent apologetic noises towards the back of Louis's head. He raised the blade, apologetic whispers slid apathetically from his mouth almost silently. "Sorry papa, I'm sorry." Tears whetted his ashen cheeks as with a quivering hand he plunged his knife to the hilt between his father's shoulder blades. Louis released an agonising yell that ricocheted off the brightly lit walls. His limp body slid motionless to the floor; lay prone in a warm pool of his arterial blood.

The commotion startled Hannah from her culinary pursuits in the kitchen. She scurried into the front room, a raging anger coursing her body. Through horror-stricken eyes she stared in utter disbelief. Her son was removing a blood-soaked knife from the motionless body of her husband. A panic-stricken scream shot in anguish from her mouth. Her overweight form waddled sobbing uncontrollably to aid her husband. Scar spotted his mother approaching, raised his hand in a bid to stop her. But the assassin, in his state of panic; forgot his hand still gripped bloodied knife. The knifes razor sharp blade slit her throat. She, like a sack of potatoes, slid lifelessly into a pool of blood, next to her motionless husband. Horror leapt into the glistening horrified bloodshot eyes of Scar; body convulsed with fear; tears of panic-filled his eerie red eyes. "But why am I crying, this is what I set out to do, mission accomplished. Now I've killed my father I'm free of his constraints; shackles." Scar blurted through sobs of partial disappointment.

With temples pounding Scar allowed a surge of dissatisfied accomplishment fill his shaking body. Accompanied by an excruciating pain, Scar felt he was dying by inches, he sank against the living room wall. The euphoria he'd been advised would follow; never did. The tragic events ensured his triumph was quickly forgotten when overshadowed by the cruel blow he'd dealt himself. In his single-minded headlong rush for freedom from his father. He'd dealt an irreversible fatal blow, to the only person that had ever loved him for himself. His loving... sweet mother; she was no more. A strange chill fell upon him, a sickening quiver gripped his stomach. His bloodstained knife dropped to the floor;

shrouded in a cloud of disbelief he rose and staggered to the door. "Mama, Mama what have I done?" He screamed in despair at the ceiling, arms gesticulating wildly his regret. Empty bloodshot eyes stared helplessly at his mother's motionless body lying in a pool of her arterial blood. Tears negotiated freely his pale cheeks; bloodshot frustrated eyes shot heavenward in disgust. "Mama, Mama." Echoed Scar's unheard scream of panic, in an awkward gait he exited the house.

He progressed his skinny body dejectedly over the windswept dusty dark streets towards the gangs H.Q. The Austrian entered the room; the godfather stared questioningly at the young assassin. "Well?" The doubting Louie queried; his thick eyebrows winging suspiciously in interrogation. "It's done my father's dead... and my mother." Scar murmured; hot tears pricked the back of his eyes before springing unbidden onto his pale cheeks. The godfather's pockmarked face broke into a twisted smile of victory. The youngster sat shrouded in disappointment disbelief. The Godfather stepped forward wrapped a comforting arm around Scar's shoulder, in a soft voice just above a whisper said. "I know exactly how you feel, the euphoria... that adrenalin injection provided by your first kill; especially as it was your father. Here!" The Italian grabbed a bottle of Brandy pushed it into the teenager's hand. "But I don't drink." Scar bemoaned. "Take advice from one who's been here... start now you will need it; this will calm your nerves, enjoy yourself; you've earned it." Louie grunted, grabbing the phone, "Deliver free booze to the town hall, the villagers of Diana Marina will celebrate my moment of victory over their hero. Louis the pagan priest is dead. A death brought about not by Mafia, but his son." The new Godfather of Diana Marina gloated.

But his moment of euphoric delirium dissipated, was quickly replaced by troubling afterthoughts. Having solved his biggest problem; he'd created an even greater one. Against Sicily's strict instructions, he'd had the pagan priest killed. Aggravating his awkward situation; he was housing the bloody assassin. Louie's fractured... fragile mind ran amok, trawled agonizingly a gamut of conflicting emotions; cold sweats of fear suddenly traced his spine. His troubled mind engaged overdrive as it strove to find a solution. How would this be explained to the Illuminati. This was his next tantalizing, explosive dilemma. "My biggest problem here is the high priest's assassin, the murdering teenager Louis's son. I'll ship the problem Scar to a Mafia office in America," Louie muttered.

Scar befriended an overweight Sylvester when landing in the states, Sylvester being an ex-Mafia outcast, a failed assassin. And on the Mafia grapevine Scar's reputation has preceded him. The mafia had summarily issued Sylvester with his final option; build up Mafia business in France or be killed; Sylvester chose the first. "I need a good right-hand man; a number one?" Sylvester's invitation danced temptingly; invitingly; in the warm night air. Scar's smirk telegraphed tacitly his answer.

31

Jean Pierre Rapes Rusha

Andre's throaty farewell to his wife filtered through the open windows through bored grunts; the noise awakened Jean Pierre. The bleary-eyed teenager dragged his lean muscular torso wearily from his bed. Kissed his cherished tattered poster of Brigitte Bardot gracing his bedroom wall. Took his healthy appetite downstairs to breakfast. "Morning mama." Jean Pierre greeted, dropping his muscled torso into a chair, in swift robotic movements the teenager ravaged toasted soldiers dipped in a boiled egg. "Jean Pierre manners, eat your food slowly." His mother chastised whilst flicking strands of greying hair from her lined brow.

In a voice from the recesses of boredom, he replied mechanically. "Okay, mama." His nondescript voice aired. On completion of his breakfast, he rose, shouting above the kitchen noise of running water against crockery; echoed his voice of farewell. "Thanks mama, see you later." The youngster edged through the front door, his vivid imagination running amok with his fictitious violent gun-toting thugs. A cold northerly wind penetrated his worn jeans as he with head bowed, progressed down the dusty street. This wild young man longed to savour the bloodthirsty turbulent excitement; the outrageous thrills his imaginary gangsters enjoyed. A skinny, unkempt youth, cigarette dangling from mouth, slumped his skinny torso against the skeletal ruins of a bombed house. His head buried in the sports section of "Le Equip." Terror leapt to bloodshot eyes when spotting Jean Pierre's muscular physique loping menacingly towards him. The young Frenchman slowed to a halt. Flashing threatening eyes dancing with menace. The Frenchman's murderous glare injected fear within the spineless misfit. "I've no money I can't afford your protection." The unshaven French youth whimpered.

The Fifteen-year-old Jean Pierre's anger rose; this illiterate punk was testing him. With the grace of an angry Sergeant Major, Jean grabbed the youth's lapels dragging him across the rubble strewn entrance into the skeletal shell of the bombed building. "Mon Ami, be scared." Jean Pierre threatened as through a laugh of evil he plunged the razor-sharp blade into boys' gut. The youths face awash with fear screamed. "No, no don't kill me. Aagh!" Echoed the victims agonizing cry, the clammy fingers of death tightened around his skinny chest. The petrified youngster released an anguished scream as blood spurted freely from the wound. Through a laugh of cold intent Jean Pierre twisted slowly his knife. High pitched shrill cries reflected the young victims excruciating pain. His skinny blood-soaked body shuddered violently; unbearable excruciating pain coursed the youngster's body who lapsed into unconsciousness. Jean Pierre withdrew the bloodied blade, carved his initials J.C. upon the bare chest of the youth. More blood gushed forth, the skinny lifeless torso coloured a deep crimson. The youth's eyes flashed open momentarily, accompanied from lips void of colour; a chilling sibilant breath of finality escaped. His eyes closed; the youth drifted into the peaceful realms of death.

Jean Pierre released a shrill wild belly laugh, his wild imagination running wildly amok. "What power they had." He scowled in admiration of his fictitious heroes. Whilst side-stepping the body of a dead crow sobbing grabbed his attention. He wheeled ninety degrees, faced the raw savage beauty of Rusha; his North African neighbour. In slow deliberation, the wild-eyed teenager wiped the blood from his blade, eyes ogled with longing her well-formed breasts.

Animal instincts festered in his gut; hormones stirred with unhealthy acceleration; his heartbeat increased. Love, or was it lust surged his body, hormone-driven desires accelerated a need; he wanted her. His rampant hormones elevated sexual instructions, injected longing; there was stirring in his trousers. For months the teenager had been attracted by her animal beauty; each sighting would set his heart beating yet more wildly. The hard exterior worn for the world mellowed, lust leapt into the ascendancy. Jean Pierre was aware her immigrant father regularly sexually abused his daughter to satisfy his sexual appetite.

The emotionally charged teenager's dilating eyes danced longingly in wild anticipation. Upon the curvature of bare flesh revealed by Rusha's torn blouse. The immigrants trembling body lay akimbo on the rubble, Jean Pierre invited his out-of-control sexual desires to dictate his advances. "That low life father of yours been mistreating you again?" Jean Pierre growled. Rusha's head dropped forward, in sorrowful tacit acknowledgement. "Trust me it will not be for long; I will deal with him and look after you." Jean Pierre whispered. She raised her bloodshot eyes filled with joy to behold the boy of her dreams. Jean Pierre's hormones stirred; cold blue eyes turned wild, nasty. In a slow menacing advance, he approached the helpless teenager; his benevolent mood turning mean. "Rusha you ready for me." Hormonal lust sprang threateningly from the Frenchman's lips, her hero-worship faded was replaced with fear. "Jean Pierre no, not again; my father then you." Rusha screeched in protestation till her throat hurt. The Frenchman's breathing became heavy, laboured, his left hand fumbled clumsily his jeans for the weapon that would inject misery into his neighbour. He entered her, the affection she'd once held for him soured, was replaced with retribution, hate. She screamed. Jean Pierre muffled her scream, once again the Frenchman forced himself upon her.

Minutes later he lay panting, a broad smile of satisfaction gracing his thin lips. The dilated wild red of his eyes exhibiting gratification; he relaxed within a self-satisfied placatory calm. The open palm of his hand caressed the smooth Black cheeks of Rusha. She lay still, petrified, as though in a coma. Jean Pierre's wild eyes flashed to his blood-stained metal blade, where they remained transfixed. "One day this baby will rid you of your despicable father." He promised in a voice devoid of emotion. Murder cloaked cold those empty eyes embracing the steel blade. Levelling his murderous eyes to Rusha Jean Pierre's threatening voice grunted, "nobody needs to know what happened today, Rusha; this is our secret... until the next time." Pressing his forefinger over her lips he rose to release a cold... sadistic belly laugh.

Rusha's body trembled with anger, a sensation releasing her from her debilitating suspended animation. Sobbing she crawled over the filthy debris strewn floor to leave the shell of a building. From a distance she'd admired Jean Pierre for years, viewing him through his thin veneer of respectability. She'd put him on a pedestal, hailed him as her hero. But during those few frantic moments of his forced sexual invasion into her. That childhood fantasy had vanished, the veneer of respectability she'd held had been replaced with a severely tarnished image. To her, he now represented nothing other than 'the devil incarnate. Bleeding hands covered her ivory-coloured tear sodden face. Retribution clung to her eyes of vengeance hooded in self-pity. Through gritted teeth, she swore an oath to herself. "One day; One day Jean Pierre you will regret ever meeting me." She blurted with burning conviction, within her aching loins lurked a savage yearning, her revenge.

The harsh crunch of gravel announced the entrance of a skinny youth, his cold ashen face housing blood-red eyes, such evil eyes ensured the newcomer a catching entrance. Enter Scar the Albino, Sylvester's number one assassin; his boots crunched progression over the bombed debris towards the Frenchman. Scar had just returned from Leicester headquarters following the sudden death of a Sunderland lady. Jean Pierre unsheathed his knife; Scar approached the challenger with his flashing blade at the ready. The Austrian's head dropped to his chest signalling the beginning of their supposedly friendly joust. Scar's adept ability ensured first blood to him as his blade ripped through Jean Pierre's fading white shirt, turning it a bright crimson. With revenge gracing Jean Pierre's scowling face, the Frenchman lunged at Scar, who deftly deflected blade.

The roar of a black Citroen quieted after screeching to a halt in a cloud of dust. The arrival of the car brought the teenager's frenetic action to an abrupt halt. The six-foot lean torso of Henri emerged sprightly from the car. Excitement and hero-worship coursed both the teenager's veins, they rushed to greet him. Henri steered his young admirers back into the ruins. In nonchalant dismissiveness they passed the bloodied body of the youth lying beside a dead crow. Henri cast an admiring glance towards the Frenchman. "I take it that is your work, Jean Pierre." Henri's voice applauded, an evil smirk of admiration nestling on his thin lips. Jean Pierre's head dropped in embarrassment to his chest. "Oui Messier, he refused to pay me for protection." The Frenchman's abashed tones of agreement echoed. The exuberant Austrian Scar pushed forward in front of Jean Pierre. "Henri welcome." Scar greeted excitedly, thrusting forward his open hand of welcome. Henri's cheeks twitched with his intense dislike of the albino, his snarling face visually displaying the pure disgust he held for the weirdly coloured ingrate. The Frenchman ignored Scar's gesture of friendliness; instead pushed a piece of a crumpled piece of paper into that open hand of friendship.

32

Louis Doubts Pagan Faith

The pain-racked body of Louis shivered uncontrollably; his trembling prone torso lay in a deep red cold pool of his arterial blood. His body temperature plummeted perilously below the safety level. Blood trickled from his open mouth; his vacant eyes stared skyward in pitiful hope. Another violent shake of his body caused more blood to spurt from his mouth. Eyelids flicked in rapid movements. His body twitched violently as though beginning its process of shutdown. With head swimming in a sea of demoralizing nausea, Louis conjured a last desperate effort for survival as the Austrian dug into reserves of energy. He summoned up his remaining breath into issuing one last desperate cry. "Please God save me." The dying man's pitiful pleas clung to the cold night air; strangulated noises floated through the open door. A passing stranger hearing the call for help; rushed through the open door to the dying couples' side.

The flustered newcomer checked Hannah's pulse; Hannah had shuffled off our mortal coil into the cold arms of death. The newcomer progressed to the blood-soaked Louis, who's breathing though erratic; was still alive. In several dexterous movements, the newcomer ripped Hannah's apron into strips; produced a makeshift tourniquet and stem Louis's bleeding. Ensuring the patient was comfortable; the stranger phoned for an ambulance. Minutes later, the vehicle with sirens blasting screeched their arrival upon the scene. As mysteriously as he'd arrived, the stranger disappeared into the folds of the dark.

Louis spent the following weeks throwing a pain-racked body on a thin hard uncomfortable hospital mattress, flirting precariously with regularity... the awaiting arms of death. The Austrian's health deteriorated, his fragile body slipped perilously in and out of consciousness; he survived. Unfortunately, his new lease of life re-introduced his former evil self. The door swung open; Louis stared blankly at the visitor. "I assume it was you who saved my life; my thanks." He croaked unceremoniously.

Appreciation, in the form of a smile, graced the face of newcomer. "That sir was a pleasure on my part, our last meeting I heard you shouted for God." The stranger stated. Louis spluttered in disbelief; his face flushed bright red; nonplussed he replied. "Messier you must be mistaken, I'm an Illuminati priest; with my son, we're practising pagans, I'm even chasing the Antichrist." Louis paused briefly, memories of that fateful night flooded his mind, "I apologize, you are right; I did." Stuttered Louis apologetically. The visitor dipped his hand into a black bag, withdrew a black book. "I've brought you a present. I'm a Christian, a Jehovah's Witness." The visitor handed Louis the Saint James Bible. Louis's eyes narrowed, were vague, puzzled. "Thank you, but no thank you, I've explained; I'm an atheist," Louis repeated in a low exasperated voice. Humour touched the visitor's eyes. "Please accept my bible, read Gods word at your leisure. Well, must be off to work I'll pay you another visit tomorrow." Shaking Louis's limp hand, handed him a bag of grapes before slipping quietly from the ward.

A welcoming silence returned to the ward; Louis lapsed into his private world of glacial quiet. With mind swimming confusedly, Louis placed the bible in his bedside drawer. Louis nodded off briefly, on awakening a curiosity welled within him. He felt urged to read that book; the hand of the pagan gravitated to the bible. He flicked open the bible to Genesis, with an overriding determination he began flicking the pages, the misplaced chronology, its convoluted writing; baffled the Austrian. He struggled to unravel its story; slammed the bible shut before almost as an afterthought the pagan blurted in frustrated anger. "My only son and atheist tried to kill me; a Christian saved my life," Louis exclaimed sourly. Hands gesticulating disbelief as they soared skyward, "what kind of human have I brought into the world." Louis questioned, shaking fingers gingerly picked up the bible, once again Louis turned to Genesis.

His understanding of the Bible had suddenly become a prerequisite. Bony fingers eagerly flipped the pages; the door swished open to a nurse. Louis blurted. "I had a visitor earlier?" "Ah! You mean Messier Adam; the Englishman." She replied whipping out a thermometer. "You know his telephone number?" "Open your mouth... Say Aaah!" She ordered pushing her thermometer to the back of his throat, "no need, told me he'll be here tomorrow." The nurse replied, withdrawing, and shaking vigorously the thermometer, an approving smile graced her lips, "you've improved, and about time too." She announced with a tad impatience; vanishing as quickly as she'd arrived. The following day Louis stared at the bright sun and scudding white clouds, when again the door swished open to Adam bearing more grapes; Louis his face in self-deprecation allowed an appreciative smile to grace his lips. "That's a remarkable improvement." Adam complimented. "I read the bible after you'd gone yesterday; it's beyond me." Louis stuttered. "And why is that?" Shot back the soft reply of interrogation. "The terminology, its interpretation; is confusing, it does not make sense." Louis issued lamely. Adam lifted his bible handing it to Louis. "This is normal for newcomers studying the bible, the book was written over two thousand years ago. The language used, differs from the present literal meanings. In fact, it is not literal, chronological, but metaphorical, symbolic; its understandable translation creates for you a problem. Anything you do not understand... ask, I'll explain." His visitor replied before his exit

Louis was placed with a problem, he found himself challenging his beliefs, his searching for the Antichrist. Was that the right choice? in his state of indecision, he was consumed within the zone of neutrality which overridingly dictated his thoughts. Days, through his inactivity were incessantly boringly, his daily reading of the bible increased, its ambiguity created yet more confusion. His pagan faith waned, the very reason for his hospitalisation, his sons' assault on him, tested vigorously his position within the cult. His avid reading of the bible transported him on a journey beyond his comprehension. His long held steadfast beliefs wandered; raised questions. Why had the Catholics not supplied this information?

On release from the hospital, Louis with immediacy swept aside the teachings of the witness; returned wholeheartedly to his pagan doctrine. But his decision to disregard the Christians advice and return to the Illuminati was misleading. Even his mingling with fellow Pagans could not douse the flame of a renaissance burning brightly within him.

His newfound beliefs transported him to a different level. This switch of allegiance would inevitably lead to confrontations; confusion reigned. Louis sank into indecision, his wildly frustrated mind juggled with his varying scenarios. With troubled mind in turmoil, he arrived at a crossroad. Still his tortured mind struggled, he did not want to challenge the powerful Illuminati. But he must choose where his religious affiliations now lay. The confounding unthinkable situation was to terminate his association with the Illuminati; end his search for the Antichrist. The troubled priest after many hours of arduous mind searching; reached the unthinkable decision. He would leave the Illuminati, disown son Scar, and return to France, to hell with the consequences. Waving his goodbyes to the nurse, he left the hospital

Frustrating months of unsettling disquiet elapsed until that mind-blowing day. Louis exited the doors of the funeral directors in Diana Marina after completing final arrangements of his wife Hannah's burial. With head bowed against the wind, he ambled to the bus stop. A familiar well blessed, young Brunette caught his gaze; jerked him from his depressed state. "Annette! How are you?" Louis gushed with schoolboy enthusiasm. Her blue eyes sparkled with happiness; she blurted coyly. "I have a son called Paul; he's seventeen."

"Seventeen years, surely that was when we..." He stuttered... emotion closed his throat, with face dressed in frustrated expectancy he stood transfixed. A snigger escaped her lips. "Yes, he's your son," Annette replied proudly. "Ah." He uttered; emotions rushed to a certain point; then stopped. "Annette we, we should have married Seventeen years ago, not many get a second chance. I beseech you to become my wife move to France with me." Louis dropped to one knee. Annette invited nostalgia, basked in pleasurable memories; happy emotions warmed her gut.

With Louis she'd experienced love, stepping forward she grasped his hands; gulped. "But I understand Hannah has just passed away." "True, but that was a mistake as I married Hannah on the rebound after losing you; I beg you again be my wife." Annette allowed nostalgic indulgence to influence her thoughts. Engraved upon her pink forehead lay deep lines of a frown... worry. A strange excitement churned her insides, with an upward jerk of her head she levelled eyes at Louis, nodded tacit acceptance then blurted happily. "Yes, why not, a new beginning, new life, new country," Annette replied. Louis's worries melted into oblivion; they embraced. He threw eyes skyward in relief, for the first time in years, he felt free from constrictions; shackles. He discarded his faith, along with the umbrella of protection afforded by the powerful Illuminati. Within weeks they married, with new bride Annette, new son Paul and daughter Brigitte. The Austrians prepared for their invasion on the Loire valley in France.

33

Scar Makes an Enemy of Jean Pierre

Scar unfolded the crumpled piece of paper, digested its instructions before staring nonplussed at the driver. "This is only an address." The bemused Scar groaned. "That's the address of your next kill, when you've completed your assignment and killed the man of the house; Sylvester wants you to report back." "Do I get to know what this man has done?" Scar queried sardonically.

"Your job is to kill him, not make bloody friends with him; I'm out of here." The driver berated in a cold sarcastic tone. Henri turned to Jean Pierre, nodded appreciation of the young Frenchman's skill. In the cold silence of authority Henri wheeled ninety degrees; loped back to his black Citroen. The car departed as it had arrived, in a thick cloud of dust.

The Frenchman Henri's obvious antipathy for Scar bothered the Austrian, not one iota. The defiant Austrian stuck up the middle finger in disrespect at the back of the departed Henri. His bloodshot eyes dilated with excitement; danced with evil upon the bloodied trusty blade. Once again, he scanned crumpled piece of paper; an evil grin sprang to his face. With a casual gait, he spun round to Jean Pierre. "I've got to go." He shouted, reddened eyes once again falling with glee towards his trusty blade, "I've work for you, my baby." Scar Gloated, strains of excitement rose; he licked Jean Pierre's blood from the glistening steel blade. Jean Pierre's moody blue eyes lit up with expectancy.

"Maybe I could assist? I'm nearly sixteen." The young Frenchman pleaded in forlorn words of hope. Scar moved towards the young Frenchman, slipping arm of comfort around teenagers' shoulder. "Next time my friend, maybe next time." He whispered consolingly.

The angry young Frenchman's face reddened when detecting evasion littering Scar's voice. Wrenching his muscled torso free of the assassin's arm; he screeched threateningly. "Look Scar I'm every bit as good as you with a knife." The Frenchman eyes hooded with hate, "and come that day I'll prove it." Jean Pierre shrieked. "But until that day arrives, stop treating me like a kid." With head drooping in disappointment and hands firmly implanted in the pocket of his worn jeans, he guided his dejected body homeward. Scar disregarded what he saw as Jean Pierre's idle threats and spun about with glee. His wild red wild eyes glowed. The Austrian immersed himself into his next project, plan how to accomplish his mission with a minimum of effort, maximum hurt. The sky darkened; threatening rain clouds rumbled over angry skies; Scar skirted the bombed buildings homeward.

The Austrian was pleasantly surprised when stumbling across attractive dark-skinned girl; perched disorientated on a half wall. He paused, smiled; sat down next to her. "And why is a beautiful young woman like you crying?" Scar queried; an unusual depth of passion entered his voice. Pulling a handkerchief from the inside pocket; handed it to her. The ebony-skinned face lined with distrust; violent memories of hormone instructed men abusing her; came to the fore. She slid warily, awash with uncertainty, along the wall, eyeing cautiously with suspicion the newcomer. Scar's thin cruel lips parted, a naïve boyish smile dressed his face, warmth veiled his eyes easing her fear, Rusha relaxed her guard; attitude mellowed. Scar queried. "What are you doing here?" He issued in conciliatory interrogation. The petulance dancing in her dark brown eyes held him with uncertainty... inquisition, before blurting. "I've left home." Came the sorrowful bewildered voice through tears, a lingering sigh of disappointment escaped her lips; anxiously she courted depths of desperation. Scar pushed hands thoughtfully through his blond hair, spotted an emotionally delicate situation that could be twisted to his advantage; a moment's reflective pause for thought ensued, he murmured. "I have a chalet you could use, I travel a lot, spend two-three months a year at the place." Scar issued in a voice of hope. Rusha's first instincts advised against accepting stranger's hospitality, but this stranger's proposition solved her immediate problem; her urgent need for somewhere to sleep. In a frightened... grateful voice she gasped almost reluctantly. "Yeah thanks, I'd like that." For the next two years, Rusha lived in comparative luxury, supported by the often-absent Scar. The Austrian being completely unaware of her connection with Jean Pierre.

34

Jean Pierre The Impatient

A desperate craving for recognition gnawed Jean Pierre's gut, this was inflamed by a growing hostile impatience. An explosive anger entered him accelerating the growing burning ambition to be number one; replace Scar. This masquerade of friendship embraced by Jean Pierre and Scar; was but a veneer of workmanlike trade-off comradeship. Their ill-conceived union was not built on the warmth of real friendship. But languished within the acceptance of a conspiratorial, mercenary agreement. Jointly their murderous twisted minds dwelt solely on honing their murderous skills with the knife. "When the opportunity arises, I will dethrone the debased, detestable Austrian." The French teenager cried his threat of intent; his angry voice issued in low threatening tones void of emotion.

Jean Pierre celebrated his Eighteenth birthday; this tender young age had not stopped him from becoming hardened; shrewd and streetwise. The mere flick of his cold blue eyes, twist of mouth; injected fear. Within this evil young monster festered a yearning, a desperate impatience for power. His quest for riches was motivated, lubricated; by a burning desire eating away inside him. These murderous thoughts instilled within him, an unshakeable belief he was good enough to achieve his ambition of replacing Scar; being the best; number one.

Within an hour's walk from that run-down chalet, he called home, on the bombed outskirts of town stood Lyon University. This magnificent edifice basked in lush green manicured grounds.

Jean Pierre eyed this building with envy, its privileged youths strutting like peacocks, its lavish gardens. He made himself a promise, vowed that one day he would escape his squalid, poverty-stricken life: be their equal. His searching gaze drifted beyond the University, to a large bungalow belonging to an Englishman, consultant Roger. The bungalow basked in half an acre of lush land adjacent to the University; his jaw dropped in admiration... excited eyes dilated. His clenched fist punched the air in jubilation; he made a grand sweeping gesture. "Mama, Papa your new home." He promised eyes blazing with a fierce determination.

35

Scar's Big Mistake

Scar's bloodshot pupils dilated with eager anticipation; he'd received his next assignment. Bright red eyes fell eagerly to the address scrawled on his crumpled paper; he'd been ordered to kill Jean Pierre's neighbour. This person being a rebellious vigilante. The immigrant had rallied groups of protestors, refusing to pay for their protection. These like-minded people joined him; in his fight to stand up against the thugs. This band of protesters refused to pay Mafia for protection; called for a halt to their domineering bullying tactics. Adrenalin coursed Scar's spine in anticipation of the kill; he needed this "high" as much as addicts needed their drugs. Twisted thoughts juggled gruesome scenarios; situations giving him the maximum of satisfaction on completion of the dastardly crime. Jean Pierre's eagerness for involvement in Scar's equation. The young Frenchman's constant whining pleas to be part of the action was to be realised. "The boy is eighteen with a heart cold as steel, and desperate to get involved. He should be allowed to enjoy the adrenalin rush provided by the kill. Tonight, Jean Pierre it's you and I to share the spoils." Scar gloated. Cocooned within self-satisfaction the Austrian progressed his skinny body towards Jean Pierre's prison. Scar's mood lightened when travelling the dusty road winding through the rat-infested bombsite, towards Andre's dilapidated chalet.

Inside the sparsely decorated dingy chalet, a forty-watt shade less bulb swung over the balding Andre straddled his chair in eager anticipation of his dinner. The ageing Frenchman threw another generous measure of cheap red wine over his tonsils; pangs of hunger gripped his gut. Bony fingers drummed the ageing table accelerating his growing impatience. Dispatching another glass of red wine; his balding head swam from overindulgence. Ann Marie staggered from the kitchen carrying a tray laden with the Frenchman's dinner. She struggled under the weight of her overloaded tray to the table, rusting hinges squeaked open the door as Ann Marie returned to the kitchen. Andre enjoying the sublime dictates of alcoholic influence swivelled ninety degrees towards the noise; and unexpected newcomer. Andre's jaw dropped open in utter disbelief. Pure raw hate of this Austrian low life; burnt like a raging inferno in his gut. Wild fury entered those tired eyes glistening with hostility.

The door had just announced the entrance of Andre's worst nightmare. The lamest excuse for a human being had just walked through the door; enter Scar. Uncontrollable anger surged Andre's skinny body. Jack-knifing himself from his seat in anger he confronted the unwelcome intruder. The veins on his neck bulged as the heckles on his neck rose; the Frenchman screamed in disbelief. "What the hell do you think you're doing; breaking into my house?" Andre slurred in strangulated accusing tones of bewilderment. The Austrian stunned by the venom of ageing Frenchman's verbal onslaught staggered backwards. "Messier! I was looking for your son?" Scar muttered bemusedly.

Anger hooded Andre's eyes, his ageing heart beat unhealthily. His bony ribcage tightened; hot blood manifested an unfettered rage. His home had been sullied. "Get out of my house, you low life ingrate; I want nothing to do with your kind." Andre's inflamed emotions blasted forth in utter disgust. Hot spit surged the burning throat of the Frenchman and a direct hit with the Austrian; hot saliva dripped down Scar's face. The Austrians ashen face twisted, grimaced with displeasure; the back of his hairy hand wiped the warm spit from his pale cheek. A piercing hot pain seared blood-red eyes falling onto his trembling hands yearning for retribution. Hate, revulsion and revenge, played havoc in the Austrians unbalanced mind. His nerve ends had tingled exactly the same as that fatal night the Mafia ordered him to "settle," their score with his father.

Scar's bloodshot eyes burnt with retaliation; his disturbed mind danced angrily with retribution. Slowly, noiselessly the Austrian withdrew his knife, advanced cautiously upon the ageing Frenchman. Ann Marie, who had returned to the kitchen returned with a food laden tray from the kitchen back into the room. Her face lit with despair when spotting Scar's knife cutting through the air, plunging into the chest of her husband. The assassin withdrew the knife, Anne Marie flung wine and pudding laden tray to the floor. She propelled her buxom body between the attacker and her husband. Scar's arm already in a second downward trajectory had no time to adjust its fatal path. Tragically, the knife meant for Andre pierced Anne Marie's heart; her limp torso slithered limply to the wine sodden tiles.

Scar stood like a person in suspended animation, his eyes cloaked in disbelief, his skinny body stiffened as he froze in fright. The terrifying thought of an uncontrollable vengeful Jean Pierre seeking revenge; sprang torturously to an already tormented mind. Bloodshot eyes stared transfixed in horror at the lifeless corpse of Jean Pierre's mother's eyes staring ceiling-ward, lying in a warm pool of her blood. A frenzied panic attacked his skinny body; self-preservation grabbed the ascendancy. The Austrian stood mortified, realising a showdown with Jean Pierre now could not be avoided.

The bloodthirsty maniacal Frenchman was bound to seek revenge; the feuding bodies would, at last, determine who was best... the number one. Fear fuelled shaking legs progressed Scar to the door of the ageing chalet; how would Sylvester react. "What will be his response when I tell him; I've killed Jean Pierre's mother. He must have realised the bad blood between me and Jean Pierre; would inevitably result in confrontation." Scar mumbled in self-pity; he negotiated wearily the dusty darkened back streets of Lyon. His troubles had just escalated tenfold, he'd killed the very woman Jean Pierre placed on a pedestal, Ann Marie his mother.

36

Andre, Ann Marie's Death

The dark of evening introduced a drop in temperature within the sparsely decorated rooms of the chalet. Rain clouds parted, allowing weak blades of moonlight flicker through the worn net curtains, illuminating the blood-soaked body of Andre. Andre opened his mouth in condemnation of his attacker; his throat tightened with emotion... restricted any sound. Torment veiled the Frenchman's eyes awash with hot tears. Through misted vision, he cast his bloodshot eyes in disbelief to the ceiling; his weakened skinny body sank to the floor. Distraught eyes beheld the motionless body of Ann Marie. The Frenchman rose to the sitting position, cradled his beloved wife's head in the crook of his arm. Anger, resentment; littered his morbid mournful tones.

"Why! Why my Ann Marie?" He agonised, revenge coursed his veins, the distraught Frenchman kissed the ashen face of his dead wife; pulled her cold motionless body close to his. His pain ceased, the cold numbness gripping his heart became, a chill spiralling outward in series of enervating shudders, pulsing that limp aging helpless body. "Why, Oh why? Why my Ann Marie." He repeated in utter disbelief. His head fell forward to his bony chest, his bloodshot eyes grew heavy. The tortured, anguished Frenchman fell into the clutches of sleep, clutching tightly... his wife's lifeless torso.

Early the following morning Jean Pierre entered the cold dark chalet. He intended asking his parents to move to a new house. He'd acquired this property within the more prosperous area of uptown Lyon. Disbelieving cold blue eyes fell upon his bloodied father cradling Ann Marie's lifeless body in his arms. A lump rose in his throat, Jean Pierre greeted his stricken father with a cold questioning stare. "Papa, what's wrong? What are you doing? What's wrong with Mama?" Questions of consternation dropped worriedly in quick succession from his dry lips. "She's, she's dead." Andre croaked in a voice of despair. "She's dead." The Frenchman iterated mournfully, motionless eyes awash with another flood of tears streaming down his already sodden cheeks in a display of unashamed grief.

Jean Pierre released an anguished howl of tortured disbelief. "No, no, this cannot be, who would kill mama?" The grief-stricken Frenchman shrieked; hot bile burnt the back of his throat. Like a heavy burden, retribution settled upon his shoulders; revenge reared its ugly head. "You, stupid ingrate, I told you not to join the Mafia; but you would insist. Now you are witness to their handiwork. This is what happens when you mix with trash; share their ill-gotten gains. What the bloody hell did you expect?" Andre injected a pregnant pause, probably to emphasise his response; continued. "You have the damned audacity to darken my doorstep, I warned you to stay away from this house. How dare you blunder in uninvited, asking the stupid question. Who did this?" Andre taunted accusingly; facetiousness littered that anguished tone of derision, his ageing face twisted with incomprehension.

His skinny body trembled uncontrollably with fury. Dilated bloodshot eyes glared at his son with pure disgust, a disgruntled voice of condemnation he shouted, "it was that pathetic species of a human that killed my beloved wife. That low life garbage! your bloody mate Scar. Like you, the scum barged into my house uninvited; made a pathetic attempt to justify his intrusion. Mouthing ridiculous comments; he wanted to meet with you."

Andre's caustic tones ricocheted disparagingly off the bare stone walls. The lump in Jean Pierre's throat swelled uncomfortably; the Frenchman's head dropped to his chest in acceptance of the dastardly situation. He fell to his knees, slipped a comforting arm of consolation around his father's shoulder; in uncharacteristic tenderness whispered. "You, said Scar wanted to see me, that surprises me as our last rendezvous was alive with hate. We parted company after an angry exchange of words, strong disagreement. That day I challenged him to fight me." Jean Pierre spat out.

In a cold dispassionate action Andre snatched his son's arm from his skinny shoulder; replied angrily. "Well, whatever! I told the Albino his rotten kind was not welcome; I spat in his face. The Austrians blood-red eyes then danced with hate; he stabbed me. I remember vaguely that it must have been on his second attempt; when your mother spotted the Austrian; blood-spattered knife in hand. She charged between us to intervene. It was that fatal downward thrust; your mother positioned her body between me and Scar for my protection." He entered an unashamed emotional pause; a lump rose in his throat. "She took the knife meant for me; straight through her heart." The Frenchman's head sank to hands; emotion overtook him, tears ran uncontrollably down his ashen cheeks.

As heartless as Jean Pierre was, the exception for him was love for his mother; this emotion was boundless, in his eyes she had no equal; tears wetted his tanned cheeks. "Why? Why?" The young assassin shrieked, grief-stricken he rose to his feet, staggering over threadbare carpet he swivelled about. Stared helplessly, at Anne Marie's motionless corpse. Into his wild blue eyes appeared a fearful hatred; he blurted in caustic threatening tones. "Scar! Scar!" The Frenchman screamed, collapsing distraught to chair. Almost instantly vaulting himself back to his feet. Fury filled those tear-filled eyes snapping heavenward; through an icy tone of hate-filled threatening conviction... he screamed. "Scar up till now you've called the shots but today you overstepped the mark; the next meet... only one can walk away." Jean Pierre issued. That mock charade of a friendship with Austrian was over, a closed chapter.

37

Disgruntled Sylvester Dispatches Scar to England

Scar's chest rose and fell sharply with increasing rapidity; he gasped for air as the hot breath of fear burned his throat. Emotionally driven terror coursed his skinny body, shaking legs progressed the trembling torso to H.Q. Terror, a negative emotion alien to scar, excepting for that gut-wrenching traumatic event with his father, it ran rampantly through his body. He entered in uncoordinated jerks H.Q and Sylvester's office. An impatient Yank snatched a Havana from the box. "Where the hell is my cigar cutters." He roared ungraciously; his 'assistant' Blonde shuffled forward handing the implement to him; Scar approached.

Consternation sat uncomfortably on Sylvester's face as he blurted. "What the hell! your early, a problem?" Sylvester challenged caustically; suspicion lacing his questioning tones. The despondent Scar dropped to a vacant chair, his bony hands cupping a worried face, "You have sorted the problem? Jean Pierre's rebellious neighbours? I take it that's what you've come to tell me, that you've dealt with the situation." The Yank snarled in probing tones of uncertainty.

Scar shoulders sagged, his bloodshot eyes alight with failure. "There was a tragic accident; I went to Jean Pierre's house as he wanted to be part of the kill, I was to let him assist me. But I was confronted by his father Andre, we struggled, I ended up killing Jean Pierre's Mother." Scar bleated pathetically; the smoke-laden air became electric with the poignant lack of reply. Continuing his futile pleadings Scar despairingly beseeched, "it was an accident you have got to help me." The Austrian sank head into his hands. "You've what." An incensed Sylvester screeched, leaping in disbelief to his feet, "you stupid, stupid... idiotic Austrian. Who is going to control the unstable egocentric Jean Pierre? You know what an explosive temper the crazy Frenchman has."

The wheezing Sylvester snatched a lungful of much-needed air. The veins on his fat neck bulged... eyes flamed red. Minor hysteria ran amok within the obese frame. A worried disgust inflamed the American who's face twitched nervously... involuntarily. Scar shook with fear, the incensed American grabbed Scar's little finger. Forced the trembling digit between sharp blades of his cigar cutters. "Let this be a lesson, make you think twice next time your stupid temper gets the better of you." The Yank grimaced; evil dressed his fat cholesterol lips. A squelchy crack followed; Scar emitted an anguished shriek. With nail intact, finger end dropped to the floor into a pool of dripping blood.

Pain creased Scar's face; his head swam with increasing nausea. Pained red eyes shot ceiling-ward; the room darkened... spun faster. He strained his eyes attempting to focus upon Sylvester; his vision melted into a blur. Inanimate objects slid into the distance as if being sucked into a vortex of black. Sylvester twisted around and roared orders to the peroxide Blonde. "Dress the wound! Blood's dripping on the carpet." Sylvester snarled in disgust, his sarcastic tones employing his usual lack of grace.

The blonde waddled forward clutching the medical box... to attend Scar. The perturbed Yank reclined in his chair, inhaling deeply on the weed clenched between his crooked, discoloured teeth. The Blonde cradled the unconscious Scar's head in the nook of her arm, wafting the bottle of smelling salts in sideways motion beneath his nose. Several minutes elapsed before Scar dozily regained semi-consciousness. The Yank held Scar in a frustrated questioning stare. "You amaze me." Sylvester exasperated; arms jack-knifing heavenward in irritation before he dropped to his knees. Podgy fingers groped inside the safe withdrawing a buff envelope. He threw the envelope onto the table in disgust, "here's a one-way ticket to England and spending money; you keep a low profile. I want neither to see, or hear from you again; until I give the order understand? And bloody well clean yourself up; you look like a tramp." The Yank fumed disparagingly. Scar, agony etched upon his face, held gingerly his bleeding little finger as his bent torso staggered from the room.

38

Nicky and Promise

Winter arrived early in Sunderland; the dark evening introduced a cold northerly wind chilling my bones. For warmth, Nicky, snuggled inside his threadbare overcoat; hands plunged to the bottom of the pockets. Selectively he negotiated a safe path through the bomb debris and craters littering Bramwell Street; towards Number 13.1/2. The ageing front door, sporting peeling paintwork; surprisingly stood ajar. "What the hell?" Nicky growled more in surprise than anger, the disturbing tones of irreverence ricocheting the bare walls like a pistol shot. Shouldering his way through the open door; Nicky stepped cautiously into the unlit hallway, "hello upstairs." I rasped to no response; my surprise turned to worry.

Worry that quickly escalated to panic; my heartbeat pounded, accelerated unhealthily. At that dreadful moment of fearful anticipation, I longed for the reply of a friendly voice. But instead from the fearsome black embracing the upstairs; the empty house resounded loudly with an eerie silence. My hand raked the bare wall for the upstairs light switch, a shade-less forty-watt bulb flashed into action, emitting a dim glow over the carpet-less wooden stairs. For a nerve-racking large space of time, I stood rooted to the spot; stark fear introduced a cold enervating numbness. I shuddered momentarily before losing the power of movement; cold sweat liberally whetted my scalp. The chilling eerie silence sent cold shivers down my spine.

The Jew from Berlin

There's always someone here I thought; rubbing grubby fingernails over my stubbled chin, "Mam, Dad, I'm home sis." Searching panicky words chased one another in quick hopeful succession. Hairs on the nape of my neck stood proud like soldiers on parade. The clatter of hobnailed boots against the wooden floorboards echoed my ungainly progress on the wood of the carpet-less stairs. With heart racing, I reached the top; staggered ungraciously into the sparsely decorated living room. Amongst the half-eaten meals and dirty cups, I spotted a crumpled piece of paper. A bitter taste soured my throat, I grabbed the note. Fingers of fear grabbed my gut, through misted eyes I read the almost indecipherable shaky scrawl. Mother had been stabbed by a scarred youth, the albino from the betting shop in John Street.

The note read. Am taking her to the General Hospital. It was signed by Dad.

Something inside me died, I gulped in disbelief allowing pains of anguish to burn my stomach. "Those bloody bookies." I choked in a growl of hate, dropping the crumpled paper to the floor my hobnail boots clattered my hurried progression back downstairs. I stepped into the biting cold North-East -sea air. Accompanied by an air of desolation I trudged in funereal silence to the bus stop. The Number thirteen bus transported my worried torso to the hospital, I arrived there at Eleven-o-clock. With my gut burning with nervous trepidation, I shouldered my muscular torso through the revolving doors into the hospital and reception. My head was reeling with negative, distraught thoughts. My stupid mouth engaged a babbling incoherence; expounding a host of meaningless rubbish before my brain had time to issue instructions.

The next few moments witnessed none stop drivel dropping in quick succession from my mouth. I only became aware of my stupidity when through a bemused stare, I beheld the nonplussed receptionist staring at me in total confusion. Explaining in slow apologetic terms the reason for my visit. She directed me to the emergency ward. Ernie, my father, face masked in concern; leant his skinny body against the wall. My sisters Ann and Pat were locked in a frightened embrace. They stared at the motionless figure of mother. The ward bristled with bustling frenetic activity from nurses in black stockings. White coated men surrounded the bed in an organised chaos, barking authoritively constructive orders. I stared in utter disbelief at the Green-line of cardiac monitor lurching in spikes and troughs its erratic progress across the screen. A blood-spattered white coat leant over my lifeless mother. With an authoritative tenderness he placed his stethoscope upon her chest. With his face masked in disappointment; he grabbed the defibrillators. "Again, let's try again." The Doctor ordered brusquely, flicking his tired eyes heavenward as though seeking a sign.

Pressing defibrillators against her bare ribcage... he grunted, "ready, charging three hundred joules." His tones relayed the message in a voice laden with hope. Everyone's eyes flashed expectantly towards the monitor; the suspense created by the funereal silence of the theatre was broken; by a soulless harsh clunk.

For a precious moment, mother's motionless body jumped into action. I savoured that wonderful moment with expectation. Fleetingly it coloured my wishful thinking that maybe there was a spark of hope. But to my horror her body collapsed into inaction onto the bed almost immediately, extinguishing that brief flickering flame of hope. The Electrocardiograph's Green light flickered momentarily; as though preparing for action. A misleading action that was not forthcoming; it collapsed into a straight line. "We've lost her." The doctor growled; his voice gravelly low; pained resignation flashed across his tired face.

Hot tears of emotion-charged eyes swept with abject sorrow to my sister Pat lying in the fetal position on the floor. Ann, my elder Sister began to shake hysterically, a sickening empty quiver gripped her stomach. With face turning an ashen white, Ann collapsed like a rag doll into a nearby chair. My distraught father Ernie cocooned in grief; slumped in apathetic limpness against the wall. Bony hands covered his face of despair, the muscles in his arm twitched nervously. His skinny body sank to the chair hugging the side of Mums bed. That desolate, grieving man invited tears to stream uncontrollably down his unshaven cheeks. He sat in helpless despair; allowing the clammy hands of fear grab his chest. Clutching his dead wife's hand, he crouched Bob Cratchett fashion over that lifeless... motionless body. Desperation, disbelief dressed his tear-filled eyes; panic slipped its tentacles into his distressed mind. That broken man slipped submissively into a glacial quiet of numbing devastation. Despondent realisation sat heavily on his shoulders.

Clutching mums limp hand: a large lump appeared in his throat. Sorrowful eyes searched heavenwards. His lips motioned speech; but no sound came forth. For the first time in his life my father clasped hands together. His balding head fell to his skinny chest; he mouthed a silent prayer. My loving mother, Nancy Isabel Nixon (nee Wrightson) had drifted silently into that dark abyss of death. No longer could I watch that gut wrenching, highly disturbing traumatic scene of morbidity; I flicked eyes ceiling-ward uttering to the god in heaven. "Please, not yet; Ma! Oh Ma no... not yet." I wailed in stuttering monosyllables of disbelief, "no please god no." I added in a cry of self-pity, panic crept into that voice of desperation, I entered a state of emotional uncertainty. The cold unwelcoming fingers of numbness embraced me in its vice-like grip. I flicked another glance at my despondent father.

Mums' death felt like a burden too heavy for me to carry, I watched in frozen silence the Doctors futile attempts to revive mother. The Doctor, defibrillators in hand, turned to the attendant staff, throwing tired eyes to his watch. "Right, do we agree?" The Doctor whispered in sorrowful finality. "Yes." Several grunts echoed in unison. "Right; time of death is..." He muttered dolefully in mechanical words of acceptance

I made a pathetic attempt at accepting mother's death as I staggered towards dad, hugging him. Frustration coursed my body; emotions ran high. I gulped to clear my throat, a sickening pain gripped my innards, something inside of me died. I shot a vengeful look to the Doctor; exhausted drained. Emptiness injected its negativity into my grieving body caused by mum's death. Something inside me did a triple somersault, held me motionless ... silent. I stared dumbstruck at the ashen face of my mother; my mouth opened to speak; nothing came forth. A white coat brushed against me; I grabbed the passer-by. "What happened Doc?" I grunted angrily. Pat, my youngest sister, spotted vengeful anger inflaming my bloodshot eyes. That sobbing figure rose from the floor to my side, slipping her skinny arms in comfort around my neck. "It's not the doctor's fault Nicky." She choked emotionally through sobs. The Doctor, fumbling with his stethoscope mouthed words of apology, closure.

"I'm sorry." He whispered, fidgeting with his defibrillator; in jerky un-coordinated movements, the white-coated figure left the ward.

A funereal silence draped the four mourners entrenched in their self-isolating morbidity. They trudged wearily their snowy path home; passing the empty Addison and Henry Streets on that clear bright night of sadness. Slants of Silver rays floated from the moon languishing against the endless cold black sea of space. A swirl of snow clouds snatched it from view; I swung my head forty-five degrees to my father... gasped querulously. "What happened Dad?" I questioned; a knot of revenge gripped my stomach. "She was attacked by a White-haired thug, scar on his cheek; that scum from the betting shop in John Street." My dad snapped in accusatory tones of condemnation. "I remember him." I grated sourly, we entered 13.1/2 Bramwell Street. Flicking the switch, the 40-watt bulb once again sprang into life, revealing once more the bare wood of the staircase. I hauled my weary body up the stairs. "Aagh." Shrieked my dad. Fingers of pain tightened his chest, he collapsed, I spun to assist. "You are okay dad, I've got you," I whispered, in that instant, another part of me died, "firstly, mother then you," I grunted. My tiny brain struggled to accept the possibility of a double death; I grabbed fathers' limp body; carried it upstairs to bed.

The monotonous regularity of rain pounding our roof tiles; injected momentary relief to my sisters and me. I embraced Pat and Ann with brotherly reassurance; gave them a brotherly kiss, bade them goodnight before both padded silently into their bedroom. Under that exterior of calm my stomach burned with the sensation of retribution. I dearly wanted someone to pay for mother's death. Commitment absorbed me; through gritted teeth I swore my revenge. That someone would pay for mothers' untimely demise; tears of self-pity flowed freely over my bristles.

The unrelenting rain-lashed the roof of Mr. Browns, our downstairs neighbours pigeon loft hugging the wall of our backyard. I stared dismally from the window; my boring past life flashing in front of me. Refracted bone slants of light glistened upon the dirty concrete of our backyard. I jerked myself back to the present. "I'll take care of dad, and I'll bloody even the score with that damned Albino." I choked. The following evening a foreboding silence hung over the Nixon family. I scanned the "Situations" vacant column of the Sunderland Echo. The police were advertising vacancies in Leicester; my eyes lit up with excitement. "Ma, the promise I made; I may just be able to honour it." I punched the air in euphoric hope.

39

Samantha, Her Problem

Samantha, Sam to her well-heeled friends, with father Roger ex Harley Street surgeon and Mother Fenella; enjoyed a privileged lifestyle. Living with this affluent family was an inherited ageing butler from Roger's oil-rich grandfather who'd died in the Bahamas. They lived in a luxurious eight-bedroom detached. The building had adjoining land of three acres of lush Surrey countryside; adjacent Lingfield racetrack.

Sam made her journey home returning from the University in France, with unkempt hair strewn over her lined brow she strode the mile-long drive to the house. She threw a drug-fuelled gaze on the row of silver birches standing like soldiers lining the drive. Shapely legs progressed her well-formed body in jerky movements; homeward. Her expensive burgeoning drug addiction was responsible for Sams unsustainable overdraft; this troubled her worried mind. She faced a huge problem that being her Father Roger, Roger was a strict disciplinarian, coveting the severe restraint of Victorian values. He had, by post issued several ultimatums, stating his wayward daughter changes her lifestyle, or harsh consequences awaited. Her stomach tightened; beads of worried sweat knitted her pink frown housed on her creased brow. She trawled relevant criteria that may solve her financially, unsustainable habit. The meteoric rise in the price of drugs meant the cost now surpassed her allowance. For her to continue this expensive habit she needed her father to increase his input. It was little wonder that lambs frolicking the fields, or starlings producing their cacophony of discordant chirps. Or even the solitary distant crack of ivory upon the bats from the cricket ground; could invade her hazy world of oblivion.

She slid the French doors open; caution dressed her perspiring face that lit up in admiration for musical appreciation. From the record turntable resounded the stirring climactic drum roll of finality; performed by Orf. It was as though the vibrant sound signalled its conclusion of her father's snooker; the black ball trickled into the corner pocket. An uptight Roger, aware of disobedient daughter's entry; placed his cue on the green baize. His troubled eyes glistened with condemnation; his angry face was decorated with disgust. The retired Surgeon held his daughter in an accusing, discomforting glare. Waving wildly an envelope in the air as though it were a sword, in accusative condescension he announced. "Sam, this letter I received not two hours ago." Angry tones proclaimed haughtily, "which is the second one this month from the bank. I will not bore you with dreary details, I'm aware you know what the damning contents inform me."

Sam's drug befuddled mind strove for words to frame a positive reply; with nothing forthcoming she resorted to girlish wiles. Dropping her head coyly; she feigned embarrassment. Roger's body shook with exasperation; grabbing the decanter he poured himself a generous measure of Brandy. Sam's blue eyes twitched nervously; body wriggled with discomfort; her normally razor-sharp mind triggered the panic button. She trawled fruitlessly her mind for a response; resigned to defeat she slipped into plan B and defensive mode. In a voice solid, trained, any BBC newsreader would be proud of she delivered her response with arrogant confidence. "Daddy I'm addressing the issue, don't make a scene; I will deal with it." Her well-timed polished evasiveness worked; she'd stalled for time and hopefully had given herself a well-earned breathing space. "Your response is yet another empty ultimatum, as usual marinated with glib prevarication. My tired mind struggles to accept your blatant ineptitude. You're a clever girl with a bright future, why? why drugs?" Roger screamed in frustrated tones. Desperation performed its giddy dance in Sams eyes shooting heavenward. "Daddy I've had a hot... tiring journey I must bathe, see you at dinner." She blurted in a caustic stinging reply. Sam's prevarication had achieved its primary objective; she'd succeeded in avoiding his assault. Roger had failed miserably to solve the burning issue. That of forcing his wayward daughter to face reality and curb her excessive spending; he cringed. Nursing a large glass of Napoleon brandy, he sank frustratedly, to the Queen Anne chair.

Quick relief washed over Sam's eyes with the realisation her normally unmovable father had relinquished ground; not proffered his normal intransigent resistance. Sam sluggishly dragged her pain-racked body up the stairs forcing one leg in front of the other. Slowly, in agonizing movements, she progressed over the thick woollen carpet adorning a highly polished winding staircase. Shooting pains attacked her slim torso; her demanding expensive habit needed feeding. Whilst admiring a Monet painting adorning the expensive wallpaper decorating the wall, well-manicured fingers grabbed her gut, she fell like a sack of potatoes to a crouched position upon the stairs; her creasing pain became intolerable. "Oh god, I need a fix." She wailed pathetically; she grasped the stair rail to aid the sluggish progression of her shell-shocked body in a series of staggers over the intricate designs of gold and wine, woven into the wool carpet. She reached the top of the staircase and passage leading to the sanctity of her bedroom.

Having endured many arduous confrontations with her father. She was only too aware of his deliberating pattern when processing negotiating criteria. Also, that his subdued state was merely transient; that his pent-up fury would return with a vengeance.

The most probable outcome, would be a sizeable reduction to her allowance. The severity of the cut depended on his wounded pride. Her greatest fear was the total withdrawal of her lifeline, her allowance. This would leave an impossible burden, having to fill that massive financial void herself. This unthinkable situation ratcheted up her blood levels. From within the deep recesses of a stressed foggy mind, her alter ego, in a drug-induced voice; challenged. "Are you going to allow this to happen?" The voice goaded questioningly, "how the hell would I cope." She groaned groping inside her Dior handbag for that dreaded syringe. Shaking hands loaded another dose of total oblivion into the needle, injected her vein. Her lifeless body plunged into the peaceful realms of obscurity. Her drug fuelled eyes dilated, shot to the ceiling; Once more Sam was at peace with the world.

Several hours later emerging groggily from the drug-induced blackout. Her troubled thoughts strayed to the obnoxious character she'd met outside Kilburn dancehall. That weird, scarred man with red eyes. Not what one could call a knight in shining armour; but this excuse for a man could be a solution to her problem. The stark reality of her dilemma prompted she loaded yet another syringe. Another swift escape from reality was realized as she slumped to the floor in another blissful release. A large expanse of time elapsed before she once more awakened from her drug-induced sleep. Shaking hands rose gingerly to caress a frown creased brow, she phoned butler Rupert to fill a bath.

Slipping her aching body into the relaxing foam bubbles she enjoyed the delightful refrain echoing softly through steam-filled air. The exquisite stirring tones of Mario Lanza's rendition. "I'll walk with God." Visions of her father brandishing his letter of condemnation; swam intrusively into her over active mind. He'd addressed her as would a General, wielding threateningly the missive as though it was a sword. The frustrating scenario plagued her fragile mind accompanied by the irritating arrogance of an uninvited hangover. "I'll have to find more money." She moaned in a voice of irritation. "Grandfather left me millions in his will." Shadow of fatigue lay under those eyes flared with frustration. "But the damn complexing legalities means my funds will be tied in probate for years. Until the legal eagles have sorted financial ramifications; that means weirdo here I come!" She groaned submerging her naked body beneath the sweet-smelling soothing bubbles of foam.

Primarily her expensive drug habit had been triggered by pressures brought about by the finals of her Economics Degree at Lyon's School of Management. Surfacing from beneath the heavily scented bubbles she reached for the bottle of Napoleon brandy poured and drank a healthy measure before releasing threateningly her warning. "Albino I'm coming for you; beware." She screamed facetiously, plunging the well-formed breasts of her naked body once more under mountains of scented foam.

Like a breath of fresh air, Sam swept, with the grace of a debutante, into the dining room where she halted, smiled confidently at her parents before with regal pomposity, stood at the chair opposite her parents. Stooped subserviently behind her unsmiling parents, stood Rupert their ageing butler. Roger shot a stare of condemnation at Sam who slipped into Queen Anne chair with seemingly unconcerned ease. She displayed an arrogant confidence, equalled only by her grand entrance. She addressed in assured tones her stern-faced sombre parents. "Evening." Her voice rang out clear, solid, hanging like a statement of intent to the warm still air. Roger squirmed uncomfortably; with guarded optimism, he initiated his prepared onslaught. "Can we concentrate on the problem at hand. Have you ever considered...?" His daughter interrupted with a haughty, judicious response. "Daddy, I did say I was addressing the issue. Did I not?" Sam replied in a cursory attempt of indulgent deliberation to wittily subdue her father's solicitous attack. She threw a challenging glance at her confused mother Fenella transmitting waves of distress, whilst crimson tinged Roger's face. The ageing Surgeon capitulated; resigned acceptance crept uninvited upon Rogers lined face. His daughter had gained the ascendancy and won the first round. With finger cutting through the air, Roger signalled tacit instructions to the butler. With a stoop of subservience, the butler slipped from the room in silent obeisance; re-appeared seconds later struggling under oversize silver salver.

The trio devoured prawn salad entrée followed by Medallions of Lamb finishing off with Crepe Suzettes. This exquisite meal was washed down with several glasses of fine red wine. An awkward silence blanketed the room; punctuated only by butler replenishing the ever-emptying Wine glasses. "Another." Sam chirped sharply as her lacquered fingernails pushed the bulbous glass forward. Several hours elapsed, beads of sweat stood proud on Sam's pink forehead, she gripped her troubled stomach. Her creased face transmitting the increasing pain.

Roger spotted his daughter's anguish; but his upper-class upbringing affording him with Victorian values expressly forbade displays of emotional intervention. Again, the room lapsed into an awkward silence, excepting for the comforting regular tick of the antique grandfather clock in the hallway. The butler, who hailed from a more mundane background approached Sam now emitting low whines of pain, she needed another fix; and quick. "Madam." The butler whispered almost apologetically to Sam doubled with pain, using well-manicured hands she waved butler away. "It's alright... I can manage." She responded in pained self-pitying tones.

The Jew from Berlin

The tactful butler proffered a curt nod of the head, squeaking highly polished shoes shuffled his obeisant respectful retreat. Grabbing a serviette Sam mopped her sweating brow, regained a modicum of composure. Shaking hands drained her glass of Wine; with her composure now but a distant memory she rose unsteadily to feet, "I'm off to bed, Mummy Daddy; we'll talk in the morning," Sam announced in clipped... forced aloofness.

Shaking legs progressed her pain-racked body from the room. Her anxiety melted when entering the safe haven of her bedroom and drug kit. In agitated unceremonious movements, she yanked back the sleeve of her dress to reveal the pitiful sight of her pale pin scarred arms. Shaking hands navigated the path of her syringe to the vein. Relief sprang to her eyes on the sinking needle as it made its target. She slipped her naked body in stuttered thankful movements her drug-stricken body between the silk sheets. Invited the welcoming oblivion of peaceful worry-free sleep.

Surrey was experiencing its hottest summer for years; Sam was in for yet another disturbed sleep-starved night. Her sleep-induced detachment from reality lasted until four in the morning. Early morning rays filtered through pristine white curtains into her room. She wrestled with sleep throwing her naked body from side to side in discomfort, sleep remained at a premium, evaded her. She rose to slip her well-formed body into a light blue Kimono; she approached unsteadily the large, bowed window.

The large orange early morning sun peeped over the horizon, flashing its welcoming golden rays, ushering in the dawn. Birds introduced daybreak with a cacophony of discordant sounds, relaying their morning chorus. From the coal Black of the West to Sapphire and Orange of the East; the sky embraced its marvellous illumination of colour. "When beholding such a wonderful sight; how can one dispute creation." The eloquent affirmations eased from her lips in a silent whisper of admiration. Then with unpleasant suddenness, her mind snapped to her present irritating conundrum; her irate father and looming financial problem.

41

Nicky the Policeman

The freezing northeasterly rain relented the storm clouds drifted across the angry sky. he bedraggled ageing postman negotiated gingerly the dirty, water-filled bomb craters littering Bramwell Street. He skirted a myriad the potholes whilst negotiating gale force winds on his debris-strewn path to Number Thirteen and a half. Due to the constant bombing of the dock area, Sunderland suffered a critical housing shortage. Each two-storey house in Addison, Henry and Bramwell Street accommodated two families. If you're numbered address ended in a half, you dwelt in the upper half of the house. The only exception was Grey Road where this rule did not apply, this being the affluent Jewish quarter, an upmarket posh road of bigger, better-quality houses.

    The prevailing north wind turned colder; the harsh greyness of day returned; black clouds hugging that angry sky parting briefly. Allowing weak rays of winter sunshine warm the postman's balding head. With his sodden blue serge uniform clinging to his cold skinny body; his bony forefinger pressed the doorbell. I Nicky, was physically exhausted having just arrived home after working a gruelling late shift at the pit. Sleep lurked in the corner of my tired eyes. Grimy dirt infested fingernails brushed through unkempt tousled hair; yawning I jarred open the door. "Sign here! I have a parcel for Pat Nixon; it's registered." The postman grunted, while his arms diligently searching his bulging sack. "And a letter for Mr. H Nixon." He added thrusting a crumpled envelope into my hand. My sleep filled eyes flashed with excitement when focussing on the Leicester postmark.

My stomach churned with excitement; I threw exuberantly my bloodshot eyes heavenward. Snatching a refreshing lungful of the cold morning air, I tore open that welcome missive. "Yes." I yelled punching the air triumphantly, hobnail boots swung my body ninety degrees then clattered my ungainly progress up the wooden carpet-less stairs to dad, "it's confirmation from the Leicester Police." I shouted excitedly, waving euphorically the crumpled piece of paper in front of dad's face. Waves of upbeat emotions coursed my spine; that lovely opportunistic window beckoned me. My euphoria eclipsing dad's sadness, excitement swiftly moved to a cold sweat, my eyes narrowed. Face muscles twitched; the gravity of the challenge embraced me; inviting me to follow the path of my beautiful revenge. Through tearstained eyes I beheld dad, my body shook with regretful apprehension, I would be leaving my grieving father so soon after mothers' death. I knew that lonely heartbroken man still struggled desperately accepting mother's demise.

My earlier ill-timed exuberance dissipated, was replaced with pangs of regret. Dad's head dropped to his chest in acceptance of my frivolous, selfish naivety. Once again Ernie, my grieving father, would have to adjust emotionally; to a second traumatic event. My leaving could exacerbate his highly emotionally unstable situation; an icy knot of anxiety formed in my stomach. I'll never forget the day dad boldly stepped forward with an outstretched hand, a lump the size of an apple lodged in my throat. His weather-beaten face registered, for the first time in weeks; happiness. "Well done son I know you'll make us proud." Acclamations of appeasement rang out in his tones of bravado; alas his saddened eyes transmitted a different message. He gripped my hand, shook it vigorously, encouraging that damn outsized lump hurting my throat; grow even bigger. Dad's stoicism inadvertently, made more difficult the task of controlling hot tears, welling behind my bloodshot eyes. A flood of emotional tears crashed forcibly through closed eyelids, soaking my bristled cheeks. I stared glumly at his vacant ashen face. This could be the final straw for him; first mum now me I sighed as I fought the rising panic gripping my stomach.

Back within the soul-destroying dark recesses of the mine, an ear-piercing screeching of steel upon steel reverberated the dust infested tunnel. The ageing wheels of overladen coal trolleys trundled speedily the well-worn track. The shrill sound of the buzzer pierced the dust-laden air, signalling the end of my final shift. Happy contentment charged my spine, I sprang to my feet with renewed energy. I'd spent four mind-numbing years, slogging in the shadows of the soul-destroying tunnels; of Wearmouth pit. At long last I was through with the mind dulling laborious drudgery within the demoralising grimy dust-filled tunnels of darkness; my guts warmed.

Struggling against incoming bodies of the following shift, I fought my way to the cage; pit head and fresh air. Emotions emanating from my newfound freedom sprang unbidden to my face, I stared at the dirty coal grime covering the darkened walls of our pit canteen. Was what I felt sorrow, euphoria, or pure relief; I broke into joyous unbridled acclamations of joy. "That's it, finished with the filthy tunnels; choking on coal dust." A sharp intake of cold breath ensued, as I inhaled a grateful sigh of relief. Cooling my buoyant mood was a shrill, frightened cry for help. It echoed chillingly on the cold air; arrested my attention.

A young female cyclist had lost control of her machine, she'd allowed her bicycle wheels to slip between the steel track guiding trams. The young girl realising her perilous dilemma; was overcome with fear. But instead following the normal course of action of throwing herself from the bicycle. The terror gripping her gut dictated the following deathly actions; she gripped more tightly the handlebars of that death machine. The bike hurtled with increasing speed down the hill and out of control within the tramlines of that steep downward slope called Stony hill. The girl released what was to be her last shrill cry for help as her machine crashed headlong into the oncoming tram; and her inevitable demise.

Several burly miners had already started their futile chase down the hill. There chase came to a sudden halt when the nerve curdling screeching of metal against metal filled the air. The miners stood awestruck as they witnessed the horrific crash. My head swam with mixed emotions; a violent sickness entered my gut. I watched traumatised bystanders, robotically peeling bloodied parts of the young girl from the front of the tram. Within minutes an ambulance screamed passed me. I bade my last farewells to workmates. It might have been an adrenalin rush, excitement, or the plain horror of the situation injecting stamina to my legs. I scampered purposefully to the bridge leading to the bus terminus.

That evening, the saddened mournful tribe of dad; my sisters Pat Ann and me. Traipsed dolefully the debris ridden Bramwell street; a burdening blanket of silence sat awkwardly upon our shoulders. Exiting Bramwell street we passed Addison and Henry Street; under the railway bridge spanning Hendon Road to "The Hendon Hotel" run by my grandfather and namesake Henry Nixon. Rising above the pub that summer evening, an orange sun sat on the horizon, it was slung low in the sky, resembling an angry red ball. An awesome sight surely confirming that belief; there is a God!

Jerking me back to reality was a rusting Ford Anglia screeching around the corner, an unshaven youth sat at the wheel. Dad and I glared at the passenger with weird coloured red eyes, scarred face, and white hair. The whites of dad's eyes turned a blood red as he shouted in cold tones of accusation. "That's the rotten sod that attacked your mother; rumour on the grapevine is that he's being recalled to Leicester." Dad accused bitterly; hot juices of condemnation burned his throat, "everybody knows he is guilty, but police cannot arrest him; due to the lack of bloody evidence!" Dads' accusations burst forth in a voice of malicious hate. I slipped a friendly arm over the shoulder of that sorrowful bent man; whispered consolingly. "Dad! I swear to you when I'm with the law; our paths will cross. I'll make sure of that and when they do; what the hell." I growled in anger; with a promising, self-impetuosity. I in a self-induced temper stormed towards the pub. Our saddened little group settled inside the snug, my seventy-year-old Grandfather, Henry Nixon; brought drinks. At the same time as dad swerved towards me. With warm brown eyes laden in ambiguity, in a low voice, he muttered. "About the police, forget what I said; don't do anything stupid young man." My overprotective father Ernie warned in mellowing, loving tones.

The following morning, mixed emotion lay on father's shoulders as he with my sisters Pat, Ann; escorted me to the station. A strange fatalism churned inside me as I boarded the train. With reckless abandon I threw my suitcase onto the rack before hurriedly returning to the window. I stared glumly through the dirty glass windows of the carriage. Memories of mother's demise clouded my mind; cloaked in misery I fought to hold back my tears. The cold north wind howled through the station; my loving... caring family shivered on the dirty cold grey slabs gracing Sunderland station. I blurted in downbeat tones of farewell. "Bye all, will write as soon as I arrive." I waved; a gamut of emotions exploded within my nerve shredded gut. I longed to cry... get off the train, but the hand of destiny strongly beckoned me. My loving family stared motionlessly at the clouds of steam spiralling heavenward; signalling the departure of that massive black machine. The shrill blast of the guard's whistle rattled through the cold wind; wheels accelerated in a seemingly backward motion. The midland bound "Pride of Sunderland" lurched forward on my journey of revenge. Hot acid burnt my throat, my aching gut churned with uncertainty; for a large space of time, I stared longingly at my family disappearing in the steam filled Sunderland station. "Bye." My eldest sister Ann croaked. Her throat closing, emotion embraced my sisters who lapsed into sobbing. My younger sister Pat hugged Ann in consolation, dad embracing a brave front could not hide the anguish dressing his face. He too in an emotionally charged voice choked his goodbyes. Clouds of thick black smoke snaked heavenward; the engine lurched forward; its departure from the station. "You take care of the Blonde-haired sod; for your mother's sake," Ernie shouted before turning abruptly to hide his tear ravaged face from his emotionally distraught daughters.

The devastating thought I may never see them again launched me into emotional turmoil. I threw one last emotional stare at the fast-disappearing platform. Waved frantically my goodbyes to my loving family fading into the distance. For the first time in my life, I was alone, nobody to confide in... tell my troubles to or comfort me when I was troubled. It was then, vengeful memories of why I was joining the police force drove its message home. My misery ebbed, almost instantly replaced by a wave of buoyant excitement sweeping over me. Swiftly followed by cold sweat tracing my spine; a heavy dose of self-pity embraced me. I recaptured happy times, focussed on the positive to sweep away dismal negativity and regrets. My loving mum Nancy never wanted me to work in the bowels of the earth. She would have leant her full support behind my decision to leave the mines. I leant back into the folds of the seat, pictures of mother and I in happier times floated before me; I smiled happily. My eyes closed to the rhythmic clickety-click of

40

Jean Pierre and Mafia

An exasperated Jean Pierre wasted seven long miserable years, drifting from one meaningless job to another. Thes futile efforts had been enacted selflessly, in a fruitless bid to please his father. The inevitable arrived; a twenty-four-year-old Jean Pierre committed himself to the Mafia. Jean Pierre decided to inform his father of his decision. The unsettled couple faced each other in the sparsely decorated front room of Andre's chalet. The air sizzled with disruptive, accusatory vibes. Rage, humiliation swept through Andre's skinny torso, tautening every nerve before unleashing his vociferous protestation of opposition to his son's unpalatable decision. Jean Pierre's face clouded in frustration; bemused awkwardness entered the young assassin's befuddled mind; faltering steps guided him towards his intransigent father. "You don't understand." The Frenchman spluttered, twisting his body to face the broken panes of the window; exasperation cloaked that handsome tanned, troubled face. The veins of Andre's neck bulged, his face coloured a deep red; harsh condemning tones delivered caustically his stinging reply. "Your right I don't understand that's the trouble." Andre screeched, "it was the bloody Mobs assassin Scar who killed your mother.

What escapes, confuses me, is your trite belittlement of my opinions on the issue." The angry Frenchman paused taking a large gulp of red wine. Ran his wiry fingers through his thinning grey hair before continuing. "That knowing full well what depths the scum, you call friends, will stoop to achieve their goals; you still bloody well joined them." Andre screeched, "and is it not suspicious, nobody has seen the sodden albino since he killed my beloved Ann Marie." Jean Pierre's blue eyes held a numbed... emotionless... impassive stare of commitment. His blue eyes stared into his father's gaze of intransigence; he launched into a meaningful reply. "And for that very reason I must join the scum if I'm to have the remotest chance of catching, killing Scar; it will have to be done from the inside. From within, it will be easier to penetrate the blanket of protection provided by the mob." Jean Pierre's head sagged resignedly to his chest. A despondent Andre withdrew his skinny body from his sons' arm; gesticulating his utter frustration, he threw his hands exasperatingly ceiling-ward. "Be it on your own head, join those thugs; I disown you." He raged, in a voice indulging intemperance.

Jean Pierre raised his crestfallen head, stared in helpless despondency at his father's bloodshot eyes clouded in sorrowful acceptance of his son's actions. Jean Pierre's options were limited, to achieve his goal; he'd to be accepted by the Mafia. He knew his father could never accept, would never be happy with his entry into the Mafia. Jean Pierres primary reason for joining the mob, was the revenge for his mother's killing; being on the inside would give him a distinct edge in pursuit of mother's killer. The Frenchman wheeled about with face decked in sorrow. He entered the world of glacial isolation; his shoulders drooped in exasperation... he left the room. A spasm of pain flashed over Andre's face. "Jean Pierre, Jean Pierre." Andre anguished, clutching his bony chest he crashed to the floor where he lay motionless. The cry of distress ricocheted the bare walls of the empty house like a pistol shot; his infuriated, frustrated son; had already left the chalet and was Mafia bound.

With his troubled mind racing with uncertainty, the Frenchman advanced hurriedly over dusty streets, leading to Mafia headquarters, and his future. With throat burning he skirted overgrown bushes, leading to the entrance of a run-down nightclub. His face lit up when spotting Rusha; he beckoned her. She flashed a gaze of hate at the Frenchman, turned and ran in the opposite direction. Jean Pierre flashed a look of disbelief but with troubled mind juggling with the needs of his father, dismissed the issue. Urgency dictated the more pressing dilemma; sorting out his future. The Frenchman shouldered open the club door; located on the Avenue Rue de Bourgogne. Sylvester, an illiterate thug renowned for employing Mafia inhumane methods; was Lyons mafia godfather. For this very reason, Jean Pierre had set the cruel American sadist apart from the rest. Himself being renowned as a sadistic... ruthless hitman. Sylvester and Jean Pierre shared the same attributes; the Frenchman held the Yank in respectful esteem. The Frenchman threaded his way between tables strewn across the dance floor. His feet hit the stairs with a rapid patter; with heart racing unhealthily, he continued his relentless progression as pounding feet carried him to the first floor. Nervous apprehension introduced fear tracing his spine; he entered the smoke-filled room. Hairs on his neck bristled, face muscles rippled with a nervous twitch. Jean Pierre threw querulous glances sweeping the smoky recesses of the room. His searching stares were to go unrewarded, no sign of Scar. His wandering gaze fell on a book strewn Oak table accommodating the overweight American. A cold chill ran up Jean Pierre spine. He could feel eyes piercing those thick smoke plumes trained upon his back; an unfriendly... cold silence blanketed the room.

A relaxed Sylvester sat with glasses perched precariously on the end of his bulbous nose. Sylvester threw piercing stares of inquisition towards the newcomer. The Yanks companion, a well-proportioned peroxide blonde; waddled her top-heavy figure until the well-endowed torso had stationed herself behind the overweight Yank. "Sit." Growled Sylvester, sending a fat forefinger cutting through the air; pointing to an empty chair. Jean Pierre slid his muscled torso into a vacant seat; shoulders tightening in discomfort, "so the feared Jean Pierre condescends to enter my little abode. By your visit, am I to take it; you wish to join my happy little band?" Sylvester gloated. Jean Pierre shifted with uncomfortable apprehension in his chair. With a swift nod of the head, Jean Pierre replied tacitly the affirmative. Sylvester continued. "we've heard about Scar's fracas leading to the untimely death of your mother. For that stupid unforgivable action, my deepest condolences are with you and your father." Sylvester's balding head dropped momentarily forward, gesturing his respect. Seconds later Sylvester's head whipped up, cold blue eyes threw a questioning glare at the Frenchman, "The Mafia is run on trust, and we have reached clear the airtime; you're aware of Scar's absence. I noticed you swept an inquisitive searching glare over the room when you entered. Now what interests me; what you had planned if you'd found him?" Sylvester questioned inhaling deeply on his weed.

Jean Pierre's brow furrowed, unbidden corrosive vibes of uncertainty eroded his confidence, he shuffled uneasily on the hard-wooden chair. His cold eyes penetrating that smoke riddled air of unfriendliness which held nothing but pure contempt from the motley crew of killers surrounding him. Each one of these soulless individuals would willing kill their grandmother if the Mafia so instructed. "That would not be a problem; we can work together." Jean Pierre spit out glibly his prevaricating mistruths, with the polished art of an experienced politician. Sylvester's podgy fingers drummed the fading worn Formica of his table. His beady eyes staring with suspicion long and hard at the young ruthless

Frenchman. The overweight Yank dredged thoughtfully strands of deep distrust tormenting his evil mind. What should I do? I don't trust him, but while he works for me, I have control over him. Sylvester thought. "Get him out of my sight; get him suited." He snarled swivelling his chair to face the blonde, "and where are my Cigars." He roared as the blonde jerked forward in subservient movements wooden box in hand. Two suited pock faced thugs escorted Jean Pierre from the smoke stenched room into the glaring afternoon sun: before melting into the milling crowd.

Three hours later, the "suits" returned with Jean Pierre, his new attire transforming him from the ill-clad village dropout; to an overdressed spiv. The Frenchman felt more at home in new surroundings. In a black shirt sporting a white tie and black suit, he melted with ease into his new image. He angled his new trilby over wild curly locks; swaggered with an air of arrogant confidence back into the half-lit room. Sylvester's yellowed teeth clamped on a cigar; gave Jean Pierre an approving stare of acceptance. "Feel better." The Yank rasped through a half-smile dressing his pockmarked face. A strange excitement exploded in Jean Pierre's gut. Beads of sweat dampened his brow, the tanned Frenchman nodded curtly his tacit reply. "Sit." Ordered the Yank, shoving a box of cigars over the chipped veneer topping the table. Not wishing to upset his host, non-smoker Jean Pierre accepted the offer. Placing fat weed between his lips; the Blonde lit the cigar. The Frenchman inhaled deeply, an explosive bout of coughing from Jean Pierre ensued before the eerie silence was resumed. Shadows of fatigue hung in the corner of the Yank's evil eyes; cholesterol lips parted in a greasy smile. "Right let's cut the crap, get to the point. I've heard flattering remarks regarding your skills with a knife. Scar informs me, you are as evil; as you are adept the blade." Sylvester paused; signalled his assistant to relight cigar, "I'm giving you a chance to prove your worth." He paused; the curvaceous blonde stooped revealing her oversize credentials; lighted match in hand. "I'm not a happy man, the south side of Lyons takings has fallen for the second month running. That is monies charged against shops for our protection. Needless to say, this has upset Sicily, they are casting doubts on my leadership; corrective action has to be taken." Sylvester grunted in displeasure whilst chewing on his half-smoked Havana. Jean Pierre's mouth opened in disbelief; excitement gripped his young face. "Mon Ami! But of course." He gushed with boyish enthusiasm. The Yank blurted. "Tomorrow select two men and... well you know what to do; now get lost and perform... make me a happy man." The Yank ordered.

The Frenchman remained rooted in his seat; unease sat upon his tanned features. He spun about to face Sylvester; groaned. "Messier; my father advised me not to return home if I joined your services." The Yank stubbed out his cigar; levelling eyes at the Frenchman he put the assassin at ease. "No problem, my friend owns the Hotel next door, you can check in their now get lost." The Frenchman rose; with a smile of satisfaction hugging the Yanks cholesterol lips Sylvester grabbed the phone, "now I have control over the Frenchman and Scar, I can control their futures." Sylvester gloated quietly to himself. Visual relief washed over Jean Pierre tanned face; face muscles relaxed. A suit leant forward on spotting Jean Pierre's watch. "Quelle Heuer est-il?" The thug enquired. "Cinc Heuer's." Jean Pierre replied glancing at his watch. "How many times, speak English you morons, I'm not a bloody linguist." Sylvester screeched. Jean Pierre on reaching the door paused in rapt admiration of his boss. "Merci Messier... I mean thank you." He stuttered in excited enthusiasm pushing open the door. His buoyant mood though was overshadowed by the nagging question haunting his mind. Where the hell was Scar?

41

Nicky the Policeman

The freezing northeasterly rain relented the storm clouds drifted across the angry sky. he bedraggled ageing postman negotiated gingerly the dirty, water-filled bomb craters littering Bramwell Street. He skirted a myriad the potholes whilst negotiating gale force winds on his debris-strewn path to Number Thirteen and a half. Due to the constant bombing of the dock area, Sunderland suffered a critical housing shortage. Each two-storey house in Addison, Henry and Bramwell Street accommodated two families. If you're numbered address ended in a half, you dwelt in the upper half of the house. The only exception was Grey Road where this rule did not apply, this being the affluent Jewish quarter, an upmarket posh road of bigger, better-quality houses.

The prevailing north wind turned colder; the harsh greyness of day returned; black clouds hugging that angry sky parting briefly. Allowing weak rays of winter sunshine warm the postman's balding head. With his sodden blue serge uniform clinging to his cold skinny body; his bony forefinger pressed the doorbell. I Nicky, was physically exhausted having just arrived home after working a gruelling late shift at the pit. Sleep lurked in the corner of my tired eyes. Grimy dirt infested fingernails brushed through unkempt tousled hair; yawning I jarred open the door. "Sign here! I have a parcel for Pat Nixon; it's registered." The postman grunted, while his arms diligently searching his bulging sack. "And a letter for Mr. H Nixon." He added thrusting a crumpled envelope into my hand. My sleep filled eyes flashed with excitement when focussing on the Leicester postmark.

My stomach churned with excitement; I threw exuberantly my bloodshot eyes heavenward. Snatching a refreshing lungful of the cold morning air, I tore open that welcome missive. "Yes." I yelled punching the air triumphantly, hobnail boots swung my body ninety degrees then clattered my ungainly progress up the wooden carpet-less stairs to dad, "it's confirmation from the Leicester Police." I shouted excitedly, waving euphorically the crumpled piece of paper in front of dad's face. Waves of upbeat emotions coursed my spine; that lovely opportunistic window beckoned me. My euphoria eclipsing dad's sadness, excitement swiftly moved to a cold sweat, my eyes narrowed. Face muscles twitched; the gravity of the challenge embraced me; inviting me to follow the path of my beautiful revenge. Through tearstained eyes I beheld dad, my body shook with regretful apprehension, I would be leaving my grieving father so soon after mothers' death. I knew that lonely heartbroken man still struggled desperately accepting mother's demise.

My earlier ill-timed exuberance dissipated, was replaced with pangs of regret. Dad's head dropped to his chest in acceptance of my frivolous, selfish naivety. Once again Ernie, my grieving father, would have to adjust emotionally; to a second traumatic event. My leaving could exacerbate his highly emotionally unstable situation; an icy knot of anxiety formed in my stomach. I'll never forget the day dad boldly stepped forward with an outstretched hand, a lump the size of an apple lodged in my throat. His weather-beaten face registered, for the first time in weeks; happiness. "Well done son I know you'll make us proud." Acclamations of appeasement rang out in his tones of bravado; alas his saddened eyes transmitted a different message. He gripped my hand, shook it vigorously, encouraging that damn outsized lump hurting my throat; grow even bigger. Dad's stoicism inadvertently, made more difficult the task of controlling hot tears, welling behind my bloodshot eyes. A flood of emotional tears crashed forcibly through closed eyelids, soaking my bristled cheeks. I stared glumly at his vacant ashen face. This could be the final straw for him; first mum now me I sighed as I fought the rising panic gripping my stomach.

Back within the soul-destroying dark recesses of the mine, an ear-piercing screeching of steel upon steel reverberated the dust infested tunnel. The ageing wheels of overladen coal trolleys trundled speedily the well-worn track. The shrill sound of the buzzer pierced the dust-laden air, signalling the end of my final shift. Happy contentment charged my spine, I sprang to my feet with renewed energy. I'd spent four mind-numbing years, slogging in the shadows of the soul-destroying tunnels; of Wearmouth pit. At long last I was through with the mind dulling laborious drudgery within the demoralising grimy dust-filled tunnels of darkness; my guts warmed.

Struggling against incoming bodies of the following shift, I fought my way to the cage; pit head and fresh air. Emotions emanating from my newfound freedom sprang unbidden to my face, I stared at the dirty coal grime covering the darkened walls of our pit canteen. Was what I felt sorrow, euphoria, or pure relief; I broke into joyous unbridled acclamations of joy. "That's it, finished with the filthy tunnels; choking on coal dust." A sharp intake of cold breath ensued, as I inhaled a grateful sigh of relief. Cooling my buoyant mood was a shrill, frightened cry for help. It echoed chillingly on the cold air; arrested my attention.

A young female cyclist had lost control of her machine, she'd allowed her bicycle wheels to slip between the steel track guiding trams. The young girl realising her perilous dilemma; was overcome with fear. But instead following the normal course of action of throwing herself from the bicycle. The terror gripping her gut dictated the following deathly actions; she gripped more tightly the handlebars of that death machine. The bike hurtled with increasing speed down the hill and out of control within the tramlines of that steep downward slope called Stony hill. The girl released what was to be her last shrill cry for help as her machine crashed headlong into the oncoming tram; and her inevitable demise.

Several burly miners had already started their futile chase down the hill. There chase came to a sudden halt when the nerve curdling screeching of metal against metal filled the air. The miners stood awestruck as they witnessed the horrific crash. My head swam with mixed emotions; a violent sickness entered my gut. I watched traumatised bystanders, robotically peeling bloodied parts of the young girl from the front of the tram. Within minutes an ambulance screamed passed me. I bade my last farewells to workmates. It might have been an adrenalin rush, excitement, or the plain horror of the situation injecting stamina to my legs. I scampered purposefully to the bridge leading to the bus terminus.

That evening, the saddened mournful tribe of dad; my sisters Pat Ann and me. Traipsed dolefully the debris ridden Bramwell street; a burdening blanket of silence sat awkwardly upon our shoulders. Exiting Bramwell street we passed Addison and Henry Street; under the railway bridge spanning Hendon Road to "The Hendon Hotel" run by my grandfather and namesake Henry Nixon. Rising above the pub that summer evening, an orange sun sat on the horizon, it was slung low in the sky, resembling an angry red ball. An awesome sight surely confirming that belief; there is a God!

Jerking me back to reality was a rusting Ford Anglia screeching around the corner, an unshaven youth sat at the wheel. Dad and I glared at the passenger with weird coloured red eyes, scarred face, and white hair. The whites of dad's eyes turned a blood red as he shouted in cold tones of accusation. "That's the rotten sod that wheels speeding over steel track; I heard myself utter in emotion filled words of sadness. "Bye Mum, Bye Pa, Bye Sis." I felt damp tears wetting my cheek; tears streamed uncontrollably as curling in the fetal position on the seat I drifted into the carefree peace offered by sleep.

Three hours and thirty minutes later I stepped from the train onto broken slabs of what laughingly passed for the platform. The platform was deserted; I'd arrived at the picturesque village station of Littlethorpe, Leicester. I trudged from broken slabs onto the clay path of the tiny station leading onto what passed as the main road, up the hill to my new home. It was six-o-clock, darkness hugged the October sky. I turned the key to enter my new abode; 17 Bingley Road. It was a small cosy three bedroomed semi–Dormer Cottage nestling in a quiet cul-de-sac. The small village comprised of, railway station, small supermarket library and school surrounded by approximately four hundred houses. A solitary broken wooden chair sat in front of the gas fire into which I slumped. A loud grumble from my empty stomach signalled hunger, I had to eat. In my excitement I'd forgotten to buy food; a sharp rap echoed from the front door.

With hunger pangs aggravating my grumbling guts, I gravitated to the front door; jarred it open. "Yes." I groaned, hunger increasing my impatience. A medium height suited man stood smiling at the door; a seven-o-clock shadow dressing his face. "Sorry to drop in on you like this but I'm Tiger... your welcoming party, fancy a drink?" The stranger laughed at the vacant look of admiration dressing my face. "Not the Inspector Tiger?" I blurted in a sarcastic tone of facetious admiration. "The same, about that drink," replied the upbeat tones of the Inspector. "Thanks, but no thanks. I forgot to buy food; I'm starving a visit to the supermarket his calling me." I squealed. "There's a dirty pub around the corner in the old market square, it is called the Old Inn; you can buy a couple of stale cobs there. I know Bob the Landlord, he's always good for a lock-in." Tiger sniggered.

42

Scar and his Newborn

A disgruntled Scar arrived back in Lyon, hailed a taxi. Handing the driver, a scribbled note of the address. Scar grunted. "Take me there." The Albino snarled, sinking into the worn plastic folds of the back seat, for the rest of his short journey. A dishevelled Scar entered his bungalow and front room; he stared in emotional gratitude at the seated Rusha's enlarged stomach. She glared unkindly at Scar's startled surprised stare, of disbelief. "Yes, Scar I'm six months pregnant, I don't want the child; arrange an abortion because I want rid." Rusha snarled, top lip curling in displeasure. Scar's eyes widened in disagreement. "Okay I'm an Austrian son of Gnostic priest, who holds no beliefs in a God; but we have a chance of having a baby; what a gift." Scar's eyes turned cold. Rusha spotted hate in his eyes; she curled in a ball on the settee before replying. "Scar I told you months ago I did not want a child, nothing's changed; I want rid." Scar recoiled with disbelief at Rusha's intransigence; anger sprang to his eyes. "You have a serious rethink my girl; you get that child aborted over my dead body. You'll bloody well have this baby. Even if that means having to look after the child myself, this child you are carrying is 50% mine. I've business in England and return there tomorrow. I'll be away for several months." He paused adding gravity to his caustic words of warning. With fury masking his ashen face, the assassin continued; voice cold... harsh, "in my absence don't you even think of getting rid of my baby. Because as God is my witness; you will end up being one dead woman. You take good care of yourself... and the baby, very good care. I'll be back for the birth." Scar barked; with bloodshot eyes soaked in hostility; he stormed from the room.

A visibly shaken Rusha, taken aback by the vicious ferocity of Scar's onslaught cowered subserviently; fear clouded her eyes. "Firstly, my father mistreats me, then Jean Pierre has his way; now you. But let me warn you Scar. My time will come, for sure my time will come; then we will see who ends up dead." Rusha spluttered as tears of frustration flooded her flushed cheeks. Revenge glistened in her wild eyes; eyes charged with retributive emotions. Two uneventful months slipped by; her pregnancy pains increased; Rusha hurried to the maternity ward of the hospital where she was kept overnight. The impatient mother had to wait until the following day for waters to break. Sleep for Rusha was at a premium till Nine-o-clock the follow morning, Rusha already having refused enema to assist birth; sat legs spreadeagled upon the blood-spattered bed clinging and biting her pillow. Her waters burst, she released screams of anguish, in a chaotic order midwives arrived with towels and warm water. A large space of tortuous time elapsed before peace hit the ward after a crying the baby was successfully delivered. Scar had arrived minutes earlier and his worried body had been placed the waiting room. The stressed Austrian spent several hours pacing back and forth that lonely, empty room. Back in the ward, the blood-covered midwife handed over a screaming bundle of flesh; to Rusha. "We find it best to lay baby upon your breast; it will automatically search for its food." The nurse advised the pain-racked Rusha. Scar fidgeted impatiently; fingers of nervous apprehension clawed his gut. In a gait of frustration, he strutted aimlessly the corridor.

Nervousness exploded into excitement when the French surgeon, thrust his bony forefinger finger cutting through the air; beckoned him to enter the delivery room. Within that emotion filled room Rusha cradled a screaming healthy son. Expectancy filled Scar, he longed to hold baby son, after donning a white gown the Austrian was allowed to cradle gently, lovingly, the seven-pound bundle; strutting proudly he shouted gleefully. "This is my son." He gloated. Tears of joy dried. With a suddenness his face distorted when bloodshot eyes were drawn to the baby's neck; and birthmark of three linked circles. "Well son, I hope they deal you a better hand than the one I had to play; come Mama is waiting." He whispered.

Rusha wrestled with torturing, conflicting emotions, she wanted to run away from her situation; but couldn't. Like it or not she was mother of a boy; she bit the end of her blood soiled sheet in frustration. A smiling Scar approached sleeping baby in his arms. Rusha's round-eyed perplexity held Scar in threatening displeasure. "You've got what you want, I've given you a son. I told you, after filling my obligations I would leave you, this changes nothing. On release from the hospital, I'm going to live life the way I want to; not as men instruct me to." Responded Rusha. "You can't mean that, you're a mother with a beautiful baby son surely that changes your mind." Replied a shell-shocked Scar. Placing carefully the infant besides Rusha; irritation, frustration gathered within him, he dropped to his knees, "please, please think again, will you marry me?" Scar begged his tortured lined pale face awash with tears.

"For years I've dreamt of being able to protect myself, from the advances of evil hormonally instructed men. That driving priority has kept me going, I've contacted immigrants affiliated to the French underground, who expressed their surprise... a woman requesting to join them. But after explaining I was a displaced immigrant dealing with a highly unsatisfactory situation; they accepted me. I'm expected at their headquarters at the end of the month. As to your enquiry, no marriage is out of the question."

Rusha replied in a harsh voice of closure. Scar proposed limply. "Maybe when you return..." The albino gulped pleadingly. "Scar I'll be gone for at least several years... maybe more so, get your act together plan a life without me; that's what I intend to do. Maybe when the furore is over, both of our needs have been satisfied." She paused, threw a smile of irony towards him; continued, "it's remotely possible our paths will cross again; maybe next time we'll get along better." Rusha spat her caustic response heavily laden with facetious sarcasm. "Your stubborn

nature will be the death of me... I know of a good home where the baby can be taken care of. When you've satisfied your urges, hopefully, you will have mellowed, warmed to the idea of motherhood; because we still could have a future together." The broken-hearted assassin choked. "As I expected this sort of reply I contacted a care home the baby has been accepted. This is where the child will be staying." Scar mumbled scribbling address of the nursing home, handing the crumpled paper to Rusha.

43

Louis and Failing Vines

Within the picturesque Loire Valley, an abundance of vineyards proliferated its lush countryside. Within this resplendent region of France, intermingled with its grape laden vineyards, stood grand, ageing Castles, and splendid Chateaus. Little wonder this beautiful valley became known as "the valley of the Kings." Sheltered within this beautiful, relaxing backdrop Louis, wife Annette, daughter Brigitte and son Paul settled. Louis's fervent hope was he and family evade probing eyes... ears and evil reach of the pagan sect. The evil, all-powerful Illuminati.

Paul gained employment as a Gendarme in the bustling nearby Roman town of "La Roche Posay." Dissatisfaction burned within the unfulfilled youngster; a troubling emotion ignited a longing; yearning for the unusual. His fervent wish was to tread the exacting path trodden by his father years previously. Paul was driven by this unquenchable hunger required to satisfy his extraordinary desires. The troubled Gendarme would mysteriously vanish for days, when making his re-appearance; explanations where never proffered.

Chenin Blanc vines became the financial mainstay of Louis's vineyard. A troublesome investment that was to be a ruinous, doomed project which unfortunately for Louis was mortgaged to the hilt. 1962 heralded a damp year, this wet weather encouraged creeping grey mould of Botrytis. This mould was to have a catastrophic effect on his vines; wipe out the whole season's fruitage. This devastating attack resulted in no financial reward for Louis's hard work; wiped out what little money he held at the bank. For the second year running, he was again to default on his loan. But to replace the lost vines, he needed to raise the necessary capital... re-mortgage property; hence he sought yet another loan from the bank which was granted. Unfortunately for the distraught Austrian, the following year eclipsed his earlier heartbreak. 1963 lurched, with equally devastating consequences, to the other extreme, the year hailed constant brilliant sunshine. The lack of moisture accompanied by the constant high temperatures produced the ideal situation to spawn the dreaded powdery mildew, Odium. Odium being the grape grower's nightmare; this mildew could decimate crops overnight. 1963 proved yet another summer of discontent for Louis; his precious vines failed yet again. No crops meant no money, no money meant default in his mortgage payments resulting in problems with the Bank.

A despairing Louis directed accusative, suspicious thoughts to the door of the all-powerful Illuminati. Could these evil people have enough power... ability to engineer his problems? Louis sank into misdirected thoughtful deliberation. His troubled mind swung from an accusatory position to access the positive. He decided against the latter, concluding the devastating results were simply down to nature. After a troubled, stormy interview with the bank... the board rejected Louis's application for an extension. The process of remortgaging the vineyard being deemed now a grave mistake; the bank demanded closure.

December 1963 the bank foreclosed on Louis's mortgage; Louis and family faced poverty. The shell-shocked Louis plumbed the depths of insecurity. He swam in vain against the tide of his financial uncertainty. His bloodshot eyes glowered sourly at his worthless vines. This latest tragedy broke Louis's spirit. With a heavy heart, the Austrian accepted he'd to bring an end to his catastrophic misadventure into wine.

Black storm clouds gathered; rain threatened; he strode in total dejection along his worthless vineyard. Into his troubled tired eyes jumped an inevitable retribution. Calloused hands tore vengefully from the ground, the worthless plants; unrepeatable profanities dropped from his lips. Brigitte beheld the broken dejected figure of her father wandering forlornly. She held that soul-destroying picture within several long minutes of agony before issuing consolingly. "Papa! Papa your lunch." Her soft voice invited. "Oui, oui." The Austrian gulped, allowing defeatist... negative vibes run rampant through his tortured mind. I'm beaten he thought sinking into the dark realms of pessimism. "We're finished." The weary Austrian snapped; bloodshot eyes stared towards the heavens. Muscles in his arms twitched, anger overcame him, with head lying despondently on his chest he plodded wearily into the house. Annette with Brigitte sat opposite the dejected Louis in eerie silence for several awkward minutes. The shrill intervention of the telephone pierced the air; fractured the prevailing funereal quiet. Brigitte answered. "Papa, Paul's been promoted, he's holding a celebratory party tomorrow night; he's invited us for drinks. I made our apologies, explaining we're busy with the vines." His wife Annette, head hanging; left the room dirty dishes in hand. "Yes, daughter we're finished, it would not surprise me if the bloody Illuminati engineered this dirty unholy mess. It's this sort of action that led... manipulated disillusioned priests; stray from the sect. I lay credit for the whole sorry mess on their doorstep. They exhibit great power; to show who is in control." Louis screamed. The ever-optimistic Brigitte clenched her father's hand, lay her head on his shoulder. "Where is my strong Papa." She whispered in consolation.

The downcast Austrian wallowed in the depressive negativity of defeat; allowed despair to further destabilise an already dejected mindset. In despair, he rose slowly to his feet, progressed in emotive disillusionment to the window.

What followed could have been a heavenly intervention. His bloodshot eyes stared in horror. An Aeroplane plummeted earthward, and certain death. The unbelievable happened, it was as though an invisible hand reached out to prevent the inevitable crash. Fifty feet from the ground the out-of-control plane pulled out of the dive; a disbelieving Louis witnessed the plane soar heavenward; climb to safety. On that wizened sad face tears dried, Louis's bloodshot eyes, previously anguished in despair; sparkled with hope. That ageing weather-beaten face broke into a smile; tomorrow is a new day he thought bravely. He embraced his daughter; whispered in an upbeat voice.

"Tomorrow is the start of the rest of our life. Phone Paul, tell him we'll attend his party; celebrate his promotion." Louis shouted.

Brigitte tripped happily from the room; Louis spun back to window the plane had disappeared. It was as though a torturous burden had been lifted from his shoulders. Fears melted, he smiled, wife Annette appeared covered in suds shouting. "Louis, the phone it's for you, Jean Pierre," Annette grunted in tones of disagreement, Annette never warmed to the cocky young thug; she nurtured a healthy distrust in the Frenchman. Jean Pierre, after joining the mafia, had been labelled the black sheep of the Dupont family. Annette handing the phone to Louis, allowed her body to shake with an evident disgust. The dictatorial hand of destiny gripping Louis's shoulder; was about to jerk him from his present tragic dilemma. To deliver him into the clutches of his old adversary, the Mafia. Once in their hands, he would face an even greater problem, the all-powerful Illuminati.

44

Jean Pierre Breaks With his Father

Jean Pierre stormed with threatening arrogance, from shadows of the darkened room to confront a cowering... terrified shopkeeper. This frightening tactic Jean Pierre had borrowed from his boss Sylvester to unnerve victims. Jean Pierre's mere presence impregnated the air with fear, his inhumane deeds preceding him. An evil scowl of intent dressed the Frenchman's cruel blue eyes when falling on the blade of his knife. The shabbily dressed shopkeeper trembled, the Frenchman was aware of Jean Pierre's cruel reputation. From the shadowy alcove of the room, discontented rumblings of an overworked freezer impregnated the chilling silence. "The uninvited intrusions of inanimate objects." Quipped Jean Pierre before leaning forward his tone changing from the frivolous to the menacing. "You owe." The cold threatening monosyllables dropped from the young Frenchman's mouth in threatening finality, "And who's this?" Jean Pierre questioned through a lingering cruel smile; his murderous gaze fell upon the slender form of a young girl. "She's my son's daughter." The balding shopkeeper stuttered, his shaking hands grabbed the girl, pulling her to the protection of his skinny body. "What a pretty face." Jean Pierre laughed chillingly, running the glistening blade down her pale cheek. "If you've not paid within the week, we withdraw our protection... I think you know what will happen." That cold... threatening message unnerved the shopkeeper. Jean

Pierre pointed gloved forefinger to the shaking victim, "a week, any more trouble on my patch; you're a dead man." The Frenchman repeated, plunging into the dark shadows; his thugs followed subserviently in hot pursuit.

Outside on the desolate dusty street, Jean Pierre entered back seat of the waiting black Citroen. "Take me to my father's chalet." The Frenchman rasped. "How is Andre?" Driver Henri questioned. "Just drive." Jean Pierre's vindictive tone spat out sourly. Henri's intense dislike for Jean Pierre grew exponentially. The confrontational, clashing personalities resigned themselves to a private contemptuous silence for the remainder of the journey.

From within a mood of discontentment mingled with frustration, in the darkened front room of Andre's run-down chalet; Jean Pierre confronted his stubborn father. "Papa. Why won't you move?" Jean Pierre pleaded agitated fingers fidgeted nervously with the hatband of his trilby. "To a Chateau bought with blood money; never." The stubborn ashen-faced Andre snarled; the ageing Frenchman fell victim to a violent coughing bout. Jean Pierre moved with uncharacteristic compassion, turned to his father, an unusual depth of feeling dressing those blue eyes. "Papa, please, this leaky old chalet; it is not good for your health." The Frenchman pleaded, but his well-meaning pleas proved futile, fell on deaf ears; Jean Pierre lit his cigar. "You're not welcome in this house, as long as you run with that, that low life mob. And since when did you start the filthy habit; smoking?" Andre screeched. "Smoking is not the only thing that's changed around here." Jean Pierre lipped derisively. "Get out of my house, take that stinking weed with you." Andre fumed; plumes of smoke idled lazily to the ceiling as Jean Pierre rose slowly. Angling his trilby over his mass of dark locks; he spun about to his father. "Papa." He beseeched, hands gesticulating frustration when the realization that his grovelling pleas had been in vain; were driven home to him. In a seamless, emotionless transition, the Frenchman's voice escalated from the pleading; to the threatening, "Papa for years you've been my guiding light, instructing how to live my life; how to act where to go. But no more, we've done it your way; for the last time. I walk the path of my future; it is my way now." His harsh tones mellowed; introduced softness, "I'd heard Louis and bad luck run hand in hand, you answered as I'd expected so I have invited him and family; to stay in your new house." He added before rusting hinges squeaked his exit.

He slipped silently from the front door into weak rays from the evening sun hanging low in the cloudless sky. The Frenchman's eyes swept cautiously the dusty, half-lit street. Those cruel blue eyes fell upon a dark-skinned elderly lady. Covering her shoulders was a ragged dirty black shawl, she manoeuvred her wheelchair laden with firewood, through bombed ruins the opposite side of the street. The old lady spun her eyes to the Frenchman; greeted the young man. "Bonjour." She cackled hands plunging into the firewood. "Bonjour." Replied Jean Pierre sourly; a shot rang out. The ageing lady slumped to the ground, gun in hand. A lean suited figure emerged from shadows of the bombed building, smoking pistol in hand. "You're one lucky Frenchman, you must have done something bad, because that immigrant bitch. Whom I've been tailing for weeks; was about to shoot you." The stranger shouted in a cockney accent. A Black Citroen screeched around the corner on two wheels, breaking to a sudden halt at the kerbside; a tall lean man stepped from the vehicle.

"Bonjour Jean Pierre." Henri greeted, shaping his thin pencil moustache; he opened the rear door of the car for Jean Pierre. The Frenchman's eyes glistening with impatience; grunted to his driver. "You're late." Jean Pierre grated, then turning to the stranger.

In a voice dropping half an octave. Jean Pierre questioned the newcomer in warm conciliatory tones, "why Messier! May I ask why you were tailing her?" Jean Pierre's eyes dropped to his watch, time was pressing; no time to wait for the strangers reply, "no matter my gratitude lies with you, I would like it if our paths should cross again. As you English say, I owe you one." Jean Pierre shouted, alert blue eyes skirting once more the rubble-strewn street for danger before slamming the car door. Leaning against the crumbling wall of the ruins the inspector muttered with satisfaction. "Oh, my friend they will; of that I assure you." Inspector tiger stared almost gloatingly at the fast-disappearing Citroen; a wry smile parting lips, "yes my friend our paths will cross once again; as sure is my name is Tiger." The inspector iterated, then approached the old lady laughing; he kicked her playfully. "You can get up Sergeant; shows over." Mayur rose adjusted his black ragged shawl; glared angrily at the inspector. "There was no need to kick me, that hurt." The sergeant growled in disgust. Tiger slipped his hand around the wiry shoulder of Mayur; together they melted into shadows of a bombed building. Tiger was overjoyed to have at last made contact with their number one suspect.

Back in their temporary office of New Scotland Yard, London; Nicky entered with tea. "Well, Nicky that operation went successfully." Tiger blurted, a smug smile of satisfaction gracing his wrinkled face; he slurped triumphantly his tea.

Back in Lyon, from the back seat of the Citroen, an anxious Jean Pierre glanced at his watch; relaxed on sumptuous white leather upholstered seats. "The boss wants to see you." Henri blurted; the car sped alongside the river Saone; towards outskirts of Lyon. Jean Pierre's thoughts drifted to the stranger, who had saved his life. "Tiger what funny names these English have. I assume he accepted the old crone carried a gun?" Momentarily his overactive mind was thrown into confusion, "who the hell is this man, Tiger? What was he doing in the bombed building? Why was he tailing her?" These imponderable, niggling questions were to pale into insignificance. Conflicting thoughts jerked him back to the fracas with his father, problems with Sylvester. "What about?" Jean Pierre snapped to Henri. Henri flicked a glance in the rear-view mirror. "Takings from protection have dropped again," Henri replied slipping gears into neutral; their car slowed gently to a halt at the kerbside. The Cours Lafayette Avenue bustled with bodies on early morning shopping. Jean Pe alighted his vehicle to struggle against the throng of oncoming bodies. Before colliding with the petite form of a blue-eyed blonde English lady.

45

Louis and New House

The telephones shrill ring reverberated the bare walls of the rundown chalet: Andre pressed the handset to his ear he heard the pleasing refrain of familiar voice hugging the line. "Louis Mon Ami, good to hear your voice; my son Jean Pierre informs me of your troubles. I hear he has invited you to my place outside Lyon. You are welcome to stay as long as you like my friend. But beware of my son he is trouble; trouble with a capital T." Andre's quivering angry voice warned; shaking hands replaced phone to the handset. Louis's forehead creased as he spluttered indecisively. "Decisions; decisions which way do we turn." The Austrian groaned sipping his wine. "Well, Papa are we going?" Brigitte chirped in girlish tones of excitement, "I hear Lyon is full of shops, and Paul has been ordered to Lyon. He's to deal with shopkeeper's complaint; regarding Mafia thugs terrorising the community. The disgruntled shopkeepers have demand protection from the Gendarmerie; they want the Mafia and their present issue dealt with immediately. Her mother Annette entered the room. "Talking about Paul, he's up to his tricks again. The boy has just returned from walkabout of two days, and again no explanation." Annette despaired, she looked towards Brigitte's pleading face; in a more conciliatory tone said, "but of course I should like to go to Lyon." Fatigue clung to the corner of Louis's bleary eyes, who announced obliquely. "That's settled, Lyon here we come." Louis said wearily as he stared forlornly through the window; despair knitted with anguish crept into those weary tired eyes levelling in disgust when visions of the worthless... rotting vines vaulted into his over active mind.

The following morning Louis and family crowded into their battered old Citroen. The sun rose high in that clear cloudless blue sky its hot rays heating the inside of the ancient car rattling its progress along the A43 through Grenoble and Chambery. Before tackling the Rue De Bourgogne and Lyon. The dust-laden car slewed to a halt in the main street of Lyon. "Mama Papa, would you mind?" Brigitte spluttered, unable to contain the excitement when spotting a myriad of shops. "Of course not, run along... enjoy yourself; if you get lost papa and are slipping into that bistro for coffee." Her mother advised laughing, pointing to a sign.

Brigitte with the sun on her back fought against the tide of afternoon shoppers. The sun's rays played on the dirty still waters of the Saone; the river running alongside the main street of Lyon. She flicked an idle glance at a Black shiny Citroen slewing to a halt the other side of the road. Alighting the car, a tall handsome Frenchman just outside the Hotel Lyon. This Adonis of a young man when stepping from the car bumped into an attractive blonde lady. The Frenchman spoke to the Blonde, Brigitte assumed he was apologising. Jean Pierre's attention was drawn to the battered old Citroen lying idle; on the opposite side of the road but mainly to the young attractive girl stepping from the vehicle. He inhaled deeply, muttered apologies to the Blonde, straightened his tie, and charged across the road between oncoming cars to reach her.

"Mademoiselle." He greeted warmly, "forgive my manners, my rude interruption but I'm eating alone tonight; I wondered might you join me. My name is Jean Pierre." With bated breath, he awaited the reply. "If you are the Jean Pierre son of Andre; then we are stopping in your cottage. I'm Brigitte; daughter of Louis." The young French girl replied laughing. "But... but that is wonderful then you must eat with me; please." Jean Pierre pleaded.

46

Sam and Drugs

Crippling pains gripped Sam's gut; she needed a fix. Beads of sweat poured liberally down her pink forehead; damp patches appeared on her pristine White blouse as a knot of anxiety formed in her stomach. She progressed in ungracious steps from the aeroplane down to the tarmac of Lyon-Satolas International airport, towards the main terminal. Relief swept over her when customs chalked her bag; gingerly she clambered onto the ageing bus that would deposit her at the family Chateau adjacent to the University, but more critically her stock of drugs.

The following day, bright French sunshine fell on Sam when entering the town museum. Rapt concentration lined her face whilst studying the ornate carvings; of a 17th century Elizabethan suite of furniture. It was during that moment of quiet appreciation, a plain young French girl crashed into her; they both clattered ungraciously to the floor. "Sorry, you alright?" The spluttering apology spilled demurely from the shy French girls' lips. Sam flicked a sour look of disapproval over the French girls shabby clothing; obviously hand me downs Sam thought haughtily. The pretty French girl assisted Sam to her feet. Sam held the slim girl in a glare of hostility, disgust; dusted her previously spotless tunic. But that warm smile of the young naïve intruder, melted Sam's abrasive mood to one of acceptance, friendliness. "Yeah, sure I'm fine except for my injured pride. Sorry I am showing my ignorance, it's my urban upbringing; they call me Samantha... Sam to you." The Blonde replied. "Pleased to meet you Mademoiselle, my name is Brigitte."

A nervous conversation ensued with a liberal interchange of girlish niceties; creasing pains grabbed the gut of Sam, her hands shot to the affected spot. Concern dressed the face of Brigitte. "Are you alright?" She blurted throwing her hands forward in a dramatic gesture of concern. "I'm fine just hunger pangs; it has been nice talking but must dash." Sam muttered, sweat gathered on her brow; hands began to shake, "I need a fix." She mumbled to herself. "It was a pleasure meeting you Mademoiselle." Brigitte replied. "I was wondering, as we're talking of hunger, tonight I take coffee in the café, around the corner. Would you care to meet?" Sam spluttered almost as an afterthought. "I've just arrived besides I am eating out with a friend tonight and do not know my way round Lyon." Replied Brigitte coyly. "Oh, it's a popular meeting place of students, it's called Rue des Maronniers; behind Place Bellacour you cannot miss it." Sam shouted hurriedly, departing the museum on route to her ubiquitous store of drugs.

Seven-o-clock rang stridently its message from the village clock, warm dark shadows of evening chased away the remaining light of day. Sam's shaking hands gripped tightly her cup of coffee; heroin glazed eyes swept the room of the Rue des Maronniers for her newfound friend. A strikingly handsome Frenchman glided into the café; the waiter acknowledged the tanned well-built Frenchman. "Ah! Jean Pierre please." The skinny waiter responded in a welcome subservience by withdrawing the stool from under the counter, and pointing to the bronzed adonis of a Frenchman. "Merci." The newcomer responded somewhat ungraciously. Sam drooled with unashamed lust at the young handsome Frenchman. "That's the young man who collided with me this afternoon." Sam mused airily. With her heart fluttering deliciously, an unhealthy adulation pounded relentlessly her ribcage; eyes dilated with the excitement stirred by her admiration. Curiosity sprang to her alert blue eyes; her fertile imagination ran rampant as the stranger ordered two drinks.

The door swung open, the Frenchman rose immediately in response, his tanned smile welcomed the newcomer. A young French lady, with close cut dark hair wearing fading denim dress; approached the handsome Frenchman and sat beside him. They lapsed giggling before engaging, conspiratorially, into deep conversation. From behind the counter the phone rang; the barman answered. He thrust the phone over counter to the Frenchman, after a short conversation a frown of disappointment clouded Jean Pierre's face. "Forgive me and please accept my deepest apologies Mademoiselle; I must leave on urgent business. But please sit, enjoy yourself; charge evening's entertainment to my bill." Jean Pierre whispered. He turned, nodded appreciatively at the barman, "Garcon, see that this young lady's bill is charged to my account." He instructed; pushing a card into the Brigitte's hand, "when you have finished, ring this number; Henri will drive you home. Once again Mademoiselle, my profound apologies." Jean Pierre hastened to the open door stopped, turned to face the female at the bar. Sam's stare fell on the young girl seated at the bar. "I don't believe it. That's Brigitte." Sam gasped in disbelief, this unassuming French naïve girl, with unplucked eyebrows, dressed in second- hand clothes. She's just been being kissed by the most handsome man in the room." A sibilance of breath escaped in a hiss of jealousy from the tight lips of Sam. Jean Pierre adjusted his trilby, tilted his head forward to Brigitte; disappeared from building. Relief swept over Brigitte when spotting Sam, who progressed drinks in hand to her table. "You do know you were just being wooed by the most handsome man; I've ever seen." Sam gushed with obvious jealousy. "Wish that had been me." Sam drooled. "Oh him, that's Jean Pierre, he's just a friend of my fathers." Replied Brigitte nonchalantly. "Yeah, now pull the other one girlie it's got bells on." Sam jeered. Brigitte's face twisted animatedly. "Pull the other one girlie; it's got bells on?" She repeated forehead lined with confusion. "Sorry, an English saying, my urban upbringing once again raises its ugly head." Sam uttered apologetically; the young French girl smiled. "Really he's a friend of my father's I'll introduce you." The naive Brigitte offered shyly wrapping her skinny fingers around the bulbous Brandy glass. "Brigitte, do that and I'm indebted to you for life." Sam responded with girlish excited gratitude.

The hours passed like minutes; the couple chatted excitedly on the obvious attributes of the handsome Frenchman. The time approached Ten-o-clock, seven hours since Sam's last fix; she wriggled uncomfortably in her seat. Damp patches soiled her otherwise pristine blouse, excruciating fingers of pains gripped her stomach. Sweats of drug withdrawal forced her to beg Brigitte's forgiveness. "You must excuse me, feel somewhat under the weather; must leave." Sam croaked. "I'll ring for Henri, Jean Pierre's driver; he will take you home." Brigitte squeaked almost apologetically. "No, I'll be fine, see you tomorrow night." Sam replied staggering from the building.

Back in the safe recluse of her chalet, the once affluent, but now debt-ridden struggling Sam; pondered her trouble littered journey. The pressures incurred by her academic journey had led her to the drugs scene, and that treacherous, slippery, road of debt. The long-awaited mid semester arrived at Lyon University. Sam longed to rest her drug addled brain from swotting for a whole two weeks. She intended to isolate herself in total relaxation. Accompanied with her stack of Heroin, she aimed for complete relaxation in fathers holiday home in Cannes. "I shall miss the girlie conversations with Brigitte." Sam mused stowing her bags into the boot of a shining Black Citroen.

The French Riviera sun rolled lazily over a clear blue sky. Sam's light blue wrap covering the briefest of bikini, fluttered in the warm breeze; she negotiated the never-ending stream of traffic pounding the road to the beach. Threading her semi naked body between palm trees lining the side of the road, she progressed over the hot sand to the edge of the sea. A gust of warm wind whipped sand into her eyes. She groped, whilst staggering blindly, to the nearest deck chair. Where she sat to await the aggravating sand working itself loose. On opening her eyes, she stared in utter disbelief; in front of her stood heartthrob; Jean Pierre. "Excuse me Mademoiselle, I believe you're in my chair." The handsome young Frenchman whispered, there followed a loaded pause. Sam with typical English haughty response sought the ascendancy; raised tanned hands to shade her eyes from sun's rays. "And here I am thinking you were a gentleman; You don't actually expect a lady in distress move?" She replied with seductive girlish charm. Jean Pierre smiled; nodded.

"Would I be so cruel, but may I?" He laughed pointing to the empty sand. "Be my guest." Sam replied, as once again her heartbeat accelerated with excitement, adulation. His eyes passed over her like a slow caress, a shiver of hope ran down her spine. An unhealthy pounding beat increased against her ribcage; emotions conjured up scenes that made her spine tingle. "Garcon." Jean Pierre commanded forefinger cutting through the air. "Oui messeur." The waiter replied curtly. "Deux Cognac, you do drink Brandy?" The handsome Frenchman questioned Sam before confirming his order then dropping his firm backside onto the sand. "Oui messeur." The waiter bowed, disappeared returning minutes later. Jean Pierre released a piercing shriek, withdrawing an oversized pebble from under his trunks; he swore in French. "Sorry, didn't catch that." Sam muttered in a girlish giggle. "It was nothing Mademoiselle." Jean Pierre sniggered playfully before sipping a mouthful of Brandy.

"We've met before!" Sam quizzed in a knowing voice, lips parting revealing evenly set white teeth. "No Mademoiselle, such a beautiful face I could not forget." Jean Pierre complimented. "Yes, you barged into me; before dashing across the road..." Sam's voice quieted. Once again Jean Pierre's blue eyes passed over her; a shiver traced her spine. She longed for him to kiss her. It must be all right, if he can make her feel this way simply by looking at her. The romantic silence was shattered suddenly. An explosion ripped through a deserted mansion, opposite her holiday cottage. "Goodness that could have been father's cottage." She shouted as sun worshippers gasped in amazement at clouds of dust spiralling from the rubble. "You joke Mademoiselle, that cottage I once longed to buy. I heard what they were asking; decided to buy downtown in Lyon." Jean Pierre replied in resignation. Sam seized the moment. "I'm resting before attacking exams. And you?" "Me Mademoiselle; I am also resting, from the pressures of work. I visit casinos for relaxation, tonight with Henri my driver we take the coast road to Monaco casino. I enjoy the thrill of the unknown; challenge of gambling... danger." Jean Pierre replied glibly. "Where do you work?" Sam quizzed raising glass to mouth. "Me Mademoiselle; for an American in Lyon." "That's where I saw you; the Rue des Marrioners café with Brigitte." Exclaimed Sam. "Brigitte! You know Brigitte." Jean Pierre replied in surprise. "Yes I...!" Sam was rudely interrupted by shouts. "Jean Pierre, Jean Pierre." Henri shouted in exasperated urgency. "My apologies Mademoiselle, my driver beckons." With agility of a trained athlete the Frenchman leapt to his feet. Henri pulled Jean Pierre to one side and whispered. "The gentleman owning the cottage, also owns the cafe; he said he would not pay. I explained there were two options; the first was pay. I think he got the message when he heard the explosion; saw his cottage crumble and knowing his café would follow. I advised him that... well let's just say he agreed to sign a new contract, Sylvester will be pleased that's the third new contract this month." Henri shouted gleefully. Jean Pierre spun round dressed hurriedly, waved to Sam before disappearing into his car which sped off in a vortex of dust.

47

Paul in Lyon

Paul arrived at the Gendarmerie HQ in Lyon; immediately was redirected downtown for his meeting with irate shopkeepers. On entry into the darkened shell of a house, Paul was approached by an irate young Asian shopkeeper. This disturbed young man advised Paul of an inhumane, vicious young Frenchman. This thug had threatened his granddaughter; a gangster named Jean Pierre. A dismayed Paul was metaphorically, placed between a rock and a hard place; his leading terror suspect was same man dating his sister Brigitte.

48

Tiger in London

The door of the London office swung open; inspector Tiger rose stroking his bristled chin; his hand shot forth to welcome the newcomer. "Morning Nicky, while you're getting accustomed to the area; sergeant Mayur Haridas will be your guide and mentor." I stared at the Malawian in disbelief... my face reddening. Tiger laughed at my bemused expression. "Don't be fooled by his baby face, the boy is lethal with a knife. Now the other piece of good news, the yard has traced a link between a thug named Scar, and the betting shop in Sunderland. The police of Bethnal Green and Kilburn are keen to speak to him; it gets better. We've received a text from the French Gendarmerie; they've only issued a warrant for Scar's arrest. They also advised us a certain Jean Pierre, who I've befriended, could prove invaluable to our cause; but the sodden trouble is he is also a hoodlum being chased by the Gendarmerie." Tiger shouted in exasperation. "How do you know Jean Pierre?" Enquired the curious Nicky. "That's the guy baby face Mayur and I, conned into thinking he was about to killed; that his life was in danger. Mayur played the old woman whom I pretended to shoot. Then persuaded Jean Pierre, the old woman was a cold assassin about to kill him. I told him I'd been tailing her for weeks. Also, that today had been his lucky day, I'd saved his life. For my service he was unbelievably thankful, but most of all could be useful." Tiger boasted in a voice marinated with hope. "I've heard on the grapevine that Brigitte, Jean Pierre's girlfriend, has flown to England; she's stopping in Littlethorpe Leicester." Mayur shouted. "I have a house in Littlethorpe, I'll track her down." Nicky responded. Tiger grinned then nodded at the silent Mayur before returning his glance back to me. "You have your first assignment now show me what you mackems are made of." Tiger grunted light-heartedly, dropping his head to an untidy heap of papers littering his desk; he moaned, "damn paperwork, I hate it." The inspector threw angry hands into the air gesticulating his frustration.

I shouldered my exit through the office door, once again Tiger nodded to Mayur who slipped from the office in hot pursuit. In the bright mid-morning sunshine, with a spring to my step. I struggled against the surging, thronging crowd of bodies, bustling in a chaotic orderliness, to St Pancras station. Then negotiated a path to the train heading for Leicester's main station. From where I could catch the 10.00 clock train to Littlethorpe and 17 Bingley Road: my haven of peace in that picturesque cul-de-sac. Mayur boarded the same train.

49

Jean Pierre-Brigitte and Ambiguity

After six months of a relationship made in heaven; Jean Pierre's feelings for Brigitte faltered, plumbed the depths of doubt. His doubts were brought to the fore by Brigitte's striking similarities to Rusha, a flame of Jean Pierre's earlier relationship. In Brigitte's company he had felt comfortable, relaxed; mistakenly though he had thought he was in love. Reciprocity was in equal measure between the couple; Brigitte had fallen under the spell of the Frenchman. Their friendship had blossomed, the couple had become inseparable until that fatal day. Jean Pierre received a summons to attend Mafia headquarters where a troubled Sylvester sprawled behind his desk.

"I suppose you are aware Brigitte's brother is with the gendarmerie." Sylvester spluttered in an accusing tone. Jean Pierre staggered back in utter amazement. "No..." Jean Pierre screeched, head dropping to hands in disbelief. "Well now you do! There is no need to tell you what action you've to take." Sylvester roared. "What the hell do you mean?" Snarled the shell-shocked Frenchman. "Brigitte's brother Paul is a bloody gendarme. Do I need to spell it out? Next time we talk, settle my nerves; tell me this relationship is history." Sylvester spat out in cold unambiguous tones.

The sun floated like a flaming red ball high in the cloudless sky at one-o-clock that hot afternoon. A disgruntled Jean Pierre basked uncomfortably within a bubble of indecision as he left the building. These negative thoughts were forcing him to accept damning accusations against the love of his life; Brigitte. Distraught he walked for hours before feeling brave enough to face her. Four-o-clock struck, the Frenchman returned home, his mind grappling with several scenarios that may solve his problem. "Who the hell does Sylvester think he's talking to? An underage naive schoolboy." The irate, disturbed Frenchman grated in discontent. His alternatives though were limited, ignore Sylvester's ultimatum; meant ejection from the Mafia. Jean Pierre could not let that happen, he'd no choice but remain inside the killing club, the Mafia. The unsettled, lovesick Frenchman trod, unhappily, that precarious lonely path.

He'd been forced to terminate his relationship with the love of his life; she had to become history. Jean Pierre entered the half-lit room in slow faltering steps. Brigitte rose from her chair in complete surprise of the unusually early entry of her lover, she spluttered. "Jean Pierre this is a nice surprise you're early." Brigitte uttered coyly; she advanced arms outstretched towards him. Jean Pierre's cold blue eyes flushed with anger. His hand shot up to ward off her embrace; she'd deceived him. "I suppose it was oversight, you not telling me your brother was a Gendarme?" Jean Pierre screamed; flamed eyes shot angrily to the ceiling in frustration. Brigitte, taken aback by his vicious outburst; answered in total naivety. "Because I did not think it was important, if it is. Why?" Brigitte responded in frightened, challenging tones. Jean Pierre paused while recollecting his thoughts, had he overacted with the condemnation of Brigitte. His head spun with negativity, reached the point of exploding. The distraught Frenchman dropped to a chair, muttered unintelligible French words of apology to the frantic Brigitte. But this latest outburst from the overwrought Frenchman had pushed their tempestuous relationship, to the edge of no return. It was Brigitte's turn to juggle these incomprehensible... contrasting scenarios. Find a solution to their seemingly insoluble problems. The young Austrian girl lapsed tensely into a funereal silence of worrying niggling thought. Her crazy Frenchman lover had just hammered one more nail in their coffin. Irritation gathered within her, the fight went out of her as she collapsed into an empty chair and started to cry. She faced the once inconceivable decision; the termination their beautiful relationship. For months she'd attempted to accommodate his volatile temper; wild outbursts. Now with her frayed nerves shattered; she was convinced that time had arrived. She'd to cut her losses, accept the fate accompli, face her 'Raison d'etre'. Cut herself loose from the uncontrollable unstable maniacal Jean Pierre.

There was a point beyond fear, you reach it after being afraid for an awful long time; unfortunately for Brigitte she'd reached that crossroad. She confronted Jean, as corrosive vibes of uncertainty played havoc with her troubled mind, something inside her broke. In an emotionally charged voice, the cold tones of finality resounded her ultimatum. "Jean Pierre, we cannot continue like this; we've reached a crossroads in our relationship." Brigitte blurted. A flood of tears encouraged mascara run liberally down her pretty ashen cheeks. Jean Pierre felt angry frustration sweep over him. He wrestled with the inner compassion competing with his outward arrogant aggression. In a seamless transformation he morphed into the devil incarnate. Fury burned his stomach; his volatile temper spiralled out of control. With head reeling, the Frenchman accessed a boiling cauldron of tumultuous indecision. Turmoil grabbed the reins, dictated the following outcome. His frayed emotions snapped, unsheathing knife from the scabbard; he pressed the razor-sharp gleaming blade against her warm mascara ridden ashen cheek. "I warn you Mon Chérie ! Don't you ever tell me what I can, or cannot do." He threatened, an inhuman evil danced in bloodshot, angry blue eyes. The air that had been charged with evil intent, waned. Now, swam with peace, love. Calm dressed his face, he'd metamorphosed between his Jekyll and Hyde personality. Horror sprung to tanned face when spotting blood oozing pink cheek of his lover.

Removing the monogrammed handkerchief from his top pocket; Jean Pierre handed it to Brigitte. Disgust etched his tanned snarling face. Hurling the bloodied knife to the floor, the Frenchman dropped to his knees in begging subservience; volatile emotional instability plagued his unstable mind. From trembling lips words of forgiveness dropped pleadingly, frustration dressed his bloodshot eyes. "Brigitte! Brigitte." He beseeched in remorseful tones. But Brigitte beset with terror had fled the room pressing Jean Pierre's monogrammed handkerchief against her bleeding cheek, her throat burned as she gasped for breath whilst running over the dusty track leading to her parents' abode. Distraught she staggered into the front room of her parent's bungalow. Dried bloodshot eyes with Jean Pierre's monogrammed handkerchief; stared in frustrating disbelief at her father Louis.

"I've left him." Brigitte blurted amidst sobs, a sickening quiver gripping her guts. "What happened to your cheek? Louis asked in astonishment. "Jean Pierre he..." Emotion unhinged her; she sank her dishevelled body to a chair. She hung between hysteria and laughter; a tightening pain gripped her stomach. "The lad, always been trouble, his quest for money and position within the Mafia has been his driving force; it is not safe for you to remain here. This will be the first place he'll look. I should have warned you, Andre told me the lad is evil; certain to bring trouble." Louis grabbed the phone, shaking hand forced the dial round. "Andre, it's Louis." The Austrian gasped, "it's happened... you did warn me. Brigitte and Jean Pierre argued, he attacked Brigitte, cut her face with his knife; she's left him and now staying with us. I need to raise money, send her away to safety out of the country if possible; could you help." Louis's pleaded. "Why she ever went to live with the man I'll never know," replied Andre.

As a troubled teenager he would stare for hours glaring in admiration, from the window of our chalet at a bombed house opposite. This shell of a house holding his attention was frequented by the Mafia, they used immigrants for their distribution of drugs. I had a gut feeling he would turn out to be trouble." Andre wheezed then spat phlegm into the fire clearing his throat, "bring Brigitte with you, she can stop in my chalet. Until Jean Pierre has settled his dispute with Scar; this is one place the lad will never come. She will be safe here; I've a little money put by." Andre's hand dove into his emergency fund. Ironically this was money left by Jean Pierre when he left home. This 'blood money' would help Brigitte escape the Frenchman's clutches. The following day Louis steered his ageing car through the rubble laden streets of derelict bombed buildings to Andre's abode, entering the front door of the run-down Chalet; shouted. "Andre, shouted Louis." With her father Brigitte entered the sparsely decorated room of the run-down chalet. Andre reclined in a rocking chair besides the roaring fire. With a cup of coffee clutched tightly in his bony hand. The ageing Frenchman stared vacantly at hungry flames leaping from blazing logs sending its smoke snaking greedily up the blackened chimney. The Frenchman swivelled his chair to face his guests; with a wad of Lira in his hand he in a sorrowful stare gazed at Brigitte. "I've changed my mind you would be safer in England not here, take this, there's enough to get you away from that rat who calls himself a son of mine." Andre clutched his troubled chest, wheezed loudly before lapsing into coughing; blood spilt onto dried lips. He handed Brigitte a scrap of paper, "this is the address of a three bed-roomed Dormer cottage in Bingley Road... number 9; it is in a cul-de-sac in Littlethorpe, Leicester. A colleague of mine lives there Jim, we fought together in the French underground; you'll be safe with him; tell him I sent you." A sombre Andre struggled for breath before adding. "There is a flight to England leaving in four hours." Andre gasped to the departing couple leaving by the front door. Beneath a cloudless sky Louis drove his ageing Citroen, carrying his daughter to the airport, and plane taking her to England and safety.

This displeasing... devastating news of Brigitte's departure unsettled the distraught assassin; Jean Pierre. The embittered Frenchman accessed a bubble of self-pity. In an aggravated act of self-destruction, he drifted on the road of self-destruction onto to that treacherous slippery slope of drink. He staggered through a drunken haze over his worn carpet to the drinks- cabinet. Through a gaze of insobriety bloodshot eyes settled on yet another well filled glass of the welcoming warm Yellow of whisky. A self-pitying tear rolled down his tanned cheek; his life had slipped into a denigrated empty vacuum. He rubbed his thick bristles as angry bloodshot eyes glared at darkened skies; the depressed Frenchman flirted precariously with doubts, uncertainty. The mantle of confidence he'd worn since a teenager; deserted him. With Brigitte he'd been alive, until that interfering American had meddled, in a drunken slur he threatened. "Sylvester, you will regret your decision by all that's holy you will pay." Jean Pierre threatened in an accusative snarl. The following morning whilst experiencing a monstrous hangover he stripped and showered; dancing with grim resolution on his red lips was retribution. As the hot spray ran down his muscular physique, visions of Brigitte in a bright pastel dress, flashed through his overactive mind. It was at that moment he made a committed vow; he would sort his problem.

The next few months passed in a blur as the French assassin immersed himself in his work, he increased takings by fifty percent, making the young Frenchman a valuable asset to the Mafia. However this presented Sylvester with a delicate dilemma. His most valuable asset was proving troublesome; he needed a plan and quick. "Why the hell has Jean Pierre not mentioned Brigitte?" The Yank fumed. "What the hell was his number two planning." Sylvester was only too aware the Frenchman would not accept the departure of Brigitte quietly, without a response. A shady plan was hatched by the American, he'd make the murderous Frenchman his number one, demote Scar; but uncertainty plagued his evil mind... what if this decision was wrong. "What would pacify the egomaniacal Frenchman." Beady eyes flashed to the ceiling as though seeking divine intervention, "and then there is Scar, I'm purposely pitting my two best assassins against each other." Sylvester released a frustrated scream; he progressed toward drinks cabinet.

As an added protection the worried Yank had begun carrying a loaded gun, sleeping with the weapon under his pillow. Clutching a glass of Brandy, he stared at his reflection through bedroom mirror. "You know Jean Pierre; you could be my successor. Why be satisfied as my Number one?" Sylvester whispered to mirror, "when I retire you could take my place; be the new Godfather." He swung head round in frustration; Jean Pierre was not a gullible child. Would the Frenchman even consider this crap? The American groaned, angrily he stuck a pacifying Havana between his cholesterol lips.

50

Jean Pierre's Confrontation

Months of dissatisfaction agitated Jean Pierre's ugly temper, visions of the conniving fat Yank ordering him to sever connections between himself and Brigitte irritated greatly the Frenchman. Retribution flashed vividly within that raging red mist of discontent. His evil calculating mind strove to find a fitting solution to his problem. The time had arrived, after a quick shave and shower, he slipped his muscular physique into a tailor-made shirt, then a black mohair suit. Pure hatred veiled those cold blue eyes that fell upon the spinning chamber of his pistol. Satisfied the gun was loaded he slotted the weapon into its holster. The Frenchman was ready for confrontation. He slid through the front door into the dusty street leading to Mafia headquarters and his quarry.

Jean Pierre stormed unannounced into Sylvester office, the portly Yank nursing a glass of brandy; sat behind an aging Oak veneered table. Terror sprang to the Yanks eyes when beholding the grimacing Frenchman standing at the open door. The mean faced Frenchman progressed menacingly in his direction. A gulp the size of a boulder slid uneasily down the fat Yanks throat. Shaking hand slid underneath the table and pressed a button. Within seconds six suits swaggered into the room, gun bulges distorting their jackets. They leant provocatively against the smoke-stained walls. The Yank retrieved his shaking hand from beneath table, travelled nervously to the butt of his gun. Jean Pierre stood tall before the Yank who shuffled with an irritated uncertainty. Fear struck the hearts of the thugs; terror sprang to their eyes when recognising who they were about to challenge. None other than the feared inhumane Jean Pierre.

Worried murmurings of discontent broke amongst the disturbed... rattled thugs. Within their petty conniving minds, self-preservation reigned, jumped to the fore. To them living was paramount, their life meant even more than their mafia vows; survival instincts advised them to take evasive action. Jean Pierre threw a contemptuous murderous stare to the thugs. In return receiving a negative response from the overweight men hugging the radiators. The Frenchman's cold eyes swivelled in accusation ninety degrees to face the oak table and quivering Yank. A forty-watt shade-less bulb swung from side to side through the smoked filled air. The murderous intent lingering in Jean Pierre eyes; was slowly replaced with caution. Jean Pierre sat and shifted confidently in his chair. The thugs merged into an agitated frightened line against the smoke-stained wall. Jean Pierre's cold eyes swivelled around, pierced engagingly each motley individual.

Nodding to them his tacit acceptance of their presence. The interrogative gaze returned to Yank sweating profusely; arrogantly the Frenchman faced the Yank, the mutual hatred introduction over. "Hy! Jean Pierre: this is a surprise. I congratulate you; takings have rose for the third week." Grovelling subservient platitudes dripped with ease from Sylvester's nervous, cholesterol lips. The hoods nodded affirmation of their boss's glowing accolades. Jean Pierre remained threateningly silent; through the friendless air, his cold eyes transmitted murderous thoughts through an angry glower. That look Sylvester had seen before. The Yank was only too aware the Frenchman was sending him a tacit warning. The feared Frenchman held Sylvester in a cold unequivocal stare; forwarded his threatening ultimatum in a glib challenge. "We all want a peaceful outcome; you would all like me to slip into the dark of the night quietly; that my friends can be arranged." Jean Pierre grated accommodatingly. Switching his evil questioning glare from the Yank to the thugs. His cold blue eyes transmitted an open challenge, daring them to disagree. Immediate appeasement was transmitted from the nervous thugs, in unison they nodded their acceptance of the Frenchman's proposal. Uneasiness descended upon the frightened occupants of that dimly lit room; worried glances were exchanged amongst thugs shuffling uncomfortably.

Satisfied he'd claimed the ascendancy Jean Pierre returned his cold blue eyes to Sylvester. The Yank winced with displeasure. His thugs in passive submission had handed the floor to Jean Pierre. Globules of sweat rolled liberally down Sylvester's forehead; shaking hand gravitated to the bulge under his jacket. "Do I have to repeat myself. Do you want this settled peaceably?" Cold harsh tones from Jean Pierre peppered menacingly the air like a threatening challenge. With blood racing at an unhealthy speed through raised veins; Sylvester's cholesterol lips pouted in angry condemnation. Fear that earlier gripped his gut vanished; a suspicious calmness swept over the Yank who responded positively. "I had planned what to say to placate you; but what the hell! Why the hell am I sweating buckets, just because you're upset. I'm the ruling kingpin round here, I do not like my number one coming in here creating havoc. This is my office... my operation, who the bloody hell do you think you're talking to? Nobody threatens Sylvester, especially I repeat; my number one." The overweight Yank shouted to claim the ascendancy; re-establish his control over the situation. Jean Pierre's eyes dilated in disbelief; he had expected trouble, only to have been promoted, "yes I said my number one." Sylvester reiterated, "now sit, shut your mouth; and listen." Sylvester grunted authoritatively, wiping sweats of relief from his forehead; his scheming diversion worked albeit temporarily. Jean Pierre's eyes filled with distrust, he melted thoughtfully into his seat before blurting. "And just what does Scar think of your plan to promote me?" The assassin shouted in scathing, facetious taunts. "Forget Scar he's history or soon will be. He had a difference of opinion with the Kray brothers. And, you know what happens to their enemies." The Yank issued coldly. On the Frenchman's lips, lay a smug congratulatory smile of victory; the Yank had capitulated. With disappointing resentment, the Yank accepted this was Jean Pierre's round. Jean Pierre swung his head around to the thugs. "You see Gentlemen, that's the way to handle a problem." The Frenchman grunted sarcastically; head jerked around to the Yank. "By the way; where the hell is Scar?" Jean Pierre questioned.

51
Brigitte Arrives in Leicester

Leicester was experiencing its worst fall of snow for twenty years. Falling temperatures invited treacherous tentacles of ice to spread over the compacted snow laden January morning. With a bag slung over her shoulder Jim's visitor Brigitte rounded the corner of Bingley Road to number nine. I, Nicky, stared from the bedroom window of number seventeen, at the picturesque snow covering the road of our private quiet cul-de-sac. Milk bottles clattered perilously against the confines of their steel crates strewn randomly across the bed of the trolley. The flimsy vehicle negotiated ungainly its slippery path cutting its route through the icy covered snow.

My eyes dilated; mouth fell open as my besotted gaze of admiration lingered pleasurably upon the trim svelte figure of the beautiful French lady. Jim, my Indian neighbour dwelling at number nine, had informed me that morning he was expecting a visit from foreign parts later that day. I was completely unprepared for this vision of loveliness. Who could have guessed this frail winsome creature; would change my life. That this scarred cheek Mademoiselle would lead me to the assassin I was chasing; help finalise my search for my mother's killer. I hurried downstairs and outside to greet her.

"Hello, my name is Nicky your one-man welcoming committee; welcome to Leicester." I gulped, she smiled sweetly, ignored my advances; gently brushed past me to enter Jim's house.

52

Sylvester Placates Jean Pierre

Jean Pierre's smile of victory faded, that face reflecting euphoria morphed into suspicion, frustration. His unexpected promotion he courted warily, questioned why. His perturbed mind became alive with unanswered questions. He slid, with caution his muscular torso into the chair facing the Yank. With a cursory flick of hand, Sylvester summarily dismissed his thugs; spun his chair to face his 'assistant' blonde. "What are you staring at woman, cigars and drinks. We're celebrating my new number one." Snarled the overweight Yank spinning the chair to face his probable nemesis, Jean Pierre. With the downbeat resignation of a man attempting to lighten the burden of his income tax; Sylvester shook his head foggily. Through bloodshot tired eyes, he held the Frenchman in a questioning stare, the muscles in his right arm twitched nervously. "Forget about Scar we can move to fresh ground, let's talk about you; the feared Jean Pierre." Sylvester paused… maybe for emphasis, warily he sipped a large swig of brandy. Whilst holding Jean Pierre in a cold penetrating stare. His mood changed, as in a state of mounting tension he bawled accusingly, "and what the hell did you think you were doing. Charging in here like a headless bull?" Sylvester's eyes flamed in angry protestation; with fat hairy paws he grabbed his cigar cutters.

The cold blue eyes of Jean Pierre threw a quick sardonic appraisal of Sylvester before spitting out his condemning, caustic reply. "You know why I'm here." Jean Pierre hanging between disbelief and anger, replied sourly, "Brigitte, she's the reason, because of your stupid order she's flown to England. Meanwhile

I'm stuck in this hole; with only you for company." Jean Pierre grated throwing another double whisky over his tonsils. He beckoned angrily for the buxom blonde to refill his glass. Sylvester slapped his forehead in despair-exasperation; stared at his number one with round eyed perplexity. Jean Pierre continued icily, "you ordered me to end the most precious relationship of my life, I did; her absence is driving me mad." Jean Pierre slid his fingers through his dark locks. While a hot bile of discontent burned his throat; his cold blue eyes threw a challenging stare towards Sylvester.

Sylvester shook his head in negativity, his overworked brain escalated into overdrive. Nervous fingers enacted staccato taps on the top of the ageing veneer of the table. His evil mind trawled for that telling, evasive reply that would placate the egotistical, threatening assassin. The Yank spoke in nervous appeasement murmuring. "Look regarding Brigitte... it could be possible I made a mistake. But let's face it with a bloody Gendarme in our midst; what would you have done? This decision I must stand by primarily with Mafioso interests in mind. But you get Brigitte to renounce her brother, I rescind my order. Is that more to your liking? You'll do well to remember that while I'm the head man, you behave like my number one; accept my judgement. That's your problem sorted." A frown rippled over his forehead while his face creased with an authoritative seriousness, he spewed out coldly. "But while we're clearing the air, I should inform you. That if there's trouble between you and scar, trouble where we do not make a profit, or I have not ordered. You are a walking dead man. Now go chase after your Brigitte in England, do what you think is right; but next time you enter my office; bloody knock." Sylvester screeched throwing a bulging envelope onto the table, "take this to cover expenses." Sylvester mumbled; sweats of fear visibly melted. Jean Pierre rose, grabbed the bulging creased envelope, whilst grunting his begrudging appreciation. The thugs re-appeared; Jean Pierre flicked a menacing glare of unconcern in their direction; shouldered past them to the door.

The Frenchman trudged through customs of Lyon Satolas Airport, over the hot tarmac and plane heading to Birmingham Airport. Back at Mafia headquarters Sylvester shouted ungraciously. "Get me Scar's number in London, the least I can do is warn the stupid Austrian ingrate of Jean Pierre's arrival." Within a sparsely decorated room, in the London safe house; the phone rang. Scar downed his Whisky, placed the receiver to ear. "Scar, Sylvester. As we speak Jean Pierre is on his way to Birmingham Airport gunning for you; beware." The line went dead. Scar's face turned even paler; his devious mind sprang into action. "I knew this day would come, just not so quickly, I am not ready for a fight with Jean Pierre and the Krays, I must curry the Frenchman's favour. I'll send a car to meet him at the airport." Scar muttered to himself in tones of appeasement. Pierre suffered the cramped discomfort of economy class, during his boring journey to England.

Screeching wheels of his plane announced its landing on the tarmac of Birmingham airport. The Frenchman shouldered forcefully through the milling crowd towards the carousel; after collection of his luggage plodded to the exit. Being advertised from the taxi rank; a large brown card had been raised bearing his name. Jean Pierre advanced cautiously... slowly to the stranger. "Jean Pierre?" The man enquired as the Frenchman approached.

"Depends on who's asking, who the hell are you?" Jean Pierre grated.

"Orders from Scar to pick you up." Came the trite response from the skinny man stroking his unkempt moustache. The Assassins eyes dilated in surprise.

"What did you say?" Astonished words echoed in disbelief. "I said Scar told me to pick you." The stranger replied almost as an afterthought. "That's what I thought you said. Take me to the headquarters in Melton Road." The Frenchman snarled. Thirty minutes later the car screeched to a halt in Melton Road; Jean Pierre alighted the vehicle and slipped driver several notes. "Wait." The Frenchman grunted disappearing inside building, it was deserted Jean Pierre returned to waiting driver. "You know why I'm in England?" Jean Pierre questioned. "You want to find this girl Brigitte, which is where I might be able to help. A friend in Narborough, informs me she frequents the pub in the old market square of Littlethorpe in Leicester; called the "The Old Inn." She's often escorted by a sandy haired male colleague. The driver raised his head in expectation of praise, instead of praising driver Jean Pierre prodded driver with another question. "Will she be there tonight?" Jean Pierre snapped in hope.

"Look pal if you are desperate to contact her ring this number, Bob the Landlord will pass your message to her." Jean Pierre re-entered the car.

"Thanks, take me to the Grand Hotel. Oh! I'm not your pal," Jean Pierre snorted caustically. On reaching the hotel located in Granby Street the Frenchman handed a roll of twenty pounds notes to the driver. "Thanks pal, I mean friend, if you ever want me to drive you anywhere it is no problem you ring this number any time Scar has put me and car at your service." The driver replied handing a crumpled card to Jean Pierre. The Frenchman entered his small comfortable room; grabbed the phone.

Bob was tired, his pub was empty so decided to shut the pub early. The phone rang; Bob slammed the front door bolt home before answering it. "Yes." Grunted the tired gravel voice. "Hy! I've just arrived in England, was wondering if Brigitte will be in the pub tonight?" "Who's calling?" Bob questioned. The Frenchman released a heavy sigh. "My name is Jean Pierre." He replied aware Brigitte on hearing his name might never want to see him again. "I'll pass your message on to Brigitte; she should be in tomorrow night." The phone clicked to a faint buzzing. The following evening Scar's driver dropped Jean Pierre in the village square. "You want that pub over there boss the Old Inn, I'm visiting a friend, will wait for you by the garage in the jitty." The driver issued before roaring off into the near town of Blaby. Jean Pierre entered the dimly lit lounge.

Bob informed Nicky of his strange phone call from a man with a French accent. It would have to be Jean Pierre Cliff surmised, Cliff sat nursing a bottle of Whiskey and two glasses. A tall handsome tanned stranger entered Cliff signalled him; Jean Pierre approached the table. "I take it you are Jean Pierre?" "That is correct," Jean Pierre responded. "Your call reached me, Brigitte is not coming, she informed me of your fractious relationship; she does not want to see you." I grated with warmth of a Sergeant Major.

"Bonjour to you Messier." Jean Pierre reciprocated in equally cold measured tones. "Forget the small talk… the niceties, let's get straight to the point. You're here for Brigitte, I'm a cop who should arrest you. Your history with Brigitte keeps you a free man… at least for the time being." Fingering his bristles Cliff continued, "question is. How do we handle the situation?" The air bristled with tension, Jean Pierre shifted to the vacant seat opposite Cliff, he struggled for an adequate response to his tricky dilemma. Into those cold blue eyes, a numbed beseeching look sprang. "Messier, I want no trouble only to apologise to Brigitte; but in person." Jean Pierre's steely cold stare scoured the room, his hand caressed the handle of his gun. The Frenchman's distress obvious. Cliff threw a good measure of ice cubes into glasses; followed by generous quantity of the house Whisky.

Cliff studied the infamous, inhumane Jean Pierre, allowing Bobs cheap whisky to burn his tonsils; he then soothed the Frenchman's fears. "It's okay I'm alone." Cliff drawled; his tired eyes transfixed on the Frenchman. Visual relief swept over the newcomer. A half smile graced his tanned face, he drained his glass of Bobs cheap Whisky; the Frenchman's face grimaced with distaste. "Messier! You call this whisky." Jean Pierre's face showed further distaste after swallowing a second glass of warm yellow liquid. I ignored his facetious but accurate comment. "I have explained Brigitte does not want to see you, she asked for my protection. I do not have to explain why, you are in the possession of the maudlin details. But more to the point she never wants to see you again." I snorted refilling glasses. The Frenchman's face remained expressionless. "Messier look inside your English heart. I travel all the way from Lyon France to beg her forgiveness; tell her this is all I ask." Jean Pierre pleaded. "Give me a phone number where she can reach you?" Cliff snarled ungraciously. "No Messier, I did not, as you English say, travel over on the banana boat. No telephone number; you being police." Replied the cautious Jean Pierre. Employing such caution had kept him alive; was the sole reason for his liberty. "Listen up Jean Pierre stop stalling; you have no bargaining power; you want to see Brigitte. Okay, it happens you have one point in your favour. I want to find Scar; now humour me; tell me how we solve our little problem?" Cliff hissed with a touch sarcasm. "Messier that scum Scar killed my mother I have first claim." Jean Pierre replied curtly. "I appreciate you've got good reasons to take him out yourself; but then so have I. That murdering Albino killed my mother also, all you need do; is tell me where I can reach him. You give me that bastards address, I promise to do my utmost to persuade Brigitte to contact you. Phone Bob tomorrow night, he will have Brigitte's answer by then." I informed the Frenchman; an unsavoury taste ran down my throat. "If Brigitte agrees to see me, set up a meet. If you are successful; then... and only then will I supply your address." Jean Pierre replied. Before I could answer the door swung open Jean Claude's hand disappeared inside his jacket, hidden in the shadows Mayur eased his gun from its holster.

Scar entered with two hoods; they approached the bar. The Austrians eyebrows arched with surprise; he'd spotted Jean Pierre; the assassin stopped in his tracks. His accomplice passed a drink, Scar raised his glass in benign mockery to Jean Pierre and nodded. An involuntary nervous twitch rippled the Frenchman's cheek; he withdrew his gun. I reached for my gun; Mayur grabs the phone whilst keeping his weapon trained on Scar. For several minutes an eerie silence blanketed the room; an impasse was introduced. The ticking of the clock in the Old Inn Lounge broke the uneasy silence; customers cocooned in fear remained motionless. It was as though; everybody in the room had entered suspended animation; tension zipped through the smoky air. The welcoming screeching of a police siren echoed through the pub. Guns waved in disarray through the air; customers sank to the floor. "Bonjour mon ami." Scar jeers, bows mockingly before disappearing through the door. Jean Pierre jumps to his feet to give chase. I barred his way. "Want to get your head blown off; go ahead." I warned, Mayur slipped from the pub.

53

Scar and Son

A dishevelled Scar arrived in Lyon to collect his son; the young boy gripped his father's hand. "Where's Mama." The youngster questioned. "I'm taking you to her." Scar replied smiling. They progressed, not to Scar's bungalow, but a dirty brick strewn bombsite the dysfunctional family now called home. Skirting the rhododendron bushes bordering the University of Lyon Scar passed Jean Pierre's chalet housing Louis. Louis, closing front door spotted Scar.

Memories of their last meet flashed through the overactive mind of Louis. His predatory instinct surfaced; cold sweat chased his spine. All this before he spotted the youngster clinging to Scar's hand, warmth and forgiveness; gained the ascendancy. Eyes dilating in disbelief he shouted. "Scar what the hell." The words dropped from his mouth in stunned amazement. Scar swivelled his head round in surprise, stood mouth open staring at his father, a cocktail of distrust intermingled with nervous apprehension gripped his skinny gut. Scar replied. "Papa!" Bloodshot eyes flashed to youngster at his side, "Meet your grandson." Through perplexed worried eyes Louis stared, Scar spotted bewilderment veiling his father's eyes, "His mother is called Rusha, hails from Malawi." Scar remarked proudly.

The prevailing apprehension clouding the mind of Louis dissipated, he stepped forward; greeted the youngster. "I'm pleased to meet you, young man." Stooping, he shook young Jean's hand; before spinning about to face his son, "Well, circumstances are rather different to last time." Louis whispered. "Yes, I hope you find it in your heart to forgive me... I'm sorry, so ashamed Papa. But the requisite, before they would accept me, the Mafia laid down was to kill you."

Louis ignored his son's remarks as he stared at the young lad. "And what is your name?" Louis enquired stooping once more to the boy. "Jean." Replied the youngster. Louis's eyes narrowed to a squint... his brow populated worry lines when noticing the sign sporting the young boy's neck. "Have you noticed those circles?" Louis queried. Scar shrugged, nodded before father with arms outstretched continued, "may I hold the young fellow?" "Maybe another day, I'm sorry Papa I'm meeting Jean's mother, she's in Lyon for a couple of days. But promise I'll return to celebrate our re-union."

54

Sam and Drugs

A perspiring Sam approached Lyon University; cramp pains creased her stomach. Globules of perspiration formed on her pink brow; damp patches spread rapidly over her blouse. "Oh god I need a fix." She groaned, her shaking legs guiding her well-proportioned form, towards the examination room and finals. Thankfulness mixed with relief, swam their giddy dance in her head when reaching an empty table. She collapsed like a rag doll, into the chair. Parading authoritatively at the front of the class, an ageing Grey bearded Professor nodded. Thirty worried students dropped their heads; accessed silent concentration. Sweaty palms nervously clutched pencils: the Professor nodded his tacit acceptance of the exam to begin; three hours of laborious mind jerking cruelty ensued.

Damp patches spread liberally upon Sam's blouse, she glanced at her watch, time was short; she scribbled furiously to complete her paper. Her agonizing stomach pains worsened; she needed another fix. Coincidentally the Professor rapped his pen on the Oak table, signalling the end of their torturous experience. Drained bodies stretched aching arms in relief, rising and plodding gratefully from their cocoon of intensity. Into the welcome rays of sunlight, the chattering students progressed from the room; a shaking Sam trailed in their wake. She staggered in a series of lurches; her excruciating pain became unbearable.

Sweating profusely; it was with thankful relief she turned key to the sanctity of her bungalow. An urgency gripped her when accessing the room housing her proverbial drugs; with a grateful sigh she plunged the syringe into her vein and blissful relief. Eight hours, later a renewed Sam headed refreshed to the Rue des Maronniers cafe. Hot sugary tea tripped over tonsils when a sour faced handsome man approached her table tray in hand; he pointed at vacant chair.

"Excuse me, may I?" The young Gendarme queried politely. "Be my guest; I'm Sam." She replied, waving gloved hand. The Gendarme nodded appreciatively; removing his hat sat. "Thank you and pleased to meet you, my name is Paul." He replied curtly, proffering hand to the Blonde. "I was wondering. Do you use this café often? I arranged to meet my sister Brigitte here, but there is no sign of her." The Gendarme spat out, digging teeth into his overdone toast. "You wouldn't mean the lovely Brigitte; whom Jean Pierre is crazy about?" Sam teased. The Gendarmes face filled with alarm. "You know Jean Pierre?" Paul gasped, mouth dropping open in disbelief. "That man is extremely dangerous, wanted by the Gendarmerie; a friendly warning Mademoiselle; stay well away from him."

Sam's head jerked awkwardly towards the stranger in consternation, disbelief, disappointment clouded her face. She shuffled uncomfortably on her chair; tears of disbelief engaged her eyes. She raised her head, levelled an apologetic stare to the uniformed stranger; applied a handkerchief to her moistened eyes before saying in a voice just below a whisper. "This has come as a bit of a shock. You must excuse me, that's the worst news I've heard in a long time; glad to have met you." She stammered emotionally, staggered jerkily to her feet and exit. What little appetite Paul had brought to the table deserted him; he bit perplexedly on a leaf of lettuce. "What a strange lady." He mused thoughtfully, in querulous raised voice he blurted. "My baby sister

Brigitte, mixing with that dangerous hoodlum Jean Pierre." Paul grated in disbelief; he placed a handful of Lira on the table.

The Gendarme rose, exited the café then headed for his meeting with the grocers. In a dingy half lit room, a motley group of concerned men sat, Paul confronted them. "You'll testify Jean Pierre threatened your granddaughter." The Gendarme questioned the grocer. "Oui for sure; I will! The lousy low life thug ran blade of his knife down my granddaughter's cheek; threatened her life. And did you know, Jean Pierre's father Andre hates the Mafia; especially now Jean Pierre has joined them. He will gladly testify against his own son; if it means bringing that scum to heel." The Grocer stated. Paul snatched the phone.

55

Brigitte and Jean Pierre Meet

Colin, our local plumber, pressed his dirty shoe to the floor on the accelerator of his white van. His tools rattled loudly against the rusting floor of that ageing vehicle as it screeched into market square of Littlethorpe village. Colin slewed his van to the kerbside outside The Old Inn pub to a halt; on the opposite side of the road Brigitte approached. She paused at the doors of the pub, brushed specks of dust from her pristine blouse; entered. Traces of fury accompanied by apprehension gripped her shaking legs; she progressed her skinny body into the lounge of the Old Inn.

Negativity slipped into the equation, refusing to meet her ex-Jean Pierre was still an option. Tired eyes limped cautiously over the half empty room; the Frenchman swam into view. She nodded tacit acknowledgment of his presence; approached him. Nicky, phone in hand, spotted Jean Pierre fidgeting. He dropped the phone to its cradle; with drinks he joined their table; started the meeting. "Jean Pierre! This is a one off; and should never have happened. 'Because if word reaches my superiors; I'm for the high jump. If there is a next time, we know what will happen then." I warned raising my beer filled glass. Jean Pierre responded with nod of agreement, swiftly moving his gaze to Brigitte; he raised pleading eyes. "Forgive me." He begged in tones of humility; his head dropping subserviently to his chest in an acceptance of his guilt.

Brigitte ran trembling fingers over her scarred face, Jean Pierre winced. A concoction of love, hate and retribution leapt into her tear-filled eyes. "You're a hot headed, calculating piece of low life...

I hate you. But grudgingly accept my family owe you a favour. When the vines failed, we had no place to go, you were there with a helping hand; you gave my father hope when it was most needed. So yes, I forgive you." She spat out in a voice riddled with contempt which dropped to a low threatening growl, "but I warn you Messier, should our paths ever cross again; I'll either kill you or be the cause of it."

Tears flooded her Brown eyes of condemnation. Jean Pierre stared at Brigitte's scarred cheek; the Frenchman nodded appreciation for her having met him; attention re-focussed back to Cliff. "I thank you Messier for fulfilling your part of the bargain, I too fulfil my obligations; then I'm out of your life. You seek the Albino assassin Scar, that low life will seek protection from the Kray brothers. These gangsters have a safe house, 101 Loveridge road Kilburn; almost certainly he will seek refuge there."

An emotional Jean Pierre stared at Brigitte. Incredulity lined his face; the face of Rusha was staring back at him. The Frenchman rubbed eyes in disbelief before re-focussing on Brigitte. Rusha's smiling face had vanished, disappeared, once again he beheld the discontented face of Brigitte. Rising from his seat, the Frenchman tilted his head forward and departed for the door. Where he paused, head went to lay on his chest, with a querulous grin gracing his tanned face, he turned to us. "Where the hell is the jitty?"

56

Scar's Seeks London Safe House

Cocooned within overbearing egotistical smugness; Scar wallowed in his one upmanship. Having escaped the long arms of the law, plus the clutches of his adversary Jean Pierre. This was a significant accomplishment indeed, first round to him over his possible nemesis. With the poise of a peacock, the Albino strutted from the cold dark shadows of Euston Station, into the sunlight; he entered the phone box. Skinny finger rotated the dial. The Kray brothers, Ronnie and Reggie sat drinking wine whilst enjoying a pre-recorded tape of Morecambe and Wise; the phone rang. "Yes." Snarled Ronnie, eyes glued to television, and hilarious antics of the comedians. The savageness of Ronnie's tone took Scar by surprise, a brief pause ensued before the Austrian replied. "Hy Ronnie Scar, I need a favour." Scar's voice reduced to a pleading whimper. "What's the favour." Ronnie snarled in suspicion. "I need a place to hide for a few days." Replied the trembling voice. "And why would you need a place to hide?" Ronnie grunted impatiently, eyes flashing to the television as Morecambe searched for a join in his partner Eric's hair. "The Leicester Police and Jean Pierre are on my tail, at this very moment Jean Pierre is talking to a copper in Littlethorpe, scheming my downfall. Can I stop at your safe house in Kilburn?" Scar pleaded. Ronnie shouted to his brother.

"Reggie! It's that Austrian bum Scar, he wants to use our safe house. Is it empty?" "Yeah! until the end of the week, the Wimbledon mob then need the house to lie low for a couple of weeks; they pulled that heist at the Elephant and castle." Reggie blurted; Ronnie handed handset to his brother. "Scar you there?

Reggie blurted savagely. "Yes," Replied nervous voice of Scar. "Go to 101 Loveridge Road, it's a boarding house run by an Irish family named Robertson with two sons Alec and Norman. From the Great North London pub, it is two hundred yards going North; you come to a bridge it's on the right. You can stop there till the end of the week." Reggie grunted sourly.

"Thanks Reggie, I'll see you alright." Scar muttered in grovelling, subservient tones. Scar was aware the Great North London pub was regular meeting place for barrow boys and thugs. It was also where the Austrian had met the Kray brothers, and beautiful Sam.

Scar knocked the door of 101 Loveridge Road. The eldest son Alec Robertson, with short cropped black hair and flashing evenly set white teeth answered. "Yeah," grunted Alec in a strong cockney dialect. "Hy! My name is Scar the Krays sent me; said I might be able to room here." The Austrian replied. Alec's head swivelled about. "Dad someone at the front door for you." The Londoners eyes then addressed Scar, "you'd better come in." Alec invited in an apprehensive, friendly cockney drawl.

Several hours later, Scar plodded wearily his way to The Great North London, once again fortune favoured him; Sam entered. Her name frequently buzzed the drugs grapevine, because of her upper class accent she was known as the posh bird. "Bonjour we meet again, welcome to our happy band of druggies; let me be of service." Scar offered Sam several small packets. Sam taken aback by strangers' generosity, stepped back in distrust. Through glazed eyes, she held Scar in inquisition, blurting caustically. "Firstly, I've not got readies on me. Secondly why would you do me a favour?" She retorted warily. "Forget your money they're on me, you have met me on a good day." Scar grinned; scribbled on a scrap of paper. "that's my number, if I can ever be of service call me; hope we meet again soon." She pushed the crumpled paper into her pocket; watched thankfully as Scar lurched unsteadily to the exit from the pub. Sam clasped hands together as though in prayer. Casting a thankful look heavenwards, she gratefully pocketed the drugs; grabbing her suitcase exited the pub. Light rain filled the late evening air; suitcase in hand Sam hailed a cab. "Heathrow." She ordered in cursory tones of impatience; snuggling into leather contours of the seat suspicion leapt to her mind.

Extracting sachets of drugs from her raincoat pocket; her eyes raised with curiosity at packets given to her by Scar. Four hours of depressing inaction ensued on her journey to her parent's holiday home based in the South of France. Breathing a sigh of relief, she entered the privacy of her bedroom housing needles and drugs. Within minutes, Sam fuelled with drugs; stared through window at Campus of Lyon University. Visions of an angry father floated in a haze of challenging confrontations; before glazed eyes. "Daddy please don't think too badly of me." Pleading words of contrition dropped with regret from pursed lips; words she'd longed for him to hear but afraid he never would. Her focus blurred; she discarded the used needle into the bin. Blonde hair fell limply over her pink forehead, the room spun at an ever-accelerating rate, inviting her into the peaceful bliss of beckoning dark oblivion.

57

Nicky's Leicester Abode

In the sparse but comforting surrounds of my Dormer Cottage, I raided the fridge to collect a beer. Snuggled into the cushions of the settee, sat in the fetal position to view Match of the day. The shrill ring from the telephone invaded the peace, jarred me from my comfort zone. The brusque tones of the Inspector resounded down the line. "Nicky... Tiger, we're flying to Lyon to keep a rendezvous with Gendarme called Paul. We leave tomorrow from Birmingham airport, meet me Leicester station ten-o-clock in the morning, goodnight." I slammed phone to receiver and gulped in dismay. Newcastle had just scored the winning goal; beat my beloved Sunderland at Roker Park.

Tiger and I arrived in Lyon Airport, where through the courtesy of a chauffeured black limousine, we were transported to the headquarters of Lyon Gendarmerie. Being a hardened Northerner accustomed to cold and rain. It was with immense pleasure I enjoyed the warm sun's rays playing on my back. In the office Paul trawled systematically through the filing cabinet in the search for more background information relating to Scar, Jean Pierre, and their movements. "Louis, Scar's father, lives just two hundred yards away; would you like to question him? Paul queried. "Would it not be better to interview Andre, being that Scar killed his wife; surely he has more reason to hate him." Tiger replied. "Regarding Andre it is bad news, at this very moment, Andre lies at deaths door in the emergency ward of Lyon's General Hospital. But Messier if you insist, I will still take you; just do not expect too much." Paul stressed, after minor protestation from

Tiger the Gendarme acquiesced to the Englishmen's insistence. He escorted visitors back to the dust laden black Citroen.

Frenetic action from nurses had their uniforms swishing in counterpoint against black stockings as they rushed in organized chaos from ward to ward. The ward Sister led us in an orderly charge through the constructive mayhem, into the peace and funereal quiet of the emergency ward. Andre's ageing ashen face creased with pain; the Frenchman greeted us with a curt nod of head; Paul strode to the end of the bed. "These gentlemen are police from England, they are here to help us Uncle Andre. Are you up to answering a few questions?" Paul questioned empathetically; a gasp of surprise invaded that air of funeral morbidity. Paul swung ninety degrees to glances of disbelief, "Yes, I'm Brigitte's brother, Scar is my half-brother. You are aware he murdered my Auntie Ann Marie also that Jean Pierre scarred my sister." Paul paused as contemptuous indignation leapt to his eyes; continue, "so yes, I've a great personal interest invested in these two. The last I heard both thugs were in London." Paul grated. "Do they have a safe house? Tiger questioned, without waiting for an answer, allowing a surge of impatience to dictate his actions; Tiger swung his head ninety degrees to face Andre. "Word is you would like to see both put behind bars Messier; your son and wife's murderer Scar." Tiger added in undertones of abject apology. Pain crept into the tired bloodshot eyes of Andre; furrows of sadness etched his face. The Frenchman lurched forward violently, coughing, blood spurted forth, the red liquid saturated his thin white lips. The frail Andre collapsed to his pillow, through renewed strength; he wheezed his reply. "You want to catch my son, forget London, forget the safe house. My son is a creature of habit, no matter where his travels take him. That troublesome boy will always return to our chalet; regardless of how much he detests it. Through his troubled teenage years, when living with my Ann Marie; he despised the chalet. Treat the building as though it were his prison. That changed dramatically when Scar murdered his mother, Ann Marie. Encouraged by an impulsive... murderous attitude he changed. Now replacing his hate for our chalet, his emotions have swung dramatically to the opposite extreme; he now treats the run-down place like a shrine. My sons burning anger for vengeance acts like a magnet, drawing him back to this house. It is here he re-ignites his burning hatred for Scar. He renews that rivalry over the very spot my wife Ann Marie, his mother was killed. This is where he religiously re-enacts his burning fire of revenge. Jean Pierre's hatred for the scarred assassin knows no bounds, that unforgiving hate will be his companion; until he's avenged his mother's death. Find Jean Pierre you'll find Scar. The irony of the situation is their confrontation almost certainly will be enacted within this chalet; I'd bet my life on that." Andre's face whitened yet further, twisted with anguish, his chest convulsed during more extreme bouts of coughing.

Once more blood poured forth liberally from the mouth of the dying Frenchman. A well-endowed nurse announced her entry when bursting her overweight figure through the swing doors into the ward, her rounded face alight in condemnation. Those accusatory eyes inflamed with indictment made it patently obvious, she was to place blame squarely upon the visitors for her ailing patients' dramatic relapse. With the charm of a Sergeant Major organising the parade ground she ordered us to assist the frail Andre to the upright position, then placed a plastic bucket beneath Andres flowing blood. Happy that Andre was relatively comfortable she rose him to the upright position whilst still maintaining the cold charm of an Army Sergeant Major; instructed the visitors to leave. Our little group trudged their exit to collect outside the hospital; Paul made his suggestion. "I know a little café where we shall have afternoon tea the English are so fond of. I met a pretty English girl there yesterday; Sam was her name." Once in the café they settled at the table; Paul poured tea the door swung open; in walked Sam.

58

Jean Pierre in London

Apprehension, distrust, draped the broad shoulders of Jean Pierre as he edged his muscular body cautiously into the front room of his Bethnal Green boarding house. One of the safety aspects of his lodgings being Jean Claude's primary concern; to be housed in the safest room. Unfortunately for the Frenchman this room was in the dingy cellar; next to thug's bedroom who ran the seedy place. The thug cordially invited Jean Pierre into his room, uncorked a cheap bottle of Whisky; Jean Pierre entered sat crossed his legs and stared coldly at the man opposite. "Don't take this wrong friend, but who are you hiding from?" The thug grated wryly, producing a half smile flashing a mouthful of yellowed, decaying teeth. Jean Pierre laughed scornfully; uncrossed his legs, grated indignantly in caustic threatening undertones. "Me! Hide; Jean Pierre hides from nobody. But since you raised the subject, it so happens I'm looking for an Austrian who is making himself scarce. He's a scarred ugly Albino carrying a death wish; I'm here to make that wish become a reality." Jean Pierre voiced in casual facetiousness.

The vertically challenged, greasy haired thug, rubbed the grimy cuff of his shirt around the rim of two half clean glasses; then splashed double Whiskies into them. Whilst running bony fingers through his dirty grey hair, he shot a glare of enquiry into the angry blue eyes of the Frenchman. "Firstly, everyone who visits this house is either running... hiding from; or in process of killing someone. Secondly, yes, I know of him; that information will cost you a hundred." The gravel voice of thug snorted. The Frenchman's eyes housed a cold threatening stare, he snarled. "I tell you for the last time messier, I run from nothing, nobody; if you want to pigeonhole me, try the latter." Jean Pierre pushed three twenty-pound notes to middle of the table, "sixty up front; forty when the jobs complete, for one hundred pounds Messier, your information better be good, you would not want to be added to my list." Jean Pierre rasped threateningly. "Word on the grapevine is, that a weird red eyed pasty-faced blonde has started frequenting the "Great North London pub" that is on Kilburn high street. Apparently, this weirdo is in cahoots with gangland bosses, the Kray brothers. These dangerous dregs of society frequent the pub between seven and nine." The thug slurred, attempted to snatch the three twenty-pound notes. Jean Pierre placed hand over notes; a frightened look embraced the thugs face who held Jean Pierre in a questioning stare, "you got a cigarette?" The thug enquired timorously. Jean Pierre threw a packet on the table; rose with a contemptuous grin dressing face. Replaced wad of notes into the inside jacket pocket; pushed sixty pounds over the table towards the thug.

"Thank you Messier but if you are wrong... well I think you know what will happen." Jean Pierre issued threatingly. "Your whisky." The thug effused pushing the dirty glass across the table. Jean Pierre threw look of disgust at the dirty chipped glass. "You have it, because if your information is incorrect; it could be your last." The Frenchman snarled through an evil half smile. "Please yourself Gov! If you hurry the tube for Kilburn is in five minutes." The thug gurgled folding notes, greedily stuffing them in his pocket. "I hope you find the guy you're looking for, Oh! And no, I would prefer not to be on your wanted list." The thug guffawed snatching the remaining dirty glass of whisky.

Jean Pierre donned his overcoat, nodded appreciatively then glided through front door, slipping into the darkening shadows of evening. "Great North London" here I come; Scar your time is short." He grated running his forefinger along the blade of his trusty knife. He patted the bulge of his loaded contingency plan... the gun under his jacket. The journey by tube, was but ten minutes to the Great North London pub on Kilburn high street; and prey Scar. He entered the tube station, which except for few unshaven drunks was quiet. The dirty train clattered its entrance into the half-lit station slewing to a halt, two drunks and Jean Pierre boarded. Arriving at Kilburn the Frenchman alighted the train onto the platform into the path of more drunks. Jean Pierre shouldered his way through the great unwashed members of the insobriety clan into Kilburn high street using shadows afforded by the dark of night; he reached the Great North London pub. The Frenchman entered the main lounge, peering through the smoke-filled room he spotted Scar passing an envelope to two men; he assumed these men were the Kray brothers. He approached his quarry, warily his blue eyes flashed searching glances over the crowded room. "So, you've hooked the beautiful posh bird; Sam?" Ronnie grated as dregs of his single malt whisky trickled pleasurably over his tonsils.

"Yeah, she was already a user, she'll run drugs because of her need and lack of funds; she will come in very handy." The Albino gloated, smiling glibly he too threw whisky down his throat.

Scar's glory was short lived, his smile of triumph disappeared. Replaced with an ugly snarl, when spotting his adversary Jean Pierre approaching the bar.

"Two double malt whiskies." Jean Pierre growled throwing a twenty pound on the beer sodden bar. The Frenchman downed his Whisky in a single gulp, swung ninety degrees to face Scar, "Scar my friend, how nice to see you again." Jean Pierre gloated tauntingly, directing a glower of hate at the Austrian. Scar proffered cautiously, his shaking hand in friendship; Jean Pierre issued a laugh of irony. Throwing his second glass of Whisky in Scar's face, "you thought you could escape; you yellow... spineless coward. My mother's dead, Papa's in intensive; you have a Leicester cop on your trail. All problems created by your own dirty handy work; then like a scared rat decided to run. And here I find you nestling up to your petty English thugs for protection. Well, you gutless piece of low life its payback time; time to find out who is number one." Jean Pierre issued coolly. A retributive anger sprang to Scar's face; he ejected his slim torso nervously from his chair running the back of his hand over his furrowed brow to remove sweats of fear. "It is my pleasure." Scar countered as challengingly he withdrew his trusty flashing blade and lunging at Jean Pierre. Who in one swift move the Frenchman swivelled adroitly his body, avoiding Scar's flashing blade? The Frenchman was however, successful in his own onslaught, plunging his razor-sharp blade into the gut of his attacker. Jean Pierre's blade turned blood red; his knife had embedded itself up to the hilt in the Albinos stomach. Blood poured liberally from the Albinos wound, whose once pristine white shirt now matching the deep red colour of his eyes.

His shaking body slithered lifelessly to the floor, resting in a warm pool of his arterial blood. The trembling barman ducked behind counter phone in hand; the Kray brothers watched in disbelief before advancing menacingly towards the Frenchman. Jean Pierre sneered at the approaching thugs, withdrew his pistol; a sardonic smile accessing his pursed lips. "Not to worry my friends, I'm not going to kill him; not just yet. That was merely my calling card, a taste of what is to come. For his crimes he must, and will suffer longer, I'll finish the job another time, Bonjour." Jean Pierre jeered in tones marinated with sarcasm, he shuffled cautiously to the door where he overheard barman whispering nervously. "Yes, Police and Ambulance."

The Krays made further threatening moves; Jean Pierre laughed at their pathetic attempts to gain the upper hand, fired shots above their heads. "Gentlemen! Gentlemen please, I'm wanted in three countries, barrow-boys from the slums of London don't frighten me. Even if this low life happens to be the mighty Kray brothers. Good evening, take care of your wounded friend; Oh! be sure to tell him; I'll be back to finish the job." He pulled his trilby over cold blue eyes; cautiously backing his muscled frame through the swing doors.

Torrential rain poured relentlessly upon the empty dirty pavements of London, but drenching the Frenchman, a multiple of sirens hailed the arrival of police cars. A sorry looking Jean Pierre, clothes soaked, melted uncomfortably into the shadows on his route to Kilburn tube station. Police stormed the ill lit rooms of the Great North London pub; the street wise Krays with associates; had spirited themselves into the dark arms of night.

"Bloody English weather." Jean Pierre complained as he stepped intor a large pool of water and onto the tube train. Thoughts of his earlier successful contacts with Scar instilled a smug self-confidence brought to him a modicum of warmth within his chilled body. The train swayed as it neared Bethnal Green safe house. He'd achieved his objective, alerted the Albino that his time on the mortal coil was short. Snapping into view swam visions of his next step. "Once I've rid the earth of that pitiful excuse of a human Scar. For her demise, I should plan when my darling Brigitte's young life will be terminated. Then its forward to a new life with Rusha." The house was dark, he entered the shadows of his room, his wet hand raked the wall for the light switch. The floorboards creaked.

59

The Confrontation

Sam staggered from the cafe under a cloud of disbelief, the Gendarmes disturbing message, like fingers of steel, gripped her aching gut. The pain introduced her to a scary place. Her heartbeat accelerated unhealthily; pounded with an intensity against her bony ribcage. Tear jerking emotions sapped her remaining energy, she placed her shaking hand against the wall of café's window. In the darkened heavens black rainclouds gathered as unrequited tears spiked the back of her eyes, before splurging forth liberally onto her colourless ashen cheeks. Bloodshot eyes flashed pleadingly to the skies in a pitiful attempt to seek divine support. Black mascara lined her saddened pale face; her pain ridden stomach knotted with tension. "Jean Pierre on the run." she wailed.

With a herculean effort she placed one shaking leg in front of the other; creasing stomach cramps increased. Light rain from darkened heavens settled on her expensive perm. That expensive perm was to have dazzled her lover Jean Pierre, sadly it was no more. Flashing forks of lightning zapped their way-earthward, threatening Black clouds grumbled angrily their progress over the dark unforgiving heavens. The light rain quickly escalated into a driving storm; under sheets of the incessant downpour a sorry looking Sam skirted the Rhododendron bushes bordering the entrance to the family villa. Yesterday's dream was tainted, that thin veneer of respectability that once protected the Frenchman had gone; her hero was but a common thug. With sodden blonde hair clinging to her face a sadness blanketed her as she opened the door. Unceremonious, clanging and gurgling from radiators resounded the walls of the empty soulless villa. The heating system burst into action, hot and cold water clashed as the heating system exploded noisily into life. A disconcerted, bedraggled Sam sank to sofa phone in hand, she had to warn her close friend Brigitte. Trembling fingers forced the dial round, her warning call went unanswered. Slamming phone to receiver; stomach pains increased. "Oh god I need a fix." She groaned, shaking hands grabbed her troubled gut.

Heavy footsteps preceded the entry of a drenched Jean Pierre who burst into the room. "I need a room for the night, could I stop here?" Jean Pierre pleaded. Sam gulped! Stared in disbelief, not only had she to contend with her habit. Now she had to house a killer. Fear sent cold sweat chasing her spine, she trembled. "But... but of course, I'll put the kettle on." The frustrated Sam stuttered, in frightened subservience she crept from the room to the kitchen. "I've come directly from the Airport." Jean Pierre spluttered sipping Whisky from a hip flask, "I'm in desperate need of a shower; that okay?" The Frenchman's words were framed more as an enquiry than question. Sam re-appeared tray in hand. "Yes, the shower is next door, I'll get you a clean towel." She blurted, consternation clouding her pretty face. The corrosive vibes of uncertainty pushed her into a bubble of scaring disbelief. Okay I'm petrified, but he's the love of my life; the sixty-four-thousand-dollar question is. Will I have the guts to save our relationship? Confusing thoughts wrought havoc within her overworked addled brain. The jets of shower water quieted; cubicle doors glided open to the exiting naked Frenchman. "Jean Pierre, you're a wanted man!" Her accusatory voice shrieked in a nervous stammer.

The Frenchman produced an ironic smile, running his towel contemptuously over a muscle-bound torso he advanced his naked body in deliberate steps towards her. Almost facetiously he snorted.

"Mon Cheri: don't fill you're pretty little head with stupid details. Get ready we're going for a drink?"

Sam, detected evasion in his voice; trembling she rose in frightened acceptance. "Yes of course it's a celebration." Sam voiced in apprehensive prevarication. "Celebration." Jean Pierre's brow furrowed querulously, "that's fine, but what is the celebration?" The Frenchman replied somewhat bemused. "I'll tell you another time, it's a long story." Sam grinned, grabbed her coat; wondered to herself what the hell she'd meant "celebration".

60

Brigitte Talks to Police

Tiger and Nicky bit anxiously on boiled sweets, hands clamped firmly onto the armrest of their seats. The huge metal torso of their plane shuddered; the powerful engines powered that immense structure forward across tarmac of Satolas Airport. The nose of the plane lifted... their ears popped; the fast-disappearing earth beneath became minuscule. Soaring skyward through thick black clouds, the flying mass of metal negotiated its course to Birmingham International Airport. Tiger sniggered at the misery masking my face. "There will be other trips." He murmured dreamily; then with a seductive suddenness his head collided gently against the seat cushion welcoming him into the welcoming arms of the escapist dark of sleep. The following morning, shimmering rays of winter sun warmed our backs as we battled against droves of shoppers, crowding the busy pavements of London. We entered Kings Cross station and the train to Leicester and my three bedroomed cottage, 17 Bingley-road. "I'll brew up." I blurted; Tiger disappeared into the lounge to phone head office. Five minutes elapsed before I, carrying tray of goodies joined him; a smug gratifying smile lay on Tigers thin lips. "Kilburn branch have been on the phone, our man Scar's in hospital. The barman of the Great North London informed police that Scar had been stabbed by a Frenchman whilst in company of the Kray brothers. This happy event took place in the pub last night." Tiger raised his head; continued facetiously, "I wonder who the Frenchman could have been?"

Embarrassment surged my body, my temperature rose, visions of my meeting with Jean Pierre flashed uncompromisingly, through my mind. My face was blanketed in apology, I crawled inside a bubble of discomfort; before grovelling in tones of obeisance. "Boss I've a confession to make. Two days ago, I met with Jean Pierre in the Old Inn Littlethorpe. Before you say anything, I know it was stupid, but with him being as desperate to meet Brigitte as we are to catch Scar. I decided to confront him for a tradeoff. Warned him this "meet" was a one off, next time we met well you can guess the rest." I dropped my head in shame to avoid the condemning anger in Tigers eyes. "You, stupid young sod, that fiendish bastard doesn't deserve a second chance. With that French assassin only one thing you can be sure of; next time you meet he'll not be so forgiving." Tiger snarled grabbing his coat; he snatched open the lounge door, "come on you jerk, I'll stand you a pint in the local pub before the Superintendent relegates you back to point duty."

That night a nervous Brigitte entered the Old Inn pub; approached Tiger and me. "Sam phoned; Jean Pierre is stopping with her at the family villa in Lyon." She glared at disbelief veiling our eyes, "the news worsens, Jean Pierre knows she's been seeing Scar. My half-brother Paul informed her Jean Pierre is wanted by the law. We know how vicious Jean Pierre is, what inhumane violence he is capable of; especially to people who stand in his way. I can confirm that from experience; as you can see... he's anything but a forgiving man." Brigitte stuttered; shaking hand ran slowly over scarred cheek. Tiger stared in emotional uncertainty; his nonplussed eyes bathed in confusion as Brigitte withdrew packet of cigarettes; asked Tiger for a light. "But you don't smoke." Tiger spluttered. "I never used to talk to policemen; times change." Brigitte replied in a matter-of-fact voice whilst inhaling deeply; a heavy coughing bout ensued. Her cheeks turned white; eyes spiralled heavenwards; like a sack of potatoes; she sank lifelessly to the floor.

61

Sam and Jean Pierre

A warm southerly breeze ruffled the blonde locks of Sam's hair. Next to her grimaced a subdued Jean Pierre wrestling with his troubled conscience demanding retributive action. The river snaked its winding course as the couple trudged awkwardly the grassy bank of the dirty river Saone. A strange chill enveloped Sam, she cocooned herself within a blanket of foreboding; eerie quiet. The Frenchman slipped into a bubble of indecision; Sam's feminine intuition sensed trouble. The couple stared vacantly at black water lapping the muddied banks of the river. Jean Pierre turned abruptly to face her.

"Sam, I have a problem, an awkward situation. Whilst I was in London it came to my attention you know a man named Scar; Yes?" The Frenchman questioned softly, threateningly. "Well! yes, he's helping me with money trouble, why?" Sam replied, knowing full well her relationship with the Albino was problematic. Jean Pierre stepped closer to her. "Scar and I, we're sworn enemies anybody, by mere association with him automatically becomes my enemy. There lies my problem." His tanned face screwed with distaste; eyes flashed with murderous intent through a steely cold look of interrogation. Fear traced her spine she shuddered; the warm southerly breeze cooled; the temperature dropped.

Frantically her mind wrestled with her frightening precarious predicament, she sought escape. Woman's intuition advised her to employ girlish whims enter prevarication, evasive action. "I've yearned for this night for so long; just you and I alone. In fact, because I've waited for so long, I'd convinced myself it never would happen." She murmured in nervy romantic overtures, "that beautiful dream was about to tread the boards of reality." She paused, confrontation peppered the air; in cold tones of condemning accusation she continued, "and all you want to do is turn it into a bloody popularity contest." She screamed... tears burst forth onto her pink cheeks; her mascara ran in scary black lines down her panic-stricken face. Jean Pierre stiffened. He passed his monogrammed handkerchief to dry her eyes. "My Cheri, do not cry." Jean Pierre spluttered voice uncharacteristically emotional. Sam dried her eyes.

"Do you expect me to break out in hilarious laughter." She gasped facetiously. Jean Pierre thrust the cold steel of his gun barrel into her ribs. "Believe me I take no pleasure in this, I must know; you and Scar."

Sam's body tightened, her frantic mind trawled varying scenarios of escape, fear gripped her mind. Luck was with her, a group of teenagers approached, in seconds they would be within hearing distance; she played her ace card.

"I warn you, remove your gun or I scream." Sam threatened, her body shook. Jean Pierre noticed the group approaching, stepped backwards; Sam continued, "there's nothing between me and Scar, truth is I'm a junkie; I needed money to feed my habit, Scar fitted the bill. The albino fed me drugs at no charge if I delivered parcels to London from Lyon Mafia headquarters. Otherwise, the pathetic pink eyed man revolts me. Now you can go to hell." She yelled angrily; her shapely legs snapped into action propelling her slender body along banks of the river. But a fitter Jean Pierre followed in hot pursuit, unceremoniously he grabbed her; a group of passing teenagers gazed on in awe. Jean Pierre smiled at them. "It's alright, just a lovers tiff... really." The

Frenchman turned to Sam, "Mon Ami please believe me I'm sorry, I never thought you were; I did not realise." He stuttered apologetically, tenderly he mopped the black lines of mascara running liberally down her cheeks, "once again forgive me, I had to know the truth, and I promise to make amends. I've to report to my boss tomorrow, then you and I are going on a holiday, to Monaco; please." His extreme mood swings, traversing from romantic to the hostile sent warnings through her frightened body. Her inability to accept his mood swings... volatility; meant she would have to get out of the relationship and escape. "Of course, I'd love to." Sam replied in the belief re-assurance, was the best policy to buy her time; her stomach festered with nervous... bitter revenge.

Jean Pierre lurched into Mafia headquarters for his confrontation with Sylvester. The tanned Frenchman dropped his muscle-bound torso into the chair facing his American inquisitor. The Yank acted cool; lit a cigar. "Ronnie phoned, updated me on the disturbance you created." Sylvester paused while he took a deep inhalation of his weed, through plumes of rising smoke he continued. "So, they are small time; and you're too big to take orders." Sylvester snarled. "I defended myself against some aggravating London thugs called Kray, some overgrown barrow boys. They may be your friends; but they are not receiving a Christmas card from me. I don't think Scar was too pleased to see me either as he went for me; I stuck him." Jean Pierre grunted sarcasm graced his curled pouting lips. "You expect me to believe that crap. Yes, the Kray's are old friends, and they are still on my Christmas card list. We go back a long way we work well together. Ronnie's told me what happened. You are one big headed Frenchman that has become too big for his britches." Sylvester fumed. Hot juices of anger surged Jean Pierre's throat; Sylvester continued, "the burning question is. What do we do with you?" Sylvester queried his hand moving to the inside of his jacket. Incensed, Jean Pierre jack-knifed from the chair, in a movement of reciprocity his hand slid to the inside pocket of his jacket.

Murderous eyes threw challenging stares to every shadow of the smoke-filled room. Six pairs of pairs of eyes, yearning for action; settled on him. Jean Pierre returned stare to Sylvester. "We have what you Americans call a standoff. I've started a job; you know me boss I always finish what I start." Jean Pierre's voice became mean, cold, hung in the air like a challenge; he swung about to face the thugs, "anybody with the courage; size up now." Jean Pierre spat in scathing, acrimonious tones. Again, his challenging words hung with menace in the smoke-filled air. Fleetingly, thugs stirred with movements of intent. Jean Pierre withdrew his gun, so did Sylvester's hoods, a standoff prevailed, "if any one of you bums has an issue with me make your move now," nobody stirred guns were placed back in their holsters, "well now that's settled I've to return to London for unfinished business with the albino." Issued an assured calm, Jean Pierre. The red-faced Yank jumped angrily to his feet. "You idiots stop this, stop this." Sylvester roared, "we're supposed to be grown men, lets behave like normal civilized people. Jean Pierre, you sit, the rest of you... well disappear. Woman! Where are my cigars?" Sylvester roared, the peroxide Blonde stumbled forward, the fractious air lost its sizzle, "alright! I know the history between you and Scar, the situation; let's say it lies in my lap. I suppose it was on the cards that the bad blood between you both was bound to deteriorate; get worse. This trouble between you and him I want settled; I want your problems sorting and quick. Either you or Scar walk through that door, the who... well that doesn't bother me. Now get out of my sight." He waved frantically. Jean Pierre rose with an air of confidence, cast threatening glances to his disappearing adversaries; shrugged his shoulders nonchalantly before twisting round to face the Yank. "You could be right boss, I'm too big for you to handle. For you that could be a problem but rest assured boss; I'll find a solution to mine. One thing I promise, when I've killed Scar, and I will, I shall return here: for you. You queried earlier as why I should settle for number one; I've just given you my answer... I don't." He grated, eyes alive with revenge, hate; all reserved for his boss ... Sylvester. Sylvester squirmed uncomfortably in his chair, puffed nervously on his cigar, channeling remaining energies into a gesture of defiance. A laughing Jean Pierre strode confidently from the smoke-filled air of that half-lit room.

62

Jean Pierre Scar and Feud

An agonised Scar lay bleeding on the stinking toilet floors of Kilburn tube station. Ronnie looked on at Scar's discomfort, an evil smile dressed his thin lips as from his hip flask poured Brandy over Scar's wounds; the Austrian squealed. Sounds ignored by the thug, laughing he poured the remains of his golden liquid over his tonsils; threw a disgruntled glower at Scar. "Get to your feet, the filth is all over the station, we've got to get out of here; you can rest when you're back on our Manor. Don't you worry about the Frenchman, I've a score to settle with him; I'll make sure you are both taken care of." Ronnie snarled in threatening tones of intent; the bloodied Scar writhed in pain on the filthy station floor; a pained smile broke on Scar's lips. "That big headed upstart of a Frenchman, this feud has to be settled." Scar stuttered through his blood-soaked mouth as he staggered from the toilet. "Shut your mouth, get in the car; the screws are moving towards us." Ronnie screamed pushing the bleeding Albino into rear seat of limousine, "you bleed on my white upholstery; you're a dead man." Ronnie added jumping into the front seat with his brother. The heavy loss of blood ensured Scar remained bedridden for several weeks.

His throat ached for the taste of Whisky, a longing propelling him from the sick bed, and towards the pub. With bandaged hand gripping his pained side, he limped over the dirty grey pavements of the A1, to the Great North London. That twisted face creased in anguish lit up; his thin cruel lips parted into a half smile. He'd spotted his latest recruit; the vivacious Sam striding towards him. "Sam." Scar croaked. She stopped abruptly in her tracks staring at the Austrians side. Scar ignoring her look of horror; embraced her. "Your limping, your side is bleeding." She squealed as with her manicured hands shielded a grimacing face. "It's the work of Jean Pierre." Scar grimaced as his hand shot to his side to sooth paining wounds. "Jean Pierre has threatened to kill me, if I as much as talk to you; he also threatened to kill you." She added, "and would you believe that when I return to Lyon; we are going on holiday together." She issued, whilst hung between an ironic laugh and terrible fright.

Tears flooded pale cheeks, her perilous position had; indeed, introduced a scary dilemma. Scar winced with pain. "As you can see the Frenchman already tried but failed, next time we meet I will be the victor; I will not fail." Scar spit out in angry words of revenge. Sam's concerned; apprehensive gaze was replaced with frustration. "I'm sick of you and Jean Pierre, the pair of you playing these stupid games with me playing Piggy in the middle. I implore you, settle this blood feud. And by the way; we're finished." Sam swivelled to walk away. Scar grabbed her, rage and humiliation swept through him; his war-torn face grimaced with a facetious warning. "But who will give you drugs, for free." The Albino leered sarcastically laughing as he limped to the pub.

63

Tiger and Nicky Question Andre

Under the dark clouded filled skies Paul entered the hospital and into the intensive care ward. "Come closer." Andre croaked, his weak voice dropping to but a whisper. Paul arched his body Bob Cratchett fashion over Andre's bed, to get nearer to his uncle's skinny withered body. "Yes, Uncle Andre, you want to tell me something?" Paul whispered in Andre's ear. The patient grimaced with pain when raising his head from the blood-spattered pillow. "I want your solemn promise you'll return me to my chalet. I'm dying, the Doctors have given me but a few days. I want to die where Annette and I spent many happy years. Not alone in some godforsaken hospital bed, I want to die on the spot Scar killed my wife." Andre coughed violently, heartbeat increasing unhealthily, he spat blood, outside the hospital angry rumbling dark clouds released its cargo of torrential rain pulsing the curtained windows of the ward. Lightning forked earthwards; Andre released an anguished cry, the worsening thunder rumbled louder, threateningly. The ward doors swished open, introducing an officious nurse barging into the ward. She with back ramrod straight, threw accusing glances at the visitors. "We're calling time on your visit today." She pushed her way forcibly through the men to Andre's bed, wiped blood from his mouth, inserted her thermometer. Paul through eyes of sorrow beheld his dying uncle, a fear gripped him, nostalgia swam in emotional waves through his skinny torso. "I give you my solemn promise uncle Andre, you'll be sleeping in your own bed tonight." The gendarme grated; his eyes smouldered with commitment. The nurse whipped her head round forty-five degrees to the Gendarme. Abruptly their gaze met, her tiny piercing eyes holding Paul in a glare of disdain; Paul snatched the phone. "That's for official hospital business." The nurse shouted in scathing accusative tones. "This is official; its police business." Paul replied, he phoned sister Brigitte. "Brigitte I'm sorry; it is bad news." Whispered Paul. "What's wrong." She shrieked loudly. "It's uncle Andre, he's very poorly; at present he lies in the intensive ward, but I am moving him back to his chalet where he wants to die." A distraught Brigitte dropped the phone to its cradle, choking back tears she stared at me. "Nicky, I have to return to France; my uncle is dying." Brigitte sobbed throwing clothes into overnight bag. I held tightly her shaking body.

"Tiger and I are on the five-o-clock train to London tomorrow; we're reliably informed the Krays and Scar; are planning their revenge attack on Jean Pierre. We need to share this information with the Gendarmerie. I'll see you next week after our meeting with Paul in Lyon." Brigitte pecked Nicky's bristled cheek gingerly, picked up her bag and disappeared through the door. "You take care when messing with those French hoodlums." I shouted to back of her disappearing frame.

64

Paul Meets Sylvester

The young gendarme groped his way through the dimly lit nightclub before an overweight bouncer barred his way. "And you want." The thug grated, eyeing the young Gendarme warily. "I phoned, Sylvester; he told me to come down." Paul replied dryly. The thug dragged Paul to a smoke-filled room and an overweight, pocked faced man sitting behind an ageing desk. "Morning Messier, my name is Paul, I phoned you earlier, I'm looking for Jean Pierre?" "ID." Sylvester growled. The heckles on the Paul's neck stood proud, the Gendarme felt prying eyes upon him as he slipped a shaking hand into the inside pocket. His stomach tensed, throat dried, he flashed nervous eyes searching over the smoke-filled room. Sylvester spun about to his blonde assistant signalling her to light his cigar before returning his gaze to Paul. "I do not know this man and if there is nothing else, I've a busy schedule." He growled, then enjoyed a deep inhalation of his cigar, sending deadly nicotine plumes of smoke surging his narrowing arteries. Paul rose in slow deliberation to his feet; nodded appreciatively. "Thank you and sorry for wasting your time Messier." He grunted dryly, spun about, spotted latest thug to enter the room. A shaft of light sprang into the semi darkened room. The Gendarme flashed an astonished glance of disbelief at the newcomer. His ghostly white skin, housing deep red eyes; the Gendarme swung an interrogative stare to the Yank, "I notice we have an addition; but it isn't Jean Pierre." Paul added querulously.

Sylvester sneered, blew plumes of smoke ceiling-ward, shot a glare of hostility to the Gendarme; the room lapsed eerily into deathly silence. Paul acknowledged the presence of Scar limping from shadows, the Austrian, face dressed in hate; lurched to the table. On passing the Gendarme their threatening gazes of hostility collided. Their mutual dislike... hatred glaringly obvious as they exchanged stares of distrust. A mental picture formed in Paul's alert mind; the Gendarme ensured he would never forget those weird red eyes. Scar stood sneering, challengingly in front of the Gendarme; he grunted sarcastically. "You want Jean Pierre... search the elephant and castle manor in London." Scar then shouldered Paul sideways, went to sit by his boss.

65

Jean Pierre and Sam

The scheming mind of Jean Pierre had ready pigeonholed the time and place of Sam's demise. Sam stamped impatiently through the door, issued nonchalantly to Jean Pierre. "While I was in London I bumped into Scar, I warned him you were out to kill him." "I bet he trembled." Jean Pierre muttered in bitter tones of facetious sarcasm, releasing a belly laugh of scornful irony. "Actually, Scar was matter of fact about the issue. He returns your challenge, when his wounds are healed, reached full recovery. Confrontation with you, settling old differences; he relishes." Sam countered. Jean Pierre's friendship with Sam had run its course; was planning how he would execute his coup de grace. In his evil mind a plan formed. "My apologies Mademoiselle I've frightened you, how can I make it up to you. We could celebrate your graduation, your diploma. I have not had a holiday in years, my friend has an empty cottage on the outskirts of Monaco. Remember, we met there a few kilometres outside Monaco; on the beach at Cannes. Please Mon Cherie! Let's hit the high spots enjoy what the highlife has to offer. The drink, the sun and relaxation; let us forget about Scar." Jean Pierre babbled in pathetic tones of appeasement. Unsettling apprehension coursed Sam's shaking body, fear gripped her gut. Negative mounting tensions had superseded her gnawing withdrawal pains.

Beads of sweat formed on her brow, she trawled frantically her overworked mind for guidance. Female intuition advised that the questionable holiday should be delayed. She cast a troubled querulous glare towards Jean Pierre. But her worries melted in a cloud of passion. The handsome tanned face of Jean Pierre; produced one of his smiles. The kind of smile any woman would kill for. Hormones surged with an uncontrolled delight through her body, intuition and mind collided in regrettable emotional disagreement. Her intuition begged her to refuse the Frenchman's offer; but her hormonal instructions advised otherwise. Her body shuddered with naked lust, a lust claiming the ascendancy. Sam again, had fallen helplessly under his spell; she accepted the Frenchman's contentious decision. "That would be lovely; yes, I'd love to." She gushed with girlish alacrity, before melting into Frenchman's outstretched arms and blissful heaven.

The following morning, lovesick Sam with Jean Pierre waited by the chalet; a black Citroen screeched to a halt. "Jean Pierre, you sent for me." Henri shouted from the open car window. "I need you to take my friend and I to Monaco." The French thug ordered. "But why are you not flying?" Henri blurted in amazement. "It's a little awkward; I'm short of readies, could you push a thousand Lira my way?" Jean Pierre whispered. "What's the Yank going to say?" Henri taunted the Frenchman. "Nothing! You're not going to report you've seen me. You'll be reporting to me in the near future as there is going to be a radical change of management. The Yank will be no more; I'll be your new boss." Jean Pierre's speech effected the correct result. "I repeat, you tell anybody of my whereabouts at your peril." Jean Pierre's cold blue eyes turned nasty. "You know me Boss, my lips are sealed. Here's what money I have, I'll send you more in a few days." Henri withdrew a large wad of notes. Sam gasped; her mouth dropped open in amazement. "Who do you have to kill to get that kind of a bankroll?" A cash strapped Sam questioned in disbelief; eyes veiled with envy.

Henri threw a knowing gaze towards Sam before pulling Jean Pierre to one side then in a husky whisper. "Boss I heard on the grapevine, your girlfriend whilst in London; associated with Scar." The driver murmured sardonically, hoping this would curry favour with the Assassin. "Thanks Henri. But she's already told me." Jean Pierre flashed a comforting smile at Sam. The Frenchman was at odds as to how he was going to resolve his dilemma. The one certainty in Jean Pierre's mind, Sam would never lay eyes upon Scar or anyone else again. Henri pushed the accelerator pedal to floor, in a cloud of dust the car roared towards Monaco.

66

Sylvester Returns Scar to London

A frightened dishevelled Scar slumped into the vacant seat facing the Yank; an ardent plea accessed those bloodshot eyes beholding his disgruntled boss: Sylvester. "Boss I had to come back; the Krays threatened that if I chose not to leave their safe house. My options would be to be dropped into the cement pillars supporting the M1." He wailed pathetically, "alternatively, they would turn me over to the cops unless I fled the country." Scar nervously sipped water. "And why should the Krays threaten you?" Sylvester queried eyebrows winging inquisitively. "There was an unfortunate incident in Sunderland, I killed a woman; the mother of a cop. They're worried that Scotland Yard, because of my Sunderland connections, will carry out reprisals on their manor." Scar's eyes rolled nervously; his skinny fingers performed a drum roll upon the Oak table. The Austrian fidgeted uneasily in his chair. Frustration dictated actions; he dropped head to cupped hands as fingers of tension gripped his stomach. Sylvester, new the value of his London relationship and was in agreement with the Krays. He allowed Scar's pathetic plea to fall on stony ground.

Sylvester's angry eyes glowered in displeasure at the excuse of a human being cowering before him. "You miserable wretch, get your backside back on the plane double quick, you go to London, tell the Kray brothers I sent you; you grovel, do whatever it takes to gain their favour. They've taken a dislike to you and they play for keeps. Your options of avoiding an unpleasant death are slim; if not impossible." Sylvester paused for an inhalation of his weed, continued, "put simply, if you are unable to befriend them; you're a dead man walking. For God's sake man use your imagination invite them to my chalet in Cannes for a holiday; do whatever it takes. I'm sure your conniving mind can work something out." Sylvester grated.

Scar stared nonplussed at the fat Yank, disbelief veiling his bloodshot eyes. His troubled mind deliberated his few options before responding in a choked reply. "Okay boss, I'll play happy families with the Krays. But mark my words I do so under duress, and I'll be back." Scar hissed sourly, dragging limp body to his feet, headed for the door. Where he paused before whipping his head about to face the Yank. "I was wondering; have you heard from Jean Pierre?" Scar queried, "since he knifed me, he's gone underground disappeared, nobody knows his whereabouts." "I've an idea of where he might be, nothing concrete; and yes, the egomaniac Frenchman Jean Pierre was here. After a disruptive conversation, I issued him with an ultimatum. But what is more important; the bad blood between you both I want it settled. If you cannot work together; are unable to reach an amicable arrangement." The Yank paused for a sip of Brandy, then in challenging tones of finality ordered, "putting it bluntly, I want only one of you to walk through that door. The who; does not bother me. But face reality you stupid Austrian, the last thing you should be worrying about is Jean Pierre. Because if you fail to make peace with the Krays, you're a marked man walking into a concrete coffin. Now get out of my sight, I don't want to set eyes on your ugly mug; until you can tell me everything is under control." The Yank roared. Scar slunk from building like a whipped dog.

The Jew from Berlin

The Austrian's journey back to London was inevitably veiled with fearful trepidation. He had heard of the barbaric methods employed by the Kray brothers. He stared from the window of the rising plane at torrential rain soaking Lyon. Pictures of unforgiving Krays flashed through his mind; he cringed. Landing at Heathrow airport he hurried to the taxi rank and Kilburn; he dove into a telephone box.

Sylvester phoned the Krays. "Hy Ronnie! It's me Sylvester, I've spoken to Scar, the stupid sod has apologised for the upset. I've put him back on the plane, he's flying to London to grovel with you pair." Sylvester's voice dropped an octave, "do me a favour, go easy on the boy, Scar and I go back a long way; he's a good lad who is at his wits end. The lad's confidence has plummeted so low he senses Jean Pierre will better him." The Yank pleaded for his colleague with uncharacteristic solicitousness. "That woman he murdered in Sunderland cost us, he needed to realise that. Your request puts a strain our friendship. Okay he can billet in the Robertson's house Kilburn. The Wimbledon gang are travelling north. They are sizing up their next job; in the Tottenham Court area." The cockney replied.

To reassure the Austrian Scar, Ronnie sent his chauffeur driven Jaguar to meet him at Heathrow. This calmed the Austrian's insecurity, reinstalled a lost confidence; Scar snuggled into white leather of his chauffeured limousine. He'd settled in 101 Loveridge road in Kilburn, when the phone sang out. Nobody knew I was coming to London; the worried Austrian reflected. Cautiously he lifted the receiver. "Yes." He whispered. "See you in the Great North London at eight-o-clock." Ronnie's tones tripped merrily down the line; jubilant Scar replaced the handset; showered. With a spring in his step, the Austrian hastened to Kilburn High Road, and pub. Ensconced within the grubby lounge of the ageing pub,

Scar placed three glasses and a Litre bottle of Jameson whisky upon the table; Ronnie and brother joined the Austrian. "I'm not sure how to apologise, this is alien to me but here goes. I'm sorry for killing the cops' mother in Sunderland Ronnie, can we make amends; shake on friendship." Scar proffered an open hand. Ronnie paused, hesitantly the thug raised podgy hand to grasp Scar's. "Before we play happy families understand that cop is no friend of ours, but we never give them reason to investigate us. You are one stupid Albino; this one time you are forgiven I iterate this one time. You are lucky to get one chance from us; you've used yours.

So, you're running scared of Jean Pierre." Ronnie sniggered pulling the trembling Albino close to him, "well that is where we can help you, the Frenchman will be visiting our other safe house Bethnal Green; but that's for later." Ronnie bragged sinking the last of the whisky. "Barman another bottle of Jameson, and a drink for yourself; I'm celebrating." Scar threw two fifty-pound notes on the bar whilst blurting. "Keep the drinks coming." The Austrian slurred.

67

Sylvester Threatens Henri

"Where the hell is Jean Pierre?" Sylvester groaned. The Yanks grievances filtered through the smoke-filled air to the ears of entering Henri. Through the smoke laden shadows of the semi lit room; Henri approached the worn Oak table and seated Yank, "you got news?" Sylvester snarled ungraciously rising, leading Henri to a private room. "Jean Pierre is shacked up with a blonde English lady; that should keep him busy for at least two weeks." Henri informed the Yank, sniggering loudly as he slowly shaped his thin moustache. "What is the address." The Yank shrieked; hot blood coursed the bulging veins of his arm. "Messier, I know not where he is, only that he's a red-blooded Frenchman in hiding with a woman." Henri lied consummately before continuing, "if you were in that situation; I ask you messier what would you do? Where would you go?" Henri questioned his boss in convivial undertones. The Yank withdrew a cigar. "Don't push it, my patience is wearing thin; this situation is getting out of hand. Ever since that egotistical Frenchman decided to take control, replace me; the world has gone mad with killings.

Death happens, which is incidental provided the demise means a rise in profits. Then the incident is justified; this stupid ingrate creates mayhem for fun." Sylvester shouted; hands scything through the air in exasperation, "in our line of work you never kill unless the price is right or ordered from Sicily." The yank threw Brandy over his tonsils, loped menacingly to Henri; grabbed his collar, "alright Henri you've had your little joke, you, and that ego maniac Frenchman; are close. The pair of you, breath the same air...

share the same space. To you he would divulge privileged information, information we mere mortals could never hope to access; I ask you for the final time. Where the hell is Jean Pierre? Or maybe you are just sick of life." Henri's face turned blood Red, the veins in neck bulged as he struggled for breath. He trembled, fear consumed him, his spine tingled in a body devoid of feeling. At that point fear deserted him, replacing his fear was an innervating cold sweat of death. His overworked mind trawled frantically for avenues of escape. Evasion from the Yanks wrath, prevarication reared its ugly head; an eerie scary silence ensued.

By divulging half-truths and withholding important details may extend his execution; save his miserable life. Henri writhed uncomfortably; cold sweats chased his spine. Sylvester would eventually find the location of Jean Pierre hideaway without his help; he had to access safer ground. Exasperation filled Sylvester; the Yank spun about to face Henri. Blood pumped through his veins at an unhealthily rate. His volatile temper rose exponentially, worry lines etched his pock marked face. Sylvester strode the worn carpet like a caged animal; paused and snarled ungraciously. "You disappear, get out of my sight, the next time we meet if you have not provided the information I need..." The tyrannical overtures dissipated when Sylvester paused in aggravated frustration, "just get out of my sight I'll phone instructions later, and when I phone, I'll expect answers." The enraged yank snarled.

Sweating profusely Henri, was just glad to be alive; he traipsed gloomily from the room. With head lying in resignation upon his chest, the forlorn figure disappeared into shadows of his bedroom. It was a fractious humid night, a storm raged, lightning flashed, torrential rain pulsed noisily the windows of Henri's bedroom. The wind whistled its friendless message through the warped window frame attacking the shade-less 40-watt bulb which swayed violently. The inclement weather ensured sleep was at a premium.

Sylvester grabbed the decanter to pour himself another healthy large Brandy; his fat hairy fingers counted the day's takings. With head swimming in negativity, he grabbed the phone... dialled his driver. Henri experienced a disturbed night which lead him to drink a half litre of Whisky. The phone rang... the Frenchman's glazed eyes shot heavenward; feet turned to jelly as he tried to answer the phone; he collapsed back on bed in an alcoholic fuelled stupor. Seven hours later an agitated Sylvester phoned again. Henri nursing a hangover picked up the receiver to the angry voice of his boss. "If you're not in the club by ten-o-clock with address of Jean Pierre; start saying your prayers." Sylvester menaced before slamming the phone to its cradle. With head pounding, Henri juggled his options. "I am betwixt a rock and a hard place nursing the problem of who do I want to be killed by Jean Pierre or Sylvester?" He sought to rise above the disturbing dilemma as shortly he would be forced into making the most dangerous life-threatening decision. Exposure of his boss Sylvester to the Gendarmerie.

68

Louis With Dying Andre

The rusting wheels of Andre's invalid chair squeaked its progression, as Louis guided the ageing chair into Dupont's run-down chalet. In the sparsely decorated front room Louis prepared a makeshift bed for Andre then lit a fire. Alongside his comrades' bed, lay a second rough structure the Austrian had prepared for himself. Andre's makeshift cot was poignantly placed opposite the spot his wife Annette had met her untimely end. A cool evening air chilled the room as Louis added kindling to the fire to combat the cold. Andre's tired eyes glazed in abject sorrow, directed themselves towards the ceiling as though seeking heavenly intervention. Emotion coursed his pain racked body, pain eased by the company of his old friend and comrade, Louis. Who with head half bowed allowed tears to mist saddened eyes, the Austrian stared vacantly at bloodstained tiles. The very spot Andre's deceased wife had met her fate; debilitating self-pity encompassed him. Louis pulled Andre to sitting position, the ailing Frenchman coughed blood. Transforming his colourless ashen lips; into a bright crimson.

The fragile bony Frenchman's body twisted and turned as excruciating pains increasing in their intensity had reach an unbearable point. That was when numbness arrested his body; his lined face relaxed... pain vanished. His body was advising him he'd reached the point of no return. That it was time for him to shuffle off this mortal coil. Hot tears of emotion swamped his bristled cheeks. Stares of hopeless mingled with desperation shot ceiling-ward; before his bloodshot eyes returned to the floor, to the blood-spattered tiles. The dying Frenchman croaked emotionally. "Ann

Marie, I can feel your presence not much longer my darling; we'll soon be together... forever." The dying Frenchman dug into reserves of energy, struggled to rise shaking torso from his cot. A chronic bout of coughing beset him; blood splurged forward to saturate his already blood-stained cheeks.

Strength deserted the ailing Frenchman's feebly body, he collapsed wheezing into his cot. With eyes alight in conviction, he clutched his ancient Army gun. His old friend and comrade Louis approached him. With staunch conviction littering his voice Louis choked supportively. "Andre. You and I fought the Germans with little more than courage and a rusty old handgun to protect us. We survived many battles whilst fighting those inhumane beasts; surely, we can survive this." Said Louis, nostalgia abounded, tears ran down Louis's cheeks; the Austrian stooped to embrace Andre's fragile torso. The weary Frenchman grated sourly. "I know Jean Pierre will return here. If only to get justice for Ann Marie. I long to join my wife; but not until I've settled with my son first. I'll do everything in my power to keep breathing until he shows his face. That foolish, obstinate son of mine is driven by stubborn pride, a trait he inherited from me. His driving force, overriding pride will dictate his return, back to where the love of his life was killed, my Ann Marie. Only when he's fulfilled that promise and rid the world of Scar; will peace return to him.

I have never forgiven him, never will while he treads this evil path for the Mafia. I and my trusty gun will be ready, to hasten his journey to that black hole in hell; I long for that day." Andre croaked as with vengeance in mind his bony hand stroked his rusty weapon. The door squeaked open; an emotional Brigitte entered. Worry lines creased her pink brow; bag in hand she crept to dying uncles' side. "How are you?" She choked. But Andre's eyes had closed, he'd lapsed into the quiet oblivion of sleep. A cold funereal silence swam unbidden through the chilled soulless air. Through bloodshot eyes she beheld the forlorn figure of Louis.

69

The Death of Inspector Tiger

The unkempt collection of barrow boys huddled conspiratorially in the London pub. I Nicky, tucked warily in the shadow of Inspector Tiger; entered the dimly lit crowded lounge of the Great North London pub. Inspector Tiger, treading the path of caution; we approached the bar with tentative apprehension. Our searching glances fell upon the assembled thugs in the centre of the lounge. Their heads shot upright; the motley crews sixth sense advised them police had violated their territory... were in their midst. Tiger and I approached the glass laden bar counter. Our elusive prey was nowhere to be seen, no Scar or adversary Jean Pierre, also absent were Scar's buddies the Krays. An exasperated Inspector Tiger cast frustrated eyes to floor. "This is a bloody waste of time; our boys will have flown the coop; they'll be back in France now." Tiger grated his voice rose with angry impatience, levelling accusing eyes at me; guilt coursed my body. "Okay, okay, I accept I'm to blame, I had him... let him slip through my fingers, but if you do not stop taking the p... I'll." I half threatened in a voice of regretful exasperation. "Or you'll what." Tiger grated, flashing a facetious... sycophantic stare that clung to the smoky air, "what do you aim to do?" Tiger challenged in comedic tones of irony.

Naivety had driven me to make that stupid call; in apologetic tones I blurted.

"Sorry boss it was irresponsible, my gut feeling is if we were to track the guy; shouldn't we keep tabs on The Old Inn Leicester and Brigitte. Jean Pierre is bound to put in an appearance, the

Frenchman is besotted with her." My eyes took evasive action, dropped sharply to the ground, avoiding contact with Tigers cold disbelieving stare.

The inspector slipped into the toilets, returning minutes later shaking hands dry. "There's no bloody hand towel in those stinking toilets. Yeah, I reckon your plan could work. It will have to wait until after our meeting with the French Gendarmerie; we're booked on the early morning flight to Lyon. "Two pints barman." He grunted in a more upbeat mood. Tiger downed the pint in two swift mouthfuls; slipped a comforting arm round my shoulders. "Don't look so bloody depressed, we'll pick up on your plan when we return." Tiger grunted turning to the barman, "same again." Tiger grunted, pointing at me said, "it's his turn."

The barrow boys gathered in a threatening group, chatting conspiratorially they emerging from the shadows before advancing in our direction. Tiger and I immersed in conversation had temporarily forgotten about the thugs. Two overweight ugly misfits led the motley crew, into their eyes leapt their murderous intentions. They sidled quietly behind the unsuspecting couple; one withdrew a knife the other a gun. He thug released the safety catch on his handgun. The faint click was enough to catch my attention. I spun about in time to catch that fatal knife cutting through air. Burying itself up to the hilt, between the blades of the Inspectors shoulders. Tiger released an anguished yell... his limp body collapsing in pools of beer and blood saturating the cheap worn carpet. A trumpeted shout of triumph filled the smoke laden air as thugs celebrated before advancing upon the lifeless body of Tiger. His motionless body lay face down in a pool of his arterial blood. Cold angry tears ran unashamedly down my bristled cheeks. I stooped my head into cupped hands; released a yell of disbelieving grief. I stood in frustrated inaction over the blood-soaked corpse of my boss. Frustration, despair, and grief united; to spin their giddy dance in my head. My arms shot ceiling-ward in frustration, bewilderment. "Tiger, Tiger." Emotional tones screeched sorrowfully, but Tigers empty eyes were void of life. His end had arrived abruptly, on that filthy floor of the Kilburn pub. Inspector Tiger lived no more; he'd shuffled off this mortal coil. Rest in peace my dear friend.

70

Rusha, the Underground and her Revenge on Jean Pierre

Rusha's driving motivation was bolstered by her single-minded quest for vengeance. This driving urge that had prepared Rusha to accept the filthy, inhospitable conditions of the underground. It was within the dirt riddled tunnels over the past two years, she'd happily called home. Even accepted the constant amorous advances, from unshaven, hormonal driven sweaty fighters of the French underground. But rather than accepting any of the amorous advances from the men, she had channeled all her energies into the physical activities such as martial arts training. Vital prerequisite skills needed for her journey of revenge; to kill Jean Pierre. The Malawian immigrant, whilst cooped within those dirty dank tunnels; spent those long lonely hours honing skills for her long-awaited confrontation with the Frenchman. "Jean Pierre, time is fast approaching; meet your nemesis." Rusha snarled; hate curdled in the corners of her cold eyes staring at the ageing wooden beams; beams shoring up those filthy dusty tunnels. Tunnels that were to, at last, launch her retributive juices, her craving for revenge. She was now an able fighting, killing machine.

What was once but an illusory concept could now be realised. Colour sprang to her cheeks, excitement tingled her spine. The well-shaped torso jackknifed that single minded girl to her to dirty booted laden feet; mixed emotions welled her gut that final day. Sorrow invaded her conscience; emotional tears spiked her tear-filled eyes. She packed her meagre belongings into a rucksack. Hot tears of emotion rolled liberally down her ivory-coloured cheeks as she approached waiting colleagues. Her emotional voice marinated in wistful desolation; bid mournfully... her goodbyes. "Messieurs! Time has come to bid my fond farewell; I truly thank you for training me; preparing me for my mission." She spluttered to the motley crew; an appreciative radiance sprang to her face when progressing along the solemn line of men. She embraced lovingly each sweat stenched body; cried unashamedly. Her head dropped to her well-formed breasts with morbid resignation; emotional sadness disturbed her. "I shall miss all of you." She cried. With tears misting bloodshot eyes she jerked head upward, back straight. Allowed booted feet to progress her sinewy frame forward. With controlled majesty, she marched from the tunnels, down dusty roads to the Lyon Gendarmerie.

Where better to go when wanting the address of a criminal, her first kill; Jean Pierre. She strolled with a confident swagger through the doors into the station. Approached the desk and bored face of young gendarme attempting fruitlessly to finish his crossword. "Oui! Madame." The Gendarme gushed, stroking his pencil shaped moustache. Allowing dilating admiring eyes bulge uncontrollably as he savoured the curves adorning Rusha's willowy cleavage. Sexual urges ran rampant through his lean torso, there was a stiffening in his trousers. Rusha smiled, took full advantage of the situation, leaned forward provocatively, encouraging further Gendarmes effusive admiration. "I wondered, could you help?" She asked coyly, flashing her eyelashes seductively in obvious incitement to the gendarme. "It's hot in here." She muttered sheepishly, slowly she removed her jacket; revealing her well-formed bust, "I've spent the last few years in Paris, and have mislaid the address of my cousin Jean Pierre. I believe he had the misfortune to spend time in your jails; he should be on your records, I just wondered if..." She paused and stepped closer to the desk allowing her well-shaped attributes to bulge within her blouse. Leaning forward her bust fell to the desk; her question hanging teasingly in the air. The Gendarme produced an embarrassing cough as she continued, "I wondered, could you point me in the right direction?" She whispered in strong seductive undertones. An ageing Gendarme strode into the room accompanied with an air of seniority; towards the young Gendarme, acknowledging the entrance of his boss; the Gendarme coughed loudly. Sent cold glares of suspicion in Rusha's direction. "Madame! I cannot supply this thugs address, but if you find this assassin contact us, we would like to speak to the gentleman." The Gendarme replied. "I thank you Messieurs." Rusha grunted sarcastically, hastening her exit to the next port of call and son.

Although a sky of blue addressed the heavens, the warm rays of the sun before falling to earth was cooled by a North Easterly wind. Outside the care home, Rusha pulled her cardigan around her chilled body as she lingered in deep thought before committing herself. "What the hell am I doing?" She frustrated wrestling with indecision; she paced the pavement. She paused, sucked in a breath of confidence, then slipped through doors into the home's reception. Where she was approached by an officious overweight nurse employing an accentuated waddle. "Yes." Nurse resounded haughtily. This filled Rusha with retributive emotions of discontent, her eyes blazed with distaste; and reciprocated with the cold emotive negativity she'd received. "I take it you did receive the phone call regarding my son." She snapped abrasively. The nurse's eyes narrowed. "But of course, Madame, and once our discrepancy has been dealt with, we can continue." The nurse replied with equally cold equanimity.

"Discrepancy! What the hell do you mean; discrepancy?" Rusha's face flushed with rebellious defiance. "Three months have lapsed since the red eyed gentleman returned the young boy Jean to us; no payment has been made since. We are not a charity; your account is in arrears. But if Mademoiselle would care to settle the outstanding amount; your son could be with you in minutes." The nurse replied. That damned Scar Rusha grimaced to herself, her blood boiled, she began to shake hysterically, torn between tears and laughter at her predicament; a calm returned within her. With a face like thunder, she checked her meagre funds before scribbling out a cheque. Minutes later the door flew open to a healthy enthusiastic; but suspicious six-year-old boy. Draped in apprehension he slowly approached Rusha. She bent down; an icy knot of anxiety formed in her stomach; would the young boy accept her as it had been so long since their last meeting her mind spun with negativity. After all this time would there be a reciprocity of emotions; shelving these niggling worries she embraced him. "I can see you are going to be big and strong." Rusha choked, "come Jean we are going home." She grabbed the well-worn rucksack; young Jean's feet hit the stone floor with a rapid patter as they disappeared from the building.

Within hours the couple, arms laden with food, left the supermarket and headed to a clutch of bombed houses she called home. "Mama! Papa brought me here you call this home." Squealed Jean in disgust. "Oui. That is correct." Rusha laughed, dropping to one knee she placed a comforting arm around the boy and continued, "but it will not be home for much longer. This Mon Cheri remains our house until its purpose has been served. A certain gentleman, I need to deal with, lives just across the way. After I have accomplished my errand, we move on to Paris; just you and I." Rusha explained running fingers through his tousled brown hair. "But my papa, Scar. What about him?" Young Jean replied, confusion veiling his youthful naïve eyes. "Somehow I do not think Papa will fit into our plans." She remarked coolly, staring at the nonplussed... bewildered youngster.

    Grimacing, young Jean grabbed the bags before traipsing behind Rusha through their entry to the skeletal building. She searched the debris littered rooms shrouded in dank cold shadows before instructing her son. "Jean, collect flat bricks like this one." Rusha pointed to bricks lying beside him. Disgruntled young Jean dolefully accepted his task, she placed bricks fashioning them into a level floor. She lay tattered blankets upon a roughly constructed bed before lighting a fire, "right young man after all your hard work you deserve dinner." Rusha remarked light heartedly cocking her head comically to one side. Young Jean scowled, with sore hands firmly entrenched in his pockets; he shuffled in disgust towards Rush adding brush wood to the fire.

71

Paul and Nicky

Hopeful expectancy sprang into Paul's eyes as through a wistful half smile he enquired. "You speak French?" He probed eyes widening, Nicky threw a sheepish look of naivety towards him. "Not a word." I replied ashamedly. "Then for our forthcoming meetings with the Mafia let me do the talking, in the meantime the driver will take you to my chalet; wait for me there." Paul disappeared into the side door of Mafia headquarters; the driver transported me to the chalet then left. I placed my backside upon my ageing suitcase, waited patiently outside the chalet for Paul to arrive from his liaison with Sylvester. Thirty minutes lapsed; a black Citroen screeched around the corner before slewing to a halt in a swirling vortex of dust. The Gendarme jumped from car, a disturbed look dressing his face. Paul stared at me; eyes filled with pleasing disbelief he blurted enthusiastically. "My meeting with Sylvester." Paul shouted euphorically. "He's the Mafia head boy controlling our assassins Jean Pierre and Scar. The air in that half-lit dump was alive with friction during our negotiations. The tense atmosphere unnerved made me feel uneasy. Blatant mistruths dropped liberally, glibly... with ease from the fat cholesterol lips of Sylvester. The Yanks answer regarding whereabouts of Jean Pierre and Scar; was misleading. The only evidence he fed me was that there was no bond, allegiance, or solidarity. Between himself for either of his two assassins; to Sylvester his own survival was paramount."

Paul muttered, sipped water. "So, he knows where Jean Pierre is hiding?" My question shot with hope from my open mouth. "As the English say, I hit the nail on the head; yes, I'm confident he knows." Paul mocked facetiously; releasing a sardonic... mocking laugh before continuing, "at the conclusion of our meeting; Sylvester tensed, his pock marked face paled; he stared right through me. Displayed obvious agitation when spinning about and yelling for cigars. His eyes were alight, with distrust, hate, when nodding to his thugs, tacit instructions to remove me from the premises. Whilst being forcibly removed from the room; the door squeaked open. I collided with a weird looking albino gripping his side. Blonde thinning hair hung over bloodshot eyes, this weird looking guy could well be Scar. It gets better my friend, news on the Jean Pierre front. Henri, Jean Pierre's driver and my snitch, informs me Jean Pierre is with Sam. They are staying in Monaco, in the holiday home of a gambler friend for a fortnight.

Henri is only too aware of the Frenchman's volatile moods swings, as on several occasions he has been on the receiving end of Frenchman's vicious tongue. My snitch also informs me; Jean Pierre will never let the woman leave alive. Odds on the blonde leaving Monaco alive are very; very short." Paul stuttered with gloomy conviction. My eyes lit up; face beamed with delight.

"That's brilliant news, both of our thugs are in France." I gushed with boyhood excitement, "I don't expect you noticed what direction he took?" I spluttered sarcastically. Paul, with a cheeky smirk addressing his cheeks replied. "You English. I left them inside the building; we have to assume Scar and Sylvester were there to talk." Paul replied before progressing to the drink's cabinet for a bottle of wine. I searched excitedly my overworked mind for our next move, swung about to face Paul. "You wouldn't know where Jean Pierre born?" I questioned in a thick Mackem accent. "Yes. In a dilapidated Chalet amidst bombed buildings on the edge of Lyon. Scar has a chalet, two blocks away on the same estate; he lives with Rusha. I also heard on the grapevine; Rusha has taken up residence in a bombed house opposite to where Andre lives. That is the house of Jean Pierre's birthplace; come I'll take you." Paul decanted the bottle of red wine; after warming the wine placed it back on the table muttering. "That will do fine for tonight." With the exuberance of excited schoolboys, we hastened to the awaiting Black Citroen. The 2.4litre engine powered its way through the dusty backstreets; into a poverty-stricken area skirting Lyon. Total surprise merged with amazement sprang unbidden to my face. "This is it?" I gasped in utter disbelief. "Messier do not prejudge this area too hastily; this estate was the crème de la crème pre-war. Before Hitler made the decision to unleash his bombers on our beloved country and bomb the area into submission.

It was due to the imminent fall of France, that Marshal Philippe Petain was made Prime Minister by President Lebrun in Bordeaux. Suspicion lay on his doorstep especially when the 84-year-old signed an armistice with the Germans, even today the Marshal is still considered to have been a Nazi collaborator. Hitler had, with his Generals, decided that it was from France; he would launch his all-out attack upon England. It seems so unreal, that within this picture of desolation, once flourished an affluent community. Snapping me back to reality was Paul's voice. "Alas as you say, and I agree with you; it is nothing more than a rat-infested bombed site. But in this is the place the Dupont family, tasted the good life; lived life for many years in the lap of luxury. Profits from his car plants enabled their rubbing shoulders with the affluent. However, these profits creating their unreal lifestyle was all too suddenly gone, all Dupont's money came from producing car parts for the German company; everything vanished in an instant. Within months of Hitlers bombing raids, the family fell dramatically from the euphoric heights of prosperity to the spiralling depths of poverty.

The following years did not treat the Dupont family kindly, with unemployment at its height, jobs were virtually nonexistent. The Dupont family were forced to scratch out a living. That was about the same time Jean Pierre became disillusioned. A brave Andre managed to keep the family intact; put food on the table by tackling menial tasks. Sadly, these labours earned him very little money; their menu was very... very basic. On more than one occasion, the Dupont family flirted with starvation. They had literally fallen from the giddy heights of being millionaires; to beggars in a few short months." Paul inhaled deeply; before a sibilance of breath released a sigh, "as you can imagine they were utterly devastated." The Gendarme muttered sadly slewing the car to a halt in what passed for a street. Alighting the vehicle, we slipped inside the chalet moving cautiously from room to room of that dirty broken-down wooden building. Paul slipped an arm round my shoulder; pointed at bombed building opposite. "See that shell of a building." He said in condemnation, "that was where Jean Pierre first tasted the might of the Mafia, according to Uncle Andre. The mafia have long since gone; that is the abode where Rusha and son are shacked up." A thick chesty cough echoed, through the dark shadows of the chalet as Paul guided me to the sound and pointed to the spot where Scar had killed Andre's wife Ann Marie. Helplessness filled us, we stared at the motionless dying Andre. Accompanying him, friend Louis squatted on a rickety stool next to the home-made bed where ashen faced Andre lay. Louis spotted us and rose, Paul approached him; they embraced. "It's good to see you Papa this is Nicky from Scotland Yard England, he's here to assist in the hunt for Jean Pierre and Scar." Paul released his grip on his father; swivelled those sad eyes to his patient, "Papa please forgive my intrusion." Paul muttered apologetically.

In a move of compassion, Nicky dropped to the floor next to the dying Andre.

"Pleased to meet you sir." I muttered with consoling subservience.

Andre winced, turning head towards me, a forced pained smile dressed his lined aging face. "Where is your inspector, Tiger?" Croaked Andre, hurt cloaking those tired eyes sweeping to the door. "Sadly, Tiger is no more, he is dead, we ran into a nest of hoodlums; on their manor in Kilburn... they knifed him." Hot bile burned Nicky's throat, condemning expletives dropped from my trembling lips; hot tears stabbed the back of my eyes. Andre still grappling with the death of his wife, empathised with my emotional outburst, his bony hand groped for mine. "I'm sorry young man, must be painful for you, death introduces the cold sombre throes of finality. Damn invasive negative emotional memories do not help." His weary eyes strayed to dried dirty blood spots; splattering the floor, "it was on this very spot that scumbag of an upstart Scar murdered my Annette." Andre struggled to stem his tears; his balding head dropped to the pillow. I cased the ageing Frenchman's body into the cradle of my arms, my eyes misted over; emotions of a different kind embraced me. "Andre... do not worry, your nephew Paul and I, will catch your thug of a son, and that bloody freak assassin Scar. In that albino I too have a personal interest in his being brought to justice... he killed my mother." A lump rose in my throat whilst making that promise to the dying man. Rusting hinges squeaked; everyone's attention was immediately drawn to the door; a disheveled... distraught Brigitte entered.

72

Police and The Kray Brothers

Angry rain clouds rumbled across the dark menacing heavens hovering over London. Torrential rain lashed incessantly the dirty windows of police headquarters. Agitated murmurings gained the ascendancy within Scotland Yard's murder squad gathered for their morning briefing. Discordant, discontented mutterings quieted when the commissioner strutted authoritatively into the room. In his wake following submissively; an entourage of chiefs. With heads bowed, they studied in rapt concentration, papers in hand. "Gentlemen, you are no doubt aware the unwarranted murder of Inspector Tiger took place within our manor, more precisely The Great North London pub in Kilburn. However, since that untimely death... good news, the de facto evidence gathered should enable us to indict the Kray brothers. It is also rumoured they are housing a French criminal called Scar." The commissioner paused, a sarcastic smile dressed his lips before continuing facetiously, "now all we have to do is catch them." His smile was replaced with sardonic grimace of irony, "the assistant commissioner will hand out details of the operation. That's all gentlemen." The Commissioner wheeled about ninety degrees to face the exit; highly polished shoes progressed him in squeaking steps from the room.

After the exit of the Commissioner the funereal silence blanketing the room exploded into excited babbling, officers perused their papers; this operation was aptly named TIGER. Uniformed officers alongside plain clothed police saturated the manor of Kilburn in their fruitless search for the Krays. The killing of their inspector had significantly raised the profile of their operation; any John doe suspected of fraternisation with the Krays were hauled in for interrogation. The Krays income generated by the borough of Kilburn was slashed significantly. Takings from Bethnal Green and Elephant and Castle were almost non-existent. Raids disrupted the Krays lifeline to nigh on zero cash. Emblazoned over the front pages of the Kilburn rag emphasised police successes in the closure of the Krays money spinning hot spots. The safe house, run by the Robertson family in 101 Loveridge Road Kilburn; came under strict surveillance.

Fugitives Ronnie and Reggie had already fled to the Northeast; seeking refuge in the dock area within the garth flats in the notorious east end of Sunderland. These flats proved to be the perfect hiding place for the high-profile thugs. As within the buildings over ninety percent of its occupants were small time thieves and crooks. The very dregs of society whose sorry existence was subsidised by government benefits. Long days of inaction dragged drearily by the Krays spent their days of inactivity in the infamous Ship Inn and Bridge End Vaults. Both pubs were known trouble spots in the crime rife dock area, aggravated mainly by visiting sailors. Several weeks lapsed, the troubled Krays returned to their flat in the Garths. The watched glumly the six-o-clock Tyne Tees news. Pictures of Ronnie and Reggie flashed across the screen, the newsreader gushed gleefully, that the brothers once mighty empire; was tumbling into disarray. Unease... dissatisfaction sat uncomfortably on their worried faces. They needed to return to the capital and quick; rebuild their domain. Ronnie threw last dregs of whisky over his tonsils; switched off television. "The screws are predicting our downfall, bragging they've severed our lifeline, the media are talking about us as though we are history; finished. We need to return to the smoke and our manor. Start money flowing, revive our lifeline, the police have moved their search further afield." Ronnie snarled. Reggie jerked head skywards in frustration as though searching for inspiration, guidance. "We need a scapegoat, someone to divert attention from us." Through a facetious snigger he continued. "That Frenchman Scar has outlived his usefulness." Reggie paused, stroked his chin thoughtfully as he swung about to his brother, "the Albino... he dove tails into the equation nicely." Reggie stared at his brother who smiled coldly through a mouthful of gold fillings and yellowing teeth. "We travel back to London; tomorrow," Ronnie sneered.

Back in their Kilburn residence Ronnie ordered his brother. "Get your coat, we are paying a visit to Loveridge Road." Ronnie grabbed his pistol. "You have not forgotten that house is under surveillance." Reggie murmured cautiously. Several hours later, the brothers barged unnoticed into the safe house; confronted the nonplussed Austrian. "Welcome Ronnie, Reggie." Scar stuttered. "I thought you were in Sunderland?" The Krays embraced a chilling silence, the air cooled putting nervous vibes into a frightened rattled Austrian. Reggie pulled up the collar of overcoat, threw a long friendless stare at the bemused Austrian; slumped into a seat. Ronnie paced slowly forward; in gravel tones grated. "Scar you're a troublesome, Austrian ingrate; that has been the cause of our upheaval. Because of your actions my brother and I were forced into hiding. Like common criminals we hid in the dock area of Sunderland. All while the cops happily decimate our living. For our desperate plight and suffering, the blame for that lies squarely on your shoulders. As long as you remain in our manor, the police presence will continue; our income will continue to fall. You've outlived your usefulness; you're no longer welcome on our patch; from today you are history in this Manor." The thug threatened. Scar gasped in disbelief, fell pleading to his knees. "I can't go back yet, you know Sylvester... he's not a forgiving man. Give me a week please, I promise I'll be gone." The Frenchman beseeched in the pathetic voice of a frightened... beaten man. "You've got till tomorrow when we return; do not be here. Oh! And before you leave; make sure everyone knows you are going."

Ronnie released a sarcastic snigger, with his brother they slipped from the safe house; into the darkening shadows of evening, "we'll do the decent thing, inform Sylvester we've ordered Scar to leave the country, you phone Scotland Yard; advise them of Scar's movements. Oh! and be sure to mention it was the Albinos knife that killed their beloved inspector. Scar the cop killer." Ronnie issued a belly laugh; turning to his brother bragged, "has a certain ring to it Scar the cop killer. That juicy morsel of information should get the law off our backs; but more importantly out of our bloody manor." Ronnie blurted angrily. Reggie grabbed the telephone. At mafia headquarters Lyon the phone rang Sylvester answered. "Sylvester, your boy has caused a big upset... cost us a lot of money; we've ordered him to leave." Ronnie snarled. A stunned Sylvester fell back in his chair while opening his mouth to complain, but no words came forth from his pouting cholesterol lips; the hoodlum sank into a chilling silence.

The London thug's unwelcome information irked the Yank; did not sit well with him. For the next several hours the telephone line between London and Lyon burned with foul expletives; sizzled with angry condemnation. "Sylvester, we are bearing costly... unsustainable losses; we lay our considerable financial loss down to your man. We have presented the Albino with an ultimatum, that by tomorrow he vacates our patch; if you are not bloody happy... then tough." Ronnie snarled with aggravated finality. "Hang fire Ronnie, I'm having trouble digesting this situation; what with Scar upsetting you lot in London; Jean Pierre freaking me out. No, I am sorry I do not want that freak to darken my doorstep again, alive.

He is trouble." Sylvester grunted. "Well put it down to our good nature, let's say we give him an alternative: he's either another body propping up the pillars on the M.1. Or we can sell him out to the cops, we have already put them on his tail. Would that sit better with you." Ronnie chuckled. "Now that my friend's is more to my liking, any one of those solutions would be just perfect." Sylvester purred, reaching for his brandy, slamming down the phone, "one down, one to go." Sylvester gloated, spinning about to face his thugs, he raised glass to lips; grunted, "now to our second problem, I want you lot to search Henri's property, you are looking for any connection nailing that driver to Jean Pierre." "Okay boss." The disappearing thugs grunted, returning beaming several hours later in possession of address of Jean Pierre's holiday cottage. "One half of my problems solved: now let's settle with the other half. Boys, we're going on a surprise visit."

73

Jean Pierre Returns Home

Henri decelerated; the dust laden Citroen slewed to a halt outside Monaco holiday cottage. He lit a cigarette, slumped back into his seat; awaited the presence of Jean Pierre. Ten long minutes elapsed, his boss appeared carrying overnight bag spattered lightly with blood, the driver perspired freely; slackened his tie. "No woman?" Henri croaked. "Shut up, I'll do the talking, you do the driving." Jean Pierre snapped. "Lighten up boss I'm only making conversation." Henri muttered light heartedly. Jean Pierre realising he'd reacted badly replied. "Okay let's say I prefer travelling light and the lady will not be a problem now." The Frenchman grunted. Henry tensed with discomfort, slipping the car into gear accelerated gently from the curb, into the main drag of traffic. Henri powered his motor for two hours in uncomfortable; disturbing silence. The Citroen roared through the dusty lanes skirting Lyon. Swiftly running through the gears, his two Litre motor responded. The dust laden car slew to a halt outside Andres dilapidated, rundown Chalet in rat infested slums of Lyon. "How did you know I wanted to return home?" A surprised Jean Pierre quizzed. "Well boss, your father being ill and Louis tending to his needs, I assumed you would want to be with your ailing father."

A pregnant pause issued a poignant silence; curiosity got the better of Jean Pierres driver who blurted, "will you be seeing Sam again?" He quizzed. Jean Pierre's mood swung in seamless transition from surprise to threatening. Blood surged the Frenchman's veins at an unhealthy rate. Anger gripped his gut. Jean Pierre unsheathed his knife; pressed bloodied razor-sharp blade to driver's throat... drew blood. "You're hired to bloody drive; not think. If I wanted you to pry into my private life; I'll ask." Jean Pierre snarled; he alighted the Citroen; displeasure etching his handsome tanned face. Henri pressed accelerator to the floor, the cars powerful engine responded, the dust laden car screeched its departure under a cloud of smoke. He sped eagerly towards his meeting with Gendarme Paul; inform him of Jean Pierre's return to the chalet. Jean Pierre's arrogance irked Henri: his gut burned with a cocktail of retaliation, retributive justices; revenge upon his boss. "One day Jean Pierre, one day I will get even." Henri growled, face grimacing contemptuously; the car slewed to a halt outside Gendarmes chalet.

74

Rusha Awaits Arrival of Jean Pierre

Numbness attacked Rusha's rear end; an agitated impatience consumed her. She awaited the appearance of her ex-lover and sweet revenge; a dusty black Citroen slewed to a halt outside Andre's chalet. Rusha's breasts swelled with excitement, before releasing gasp of disappointment. The occupant was Louis... not her target Jean Pierre. Andre struggled onto his wheelchair; Louis steered the fragile Andre into the chalet. A warm autumn breeze chased black clouds hugging a darkened sky, thunder resounded ominously, lightning forked illuminating the pouring rain. "Mama, I'm soaked, can we go inside now?" Bemoaned young Jean. A second car screeched to a halt in vortex of dust; in front of Andre's ageing Chalet. The driver alighted his vehicle shaped his pencil moustache. Made hurried entrance into the Chalet; re-appearing several minutes later to drive away. Yet a third black Citroen slewed to a halt, a Gendarme accompanied by suited gentleman stepped from the car. Rusha wheeled about to fidgeting son; snapped ruefully. "You're right Jean; this can wait for another day." She guided her offspring into the ruins and makeshift room. Within minutes she'd a roaring fire warming that skeletal shell of her home. Early the following day, Rusha with son slipped from the building back into shadows, lurking... watching, patiently from the safe cover of the bushes. The soul-destroying hours of inactivity proved agony for young Jean; the hyperactive youngster rubbed miserably his empty stomach. Hunger attacked them, they returned inside the ruins, Rusha heated and served pasta and fried chicken over her makeshift fire.

They ate in silence before returning to the bushes, evening approached; together they stared in awe at the twinkling stars. Screeching car tyres attracted attention of Rusha; a dusty black Citroen shuddered to a halt at the kerb. The doors of Citroen opened once again to a tall lean man shaping Hitler type moustache exited and opened rear door. An excited Rusha invited a cruel sadistic smile of intent when recognising the passenger. She gasped with delight as her target alighted the car, the infamous Jean Pierre. Beads of sweat gathered on her brow, with fingers trembling she withdrew her gun from its holster, released the safety catch. She lined Jean Pierre within the gun sights. Her hands perspired, trembled with anticipation, her long-awaited moment of fulfilment had arrived. With the cool of James Bond, her dark ivory fingers caressed gently the trigger. Her guts warmed with excitement; adrenalin surged her body; tingled her senses. Seconds drifted seamlessly into minutes, for what seemed like an eternity she had her weapon trained on the victim Jean Pierre. The moment she had trained for many years had arrived, retribution was to be hers, the forefinger pulled the trigger back. Indecision filled her, she shuddered; a sweaty forefinger released her grip on the hairpin trigger.

She dropped wearily to the bushes perspiring freely, frustration gripped her gut. She replaced the safety catch of her gun, placed the weapon back into holster. "What the bloody hell is wrong with me." She whined, ushered her son back into the ruins. Jean sidled up to her upon the bed, she pulled him close. "What's wrong? Why were you talking to yourself Mamma?" Questioning words of naivety sprang in an innocence query from the youngster's lips.

Rusha grimaced, defeatism dressed her face, abject misery had replaced her excitement. She turned; stared wistfully at Jean. "Well son I came here to kill a man, a cruel man who abused me." She trembled; instability urged her to smoke. "Which man. And what do you mean abused you?" Young Jean probed in boyish curiosity. "He's an old boyfriend who took advantage of me... calls himself Jean Pierre." The name dropped from her lips in dribbles of pure cold hate. "Jean! That's what they call me, you mean he is my father?" The boy quizzed. Rusha laughed. "Well, you are his son, but that is not why I called you Jean. Jean Pierre used to be my hero, but long ago he fell from those dizzy heights; now he wallows in the gutter. Jean is a popular French name, I've lied to Scar, pretended to him that he was your father, which by the way is our secret. The man I'm out to kill, your father, raped me in a bombed building: that is when my love turned to hate." Hot juices of emotion burned her throat; further words failed her. "That man I don't like." The young boy winced. "That's good my son, because now I have my little warrior to fight by my side." Rusha whispered affectionately throwing an emotional embrace round young Jean's shoulder.

 The night air cooled the dark of evening, out went the remaining warmth of day. Rusha swilled the warming heat of hot coffee over her tonsils, outstretched hands grasped at escaping tongues of heat spewed out by the roaring fire. "Tonight, you screamed. Why?" Young Jean queried throwing another log on the fire. "Frustration, for years I harboured a burning desire to kill that man, yet when it came to pull the trigger, I froze; years of training vanished." Rusha whimpered despair dressing her face. "You're funny." Young Jean giggled; he slipped between homemade blankets to invite the peaceful realms of sleep. The dark of night brought with it, an unnerving chill, introducing a colder atmosphere into the skeletal building. Rusha stoked dying embers of wooden logs; the fire exploded into life. Her brow furrowed with bewilderment. "Why could I not commit to that damn final act? Why the hell could I not kill him? For years I've prepared for this moment. Could it be I still love him. Could it?" She cursed; her distraught mind grappled with the unthinkable. She glanced at sleeping son; whispered emotionally. "I'm sorry my young hero; but it is possible that I'm still in love with your father?" She stared through the jagged hole that once housed a window. With bemused confusion, she stared in mesmerised wonderment at the innumerous twinkling stars decorating the black abyss.

75

Scar Threatens Sylvester

The cold mist of evening settled upon Scar's shoulders as he negotiated empty dusty back streets leading to the club. Sylvester, reflected upon his dismal failure; dissatisfaction enveloped him. He, with thugs had returned from Monaco, and unsuccessful venture to south of France, in their search of Jean Pierre they found only the bloodied body of a dead woman. Misery dressed those cholesterol lips draining Brandy; self-pity engulfed him. He grabbed his private accounts book to check club's income; tired eyes sparkled with glee when falling on final total. He grabbed bundles of notes and counted them into hundreds. Whilst placing the packaged Lira into elasticated bands; a package fell to the floor. He dropped overweight body to floor, to recover it.

The loud squeaking of hinges encouraged the Yanks head in direction of the office door. The door burst open to Scar; with evil dressing bloodshot eyes; the Austrian entered... glowered at the Yank. "Evening Boss, there is no need to get up." He snarled in tones littered with condescension, "I have just returned from London, your friends; the Krays kicked me out. Then they laughed in my face; that hurt, really hurt. But then, you already knew what they had planned. Didn't you? But what hurt even more, is that you'd informed them; you'd rather see me dead than return to France. The unforgiving sods put the cops on my tail. Now boss, I'm sure you are aware, since we hooked up in America, I've always looked up to you! Believed your every word." Scar paused, gulped Brandy from an uncorked bottle then resumed, "tell me what they said is not true, I might re-think my actions; let you live." Scar growled; menacing accusations filled smoke filled air where they hung there like a threat. Terror sprang to Sylvester eyes, sweat streamed in anxious beads the Yanks forehead. His face distorted in fear, cholesterol lips pouted in disgust.

Scar approached his boss with his red eyes glowing with menace, he ran his skinny finger down the razor-sharp blade. The Austrian, eyebrows raised in anticipation, he licked the gleaming blade. The trembling Sylvester rose shakily to his feet; grabbed the bottle of Brandy from Scar. Poured two drinks handing one to Scar. "You've got the story all twisted, yes, I did tell the Krays I wanted either; you or Jean Pierre to step through my door. It was that mad Frenchman, he suggested it because he wants to be my number one. Jean Pierre, instead of him returning to England; paid me a visit. Threatened, unless I phoned the Krays, telling them to dispose of you; I was a dead man. I knew the cops were intent on arresting a body for the murder of their inspector Tiger; they needed a scapegoat. The Krays said they were going to provide one." Nervously Sylvester swung round to face his peroxide Blonde, "fetch my cigars woman." He roared. The angry Austrian dropped his skinny athletic torso into the seat facing the Yank; his cruel thin lips parted in an ironic laugh.

Bony fingers again played over the razor-sharp edge of his lethal glinting blade. Something the size of a boulder came to Sylvester's throat; he gulped. Stark fear knotted his stomach; it was the dread you feel when you know your end has come. He snatched a handkerchief from the top pocket of his jacket, mopped the perspiration liberally wetting his brow. His ugly trembling cholesterol lips parted in disbelief at his rapidly, deteriorating situation. The man he'd rescued from the clutches of the Mafia; was about to kill him. Death stared him in his ashen face; he panicked. His mind exploded igniting emotional instability. The overweight American lapsed into turmoil; frantically he grappled fruitlessly to find a solution to his crisis. In subservient pathetic movements his obese torso dropped to the floor; he released in grovelling tones; his whining plea for mercy. "Scar, Scar, please you can't kill me we're partners; I gave you your break. What happened to you when the Mafia decided to offload you in America? Who stood up for your interests then?" The Yank squealed uncharacteristically. Scar squinted through cold empty eyes, unmoved by Yanks inept pathetic performance; he released a sinister mocking laugh. "Sylvester, you needed an assassin, I fitted the bill; that suited you and me. You are aware I detest weakness: in anybody. Now get to your miserable feet; tell me where Jean Pierre is." Scar screamed running his glistening blade against the Yanks throat. "He's home tending his dying father; Henri dropped him at the chalet; not two hours ago." Sylvester's voice quivered. "Well fat man today is your lucky day; you've just bought yourself time. I'll check your information, if you're wrong: I'll be back, then partner you are a dead man." Scar loped through the door. A light, warm breeze filled the air, Scar arrived at the chalet before melting into the shadows.

The chalet lights blazed; grunts of disagreement echoed from inside; men argued. "You're not welcome here. Louis is helping me," an ailing Andre Grated wearily to Jean Pierre. "Papa Louis has gone home and I'm staying you're too ill to be left alone. Please stop this infernal rowing, if not for your sake; Mama's." Jean Pierre pleaded; he dropped to knees. An incensed Andre raised fragile body from his bed. "Don't you dare drag your mother into this." Andre released a squeal of anguish, clutched his painful chest. Like a rag doll the ailing Frenchman rolled limply from his makeshift bed to the blood-spattered floor. A pistol shot rang out, the bullet passed cleanly through the chest of Jean Pierre and thudded into the beam. The Frenchman fainted, slid unceremoniously to the floor. From the broken window, Scar recognised the ebony face of the female attacker; as he entered the chalet approaching the injured couple. For a fleeting humane moment, Scar dropped his guard; emotion moved him. Pictures of he and Jean Pierre, in happier times warmed his insides. He smiled momentarily at the wounded Frenchman, in that moment he viewed Jean Pierre as a friend not his enemy. Slowly life ebbed from the Frenchman, Scar embraced an emotional indecision; feelings for the man he once knew, surged his skinny body. This was his opportunity to put Frenchman to rest for good; that surely would prove who was number one. But would it prove the albino was the best? Would people say that in order to prove his superiority; he shot an injured man. Deep in thought he slowly approached his would-be nemesis. Tearing a strip from Jean Pierre's blooded shirt he shaped the dirty fabric into a tourniquet.

The Frenchman's eyes opened, through the heavy mist Jean Pierre issued a stare of disbelief; his sworn adversary Scar was dressing his wounds. The Frenchman attempted to rise and push the Austrian to the floor. This enraged Scar who grasped Jean Pierre's throat in a stranglehold. The Frenchman coughed, struggled to breathe. That tanned face turned a blood red; to the delight of Scar who released a cold sinister laugh. "Mon Ami!" Scar shouted in gloating contemptuous dislike, "you are still an ungrateful wretch; tell me why I should not end our feud now; kill you and have done with our dispute." Scar threatened tightening his grip over the Frenchman's bony throat. "This is the only chance you'll ever get, while I'm injured; don't do me any favours." Jean Pierre gasped; his eyes closed... body went limp. The Frenchman lapsed into the black abyss of unconscious. "Do not worry my friend I never aimed to." Scar gloated to the unconscious prone

Frenchman, "no we'll finish our differences standing face to face; that way we prove who is number one." Scar muttered, placing his coat under Jean Pierre's head, the Frenchman stirred; regained consciousness stared through blurred vision at a nonplussed Scar. "Messier. My apologies for overreacting to an indelicate situation; I should be thanking you for saving my life. But while we are on friendly terms, talking to one another Mon Ami; let us be realistic. You and I, both are wanted by the Gendarmerie and English police. We both need of friends; you need me as much as I need you. Everybody is chasing us; our problem is we have nowhere to hide... nowhere to run to. This could be our last battle, our final act so why don't we make a pact, stand shoulder to shoulder to fight the enemy; united we are stronger.

And once the enemy is defeated, you and I can fight like grown men to the death; that way we'll prove to each other who really is the best." Jean Pierre croaked; more blood pumped forth onto his crimson chest. Scar re-applied the tourniquet then scratched his bristled chin; the Austrian relapsed into deep thought. "Okay Number two you're right; united we will stand against our enemies. For that task neither of us could wish for a better ally to protect our backs. Then your sworn enemy who would rather kill you himself. I agree your stay of execution old friend; until the fighting is finished. Then Mon Ami, you and I can settle out our grievances." Scar grunted with an air of confidence. "That is good, together we were always a formidable team, I'm sure that once again; united as one we can be." A weakened Jean Pierre smiled faintly, from the deep reserves of his energy Jean Pierre summoned up strength to shake Scar's hand; this sealed the most unlikely pact ever enacted in French history. Scar went to shake the outstretched hand, the Frenchman's hand dropped to the floor; Jean Pierre once again was taken by the peace of darkness. That was the day the most unlikely alliance in history began between the two worst enemies France had known since the civil war: and Madame guillotine.

76

Henri Snitches to Law; Jean Pierre Returns

The morbid vision of Tigers death haunted me; I sat with unease on my wooden chair glumly pushing my continental breakfast round the plate with a fork. From opposite, Paul observed my self-indulgent display of self-pitying grief, he attempted to soften my pain. "It is blatantly obvious you still miss Inspector Tiger; unfortunately, my friend your pain will not get any easier. But what might help initially is to bury yourself in work." Paul muttered in tones of conciliation. Nicky attempted to compartmentalize his immediate problem. "Back to our earlier discussion, the first visit should be to Louis and Brigitte, from there to chalet and confrontation with; Scar and Jean Pierre." Paul questioned. "Do you agree?" The Gendarme said through a boyish smile, sipping his coffee, his questioning eyes burned into Nicky searching for confirmation.

Nicky shovelled the remains of breakfast into his mouth. Streaky bacon laced with beans spewed from my mouth as he grunted agreement. A clatter of leather on wood caught our attention, the dining room door burst open to a breathless Henri. "Messieurs I'm glad to have caught you." The driver blurted, "last night I returned from Monaco with Jean Pierre; minus his woman, I drove him to his ailing father at the chalet. Also, I've heard that Scar arrived in Lyon, there he met with a dark-skinned woman, possibly his accomplice; it is rumoured they plan to kill Jean Pierre.

An excited Paul jumped to his feet and grabbed Henri. "You sure about Scar and this." The Gendarme grunted. "But of course, Messier but please be warned, when you and your English friend approach the chalet be cautious; they are both armed. I must take my leave as I drive Sylvester to the bank, Bonjour." Henri blurted, turning, and scampering from the building. Henri reached the safe confines of his car, sat back relaxed and stuck a fat cigar between his lips. Producing a self-satisfied grin lit the cigar, gloated at his scheming plan, "with Jean Pierre and Scar out of the way, only Sylvester stands between my running the club. And me becoming the new Mafia's godfather of Lyon. Everything is set for a grand finale, well done Henri." The self-congratulatory praises echoed in tones of commendation.

Meanwhile in the Bistro silence returned, a perturbed Paul turned abruptly to face me. "This changes our plans, the possibility we'd face four guns, taking on that many would be foolish; we're going to need back-up." Paul grated an avenging look danced in his eyes. "Back up. What for? It is only a woman and three thugs I'm sure we can handle them." Nicky screamed with youthful impatience. Paul jerked his head towards me in a defiant gesture. "Well at least let me call on my father." Grated Paul: we set a course for his family. The bungalow was shrouded in silence, we entered, confronted Louis, and told him of our plans. "What the hell do you mean you're going alone, there's a possible four killers waiting for the two of you." Louis fumed, "I'm coming with you." The ageing Frenchman added grabbing his rusting gun, checking the chambers. "And what about me." Chirped the young Brigitte. Nicky moved to the side of Brigitte soppy eyed; the lovesick cop whispered. "After all this is over, I would like to think you and I could... I was going to ask you in Leicester, but with Tiger getting killed everything went crazy." Awkwardness invaded my voice; I dropped to one knee, "will you?" A bullet smashed through the pane of glass, Paul and I ran to the door to spot an ill-dressed thug disappearing around the corner

77

Scar and Rusha Plan Showdown

The crushing of gravel awoke Rusha, she scrambled from her makeshift bed to protect her son, the slender figure of Scar entered. "What are you doing here? How did you find me?" Rusha screeched confoundedly. "In your position this is the first place I would have run, not to my bungalow; but here. But listen up, I've only got a minute I'm staying next door with Jean Pierre." Rusha interrupted. "You're stopping with Jean Pierre, that, that..." Rusha repeated in a scream before Scar cut her dead. "We've made a pact, to stand united; both Jean Pierre and I know it will be only days before the Gendarmes find us. Our unison is based on the well-worn theory; two guns are better than one. But when this charade has run its course, Jean Pierre and I intend to hold a duel; settle who is number one. When the battle with the Gendarmerie is over, I'll step outside under the pretence of lighting a cigar, instead I'll ignite the flame of my lighter three times. That is when you make your move to the chalet and stay outside. I will re-enter the chalet and challenge Jean Pierre to a duel; when we're prepared to fight you shoot Jean Pierre through the window. Are you alright with that?" Scar's voice dropped half an octave to a whisper; he smiled.

Rusha's eyes reflected frustration, impatience, was she still in love with Jean Pierre, could she go through with this charade? "You are a coward but keep your end of the bargain, I'm sure the rest will take care of itself." She grated rubbing the butt of the gun; Scar traipsed back to Jean Pierre and the chalet. Rusha sat in deep thought. "I've been waiting for this so long, it hurts, when we've disposed of Sylvester, shared the money from the fat man's safe; my boy Jean and I will escape to Europe live in comfort," Rusha mused out loud. "But you take one step out of line; you are one dead Albino." Rusha gloated, patting the head of her Eight-year-old as a confident Scar padded to that doomed fatal chalet and Jean Pierre.

78

Nicky, Paul and Sylvester

Rusha hastened passed Sylvester's club... Paul spotted her, she spotted the Gendarme and started to run faster; we gave chase. Inside the Yanks once feared club, lay an empire that had crumbled; Sylvester lay in sorry disarray. For the second time in his life, Sylvester had been humbled; the Yank left his office to address cronies. "Scar has returned," Sylvester gasped, "he will make life difficult for us so before he or Gendarmerie return, we'll make ourselves scarce. We have enough money to escape France." The Yank exclaimed, clutching his money bags he pushed his overweight figure to exit of the club stepping into morning sunshine flooding the front of the club.

Sylvester stopped, stared in disbelief, as a dark-skinned lady ran past his club; with Paul and I in hot pursuit. Paul spotted the obese figure of Sylvester, called a halt to chase of the immigrant, diverting us to overweight body of the Yank. "And where might you be going with that money?" The young Gendarme questioned facetiously... his querulous tone laced with hostility. Sylvester's fat cholesterol lips pouted with indecision, the distraught Yanks mind grappled with panic, turmoil, groped for pretentious... ambiguous criteria that would divert the Gendarme's interest; Sylvester stuttered awkwardly.

"Good day, it's yesterday's takings my boys are escorting me to the bank." Perspiration ran in rivers over the furrows of worry lining the Yanks brow; Sylvester stared blankly at Paul. "And how long have your "boys" been escorting you the bank?" Paul quizzed through eyes hooded with distrust. Sylvester trawled his befuddled mind for an excuse, none was forthcoming; he blurted hesitantly. "Forgive me... I forgot my car keys." The yank replied in a nervous response before disappearing with his mob inside the club, Paul and Nicky loitered impatiently outside the club for ten minutes, Paul moaned as his hands shot to the sky in despair. "Nicky we're wasting our time, we've got nothing on him; he could be telling the truth. We'd have more success chasing the Black girl; she could lead us to Scar." He grated, an abandoned hope littered his voice. Inside the shadows of the club Sylvester snarled at his henchmen. "The bloody Law's outside... a slight change of plan we wait till tomorrow to execute our escape. You all bed down in the billiard room... get a goodnight's sleep." In the meek silence of obeisance, the motley crew trooped away; their future had just taken a nose-dive

79

Rusha Kills Sylvester and Scar

Stabbing pains seared Jean Pierre's gut; his handsome tanned face now bore a grimace. His shaking hands gravitated to his blood-spattered wound; a restless Scar looked on. The impatient Austrian felt twinges of indecisive exasperation. Creasing stomach pains reminded Jean Pierre of his hunger, the Frenchman struggled to his feet and cold stew. Scar squirmed, turning to face his adversary, he grunted sourly. "I've an errand to run, should only take a couple of hours, it's much too early for anything to happen." Scar mused; a sardonic smile dressed his thin lips. Jean Pierre glared at the albino. Nodded his begrudged approval whilst robotically shovelling spoon to mouth. He paused eating, distrust tortured his worried mind. "This errand that is so important. What... is... it?" Jean Pierre stuttered through a mouthful of cold food. "I thought I'd mentioned it earlier," Scar lied glibly. "I've to settle a score with our boss Sylvester. I want to refresh my plan of attack and I need fresh air. Nothing to worry about; shouldn't take too long. While I'm gone you look after your wounds; I do not want an invalid covering my back." Scar chortled. "Be sure and bid the scum bag hello from me." Jean Pierre issued sarcastically. Scar smiled and nodded his tacit reply and releasing a belly laugh of derision before disappearing outside the decaying building.

The late Autumn breeze ushered a chill into the evening air. Suspicion filled Scar's beady eyes that threw cautionary scans the length and breadth of the deserted dusty streets before slipping into the bombed building opposite Jean Pierre's chalet. The Austrian groped through the eerie dark shadows gracing the skeletal shell.

He stumbled over the brick strewn floor towards a pool of yellow light afforded by a single candle illuminating the figures of Rusha. He threw a cursory glare in their direction, from a faintly husky voice he almost ordered. "Rusha you ready, a slight change of plan we will visit the club; settle up with Sylvester. Historically, this is the time the greedy rat will be absorbed with his end of weeks takings." Rusha kissed her sons' forehead, settled him onto his bunk. "See you soon." She issued softly before turning to Scar, "I'll never be more ready." Rusha grunted solemnly, checking the chambers of her pistol. The couple stepped from the bombed building, once more his wary eyes swept cautiously empty dusty roads.

With the cold North wind chilling their backs Scar and Rusha plodded the back roads to Mafia headquarters and prey. Sylvester satisfied himself enough time had passed for Gendarmerie to disappear, clutched bulging bags of cash. Waddled towards the exit but uncertainty clouded his mind so returned to his office. Scar and Rusha slipped into the club; Sylvester's bodyguards pre-occupied enjoying a glass of Brandy did not notice two furtive figures slip by them. The Austrian spotted the bulky form of Sylvester in the office; Rusha slipped into the shadows and attached the silencer to her pistol. Sylvester swept a nostalgic gaze of farewell around the ageing furniture. Uncharacteristic emotion swept over the Yank, he reminisced. He visited pleasant memories before sweeping a last sorrowful stare of regret into every nook and cranny of the room, muttering wistfully. "Wherever I end up, I hope to experience similar happy emotions; I had in this room." Sadness touched his face... tears pricked the back of his bloodshot eyes; he replaced his fat rear end on the chair. Increasing nostalgia overwhelmed him, as pleasurable reminisces swept over him.

His Blonde 'assistant' after taking several sleeping pills had retired to her bed, Sylvester decided to enjoy one last emotional cigar. A slimy smug grin dressed his cholesterol lips. An exhalation of smoke drifted to the ceiling; the door burst open. Dread sprang to his eyes; he shot frantic worried glances to the newcomer; he sought prevarication. "Scar, did you find Jean Pierre?" The overweight Yank stuttered in pathetic subservience. "Oh yeah I found him, we're even on talking terms." Scar drawled facetiously, "you see old man, Jean Pierre and me. Well, we've made a pact which does not include you." The assassin paused, poured a Brandy, threw it over his tonsils. The warm yellow liquid warmed his insides; the Albino threw an evil sardonic grin of contempt at the overweight trembling Sylvester. "The only reason I came back is to kill you, take your money. Not to exchange niceties; shut your slimy mouth, hand over your cash." Scar drawled, dropping his skinny torso into the seat opposite Sylvester. Sylvester's eyes dilated... glazed over in disbelief, the Yank sucked deeply on his cigar. Sending yet another cloud of nervous nicotine inhalation; surging through miles of his thinning arteries.

Cocooned within fear, the yank juggled nervously scenarios that would enable his escape from his perilous situation. He trawled into reserves of energy to summon courage. "Have you gone mad, outside I've five men armed to their teeth." He shouted in words of bravado, "you think you can walk in here, threaten me at will. This my boy is my outfit, my office, my regime. Here I am king I give the orders, so welcome to the real world. And dream on, there's no way you get your grubby little hands on these bags." Sylvester paused, shaking hands reached for his drink. Took another deep inhalation of his weed before continuing, "Okay Scar we go back a long way so for old times' sake, I'll give you five grand cash now." Sylvester paused again, beads of sweat stood proud on his brow, "if I were in your position, I would think that a very generous offer?" Sylvester grunted in a placatory plea.

An appreciative modicum of confidence warmed his fat stomach in anticipation of an empiric victory. But the moment of exultation lasted briefly. No sooner had the words dropped glibly from his cholesterol lips. Yet again the door swung open; the smug smile of triumph hugging his fat lips faded. Rusha entered with an exaggerated swagger, blowing smoke from her gun barrel and replacing the silencer in her pocket. Sylvester's hand slid furtively beneath the table. Rusha spotted Sylvester's fat paws diving under his desk she threatened. "Don't waste your strength fat man, you can push your little bell all you want there's no one outside to help you; you're all alone," Rusha sneered, "so you're Jean Pierre's boss, the sad old man who creates drug addicts. Who wallows in the delights of adrenalin rushes; provided by killing? Well, there is good and bad news, the bad news for you is you'll not be killing any more. The good news, for me is your number one Jean Pierre will shortly follow you." Rusha released a hollow laugh of contempt, placed her gun against Sylvester's head, "but before I kill you, I overheard part of your conversation; I take it you offered some deal to Scar." Rusha spat out in low vehement tones of accusation. Scar whipped his head round in disbelief; from a scary white face he levelled bloodshot eyes at her. "Rusha what the hell do you mean." The Austrian snarled, "you don't think I would make a deal with this weasel." Scar spotted suspicion lurking in Rusha's eyes. Sylvester spotted his opening, a chance to even the odds; the Yank released a scornful laugh of derision at Scar's plight. "Yeah, you're right he wanted to make a deal, I told him no, I taught the snivelling punk everything about the business; this is the way he repays me." The Yank snatched a quick glance at Rusha; the cold impassive grimace adorning her face did not bode well. His head dropped in resignation; his ploy did not work... his end was nigh.

Accepting he was to shuffle off this mortal coil, Sylvester set his devious mind to work, what the hell he thought why not take Scar with me. Scar scowled angrily at Rusha, in disgust wheeled ninety degrees to face Sylvester. "Stop your lying fat man, Rusha and I came for your money; hand it over." Sylvester remained motionless as though he were in a coma. Scar re-issued his demands, with patience exhausted Scar tried to grab the satchels from the quivering submissive Sylvester. The Austrian released a belly laugh as the American dropped his money bags to the floor, followed by Scar. Greed danced liberally in his eyes as the Albino investigated his haul.

The Yank jerked himself from the futility of his funereal morbidity; whispered a hopeful plea. "There's more where that came from." Sylvester cried in a hopeful wistfulness. "What do you mean more." Scar blurted... eyes hooded in suspicion, "I've twice as much again in the bank." Sylvester babbled hoping to delay his execution. Rusha invited a sneer to lace her stare holding Sylvester in a glare of inquisition, derisory tones spat at the Yank. "You're a fat lying toad, unreliable and untrustworthy; I don't like you." Rusha grunted pressing the barrel of her gun against Sylvester's temple, "I've already checked the clubs accounts, you withdrew every cent, there's no more money." An acid tone from Rusha's surly tones accused. Angry frustration lurked in those murderous eyes of Sylvester's staring in desperation at the ceiling, exaggerated bitterness; retribution veiled Rusha's face as Sylvester threw out another excuse. "They are the club accounts. I do not reveal private finances through club ledgers you understand, for tax reasons." Sylvester shouted. The wild-eyed Rusha, already embracing a healthy dislike for the Yank released a belly laugh as she wrapped herself in a bubble of calculated, hateful deliberation. Coolly she re-applied the silencer to the barrel of her pistol, applied pressure to the hair trigger, the guns silencer hissed with action. A bullet whistled through the air embedding itself into the side of the Yanks face; blood spurted liberally from the hole that once was his temple. Rusha smiled triumphantly before turning the smoking gun from the Yank, training her weapon on Scar. Rusha's cold slate grey eyes of accusation planted themselves squarely upon the Austrian. Momentarily she switched her gaze to the dead Yank, lying in pool of his arterial blood; before returning a harsh stare of accusation towards Scar. "So, you now make deals behind my back, you, ingrate."

She paused, maybe for effect. But more likely to languish in her moment of joy; she released an evil smile of irony, "but don't feel too bad about your scheming treachery; our so-called relationship was always going to end up this way. You may have guessed Jean Pierre was my heartthrob, the love of my young life. After he raped me in that bombed building." She grabbed an emotional intake of breath, tears spiking the back of her eyes forced themselves onto pallid cheeks, "that single action turned me against men, all hormone instructed men I hate them; and that includes you." After a slight pause she continued. "Give me your gun," Rusha ordered and pointing the weapon at Scar's heart. But the sight of so much money lying on the floor consumed Scar; made him oblivious of threats levied against him. The Austrian now totally absorbed in feeding his financial frenzy paid little heed to her threats; Lira signs flashed with total greed to his eyes. Scar licked his blood red lips with relish, long bony fingers flicked impatiently through bundles of money just waiting for him to pick it up. Rusha recoiled the hammer then released the hair trigger. The clicking noise released the Austrian from his insatiable greed, he re-focussed his attention.

A chill traced the Austrians spine, his gun was trained on the nape of his neck, hairs stood erect, like soldiers on parade. His thin lips dropped open in disbelief, pure fear engulfed him. Terror sprang to those bloodshot eyes locked onto the cold deathly stare of Rusha, and facing the wrong end of the gun barrel. "What do you think you are doing?" Scar stuttered in disbelief, "stop fooling around we had a deal, remember who's boss here. Who will support our son?" Frightened, concerned pleas dropped pleadingly from Scar's quivering lips. Unmoved by the assassin's emotional outpourings; Rusha steadied the gun. "Our son! You fool you mean Jean Pierre's son. And with Sylvester's money we do not need anybody's support," she mocked impassively.

Scar's dire situation signalled disaster, the tables had been turned, he trembled; strove to be brave and prepare himself for the worst. Was it his turn to shuffle off the mortal coil...? Meet his maker?" His body shook with fear, the assassin

dropped to knees convulsing with uncontrolled sobbing. "Your joking; our son was fathered by Jean Pierre." Scar screeched in disbelief; instability entrenched him. His grieving mind embracing self-pity snapped; greed re-entered the equation. His blood red eyes danced with maniacal glee. Once again, his eyes dressed in insatiable greed fell upon bundles of Lira. Inborn negative frailties surfaced, corrosive vibes of uncertainty consumed him, grasping bundles of Lira; he massaged his face lovingly with the notes. That once impregnable shield of self-belief invincibility, that for so long had served him so well; disintegrated... vanished.

Rusha dropped her weary body into a chair, released a derisory laugh of scorn that quickly evaporated, the facetious outburst was replaced by pity. The sight of the once confident Scar reduced to crazy bizarre antics saddened her. She vaulted to her feet; boredom dressed her ebony face as sneering she issued coldly. "Well, I've to go now thanks for the cash; I'm sure Jean will appreciate it. But before I kill you, to show you I'm not completely heartless. I heartily give you my sincere thanks, rescuing me from the clutches of Jean Pierre. But come on Scar take a reality check, you really think there could ever have been strong emotional attachment between us. No, I doubt that any real form of true love, no what took place was a convenient arrangement of necessities; I needed a place to stay you fancied me, needy goals of the time. We met and were in need of something, someone, our arrangement solved the problem. We have moved on and now faced with an entirely different situation. One that was bound to arise, I'm afraid that moment has arrived; from now on it's just my son and me.

Together we will kill that rapist Jean Pierre, but before sending you to your creator. You must know that I never did trust you, one last thing, it was me who shot Jean Pierre through the window. I sort of guessed how this scenario would play out so wanted to give myself an advantage." Rusha released a cold laugh, in one seamless movement fired a single bullet from Scar's gun which cut through the air with a silent hiss. Embedding itself deep into Austrian's temple. Scar's limp body slithered unceremoniously to the floor on top of the blood-soaked Sylvester. Rusha replaced the gun in Scar's hand; taunted facetiously, "boys will be boys, fancy killing each other." Her tones echoed comedically. Then with a confident majestic stride, sweeping all the loose money into bags she progressed from the club, spine tingling with accomplishment. Sylvester's attendant Blonde awakened from her afternoon siesta by the fracas came running to scene. After releasing a terrifying scream phoned the Gendarmerie.

The last of the Dupont family meets his maker

Amidst the devastating proliferation of skeletal buildings littering that filthy rat-infested bombed site. Lay Andre's dilapidated... broken down chalet; he lovingly called home. In the dingy sparsely furnished front room, Jean Pierre lay writhing in agony on the blood-stained tiles of the floor. Blood seeped liberally through his roughly made tourniquet; the burning pain searing his chest became unbearable. A dull thud echoed from adjoining room immediately his overworked mind re-focused attention upon his father. Re-directing his morbid self-pity towards Andre; his own pain evaporated, vanished.

Struggling to his feet he progressed his pain racked body in staggered movements towards the prostrate Andre. Ironically his father lay on the very blood- spattered spot his wife had lain after Scar had killed her. Through misted bloodshot eyes his probing gaze of helplessness fell upon the prone skinny torso of his father Andre. "Papa, Papa." Jean Pierre screeched in despairing, emotional tones; hot tears of sorrow peppered his tanned cheeks. His pain racked body dropped like a sack of potatoes to the blood-spattered floor alongside the lifeless corpse. Anguish lined that grief-stricken face of Jean Pierre who cradled lovingly the grey head of his father in cupped hands. The Frenchman opened his mouth to speak, a sour taste gripped his throat, but this overpowering emotion ensured a funereal silence ensued. Rampant conflicting emotions engendered irritation; negative emotions jerking him back to reality. His gold-plated Rolex watch registered two hours had elapsed since Scar had left. "What the hell has happened to that slime bag, the Austrian should have been back by now." Jean Pierre's maudlin mood conjured up memories of his past evil senseless killing, maiming.

Pangs of remorse gripped his gut as visions of his earlier inhumane torturing of helpless victims flashed through his mind. He'd wronged countless innocent victims; vivid recollections of his evil past made the Frenchman shudder with disgust. The Frenchman's human side surfaced, he decided for once in his life he would do the decent thing. Swung his head in direction of his mother. Her decaying corpse lay in the freezing cold of the cellar. "Neither you Mama nor Papa will rot in some filthy cemetery; I will not allow anything to prey on your rotting flesh. Both of your lifeless bodies will have a private cremation right here in your beloved chalet. Your worthless son will personally perform this ceremony." Sobbing uncontrollably the Frenchman dropped to his knees, regrets, retribution settled on his shoulders like a wet blanket of doom. "I'm sorry not to have been the business son; you wanted. This time I swear by all that's holy; to keep my promise." Pain returned he grimaced, shaking legs advanced him from chalet to the outhouses. Returning moments later with several cans of paraffin which he lay to one side.

Respectfully he placed the dead body of Andre on a makeshift funeral pyre alongside the now smelling corpse of his mother. Poignantly the pyre was placed directly over blood spattered tiles marking the spot his mother had been murdered. A reverential emotion gripped his pain racked body. In morbid quiet he solemnly draped a worn blanket over the cold lifeless bodies of his parents. Autumnal shadows of evening fell, the temperature dropped another degree. Jean Pierre gathered more dirty tattered blankets... wrapped them around his parents. He lay on the blood-spattered floor besides his dead parents awaiting the arrival of Scar. He drifted into the comforting peaceful oblivion of sleep.

Warm early morning sunshine pierced the frayed curtains covering the dirty cracked panes of the windows. A cold North easterly breeze whistled through the warped wooden frame of the window. The chilled body of Jean Pierre stirred; he rubbed sleep from his eyes. Blood spattered hands soothed his paining chest, still no sign of Scar. Sorrowful eyes fell on the blanketed corpses. "Morning Papa, Mama." Jean Pierre whispered quietly; the wounded Frenchman breakfasted on dry bread in sorrowful solemnity. In a herculean effort he lifted his aching wounded body to his feet, in jerky limping movements he prepared to execute the act of finality, to cremate himself with his parents in that prison of a chalet. Self-pity consumed him when grabbing that menacing can of paraffin. Loosening the lid, he doused the explosively volatile liquid liberally over wooden beams and blankets covering his father, Mother and self. The self-professed atheist clasped hands together; his tearful searching eyes soared pleadingly heavenward. For the first time in his misspent evil life the Frenchman muttered a short prayer before grabbing a box of matches. He withdrew a match and was about to ignite it; the door squeaked opened.

80

Louis, Paul and Nicky Head for Chalet

Louis in fatherly tones managed to convince his daughter Brigitte to remain at home; begrudgingly she nodded tacit acceptance of father's wishes. With son Paul and policeman Nicky, the trio hastened towards the chalet; Paul's intercom bleeped informing him of shooting at Sylvester's club. A diversion was made to the venue, inside the dark dingy club lay five dead thugs. Progressing inside the office, they found the motionless body of Scar lying on top of his dead Mafia boss Sylvester. Paul stared at the two dead corpses and the gun in Scar's hand; he snarled in sardonic cynicism. "Looks like an open and shut case, the evil low life killed each other." I nodded agreement, Paul rang head office, informed H.Q. updated them of their movements; headed for the chalet. Nicky grunted to the Gendarme. "With Scar out of the equation we should still be ready to face strong opposition. You think we'll need back up?" Paul shot a knowing facetious grin at me. "You could be right; we may need them." He chuckled and rang H.Q.; we proceeded to the chalet.

81

Rusha Returns to Chalet to Kill Jean Pierre

That morning bright sun's rays fell upon the ramshackle chalet as the ageing front door slammed shut. Jean Pierre presumed the noise was to introduce the return of his adversary Scar. So did not bother to look round as he emptied his cans of volatile liquid. "Scar where the hell have you been?" Queried the Frenchman edging his injured body to front room; his eyes dilated in astonishment. Standing in front of him was not the Austrian assassin. Surprised eyes beheld an Olive-skinned beauty. The girl who for the last few weeks, had replaced Brigitte in his heart. This new heart throb presented herself before him, the beautiful Rusha. The Malawian immigrant flashed a threatening stare to the crippled Frenchman, staggering his approach towards her. "Well, at last it is the great Jean Pierre come to greet me. And who this time will come out as top dog I ask myself." A smile of irony, a touch of poetic justice twisted her lips, "this time it is I who have the upper hand; I hope you enjoyed my bullet." Rusha snarled; tying Jean Pierre's hands before snatching her gun from inside the worn leather flying jacket, "now Jean Pierre would you like to rape me again I ask myself." She taunted facetiously, vengeance sprang to her eyes; cruel lips tightened with sarcasm, "you do remember that bombed building; that rape; you said, and I quote. What I'm about to do will be our secret." She added icily, sardonic humour laced her laconic tones. She withdrew a pack of cigarettes selecting two, offering one to

Jean Pierre. His face twisted with bemusement. "But you don't smoke!" Jean Pierre spluttered.

She laughed tauntingly whilst waving menacingly her gun in his direction. "Times change... now Sit." Rusha ordered, binding Jean Pierre to a chair, with controlled coolness she sat opposite her victim. "Before I kill you, satisfy my nostalgic curiosity. As a young girl I idolised you, my curiosity often wondered what your bedroom would be like; which room is it?" Before you took advantage of me, I dreamt of you and I getting married, being in your bedroom; snuggling in warm embraces together." She hissed unforgivingly. "My bedroom is top of the stairs on the right." Jean Pierre grunted, pointing the way. "I was expecting Scar." Jean Pierre whispered... face twisting in partial dismay. "Ah Scar, well he along with Sylvester has been detained; now your bedroom." She ordered. "Release me, let me show you." Jean Pierre grunted. She untied the ropes; he grimaced; hand shot to his paining side; he rose from his chair to lead her upstairs. "That was my calling card." She issued coldly staring at the bloodied tourniquet. They entered the small sparsely decorated room, cobwebs hung from every nook and cranny of the darkened room. Beside dirty cracked windowpanes lay Jean Pierre's partially made bed, he withdrew a well-worn book from beneath the pillow. A book, that in his younger years had been his bible, shaped his life; the title "The Valentine's Day Massacre." "What every young thug should read." Jean Pierre remarked glibly

A wistful smile sprang unbidden to her lips, tears of emotion ran down her ebony cheeks. She cast inquisitive stares into every corner of that room, her heart sank; regret cloaked her like a wet blanket. Rusha had reached a crossroads, entering this poignant moment, she cocooned herself within an emotional bubble. Emotionally disturbing memories of what might have been seeped dreamingly her memory banks. Introduced chaotic turmoil about to wreak havoc within the unbalanced mind of that cow eyed lovesick girl. Hot tears pricked the back of her eyes before splurging out upon her Ivory coloured cheeks. "Jean oh Jean, it could have been so different." Her voice choked emotionally, "for the last few weeks you've been uppermost in my thoughts." She paused tears misted her eyes, "the irony of our situation is, I tried to suppress such thoughts. I came here with every intention of killing you. Instead, those thoughts have re-emerged I believe I'm in love with you." Rusha blurted in sorrowful words of conviction; indecision flushed her dark cheeks; she blushed.

That cold murderous look that had addressed her eyes vanished, was replaced with warmth. Jean Pierre advanced with deliberate cautiousness towards her; he whispered tenderly. "And I love you." The Frenchman replied with equal emotional intensity. "I do not think I ever stopped loving you, I had you in my gun sights; but was unable to pull the trigger." Rusha murmured coyly, they embraced. Outside the chalet, a young Jean paced impatiently the street like a caged tiger, he waited with growing irritation for his mother to re-appear. Frustration mounted within him; impatience urged him to make a move. Young Jean shouldered open the door to enter the chalet; he stumbled over empty paraffin cans. The noise startled the lovesick couple; hand in hand they crept down the stairs.

Rusha felt her face burning with distress when spotting her son, abject horror dressing his young face. The youngster stared in utter disbelief; his mother was standing hand in hand with Jean Pierre; the very man she'd taught him to hate... he winced. A cocktail of hostility, antagonism, danced rampantly with misplaced allegiances through his young mind; revenge sprang to his face. With a raging anger burning inside him young Jean grabbed the

The Jew from Berlin

box of matches lying on the chair besides him. In an effort to redress the situation Rusha jerked her hand from the Frenchman's forcing the unwilling Jean Pierre back onto chair. She bound Frenchman's hands loosely.

Young Jean approached the bound Jean Pierre, eyes burning with retribution. "You, you put my mother through hell." The young Frenchman grunted; eyebrows raised in condemnation, "what's that smell... Paraffin?" The young boy queried; wild bloodthirsty eyes fell to his hand holding the matches. His murderous confused gaze transferred to his mother. She stood holding hands with the very man he'd been taught to loathe. A strange excitement stirred his mixed emotions; a sour taste lodged in his throat "enjoy." The youngster enthused in sour emotional tones.

Rusha's face twisted in disbelief; panic stricken she dashed forward. "No son there's been a change of plan, I've decided not to kill him." Rusha spluttered hastening back to the Frenchman; clutching him tightly. Young Jeans eyes twinkled dangerously. "But mama we had it all planned. You taught me to hate this man." Jean screeched scathingly. She approached young Jean, dropped to her knees in from of her young son, hugged him; emotionally she choked quietly. "I know son my intentions were misguided; the situation has changed; we've decided to marry." Rusha blurted through nervous sobs. Pure disgust, hatred veiled the young Frenchman's eyes as he warned in a chilling voice. "I'm sorry Mama, after what you have taught me that only happens over my dead body." Young Jean threatened throwing a lighted match onto the saturated wooden beams. The building exploded into a blazing inferno, flames snaked hungrily up the dry beams of the chalet, the youngster crept out of the door a cruel smile hugging his thin lips. With tears streaming down his pallid cheeks, abstractedly he stared at tongues of flames licking voraciously the dry wooden structure of dilapidated chalet. Rusha dashed to untie Jean Pierre's hands; questioned him angrily. Where did the bloody paraffin come from?" Shrieked an exasperated Rusha, through the thickening smoke she struggled to breath as she untied the hands of Jean Pierre.

The raging inferno blazed out of control; the heat intensified became unbearable as tongues of flames licked hungrily ever closer to them. "My mother and father lie dead in the next room I'd saturated the place with Paraffin. I was going to set the chalet on fire, cremate my parents and myself." Jean Pierre stuttered, "that boy Jean has a lot to answer for; but you are back in my life, so I have a lot to thank him for." Jean Claude stuttered awkwardly; as the heat of the fire increased.

A strange calm consumed the Malawian. With remarkable cool she accepted she was with the love of her life, and there was no escaping from that impenetrable wall of fire. That her and Jean Pierre were about to be cremated, alongside his parents. In those last frantic moments, she turned to Jean Pierre. "About Jean, I was pregnant when I moved in with Scar, but being aware of the hatred between yourself and Scar. I kept quiet even pretended Scar was the baby's father." She screamed; as tongues of flames licked her clothing. "I thought Scar was the father of the boy, you call him Jean and Scar did not suspect anything." The bewildered Jean Claude's throat closed momentarily before issuing. "Rusha my love we are about to die." In frenzied tones of finality, the couple attempted to talk down the perils of their fatal predicament. "Scar was too consumed with power, money, when Jean was born, which I was going to abort; Scar insisted I keep the baby." Jean Pierre stared lovingly into the eyes of Rusha; they embraced tightly almost in ignorance of the blazing inferno. "What irony, for years, the

Gendarmerie and English police unsuccessfully chased me without any success; it took my own son to run me to ground. When we die, I could not think of anyone I'd rather die with than you, my love; my Rusha."

The heat in the burning building became intolerable as avaricious flames licked hungrily at the flesh of the doomed couple. Anguished screams from the doomed couple resounded in their throes of finality. The deadly flames engulfed the screaming couple, the stench of burning flesh proliferated the smoke-filled air. The charred bodies of Rusha and Jean Pierre melted to the floor. The ageing wooden beams of the chalet; burnt like a crisp; collapsed on the charred couple. It had taken the Frenchman's death, for his wish to be granted, release from his prison. In the middle of that stinking, smoking dining room, where once an affluent Dupont family ate their meals; lay two more dead bodies to join Jeans parents. The immigrant Rusha; and last of the Dupont family. Rusha's vengeful son Jean strutted with pride the green grass, he sat to admire his handy work; whilst holding tightly the satchel of money. "One day I'll show the world who is number one." He gloated then adding in tones of reflective sorrow. "If only Mama had been reasonable, not taken that thugs side she'd be alive now and with me. We could have left this place; enjoyed this money. But mama at least has died in the knowledge that it was her little warrior that killed that man she so hated.

82

Paul's Wandering Uncovered

We slewed our Black Citroen to a halt, stared in disbelief at charred smouldering embers that had once been home of the Dupont family. "I think we're a little late." Paul grunted sarcastically; an ironical acceptance of mission accomplished dressing his tanned face. Alighting our vehicle, we strolled to the burnt-out chalet. The charred thick oak beams were still flickering with the last vestiges of the flames. We moved cautiously through the fire blackened wood, into the main room of the building. Nausea created havoc within Nicky's stomach; the stench of burnt flesh filled the air; his stomach exploded. Vomit spewed freely onto the charred wood when espying four charred bodies. Paul trailed behind me, sardonic smile dressing his face. Louis and I spotted charred remains of a book; I picked it up, the title read. "The Valentine's Day massacre."

The thick smoke hugging the burnt-out building overcame us. Louis and I staggered outside Paul followed. Noises from the bombed building opposite caught our attention, a youthful hysterical laughter ricocheted the crumbling walls of the skeletal building. We entered the crumbling skeleton of a building, Louis spotted young Jean sporting a birthmark of three red circles on his neck. He grabs Paul's gun, shoots the youngster who slumps to the ground. Young Jean released his grip on his money satchel as Louis shouted in condemnation. "Scar had the same mark on his neck, it is a sign of evil.'

Louis hands the gun back to Paul who slips in a pool of paraffin, soaking his uniform. Paul reached inside his pocket for a handkerchief to clean his face, a sheet of folded paper dropped to the floor. Louis recognised the bold typing across top of paper as belonging to the Illuminati Grand Council. He stared long and hard at his son. Louis's face masked in disappointment his mouth opened to speak, angry emotion tightened his throat; robbed him of words.

"Yes, Papa those days I went missing I was visiting the Illuminati, pleading for the unfilled position of head priest; the position you vacated.

Did you know you were never replaced? The letter you're looking at is advising they have at last found that person, me; they want me to replace you. They have this crazy idea I could be the Antichrist you were searching for. After you left Diana Marina Italy, the Illuminati made peace and merged forces with the mafia. I have been charged with finishing the job my stepbrother Scar failed to complete. I travel to Italy next month and your old post." Paul released a sibilance of exultation. Eyes flushed to a murderous blood red; Paul released a cold murderous laugh; primed his gun... took aim at Louis. "And now to complete that mission I have to kill you." Paul gloated as the wounded young Jean stirred; through misted vision he spotted the Gendarme pointing a gun at his grandfather. The blood-soaked youngster having been fed with hate for authority; grabbed the blazing money satchel from the fire. Twisted his pained racked body he threw the burning satchel at the Gendarme shouting. "Vive Le France." The young voice babbled incoherently.

The paraffin-soaked uniform exploded into a ball of fire; the gendarme became a blazing inferno. Young Jean released smile of accomplishment when beholding blazing body of the Gendarme. The young Frenchman collapsed to the floor releasing a sibilant breath of finality. The dark arms of death snatched his young body, a body that would be re-united with father, Jean Pierre. Louis and I stared astounded at the ball of fire; I threw arms heavenward in a gesticulation of helplessness. Burning question gripping my gut was, should we quell the fire consuming Louis's already dead son Paul. Louis slipped arm around my shoulder, guiding me away from the scene. "Nicky, I think it better this way, the blood money was put to good use." We paused, turned about to face burning gendarme, stood in funereal silence watching the self-proclaimed future antichrist smoulder.

83

The Finale

"My life has gone full circle from Gnostic to Christian." Louis reflected emotionally dropping his body unceremoniously to the grass, head in hands.

"Full circle what the hell do you mean?" Nicky grated querulously. "And what did Paul mean the Antichrist?" I questioned face screwing in interrogative frustration. "It's a long story and will keep for another time, let's celebrate the fact Inspector Tigers death was not in vain. What do you say to collecting my Brigitte going for a drink; and planning your wedding." The Austrian laughed. I responded nodding in the affirmative. A shiny Black Citroen pulled up; an elegantly dressed gentlemen alighted the vehicle. The gentleman dressed completely in Black, excepting for white silk handkerchief adorning the top pocket of his suit. The stranger flicked dust spots from his pristine suit and approached whilst nodded tacit acknowledgment of our presence. A suspicious Louis threw a concerned state of suspicion at the newcomer. "Yes! you want something?" The Austrian grunted abrasively "But of course, messier, I believe I'm speaking to a messier Louis, am I not." The stranger queried politely. "Yes, that's right, and you are?" Louis replied curtly in tones of hostility. "Actually, I came to see your son, but I see that is already too late." The Frenchman put a white handkerchief to his mouth; looked disgustedly at the charred body. "Well now we are sorted, my friend and I are to move on; cheerio." Louis advised the stranger, shouldering Nicky abruptly from the scene. "Ah! but Messier, I came principally to inform your son a mistake had been made; that

I had to approach you." The stranger nodded, before releasing a wry smile, "you see I'm the grand master of the Illuminati." Louis stood back astounded a strange chill befell him, mounting tension urged him to speak. "But... but." He stuttered in a childlike utterance; words failed him. "You see messier we offered Paul the high priesthood, but after careful deliberation, the grand council decided our pre-emption of him being the Antichrist was wrong; therefore, your son cannot fill position you vacated."

"You're not suggesting I return." Said Louis flabbergasted eyes widening in astonishment. "We hoped you would give the matter your deepest deliberation, consideration; and yes, we did have that in mind." Came the reply in form of a plea, "and who is this fine young man?" The stranger added straightening the silk handkerchief adorning his top pocket. "This is Nicky my daughter's fiancé. But thank you; and no to your invitation." Louis retorted with calm authority. "But messier you have not even asked why we came to this decision. Are you not in the least interested? Blurted the Grand Master. "Okay! Why after so long?" Louis questioned impatiently. "Well messier, when you left our organisation, after you having increased profits so substantially. Also converted multitudes to the Illuminati; you could say we were mildly outraged. Wanted to get even and reached the decision to kill you; but we could not do this directly. We attempted to bankrupt you; we were even instrumental in your vines being poisoned; but Jean Pierre came to your help. We contacted the underground to have Rusha trained in the arts of assassination to kill you. Finally, we hoped Scar would finish that job for us. Due to his indelicacy, he proved comprehensively incapable, the job was beyond him; he should have killed you... he failed." The Grand Master paused took a swig from a hip flask re-commenced. "We arrived at the conclusion, if we are unable to kill you, encourage you to re-join us; as my assistant." The stranger removed his trilby, wiped beads of sweat from his forehead. "Louis you cannot go back to this, this cult." Nicky blurted. Louis walked towards Paul's charred body; removed his gun. "Messier there is no need for that." The stranger issued in warning tones; hands gesticulating disappointment pointed heavenward. Louis levelled Paul's gun at him. "Sir through your organisation, or because of it, my son Scar turned against me; tried to kill me. You filled my son Paul with hatred for me. I only have my daughter Brigitte left; whom I now want to see safely married.

There are two answers to this scenario. One is you walk away, never bother me again; two is I kill you now where you stand." Louis grated. "I beg you to reconsider, even my friends the freemasons would like to welcome you on board." The strangers replied before his head dropped to his chest as though in resignation. "So, you want to die." Louis hissed; muscles twitched like snakes in his gun hand. The Grand Master raised his head laughed mockingly before threatening Louis. "Messier, messier you sadden me, before you act too hastily look yonder at that second car, that vehicle houses five Mafia gunmen, brought along as a cautionary measure in case a situation like this arose." The gunmen alighted the car guns in hand. The Grand Master paused, murder leapt to his eyes; in caustic tones of warning, he continued "Now lower your gun and back off." He snapped in cold tones of anger. The confused Louis shouted indignantly. "You and your hired gunman can do what the hell you like, my future son in law and me; we are going to arrange a wedding." Louis laughed facetiously, threw the gun back at his dead son Paul. Slipped a friendly hand over my shoulder; we left with Louis saying to his future son-in-law. "You and I will arrange a wedding."

I recently watched the powerful G20 leaders gather for the 2017 conference in Davos, several of them shaped hands in the Illuminati sign. I asked myself. COULD THEY BE BACK?

Available worldwide from Amazon

www.mtp.agency

www.facebook.com/mtp.agency

@mtp_agency

www.ingramcontent.com/pod-product-compliance
Ingram Content Group UK Ltd.
Pitfield, Milton Keynes, MK11 3LW, UK
UKHW032101150325
456262UK00002B/244